Perfidious Tides

Pelham Pugh

For my family and their unwavering support.

Copyright © 2024 by Pelham Pugh

ISBN 979-8-9915351-2-0

www.pelhampugh.com

All rights reserved.

No part of this publication may be reproduced, distributed, or transmitted in any form or by any means, including photocopying, recording, or other electronic or mechanical methods, without the prior written permission of the publisher, except as permitted by U.S. copyright law.

The story, all names, characters, and incidents portrayed in this production are fictitious. No identification with actual persons (living or deceased), places, buildings, and products is intended or should be inferred.

Chapter 1

Six men sat in a dimly lit room, their faces illuminated by an eerie glow cast by a lone bulb suspended by a long wire from the ceiling. Three were clad in somber business suits, two in worn overalls, and one in a dark green army uniform denoting his rank as captain. Outside, a storm raged, its fury echoed by the occasional lashing of tree branches against century-old windows that creaked with each powerful gust.

Despite the tempest outside, the men, unperturbed, gathered around a long table strewn with papers. Among them, a figure stood out - a short man with tightly cropped graying hair, unmistakably the leader, despite his diminutive stature.

"Next one up," the man announced, his voice cutting through the stillness, "Vernon Frank Bruce, Panama City Beach." He placed the sheet of paper onto the over-polished table in front of him, prompting each man to scrutinize their own documents before nodding in assent.

"Another college kid," the army captain grumbled, his frustration evident. "Mac, how many of these are slipping through?"

Mac Tate, the politician of the group, shook his head slightly. "I know the boy's father, works at the paper mill down near the port."

A chuckle rippled through the group, save for the captain, whose scowl deepened. "Gentlemen, professionalism, please," the captain interjected, his voice edged with impatience. "I need soldiers."

Mac, unfazed, reassured him. "We'll get you soldiers, Captain. Now, let's discuss the deferment for young Vernon Bruce."

As the discussion unfolded, tensions simmered. The captain's insistence on duty clashed with Mac's familiarity with the locals, each man advocating for his own perspective. Amidst the debate, a silent figure, clad in bright new overalls, at the end of the table, leaned forward.

"He has a brother, just turned eighteen," the man in overalls mentioned.

Mac nodded, feigning surprise. He was already aware of the sibling, but wanted someone else to mention the kid. His fingers grazed his chin thoughtfully as the others conferred.

"He ain't listed," the other man in overalls remarked, his drawl slow and deliberate and his bibbed garment faded and torn from years of labor in the hot Florida sun.

Mac's brow furrowed as he thumbed through the papers, a pretense to cover his tracks. "Let me check," he said, rising abruptly and excusing himself.

Outside, he retrieved the *missing* document, returning with a triumphant wave. "Found it!" he exclaimed, distributing copies to the assembled men.

"Ronald Frank Bruce," Mac read aloud, his voice steady. "Eighteen. No deferment, no college, works at the beach."

The revelation sparked interest, the captain inquiring about potential medical exemptions. Mac dismissed the notion, citing the boy's full recovery from a prior high school baseball injury.

"Does he have his draft card?" the captain pressed.

"He'll have it tomorrow," Mac assured him, his tone final.

Amidst nods of agreement, a lone dissenting voice rose from the end of the table. "This ain't right," Weston McPherson protested, adjusting his tie and hints of sweat appearing on his forehead. His objection met with a stern rebuke from Mac Tate.

"Please, Weston. You can't save every kid that comes across this table," Mac scolded him. "We can spare his brother, but not him."

Mac reached into his shirt pocket and pulled out his reading glasses. He didn't really need them, only using them for effect. He read the kid's address and, once again, noted he had no deficiencies. He looked sternly down the table, nodded to each man, and called for a vote. Five hands shot in the air, but the objector didn't move. Mac pulled his glasses to the end of his nose. "You know, Weston, I like for this to be unanimous," Mac said, staring at the man.

A bolt of lightning flashed in the window and thunder crashed seemingly before the streak vanished, indicating the storm's intensity. Mac smiled at Weston. "See, even God wants this to be unanimous." The rest of the group, excluding Weston and the army captain, burst into laughter.

The man with new overalls slapped Weston on the back and said, "I'm ready to get home out of this storm. Let's vote again."

Once again, five hands shot into the air. Weston raised his slowly, shaking his head from side to side as he did. Outside, a limb lost its battle with the wind, cracked, and fell to the ground beneath the massive oak standing guard since before the civil war. Mac stood and motioned around the room. "Time to adjourn then?" Each man nodded in approval, and the meeting ended.

Usually, a couple of them hung around, swapping local gossip and telling lies, but with the storm raging outside, they all grabbed their hats and headed towards the double doors leading to the hallway. As Weston angrily slapped his hat into place, Mac grabbed him by the shoulder. "Let's talk a minute," he whispered into Weston's ear.

Weston reluctantly stayed behind, leaning on the edge of the table. Mac stood in front of him. With Weston leaning on the table, he and Mac were able to look each other in the eye.

"I know what you are going to say, Mac. Save it," Weston spoke first.

"Look, West, you know how the captain is. If we want to keep our *good* boys alive and home, we must make compromises. Right or wrong, it's for the best," Mac responded, holding his palms outward.

Weston leaped from his leaned position, shook his head, and his voice cracked slightly as he responded, "It ain't right, and I can't do this anymore."

The old politician took Weston's vacated perch on the side of the table. He placed his hands on the edge next to him, tapping his fingers against the cold wood. "I picked you for a reason, West. People like you, respect you, and most of all..." He pointed his finger at him. "People *trust* you."

"How long do you think they'll trust me if word of how we do things in here gets out?" he asked as he walked over to the window and traced a raindrop along the windowpane with his finger. He whirled around and walked back over to Mac. "They won't. Not one bit. Not on the street, not at the café, and, more importantly, not in my church."

"Look, West, I understand. Believe me, I do. But we are doing the right thing for everyone. Most of the boys we're giving him, they'd never amount to anything," Mac said dismissively.

Weston slammed the stack of papers he still held in his hand on the table and slammed his fist on top of them. "What about this Bruce boy? He not going to amount to anything?" He picked up the sheet and waved it in Mac's face. Mac swatted the paper away and stood up, grabbed Weston by the collar of his shirt and eased up on his tip toes so they were almost nose to nose.

"I don't care if you are a preacher. You best be careful how you speak to me," Mac warned him. Weston grabbed Mac's hand and shoved it away. He didn't say anything, but the two stood, toe to toe, with only the sound of howling wind breaking the silence. Weston finally shook his head again and briskly walked away. As he opened the two doors, he heard Mac say, "*Nothing* leaves this room." Weston didn't acknowledge him and kept walking.

The side door flew open, and the army captain strode through, marching towards Mac, who remained in the middle of the room, staring at the doors that had just slammed shut behind Weston.

"Problem?" the captain asked as he stood beside Mac. The politician pursed his lips, shaking his head.

"No," he replied curtly, and left without saying anything else.

Later that evening, after the storm moved on towards the Alabama line, Weston swayed back and forth in his front porch swing, watching lightning fork across the sky in the distance. No thunder followed, the storm too far away for the sound to reach his ears. The air, cooled by rain, comforted his skin as he moved with the motion of the swing.

Across the dirt road, a couple of frogs ventured from the depths of the swamp and talked to each other and in the darkness, he saw a couple of lightning bugs in the pine thicket lining the dirt road. It had been hot for late May, even by Florida Panhandle standards, and creatures of summer had already begun making their presence known.

He sat in darkness, leaving the front porch light off. The house was empty because his wife and children attended a youth event at another church. He loved his family, but also liked to be alone, especially after a day like today.

Guilt filled his mind, and he couldn't get the name Ronald Bruce out of his thoughts. The kid was only another in a lengthy line that he had sentenced to death on that awful draft board. When he took the job, Mac promised him he was doing the community, if not the whole Panhandle, a great service. That was a lie. Mac was using it to line his pockets with cash. He didn't care anything about the families he tore apart.

A strange sound caught his attention at the edge of the yard. He stopped the swing and eased to his feet, straining his eyes in the darkness, trying in vain to focus on what had caught his eye. He eased down the short steps to the ground and carefully made his way to the area where the sound originated. He kicked at a bush, and nothing happened. He kicked a little harder and suddenly the bush shook ferociously. One of his feet hung on the side of the bush, throwing off his balance, and an armadillo scampered past his other foot, nearly knocking him to the ground. When his heart rate settled and he caught his breath, he laughed and turned back towards the house. *So much for monsters in the night*, he thought to himself.

After only one step, an arm grabbed him from behind and Weston felt hot breath on his ear. Before he could scream, a thick blade slid across his neck, and he tasted iron in his mouth as blood careened from his lips. His last thoughts, before his consciousness faded, were of his family. He hoped they wouldn't be the ones to find him.

Chapter 2

Most times, changes in life arise when you least expect them. The same day that featured a muggy morning with a brightly shining sun evolved into a day that ended with an afternoon downpour from a summer thunderstorm. That same day began with optimism but ended with a young man holding a piece of paper with life-shattering words. A piece of paper bearing the symbol of the Selective Service.

Ronald Frank Bruce, or Rof as he was known, was the younger of two sons. Two sons that grew up not far from the sandy white beaches of the northern gulf coast. Rof filled his days with carefree flirtations with young girls along the beach that came down to the gulf with their parents. He worked at a small ice cream shack fittingly constructed as an ice cream cone. They were littered up and down the beach peddling the soft, creamy treat to sweaty tourists.

On the day the card arrived, Rof wasn't at home. He was busy charming his daily sweetheart and leaned on the cone shaped structure with his arm around her and his boyish voice in her ear. Her hands twisted the ends of her long blonde hair, and her smile told Rof all he wanted to know. He leaned over and whispered something else into her ear. The girl giggled and looked up into Rof's eyes, and a mischievous grin spread across his lips. The night was theirs.

His mother left when he was five and his brother was eight. They never saw their mother again after she slammed the screen door and began walking down the dusty driveway, not even saying goodbye to her sons. On that day, their family whittled down to three. Their father was a hard-working man in a paper mill located near the brackish bay where the Apalachicola River spilled its muddy waters into the gulf. He made a good living, even if it came at the expense of raising his two boys. He was never home, but older brother Vernon Frank Bruce, always known as Vern, tended to fill the void.

Vern was not a daydreamer like Rof. He couldn't be. In the absence of a mother and the unintentional neglect of a father, he had to be a rock for his brother. Vern always held a book in his hand and a pencil behind his ear. Holding no desire to work in the paper mill alongside his father, he held visions of one day becoming wealthy and wielding power. He wanted to be one of the higher ups of the community, one of the businessmen, complete with a suit and tie and have his lunch down at the Captain's.

The Captain's was a restaurant right on the shimmering Gulf of Mexico where fishermen dropped large nets of fish each day. Every day hundreds of small vessels left the tiny port like an army of ants and returned with red snapper, grouper, trigger, mahi mahi, and a variety of other types of fish according to season from the emerald waters of the Gulf of Mexico. The businessmen that owned the hotels, the gift shops, the gas stations, and all local businesses, big, small, or corporate, would gather for lunch. They often sat together, telling tales, casually eating their lunch and slapping each other on the back. Vern had noticed the reverence they were given. Everyone spoke to these men as they strode past the dockworkers, mechanics, and fisherman struggling to make a living in hopes of gaining favor in their next loan or purchase. Each "A" that Vern made in college was a step towards joining those titans of the Panhandle. That was why he filled all of his days with his nose in a book. He loved to study. He loved to learn. Rof was a carefree playboy, filling days with different girls and parties. Vern filled his with knowledge. The brothers couldn't be more different.

 Vern stood on the porch of their wooden home. It was a hot, humid day and clouds began to form on the horizon. Thunder erupted in the distance as Vern studied the paper in his hand. It was 1969, the so-called summer of love. Protests to the war in Vietnam were reaching a boiling point. Lyndon Johnson vacated the White House, succeeded by Nixon. His campaign promise to get the United States out of the war was long forgotten. If anything, Nixon sank the United States deeper into war. Vern disliked the whole damn political system, especially around the panhandle where he called home.

 The politicians of the area were old Dixiecrats, and he despised them. The people holding power here also held a lot of sway in Washington. They were behind the war all the way and the resulting draft. He held the paper to his eyes once more and shook his head. Here was a piece of paper that summoned not only Rof into the damned thing, but the whole family. The men who were drafted tended to be, if not outright poor, part of a struggling working class that couldn't seem to get ahead. Vern's face tightened as he thought about how curiously the whole draft lottery worked, and he loathed it. He leaned over the edge of the porch and spit into the ground, envisioning Nixon's face. Pops, as they called their father, would be home later than Rof. He never was home before his little brother and usually arrived after Rof left to begin his nightly conquest. He ran his fingers through his thick, black hair. He could see headlights in the distance. A sigh escaped his mouth, and he thought about how difficult this was going to be.

  Rof left his little North Carolina cutie with a promise to return that night. Her cute little smile wouldn't leave his thoughts. He hung his arm out of his old truck's window and went up and down as if his hand were riding an invisible wave. She promised that she would ditch her parents and meet back at the county pier at ten. Rof held no intention of missing this date. His plan was to come home, shower, eat very quickly, listen to a lecture from his brother and head back to the strip. A grimace came over his face as he thought about his brother. Big brother was always telling him what he should do. He cocked an eyebrow as he wondered if Vern would ever mind his own business.

  As he pulled his old fifty-eight Chevy truck to the front porch of their modest wooden home, Vern rocked back and forth in an old rocking chair. He turned off the engine and began snapping his fingers to the rhythm of the chair. He expected Vern to be outside, as Pops had yet to join modern times and buy an air conditioner. He figured the old man just liked sweating. There was always a nice breeze in the afternoon that swept across the swaying grass field in front of their house, or a summer thunderstorm with its cooling rain and ferocious display of lightning and thunder. Today looked like rain as he could see lightning over the tall, narrow pine trees and hear the thunder crack ever so closer from the distance. He welcomed the rain. It would be a better backdrop for his evening activities if it were cooler. Miss Carolina would want to snuggle up a little if it got a tad cooler on the beach. But for now, he took off his dark, pointed sunglasses, threw them on the dash, and turned his attention to his brother. He could tell Vern didn't look happy, but what else was new?

   The old truck hissed and popped a little as Rof closed the door with a creak and moan. The first heavy drops were beginning to fall, and he didn't want to get soaked as he picked up his pace. With a huge step up onto the porch, he always bypassed the steps, Vern extended his hand and as the card dangled from it, Rof noticed it trembling as the card shook ever so slightly in his grasp. Vern did not make eye contact with his brother. He didn't want to. As Rof read the card, his face reddened. This was the worst of nightmares. So many young men left and so few came back. To Rof, Vietnam meant death, so this card was death. His head began to shake, and he waved the card in front of Vern. Vern didn't know what to say to his little brother. He sat there expressionless, his face like stone. There wasn't much he could say. The falling rain beat against the tin roof and became almost deafening. Rof slung the card into the rain and as soon as it landed, the words printed on its surface began to smudge.

"I knew I should have stayed at the beach," he managed. The silence was deafening for a few minutes. The only sound permeated from the now pouring rain. Vern held the silence for a few moments longer before he managed to speak.

"It's just one of those things, Rof. You go, you deal with it, you come home. Hell, some boys don't even go over there. Some get stationed in Kentucky, some in Georgia." He felt as though he told the truth, but his face could not hide his true feelings. His eyes watered, but he would not allow his little brother to see tears.

"You know as well as I do, I ain't got no skills. I sell damned ice cream. We ain't rich, we ain't got shit. I'll be on the first plane they can get me on," he said as his eyes began to swell. Both brothers sat for a second in another round of silence. Lightning flashed and before the flash disappeared into the night, the ground shook with the resulting thunder and it caused both to jump slightly.

"Pops will be home around midnight; you be home by then. I know you're going out. Just don't come home drunk. We need to talk this out." Vern's voice stiffened as he talked and it steadily angered Rof. He hated it when his brother became condescending.

"Don't want none of your damned lectures, Vern. This ain't your life we're talkin' about."

Vern didn't want to argue with his brother. This was not the time. He just nodded his head as Rof brushed past the rocking chair Vern was still occupying and slammed the door as he went in the house. Vern scratched his forehead and once again ran his fingers through his hair. He glared into the rain. The pine trees swayed heavily in the wind and Vern said aloud, "Should be me."

Ten thirty and no Miss Carolina. The evening had gone from bad to just completely awful. Rof sat on the glowing white sand near the first set of giant timbers that held up the massive pier. The gulf was calm on this night. The thunderstorms that rolled through resulted in an eerie silence settling in. A couple strolled by, swinging their arms together through interlocked hands. Rof just sat there and wondered why the young blonde stood him up. Perhaps her mother and father had gotten wind of their plans and put a stop to them. He could see in his thoughts a burly father pointing his finger at his young daughter and forbidding her from seeing a "beach bum." Or she might have gotten cold feet, he thought. Wouldn't be the first time that happened. In fact, it happened all the time. He played the odds. Sometimes he would make this date with three girls on a given night. Only on a few occasions had all three shown up at once.

Rof was quick-witted and had a certain charm that would allow him to wiggle free on those nights. Most often, those turned out for the best. The warm breeze off the gulf blew his bushy blond hair back. Not tonight, he thought.

With no young beauty to occupy his mind, his thoughts returned to that damned draft card. Pops would be home in an hour or two and Vern would give him the bad news. He took a deep breath and blew it back towards the ocean. His father would echo Vern in telling him it was time to grow up and do his duty. He was old school like that. God, country, family in that order. *My God*, he thought, *I will be gone in two weeks*. He closed his eyes tightly and thought in two weeks he had to report to Fort Benning in Columbus, Georgia, for basic training. How in the world could he let this life go in two weeks? The distant light of a fishing boat appeared way out on the gulf's horizon. It seemed to blink just like the stars. Rof watched it as he thought and wished he were on that boat, setting off to Mexico or the Caribbean. Anywhere but here. He turned quickly when a soft, cold hand touched his shoulder and jarred him from his thoughts.

When he turned around, he saw the small, round face of Susie Brannon smiling back at him. Her father owned a little mom-and-pop motel up on the strip a short distance from the pier. The strip was a stretch of Highway Ninety-Eight that meandered down the beach and was home to most of the small motels and restaurants Panama City Beach had to offer. Susie made her way down to the pier most nights. She was often the distant witness to

Rof's nightly conquests with the visiting girls. During the off season, which wasn't very long these days, Rof's attention would turn to her. She wasn't exactly the most beautiful local girl, but she was pretty. Her frame was short and lean, with long brown hair. Rof didn't feel like talking, so they wasted little time. After all, he had to go back home soon and face his father and brother and the conversation he really didn't want to have. He eased his hand to her face and pulled her in close.

 Susie's perfume filled the room when he opened the front door and found his father slouched in his favorite chair. Pops' gray hair was only slightly visible underneath his cap and his green eyes were fixed on the floor. Vern wasn't there and a sigh of relief escaped as Rof noticed. It surprised Rof a little that his know-it-all brother was absent. Usually, Vern was at the kitchen table with a book in his hand and a stern look on his face, but not tonight. There was no sound in the house, just the creaking of his father's chair. Rof didn't snap his fingers to his father's chair as he did Vern's that afternoon. He kept his hands in his pockets and struggled to look at his father.

 "Vern told me," his father finally spoke, his voice a little scratchier than normal. Rof thought it sounded like he had been crying, but he knew his father better than that.

 "My duty, right?" Rof replied, already knowing his father's response.

 "Son, I don't know what to tell you. Of course, it's your duty. Your country is calling, and you have to answer." Pop's voice began to crack faintly. "I don't want you to go, though. I'm selfish like that. I guess every father is that way. But I have to bury that selfishness. Hell, maybe by the time you get there, it will be all over. Nixon promised."

"Yeah, maybe so." Rof took his hands out of his pockets and cracked his knuckles. "I'm scared though, Pops. Never thought I would get picked. It's just the three of us. We're all we got," Rof said as a thought suddenly entered his mind. *Vern is in college; he got a deferment.* "Bastard!" he let slip before he realized it.

This outburst caught Pops unaware. He stood up, took off his cap and looked his youngest son in the eye. Their eyes locked instantly. "What the hell?" he snapped at Rof and slightly shook him.

"This is all Vern's fault! He should be going!" Rof was getting angrier by the second now. His eyebrows arched and his face once again turned red in rage. "He is the older brother; he should have been picked before me. The bastard would've if it weren't for that damned college!" Pops' face also reddened, but for just a second. His face became emotionless, and he drew in a quick breath, holding it for what seemed like an eternity to Rof. It seemed all the life was instantly drained from his father's wrinkled face. To see his father like that sent Rof into a full rage. He wanted to confront his brother right then and there.

"Where the hell is Vern?" Rof asked, his voice dripping with hate.

"He left tonight. Packed up his things and left to live at the college. He knew sooner or later you would blame him, and he didn't want to be around. He loves you, son; he's been here for you when I couldn't. Don't blame him, don't drive that wedge between you. I'll tell you the truth, right here and now. You ain't got nothing in this world if you ain't got your family. Wives, husbands, friends, they all go away at some point. All you two will have is each other. Brothers."

Rof was having none of it. He stormed out of the room in silence. Now his father couldn't hold back his tears. They streamed down his face, and he shook his head. He knew on this day both of his sons' innocence was lost. Rof would never be the same. Neither would his relationship with his older brother. Pops walked out onto the porch, and he could hear his youngest son cursing the name of his firstborn. With the porch light off, he slipped into the rocking chair and twisted open the whiskey jar. He didn't need a glass.

Rof didn't stay in his room for long. Not wanting to face his father again, he left through the back door, slamming it so hard, the house seemed to shake. He slid into his truck through the open window and sped out of the yard, slinging dirt from the spinning wheels. He didn't see his father on the front porch. His thoughts were consumed with Vern. He couldn't let that coward off this easy. If he had to drive all night to Tallahassee, he would. When Vern woke up tomorrow morning, he would be there to greet him. Staring into his face, nose to nose. "Good morning, you coward son of a bitch, and thanks for nothing," he would snarl at him. Vern knew what he was doing all along. Getting that deferment for college. He hated the war, the government, the president, everything that his father stood for and believed in. But he, Rof, was the bad guy. All his brother wanted was to make money. All he wanted was to be a big shot. Vern couldn't fulfill his dreams dying beside a god forsaken muddy river halfway across the world. No, he would send little brother for that. Why not? Little brother was a no account anyway. Rof envisioned his brother telling his rich friends at the university how his little brother filled his days selling ice cream on the beach and his nights entertaining the girls in bikinis. He reached for the glove box and pulled out a crumpled pack of cigarettes. The smoke he released from his lungs floated out through the window and Rof's grimace turned into a wide grin. "It may take some time, brother, but I'll pay you back for this," he said through gritted teeth and that wide grin. He wasn't going to Tallahassee; he was going to drink the night away. He would go by and pick up a bottle from a bootlegger that didn't mind selling to anyone, twenty-one or not. Rof didn't know where he would end up that night, only that he wasn't going to be sober.

    As the old Chevy thundered down the road, thoughts raced into his mind nearly as fast as the truck sped down the pavement. Each time he inhaled the smoke, and he let it escape his lungs, he cursed his brother's name.

Chapter 3

Vern hadn't returned home since that fateful evening on which Rof received his draft card. He couldn't. He knew his brother blamed him and he just didn't want to face him right now. He just sat there, staring into nothing, his mind wandering. He stood up and took a picture from his desk and stared at it for several minutes. It was a picture of his family, all three of them, standing with some fish they'd caught on one of their many trips to Holmes Creek. He returned the picture to his desk and sat back down, sighing as he did. Maybe somewhere deep down inside his soul, he had hoped the conflict in Asia would miraculously end by the time it came calling for Rof. Entering college and forgoing his turn gambled with his brother's life. He looked at the ceiling in disgust as shame enveloped him when he thought about that wager. He had bet his brother's life and lost. Now that debt stood due.

Vern called his dad at least every other day during his exile in Tallahassee. It just so happened that the friend who let him stay in his apartment had a phone. Few college students could afford that luxury. On one of those phone calls, Pops told him which day Rof was supposed to ship out and head to Georgia for boot camp. That day was fast approaching. In fact, it was tomorrow. On the phone with his father, he had lied and told him he would be there. He bit his lip as he did so. The pain masked the lie. He didn't want to let Rof go away without at least trying to patch their relationship, but Pops told him that it wasn't going to be easy. Rof had grown even more bitter and somber over the past two weeks. He blamed his older brother even more, and one day replaced the other. Vern stood up again, grabbed his keys, and took one more look at the picture. He was going to make things right, and he stormed out the door.

    Rof stopped showing up at the ice cream stand and he quit flirting with the vacation girls. The bushy blond hair that he at least did try to keep combed became longer and more unkempt. Ever since Miss Carolina had stood him up, he spent more time with Susie and more time with the bottle. On the night before he left for Georgia, he held Susie in one arm and a bottle of whiskey in the other. On previous nights. each time he turned the bottle to his mouth, he thought of Vern and his face burned with anger. But tonight, it could very well be the last he spent with Susie curled up in his arms. Tonight, with each swallow of liquor, however, his thoughts would turn away from Vern and back to Susie's young, pretty face. Why not get drunk and try to forget what was coming? Why not enjoy the last night he may ever spend on his beloved beach? Susie wasn't much, but she was there. Never a big conversationalist, Susie made up for it in other ways, and that was exactly what Rof needed right now. The last day had snuck up on him. He could've spent it with Pops, but he knew his father didn't want that. The old man just wanted Rof to be happy on his last day at home. Susie could make that happen; Pops could not. He lifted her face up by the chin and smiled down at her as her brown eyes glistened in the moonlight.

As the sun began to rise behind them, Rof and Susie parted ways. His last thought as he watched her walk away, with her hair blowing in the slight morning breeze, was he may never see the young girl again. In the two years he would be gone, Susie would probably move on. She would either leave for college, as she was only sixteen, or get married and settle into a life of a housewife with kids. Before she walked away, they said their short goodbyes and made vain promises to write that neither would keep. The sun began to reflect off the emerald-green waters and there was no movement in the ocean save a bird dipping into the water, searching for its morning meal. Rof brushed his hair back and peered over the still water. With one last deep breath, he turned around and faced his future.

Vern turned the key in the door's lock and slowly opened it, took a look around and closed his eyes. On the drive home, he'd envisioned Pops and Rof ambushing him upon his entrance. The room was empty. Pops' chair stood still, and he didn't hear any noise from the kitchen. Neither was there and Vern opened his eyes and fell into Pops' chair. This emptiness gave him time to think. He sat back in the chair and the acidic paper mill smell imbedded in the old chair wafted upward and engulfed him. Even though the smell was putrid, he loved it. Long ago, Pops became immune to the smell. He was inundated with the fumes every day he worked at the mill. Vern remembered when Rof was very young and held his nose as he sat in his father's lap. A smile flashed across his face as he thought back to when he and Rof were kids. It was like Rof was tied to his brother with a rope and followed him everywhere. They were inseparable. It helped that they lived out in the middle of nowhere and there were no other kids in sight most days. The two of them spent countless hours wandering through the pine trees and nearby swamps. Rof would climb onto Vern's back as the two waded across the deepest parts of the swamps without hesitation. His big brother wouldn't let anything happen to him. Now look at them, he thought as he began rocking in his father's chair. How in the world would he be able to smooth over the feelings Rof had? What could he say? He didn't start this war, nor did he make the rules. Rof could've gone to college and got a deferment. He chose not to. Even as his mind raced with these thoughts, he realized he really didn't believe it. Rof was never going to go to college.

Rof had never cared for school. He was the typical kid who grew up in the shadow of the sugary white sand and gleaming waters. There were too many distractions. He wanted to play, and play he did. In high school, he didn't care about studying, he only cared for baseball. He was pretty good at it too, making All State at one point. One torn ligament, though, ended whatever chance he had. Barely graduating this past spring, he was all-in on the beach life. Vern looked out the window and noticed the dust billowing up on the sandy dirt road. Pops never drove fast enough to kick up dust. It had to be Rof. Vern stood up from his father's chair and made his way into the kitchen. He didn't want the first thing Rof saw to be him, sitting in their father's chair.

The old chevy truck came to a stop, and the door didn't open for a few minutes. It was eerily silent. Even the birds seemed to know what was going on and chose to hold their songs. Vern stood in the kitchen, motionless, trying not to make a sound. He didn't realize it, but he held his breath during those seemingly never-ending minutes. He wanted to run to the truck, open the door, and put his arms around his brother in a tight bear hug, but that wasn't their way. They weren't the type of people to show their true feelings physically with each other and, god forbid, they hug. He waited for Rof in silence.

Rof put the transmission in park but left the engine running. He peered at Vern's car and wished it would disappear. He didn't want to see his brother. Rof hoped he could spend the evening with Pops and not have to deal with his older brother or even hear his name. His hands began to sweat as he sat there. *Might as well get this over with*, he thought, and the truck's door opened with a loud creaking sound that must have awakened the birds as they began to sing once more.

As the two brothers met in the kitchen, neither spoke for several minutes. Vern was the first to speak. The words seemed hard to form, but he managed to speak, slowly, as, "I'm sorry," was all he managed.

Rof wiped his hands on his pants and stood there in deep thought for a moment. He hesitated and thought about what Pops told him about family, but he had to say what he felt. "You're sorry. That's it? You drove all the way back here, and that's it? I'm probably a dead man and it's your damned fault. I'm taking the older brother's spot. Hell, you should be on your knees thanking me, you coward. It should be you going to the jungle." Rof's voice grew angrier with each word, his already tanned face turning darker.

Vern couldn't speak. He stood there, not looking at his brother, but at the floor. Rof continued, "I ain't got anything else to say to you, Vern. Just go back and leave me the hell alone. Go live your life. Go find your fortune. I'll see you in hell. Hope you're happy."

Vern, at first feeling guilty, tilted his head as he bristled at the mention of him being happy about his brother's situation. "What the hell do you mean 'hope you're happy'? You think I'm happy you were drafted instead of me? I'm not happy, you little bastard. Do I wish it was me?" Vern paused as thoughts raced through his mind and his gaze turned from the floor to his brother's eyes. "No. I don't wish it was me. I did what I had to. You could have done the same. You even coulda went to a trade school for at least this year and bought yourself some time. I love you, little brother, but I told you." Each word from the brothers stung the other a little more and without realizing it, both had clenched their fists.

Rof stood, not moving, taking each word in. Vern was right, but he didn't want to hear any of that right now. Especially from him. Rof watched his brother, standing there with that condescending look it seemed his face always held. He couldn't believe that Vern had taken that route. Rof thought about it for a second and reconsidered. He really hadn't expected anything else from his brother. Since they were kids, Vern dragged him along and set his path for him. It was never the path he wanted; they followed his big brother's. Slowly and deliberately, Rof unclenched his fists and took a step back.

"Said all I'm going to say, Vern. Either you get out of here or I am," he told his brother. Vern still stood with his fists balled up, ready to strike. This was not the way he wanted this to go, and here he was wanting to throw a punch while his little brother stood with his hands out in front of his body in retreat. Rof continued, "You say you love me, but here you are putting this squarely on me and nothing for yourself? Vern does no wrong, huh? You love me?" Rof asked sarcastically as he waved his open hands in front of him. "Brother, I despise you and deep down, always have for a while now. I hate the person you have become. I'm going to hate you every minute that I'm away, but I'm going over there and do what I got to and survive. I'm going to come home just to *spite* you. When I do, I'll make sure your life ain't worth shit. I hate you." Rof turned his back and walked away from Vern. He didn't look back.

Those words stung Vern like nothing ever had before in his life. He hung his head, staring back at the wooden floor and said nothing. What was said, now etched in his mind, could never be forgotten. Neither of them could take back anything said on this day. He walked past Rof, who stood by the door, looking into the distance, watching the pines sway across the field, saying nothing. Two steps past his brother, he looked back, regret sweeping over him. Vern felt his shoulders slump, and he wanted to say he was sorry. Once again, he wanted to embrace his brother, as this could possibly be the very last time they spoke, and he didn't want to leave it like this. Yet he could not. The words spoken by the brothers would from this point put a wall between them. Vern closed his eyes once more, shame overwhelming him. He wanted to scream and opened his mouth with that intent but all that came out was, "Tell Pops I'll call him tomorrow." Rof said nothing. The door slammed shut and once again there was silence. The birds, somehow realizing now was not the moment for song, made no sound. Vern sat down, closed the door, and started down the sand road. No dust billowed up behind him.

    At noon Pops took his youngest son to the bus station and with very little said between the two, Rof boarded the bus to Fort Benning. He looked out the window and started to wave goodbye, but Pops had already turned his back and started walking away from the bus. Rof fought back a tear. Bruce men didn't cry. He wiped away the moisture from his eyes and sat back in his seat. He squirmed to find comfort but found none. As the driver pulled away, he thought he saw Susie from the corner of his eye and struggled to look back through the small window but if she was there, he couldn't see. He sat back in the uncomfortable seat and a slight tear rolled down his cheek.

Vern did call his father the day after Rof left. He told him everything that was said between him and his brother. Rof told him nothing of the encounter, only that Vern had been home, and he would call his father. The old man shook his head as Vern told him what was said. He looked down at the same wooden floor at which Vern stared the day before. Without saying goodbye, he hung up the phone and walked over to a desk in the corner of the room, opened one of the drawers, pushed back some papers, and pulled out a picture. It was faded and had at one time been torn in half. A piece of clear tape held it together. A beautiful, sandy-haired woman's face stared back at him, a mischievous grin on her face. Pops looked through the window and held the picture for a while before his face tightened and he tore it into pieces. This time, there would be no way to repair it, and he flung the pieces onto the floor.

Vern drove back to campus that day without stopping. His usual radio station blaring his favorite music was silent. He just wanted to think. Alone, his tears were not held back. His eyes burned as the humid Florida air blew through the open window. The Bruce men were not supposed to cry or show any emotion other than contentment and anger. Sometimes there was no boundary to the amount of anger emerging from Pops. He was a quiet man, never saying much, but if you wronged him, his temper became like that of a volcano. Every other emotion they buried deep inside. When it bubbled to the surface, it tended to erupt like a violent volcano that appeared in anger, and it was just as extreme. Whether it was overwhelming sadness or violent anger, it was ferocious, but it was always brief. Vern felt so alone as the highway whined from the friction of the tires speeding down the road.

When he pulled up at the apartment on the edge of campus, his tears gone but the redness in his eyes telling all, he noticed his roommate looking out the window. A smile spread across Vern's face. He could recognize her slender silhouette anywhere. He couldn't let her see him like this though. His eyes were swollen and there was no hiding the evidence of his emotional outburst. As he tried in vain to clear his eyes, he realized that she didn't care one bit if he cried. He had told her what was going on back home with his brother. He told her he was torn between guilt and anger. Guilt that it should've been his name on the draft card and anger that his brother hadn't done something to avoid it and placed the blame entirely on his shoulders. He glanced back up at the window. The curtain closed and he could no longer see her figure in the window. He didn't get out of the car. Instead, he sat there, watching people walk by, seemingly without a care in the world. He snarled at that thought, jealousy overtaking his other emotions. *Damn them*, he thought, *they just don't know.* One in particular caught his attention and once again, Vern smiled. It was Patty Lee.

Patricia Clark was not like the girls Vern had gotten to know back in his tiny hometown or like the beach girls down on the coast. He had never cared about them. Of course, he had a girlfriend or two, but nothing ever serious. Brief encounters with vacation girls had happened a time or two, usually facilitated by his brother. Patty Lee as she was called, her middle name was Lee, was not from the Panhandle. She was from the prestigious West Palm Beach area. Her family made their fortune a long time ago developing the southern Atlantic coast of Florida. Unlike most real estate developers of that area, they were not thought of as carpetbaggers by the native Floridians. They weren't from the North just coming down to sunny Florida to make their fortune and run. Her father's family was from Alabama, and a couple generations back they'd settled in the quiet interior of the peninsula. At that time, the Civil War was freshly over, and the area was nothing but swamps, scrubby hardwoods, and pine thickets. The Clark family wasted no time getting to work.

Originally the family were farmers. They raised the lean, tough Florida Cracker Cattle that thrived in the hot swampy area and thick pines. The breed thrived on the vegetation of the area and needed very little care. This gave the Clark's time and money to clear land and import the larger varieties of beef cattle. They also planted vast orange groves. Her grandfather had bought a couple thousand acres. He cleared it, drained it, and planted the orange trees. That hard work paid off when Americans came out of World War II and had extra money to spend on luxuries such as orange juice. They hit the proverbial jackpot. It wasn't long before big corporations came into the area and bought up the independent producers. Her grandfather was an enterprising individual and saw opportunity on the coast just to the east. He sold as quickly as he could and left the heart of the peninsula behind. The Clark family invested in beachfront property and like the orange fields, they were one step ahead of everyone else. Americans now had money to spend, and new ways to travel.

When the automobile became an item the average family could afford instead of a luxury item for the rich, people left home on vacations. They flocked to the sunshine and year-round warmth of Florida. It seemed the Clark's became millionaires overnight and the family, from that point forward, was set for life. Not only that generation of Clarks but those to come. Her grandfather had one son, and that was Patty Lee's father. When Patty Lee began to choose colleges, her father was appalled that she wanted to go the State University in the Panhandle. Some considered the Panhandle of Florida an extension of Alabama. The state the family fled to find a better life. Miami was home to an outstanding private institution. Why not go there? She quickly informed her father she was going to school in Tallahassee, and she would have no more talk of Miami. As usual, Patty Lee got her way. Her father's only request was that she not bring some redneck home with her. It didn't matter if Vern wasn't quite a redneck, he was from the Panhandle and that was enough for her father not to like him.

Vern was not the typical guy that usually interested Patty Lee. He wasn't very athletic and always had his nose in a book. He did, however, seem to have a drive deep within himself to be more than he was. He had ambition. That, more than anything, attracted her to the young college student. She knew he wasn't rich. In fact, he had very little. The only reason he was able to go to college was his father's never-ceasing work schedule. As a foreman in the mill, Pops made good money. Enough to send his son to the college and help pay some of his bills. She noticed that this made Vern work even harder in his studies. He didn't want to let his father down. She was just the opposite. She thrilled herself at disappointing her father. It would be years before that would change for her.

If Patty Lee's father knew she was letting Vern stay with her, he would be furious. She didn't care. She was independent, sneaky, and spoiled. She always got her way and if her father discovered their living arrangements, she would use the power she held over him. She was an only child and always got what she wanted from him. She didn't go to the private school in Miami because she knew the reputation the state college had for parties. It did not disappoint. It was at one of these parties that she'd met Vern Bruce. He was there with a couple of people from one of his classes and wasn't fitting in. He was pretty much alone in a corner, staring sheepishly at the floor and was just about to leave when she'd noticed him. It was just blind luck that they met. She probably wouldn't have noticed him if he wasn't standing all alone in the corner not making eye contact with a soul. Curiosity had gotten the better of her and her inquisitive nature had to know why. She strolled up to Vern, playing with her hair as she did, and struck up a conversation. Vern fidgeted, barely made eye contact, and she could see sweat forming on his forehead. She was truthfully unimpressed with the quiet young man and decided he wasn't worth any further effort. It would be weeks before they would meet up again and this time it was very different circumstances that brought them together.

Chapter 4

Rof did not adapt to military life very well in the beginning. Back home, he never got out of bed before nine. In this place he was up before the sun, dressed, bed made up and ready for inspection. The local doctors didn't do a particularly good job repairing the torn ligament suffered in high school and that limited his physical activity. Every morning when he stepped out of bed, his knee popped into place and the first few mornings here were no exception. Today was the first day that didn't happen. The daily regimen of exercise seemed to help and for once, he didn't wince with his first step.

Without the pain to think about the first thing, he thought about home. When he stood up, he just stood there for a second, staring into nothing. He smiled, however, when he thought of Susie. He didn't think thoughts of her would bubble up here, but each day brought her smile into his thoughts. He smiled each time the image of her pretty face popped into his mind.

It helped that he didn't receive any letters from home. Each time mail call came, Rof's name wasn't called. Pops was not the type to write a letter. When he envisioned Pops sitting at the old desk in the living room, writing a letter, he couldn't help but laugh. Rof missed home but that didn't stop his determination. Now, a wide grin appeared each time he faced adversity. Rof renewed his promise to his brother each time.

Even though he did not like the military, he adapted quickly. Rof never really had a strict routine before, but now he enjoyed it. He arose each morning knowing what the day would hold. Repetition helped the time pass quickly. Within a couple of weeks, even though he was out of shape to start, he began to excel in physical training. His body, young and adaptable, quickly returned to its state during his high school days. Rof became one of the fastest in his barracks. Even the hard-nosed sergeant noticed when on one of their long runs, Rof turned back to help one of his friends that fell and writhed in pain, seemingly unable to complete the run. If he didn't finish, the whole squad would suffer. Without thinking he turned around, picked the young soldier up from the ground and the two of them finished the run, together. That day, he became the leader of his squad. When the squad made it back to the barracks, one by one each squad member thanked Rof, or Private Bum as he was known.

 He didn't like his new nickname. Rof was his nickname, one he held since he was a small boy and the one he had intended to keep. His fellow soldiers, however, thought it sounded stupid. Kind of like a dog barking they joked. Those first few days when he met someone and introduced himself, they all had the same question. "Rof? Like a dog barking?" He let it slip during one of those first confused days that he was a just a beach bum from the Panhandle. The name "Bum" stuck. Even the drill sergeant picked it up. He was dubbed Private Bum, and it stuck.

 The thing that surprised Rof during those eight weeks was how fast time moved. To an eighteen-year-old, eight weeks seems like an eternity when you are waiting to graduate high school.

Each day counted down as the one before it. In the army, there was no time for that, and time passed quickly. Mornings of physical training, team building, and survival training blurred into one another. Most days, Rof didn't know what day of the week it was. He really didn't care and before he knew it, the last week arrived. He graduated Basic Combat Training and then it was on to Advanced Individual Training. Soon he would know where his path in the Army led. The big question in Rof's mind was the same for each person graduating basic. Would they go to Vietnam? Most would, only a select few lucked out and were stationed stateside.

    Towards the end of the last week, Rof sat on his neatly made bunk as mail call arrived. He had long since given up as his name was never called. When the other guys on his squad heard their names and received their letters, Rof picked his head up and glanced at the guy handing them out. There were only two left to distribute. He wasn't really listening when the guy looked at the letter twice and said, "Ronald Bruce?" The men looked back at Rof, they only knew him as Rof or Bum. Who was Ronald? A few snickered as Rof sprang from his bunk, grabbed the letter and held it in his hand. Had Pops written finally? Was it another admonishment from his older brother? He grimaced. If it was, he would just tear it up immediately. He didn't want to hear Vern's voice much less read his words. Shock swept over his face for a second when he saw who sent the letter, but it didn't last long. When he read Susie's name, he could smell her sweet perfume, and the shock gave way to a broad smile. The whole time he had been at the Fort, he told himself it didn't matter if anyone sent him a letter. However, just reading her name made his soul fill with happiness but there was a small part yearning for word from his father.

Rof didn't expect Pops to make the trip up to Fort Benning for his graduation. Just as in letter writing, this wasn't his father's style. He hoped his brother wouldn't show up, and he didn't.

The letter from Susie haunted his mind as he stood in the burning sun. Sweat poured from the side of his face as a faceless superior officer he had never seen before spoke behind the elevated podium. He didn't hear a word the man spoke as the words written by Susie in her letter echoed though his thoughts. He was going to be a father. In her letter she told him that she was pregnant. He was the father. She wrote that she hadn't told her family and the thought of doing so terrified her. Susie's mother and father were very old-fashioned, and she feared losing them when they found out. She confessed hope that Rof would have a break before he shipped out and they could get married. Rof wanted no part. When he read those words, he knew he loved her and temporarily felt excitement in the fact he would be a father. Those feelings faded quickly, however. His face hardened, and he wished she had never told him. He had enough on his plate without worrying about a young wife back home and a baby on the way. As the old officer concluded his speech and pronounced them graduates, the words he wrote back to her raced through his mind. He told her he would have no break and when he arrived wherever he was going, he would write. He knew it was a lie. The truth would be too painful for the frightened young girl. At that time, he truthfully didn't know where he was headed, but after the graduation ceremony ended, he found out.

In 1969, there seemed to be a rush to move draftees to Vietnam as quickly as possible and with as little training as possible. Usually after basic they were sent to AIT and then assigned further depending on their specialty. There was a need for men "in country" as it was called. Especially in the infantry as the loss of life mounted daily. Rof was assigned at once from basic into the infantry and his orders sent him to Vietnam.

His hopes of remaining stateside were dashed the day of graduation. He barely held back tears as he learned that in three days, he was to board a plane for Vietnam. Rof didn't want to show emotion in front of his men. Bruce's didn't do that. They waited until they were alone. So, as he sat on the floor, alone next to his bunk, he finally let his tears flow. His head in his hands, Private Bum wept as a small child that met their first skinned knee. The army gave him three days to see his family but declined. He didn't want Pops to know where he was headed. He would write a letter and tell Pops he was going to AIT. He would lie to his father to spare him a couple of weeks of pain. He would tell Vern nothing. He didn't deserve it. As he said his brother's name aloud, his tears stopped and hatred welled up inside him. That same grin crossed his lips as the promise appeared from his memory. When he made it to Vietnam, he would once again write his father and confess the truth.

The day he left, he found a secluded spot on the half circle building that served as their barracks and sat in what little shade he could find. His hand trembled as he wrote a second letter to Susie. He couldn't wait on Vietnam for this letter. Rof peered at the sky before he began to write, gathering the words in his mind before he placed them on the sheet of paper. Taking a deep breath he began to pen the words. He promised the scared pregnant girl they would marry upon his return. He also promised Susie he would be the best father he could to his son or daughter, whichever the case may be. Now, on his day of departure, the thought of becoming a father didn't scare him as much. Rof cupped his hands together and imagined holding his child within them. In his letter, he asked her not to write to him while he was gone. He wanted no distractions over there. He didn't mention his promise to his brother. In fact, at that exact moment, he wasn't thinking of Vern. He thought of only Susie, standing beside a runway with a baby in her arms. That vision replaced his desire for revenge. He would survive for his child. Standing up and folding the letter so that it fit in his pocket, he picked up his bag and began his journey.

Vern made the trip home the weekend after his little brother had slipped away to Vietnam. Enjoying a rare day off, Pops rocked in his chair watching a baseball game on the television. The season was winding down and his beloved Atlanta Braves, having become the first Major League team in the Deep South a few years before, stood on the verge of winning the newly formed Western Division of the National League. The weather was cooler. In the Panhandle of Florida cool was a relative term. This time of year, if a person wasn't pouring sweat due to the humidity, it was considered cool. Even though it was midday, Vern thought he felt a cool breeze lifting the curtains as he stepped inside.

"You heard anything from Rof?" he asked his father.

Pops didn't turn his gaze from the television. He just said, "Nothing more than he was supposed to ship out for AIT this weekend and he would let me know when he got there. Didn't even say where he was going for training."

Vern raised an eyebrow and sat down on the couch next to his father. Facing the floor and his voice low he said, "I don't know if me and him will ever get past this, Dad." Pops turned his attention to his oldest son. He couldn't remember Vern ever calling him Dad. His face had been indifferent but suddenly there was a sadness that swept over it. He hoped his sadness wasn't that apparent to his son, but Vern detected it at once and shook his head slightly. The thought of his father in pain turned his own mood a little darker. Pops, never one to wallow in pity, turned the conversation back to one of hope.

"Yes, y'all will," he responded with as much certainty as he could muster. "You boys are brothers. Blood. If you ain't got each other, you got nothing. If you two didn't learn anything else from me, you should've learned that."

It was the same speech about family that Pops always gave, and Vern nodded just to make his father feel a little better. He wished he believed that blood would win out and he would reconcile with his brother, but he didn't feel it in his heart. He turned his face from the floor and looked his father in the eyes. It was time for some better news. He smiled and told his father he was going to get married. He was bringing Patty Lee home next weekend to meet him. Pops smiled back and tried to seem happy for his son, but the more Vern told him of his new bride to be, he was skeptical. A family trait of the Bruce men was they couldn't hide their true thoughts from shining through their facial expressions. They didn't show much emotion except in their face. Pops couldn't hide his skepticism behind a fake smile.

"This girl is from the Atlantic Coast?" he asked his son, still trying to put a fake smile on his face, but his forehead wrinkled involuntarily with worry.

"Yes, Pops, she is from West Palm Beach. Her dad is a big real estate guy down there."

"Real estate? He builds houses? Is he a contractor?" he quizzed his son. The old man didn't put much faith in people who didn't work with their hands.

"No, her family invested in coastal land a long time ago. Now they develop and sell. He hires contractors, though," Vern responded, hoping this would at least ease his father's concern.

"Huh," is all the old man said, and that was that. Vern's smile faded slightly as he turned his attention to the ball game still playing out on the television.

Rof marveled at the sheer size of the C-141 aircraft as he stood outside the beast waiting to board. The air of California contrasted sharply with the hot, humid Panhandle. He tilted his head back and let the soothing air flow through his short, sharply cropped hair. He almost cried the day his long flocks fell victim to the army's clippers and lay at his feet on the floor. Now he was glad it was gone. He enjoyed feeling the breeze.

Rof kept to himself for the most part since he'd arrived on the West Coast. He didn't venture too far from the base, and he didn't want to get to know any people here as there wouldn't be time to really make friends. There weren't very many soldiers on the plane, and he felt that was unusual. *But what do I know?* he thought to himself. When he landed, the officer accompanying them from Georgia stood and matter-of-factly told them they would fly from this base to Hawaii in a few short days. From there, he offered nothing else as the orders were classified. That was all he said, no small talk, just orders. Rof was not told where and when he would get "in country." When the signal was given, he looked around one last time at California and in a line the men ran onto the plane, their destination, besides knowing they were going to Vietnam, unknown.

With a massive thrust, the cargo plane thundered down the long runway. Vern felt the g-forces increase throughout his body and his face bore the fear he felt inside. His hands began to sweat, and his breathing increased. The men all sat in jump seats in a row, only a thin sheet of metal between them and the violent forces outside. Looking down the line, inspecting his men, the officer noticed Rof's chest rising and falling as he struggled to contain his breathing.

"Easy, Bum," the officer said. "This ain't the bad part." The officer seemed to delight in delivering the message and it made Rof feel even more concerned. He looked over at his fellow soldiers. They all had their eyes closed and Rof did the same. With his eyes closed, he pretended he was back on the school bus riding down one of the bumpy country roads back home. He felt each jolt as the plane fought the turbulent air, trying to climb. He closed his eyes tighter and thought of nothing but home.

The plane vibrated, popped, and creaked the entire flight to Hawaii. A couple of times, Rof felt the bottom of the plane seem to drop from below his feet. There were no windows in the rear of the colossal plane so he couldn't see the ocean. He could only see the soldiers strapped in on the opposite side of the plane. He kept his vision straight ahead and didn't try to look down his own side of the plane when he opened his eyes. The others had small conversations here and there but for the most part everyone was quiet. There was no doubt the other men were just as scared as he was, but most hid it a little better. He promised himself that if he made it through all this alive, he would never fly again.

Landing without problem in Hawaii to refuel, the soldiers were not allowed off the plane. He did catch a glimpse of some palm trees as the rear hatch lowered during the fuel stop but once the plane filled its tanks, they were airborne once again. This time as the plane made its bumpy ascent, he could feel what little breakfast he had before leaving California creeping back through his esophagus. With a gulp, he choked it down. He was successful, but he could taste bile, and he figured that wouldn't be his last bout with nausea today.

There was still no word to the enlisted men strapped in their seats where they would eventually land. He began to question if they were even headed to Vietnam. Why the secret orders? Why so few on this flight? Some GIs were flown commercially to Vietnam. Why were they different? They had been airborne for hours when the flight violently changed.

Suddenly and without warning, the plane shook more violently than it had before. The straps that held the cargo going with them on their journey began to stretch with each awkward movement of the massive plane and the cargo shifted, stretching the boundaries of the straps themselves. Rof reached down and with sweaty hands tightened his seatbelt. His forehead began to bead with perspiration. Over the whine of the engines, he could hear popping noises. He tilted his head towards the sounds, trying to figure out what they were. At first, they were faint, but they began to become louder with each passing second. The sounds escalated, becoming more numerous. Something was very wrong. The sounds from the engines seemed to fade and Rof made the decision to remove his seat belt. If this thing was going down, he didn't want to be strapped in and drown without a chance to save himself or the people around him. The soldiers around him were crying out, wanting to know what was happening, but the stone-faced officer said nothing. His hands folded together in prayer, paying no attention to those in his charge. Rof, standing, if unsteadily, hung onto one of the ribs holding the airplane together and shouted for the men to also get out of their seatbelts, but before any one of them could oblige, the plane started a steep descent, throwing Rof violently forward.

The C-141 was one of the sturdiest planes the United States military used for troop and equipment deployment. The massive plane could fly on two engines, and they were down to those two. Flying without half its engines had been done before, but barely and not for long. They pilots' orders were for strict radio silence as they were flying over forbidden territory, and they hoped for no more problems. The two pilots checked their instruments and voiced confidence in their ability to bring the ailing bird home. Their destination in the South China Sea spanned only two hundred miles away on two engines, they would save fuel so they decided to dump as much as they could to ensure they could make it. Their confidence didn't last long.

Engine number three, heavily damaged, began to sputter and the pilot, looking from his window, indicated smoke. It was only a matter of time before it suffered the same fate and stalled. When the engine finally and suddenly went silent, the C-141 began to nosedive.

As he was thrown forward, his head hit a piece of steel and began bleeding profusely and it felt like someone had split his skull with a dull axe, but he was still conscious. As blood began to obscure his sight, he thought of his father. The old man was going to take this badly. He could see the hard lines that cracked his father's face from long years in the mill and in his mind's eye he saw the pain he would endure. Time seemed to stand still as thoughts rushed through his mind and Rof saw the vision of Susie and a young child standing next to her. He tried to focus, but the vision receded the more he tried to keep it in his mind. The plane sounded like a siren as it accelerated towards the ocean below. As the vision of his lost family faded, he could see Vern, his arms folded and shaking his head. He cursed his name and before the plane slammed into the ocean, he renewed his promise to survive. Before he blacked out, the pain of not knowing his child flooded his mind. As suddenly as it started, it was all over.

Chapter 5

Vern watched the evening news each and every afternoon without fail. Each day, his anger rose with the sight of young men being hauled to helicopters, bandages wrapping bleeding wounds on gurneys. Each day held the fear of receiving the dreaded news that his brother was dead. Not a day passed that he didn't think of Rof and the way they'd parted. Most mornings, he awoke covered in sweat and his brother's final words ringing in his ears. There was so much hatred in Rof's blue eyes that day. So much rage. When he passed someone on campus that resembled his little brother, guilt would wash over him.

One day as a shaggy-haired guy resembling Rof strolled by with his arm around a pretty girl, it was more than Vern could take. He swore it was Rof's face, and he nearly ran over to hug the stranger. That day he swore that he would reconcile with Rof, no matter what. He just wanted his brother home.

He wondered if Pops knew where Rof was stationed for his AIT. He was going home this weekend, and he would find out and write to him. *No better yet,* he would go there and apologize to his little brother in person. He couldn't let him go to Vietnam without the two making peace.

His attention turned back to the television just in time to see a reporter on the deck of an American ship reporting that a cargo plane had gone down in the South China Sea and that search and rescue operations were underway. It was a scene that played out daily on the screen in front of him and Vern didn't pay too much attention to it. If he did, he would just get angry and he really couldn't help the situation. *This damned war*, he thought. There was another protest on campus soon and that would be where he could play his part. He had been part of several rallies on campus, and one reminded him of Patty Lee.

When Vern thought of his fiancé, the guilt seemed to ease, if only for a while. Patty Lee wanted to talk about nothing other than the wedding coming up. Each time she did, he would take her hand and pretend to listen. The guilt may ease, but Rof never really left his thoughts. The wedding would provide a distraction and offer him a day of happiness, but he knew what would happen. Rof would be with him that day. He was sure that as he held Patty Lee's hand, he would glance into the audience and see his brother's face. Vern closed his eyes tightly and through the kaleidoscope of colors, Rof's face came into focus. It was inevitable.

As his eyes came back into focus upon reopening them, another face invaded his mind, and he shifted in his chair. The face of Patty Lee's father, Daniel Clark. Tall, fit, outgoing and outspoken, Old Man Clark as he was known, hung in Vern's thoughts almost as much as his brother. Even though he had the same type roots, Old Man Clark wanted more for his daughter than some kid from the Panhandle.

When she told her father about Vern, he leaped from his desk and paced frantically around the room. He was almost in a full rage when he yelled that she had done exactly what he told her not to do. When the old man calmed down and sat back down, he shook his head and turned around in his chair to peer out of his office window. The swaying palm trees below him in the parking lot seemed to calm him and he turned back and took his daughter by the hand. She told her father of Vern's ambition and his drive to be something other than just another beach kid. Patty Lee went over every detail when she came back to school and warned Vern that her father accepted it but didn't like it. Vern shifted in his chair again. If he was going to be successful in business, he had to be able to win people over. He sighed and thought, *If I can win this man over, I'll do just fine*, and at that moment he snapped his fingers and committed to just that.

He heard the lock on the door thump and Patty Lee burst through the door in tears.

"Daddy said he would not pay a dime for our wedding!" she exclaimed as tears rolled down her face. "NOT ONE DIME!" Vern's leaped to meet her, and she seemed to collapse into his arms.

"I thought he accepted it," Vern said, his confusion showing in his voice.

"He accepted it," she replied, "but he doesn't want any part." Patty Lee's tears began to soak through his shirt as she buried her face into his shoulder.

Vern's face didn't change, and his voice, the confusion gone, calmly said, "Patty Lee, let me talk to him." He began to stroke her hair, trying to reassure her. "This weekend. In fact, right now. Let's go down there and I'll show him what kind of son-in-law he'll get. We'll get this straightened out." Vern pushed thoughts of the protest and going to see his father to the back of his mind. He had a couple of weeks before Rof would leave. He had time. Patty Lee finally stopped crying and with a kiss, her crisis ended, and the tears stopped almost at once.

Instead of heading west towards the Panhandle, the nearly new Mustang headed east on the new blacktop of Interstate Ten. Patty Lee propped her right hand on the steering wheel and held her other out of the window, dancing it through the air. She had not yet allowed her fiancé to take the wheel of her beloved blue car. Most people wanted new red Mustangs, but not her. She wanted blue. She said it just matched Florida and the blue waters of the Atlantic. She hadn't grown up with the emerald-green waters off the northern Gulf Coast but with the dark blue waves of the Atlantic Ocean. Tallahassee behind them, there was nothing but pavement, swamps, and pine trees lining the newly opened road. They were almost halfway to Jacksonville before they spoke more than a couple of words to each other. Vern had been lost in his own thoughts, his window rolled up and his gaze locked on the flat, scruffy landscape speeding by.

"What are you going to say to Daddy?" she asked so quietly that he almost didn't hear her. Vern kept his gaze on the passing vegetation and sat silent for a few seconds before answering, collecting his thoughts and his words. He smiled, if only half-heartedly, and turned his attention to Patty Lee.

"The truth. I love you and want to marry you." He paused for a second and placed his hand on top of her leg. He thought he felt it tremble. "I'm not the hick or beach bum that he thinks I am," he said, the words slipping carefully off his tongue. Vern turned his head and looked back out the window. The trees changed from the long, slender pines to thick, wide oaks. Signs were scarce on the new road, but the sight of those trees indicated they were approaching the town of Live Oak and about halfway to Jacksonville. They were making excellent time, but to himself, he wished for a longer trip.

Patty Lee pursed her lips and didn't take her eyes off the road, "I don't think that will be enough. Can you cut back on your accent a little?" Patty Lee flashed a smile in Vern's direction, and he didn't return it. "Are *you guys* not from Alabama originally?" Patty Lee chuckled and said yes but that was a long time ago. They considered themselves native Floridians, South Floridians to be exact. Vern laughed, and he took his hand off her leg and rubbed his chin.

"I want him to know that I will be dedicated to my plans in business but also that I will never ignore you. You, our future kids, will be my priority and everything that I do will go towards that goal of giving y'all..." Vern caught himself, "*You guys* everything," he said as he looked back at her and directly into those brown eyes that had captivated him as the first time he saw her.

Patty Lee raised an eyebrow; she hadn't even thought that far into the future. Kids? Their kids? She rarely thought past the current day. The thought wasn't terrible to her, however. She had always wanted a daughter. She had envisioned her daughter dressed up like a baby doll following her mother's pageant footsteps. She glanced back at him, and Vern had this crooked, silly little grin. "Mention grandchildren to Daddy and its fifty-fifty." She laughed as the words escaped her mouth. As a sign showing eighty miles to Jacksonville sped by, Vern, feeling he was not ready, wanted to get to West Palm as quickly as possible.

The Secretary of the Army has asked me to express his deep regret that your son, Private Ronald Frank Bruce, died in route to Vietnam on December 2, 1969, as a result of an aviation accident. Please accept my deepest sympathy. This confirms personal notification made by a representative of the Secretary of the Army.

William Bower Vernon Major General USA The Adjutant General

Department of the Army Washington, DC

His hand trembled as he held the telegram. It had to be some kind of mix-up. Rof wasn't even going to Vietnam yet. He was in North Carolina for his training and that would take at least six weeks. It had been only two. Instead of tears, Pops face reddened, and his anger boiled. When he found out who was responsible for sending a telegram like this to the wrong person, there was going to be hell to pay. His hand shook as he dialed the phone trying to reach Vern at school. His son left a number for Pops to call in cases like this.

It just so happened that two older ladies out on the main road were on the party line, a line shared by members of the community, when he picked up the receiver. Usually very polite, his voice seethed with anger as he asked them to get off the damn line. Church gossip could wait. He had to contact Vern.

Vern was almost in West Palm when the phone in Patty Lee's apartment back in Tallahassee rang repeatedly. Patty Lee finally relented and let him drive her new car. He had taken over just south of Jacksonville. During this part of the trip, Patty Lee had taken a long nap and Vern had time to think. He pressed the accelerator until he felt the carpeted steel under his foot and the Mustang responded with more power than he had ever controlled. The wind blew through his neatly cut hair and a smile swept over his face. He thought of Patty Lee and the future. The smile left his face momentarily when he thought of facing her father but mostly, he thought about Rof. He had hoped to see him this weekend. He wanted to mend the fence as well as he could. He passed several cars without lifting the accelerator. He had to make a good impression on his future father-in-law. As that thought crossed his mind, Vern glanced in the rearview mirror and saw blue lights behind him. Patty Lee awakened and saw the lights in her mirror. She smiled and said, "I'll tell them to call Dad if they try to give you a ticket. Don't worry." Vern grimaced. *Damn*, he thought, *that will be a great first impression, getting me out of a speeding ticket on his daughter's brand-new Mustang.*

Pops called and called and with a deep sigh gave up. He buried his head in his hands. He didn't know where Vern went, but he couldn't waste any more time. The only other person he knew to contact was the sheriff of the small county.

Charlie King had been the county sheriff for the past twenty or so years. His hair had grayed over the years, but he seemed to be in surprisingly good physical shape for a man of over seventy years. You could still see the shape of muscle under his uniform. Everyone in the Panhandle knew him and everyone respected him. Unlike most southern cops of the time, he hadn't been caught up in the battle of the races. The panhandle wasn't home to many Black people, and those that lived there were in the larger cities. Things like that were not really a problem for the small county sheriff.

Pops found Charlie in the usual place—a truck stop found near the new interstate where it crossed the state highway leading to the Gulf's white, sandy beaches. Charlie could be found there and not in an office. He was sipping strong black coffee when one side of the double door opened, and Pops walked in, looking frantically for the sheriff. Looking up from his newspaper and coffee, Charlie was taken aback when he saw Pops rushing down the aisle towards him. Pops always kept to himself and the only communication between the two had been courtesy stops during election years and they had been brief.

"How's it going there, Mr. Bruce?" Charlie asked before Pops reached his corner booth.

Pops didn't say anything, but Charlie could read the concern on the old man's face. He handed the telegram to Charlie, his hand still trembling. Charlie's weathered hand took it and read it twice. It wasn't the first time he had seen one of these.

"Damn," was all he could muster. He hated that he was the person people came to in times like this, but it was the job he had chosen and on the other hand, he appreciated the respect.

Pops, a quiver in his strong, husky voice said, "It can't be true, Charlie. I heard from him two weeks ago. He was supposed to be training in North Carolina. It's supposed to be weeks before he was to go."

"Huh, maybe it's a mistake. They may have the wrong guy. You know how much they foul up in the government.," he replied. "What do you want me to do?"

"I can't get ahold of Vern. He would know what to do. Please call someone. I don't know who to call. Please find out if my boy is dead." Pops couldn't hold back the tears as they streamed down his face. A couple of them dripped onto his white shirt. Charlie nodded his head, stood up and put his hand on Pops' shoulder. He knew who to call.

"I'll call Mac Tate. He'll be the one to find out," he told Pops trying to reassure the broken man in front of him. "I'll know by the end of the day, Mr. Bruce. I promise. By the way, do you want me to track down Vern and let him know what I find out?"

Pops lowered his head and let the thought run through his mind. The tears were short-lived and stopped. He apologized for crying and Charlie just shook head as if to say he understood. "Get him home, Charlie. Don't tell him why though." Pops turned and started walking towards the door, his head low and staring at the tile floor. He could hear the people around him whispering. He shook his head and shuffled out the double doors.

Vern and Patty Lee were sitting on the enormous home's back patio overlooking the Atlantic Ocean. They shared a loveseat-style chair but sat as far from each other as possible. Even though he had grown up near the ocean, he never saw homes like this. This was a mansion. From the large marble pillars surrounding the front door, to the spacious living room, Vern was amazed. He glanced around while waiting for her father to join them, shaking his head as he took in the beauty of the majestic home. Pops made a good living, but they were considered poor by this man's standards. He must seem like a toothless county bumpkin to this man. It was a cool day but sweat began to bead on his forehead and his palms were fast becoming moist. Vern wiped them constantly on his pants, hoping they would dry before having to shake Old Man Clark's hand. The calm that came over him in the car was gone and he was now more nervous than he had ever been in his life. He looked over at Patty Lee. If she was nervous, she didn't show it. She looked back at her fiancé and smiled as if to say, "It will be alright." The door opened and the old man appeared. He wore a baseball cap, white shorts, and shirt. Vern guessed he was on his way to play tennis. Later he would recognize this as the preferred outdoor costume of West Palm's wealthy.

Vern stood to greet him and as he stood, he wiped his right hand on his trousers once more and extended it in the same motion, hoping Mr. Clark wouldn't notice. "Mr. Clark, my name is Vernon Bruce, sir. It's a pleasure to meet you," he said, with the most confident voice he could muster. In his head his voice sounded like the bumpkin this man thought he was. The more he tried to hide his accent the more it became apparent. Mr. Clark didn't extend his hand for a couple of seconds. A stern look on his face, he studied Vern's face for any information his expression provided. The seconds ticked away, and Vern felt the sweat on his hand once again. When he finally extended his hand, Vern took it and shook it firmly. He exhaled deeply, releasing a breath he didn't know he held.

"Sit down," he said after the handshake ended and motioned towards the seat Vern previously occupied. The young man did as instructed, and Mr. Clark took the seat next to the couple. Mr. Clark studied the young man sitting in front of him, saying nothing, but Vern felt the old man's eyes studying him, hoping for a weakness to exploit. Patty Lee smiled and tilted her head as if to say, "Enough." One look at his daughter's smile and his expression of stone turned into a smile instantly.

"Daddy, how have you been?" she asked, already knowing the answer and her smile still entrancing her father.

He glanced at his daughter and back to Vern, "Good," he replied curtly, his smile vanishing as he turned to his future son-in-law.

Vern eased a few more inches away from Patty Lee and shuffled his feet. Taking a deep breath, he decided to take the initiative. "Mr. Clark, you don't have to worry about Patty Lee's choice to marry me. I don't want you to think of me as a product of where I come from. Yes, I'm from the Panhandle. Yes, I grew up on the beaches of the Gulf. No, I am not a redneck or a country bumpkin. I'm more. I'm determined to be somebody. Patty Lee is going to be my partner, not only in life, but in *our* business."

Mr. Clark seemed to be bewildered by this kid in front of him. He bit his lip and again, didn't respond for what seemed like an eternity. The silence was deafening but Vern held his ground and his eye contact with Patty Lee's father. He bit his tongue and fought the inclination to yell, "Just say something, damn it!" The old man's face changed, and his body seemed to relax. What started out a small chuckle deep within him, evolved into a boisterous laugh.

"Son, you got some nerve!" he exclaimed as he stood up and once again extended his hand. This time he shook his future son-in-law's hand without hesitation. Patty Lee's smile, which seemed insincere at first, spread across her face and she stood up and put her arms around Vern and her father. She winked at Vern and slightly kissed him on the cheek.

Mac Tate was the personal secretary, campaign manager and best friend of the Panhandle's congressman. If you needed something, you didn't go to the congressman, you went to Mac. Mac got a call from Charlie about an hour before. Making a few calls himself, it didn't take long to find out that it was indeed Mr. Bruce's son that had been killed in the crash. Apparently, the soldier lied to his father and brother. It didn't matter to him why; it was none of his business. He picked up the phone, called the sheriff and told him what he had found. He also informed Charlie that he didn't have to tell the grieving father that his son was indeed gone. The congressman's office would do it. He asked Charlie to track down his other son as Mr. Bruce requested. He had a hunch where the young man was and gave the sheriff what information he knew. When the conversation ended and both men hung up the phone, Charlie whistled. He wondered how in the world did Tate know where Vern Bruce might be? The old law officer shook his head. Deep down, he didn't want to know.

Vern received a call from the sheriff the morning after his conversation with Patty Lee's father. The phone rang a little before sunrise. To maybe impress his future father-in-law, he had planned to get up early, before daylight, anyway, take a jog and be dressed and ready for the day by eight. The phone call interrupted his plans, however.

He never expected he would have to answer a call from Charlie King while in West Palm. Charlie wouldn't tell him over the phone why he needed to get back, but his heart dropped, and he feared the worst about Pops. Immediately after hanging up the phone with the sheriff, he dialed his home and when the phone rang several times, his heartbeat increased to the point he felt it would explode. When Pops answered the phone, relief overcame him, and his legs felt weak. That relief vanished in an instant.

Pops voice quivered when he told his oldest son about the telegram. There had to be some mistake, he told Vern. Rof was in North Carolina. The telegram said he died over the waters of the South China Sea in a plane crash. Vern's mind flashed back to the news he saw a couple of days ago and remembered hearing about the crash. He just shook his head thinking there was no way his brother was on that plane. There couldn't be. He told his father he was on his way home and hung up the phone. "Be careful, Vern," he heard his father say before the handle was firmly on the receiver. He stood there to catch his breath and let his heart settle. His legs were back under him. He would borrow Patty Lee's Mustang and be home by that evening.

Patty Lee offered no resistance when he told her what he had to do. He thought she might want to go with him, and he was ready to quell that notion quickly. She hugged Vern tightly, and she knew this was something he had to do alone. If they were married, it would be different; of course she would go. She had yet to meet Pops, but she didn't want to do it in this manner. She kissed Vern, and they held the kiss as long as they could. The couple said their goodbyes as he fired up the baby-blue mustang and started down the long driveway. In the rearview mirror, he saw Patty Lee waving.

Vern pulled up to the front porch of his father's house right as the sun began to set behind a gray, dull sky. It started raining heavily as he sped through Tallahassee, and it had yet to let up. It was cold rain, and it matched his mood. Before he stepped out, he noticed another car parked near the front of the house. A black Cadillac with government license plates. Must be Mac Tate, he thought to himself. The most important man in the Florida Panhandle, never mind the congressmen. They come and go. The one constant in Panhandle politics was Mac Tate.

Mac was seated on the couch and Pops was in his chair as Vern opened the screen door and stepped in. Even though it was cold and rainy, Pops always left the front door open with only the screen door shut if he expected someone. Vern shook off the cold, but he bypassed the fireplace as he lowered himself to a knee so he could look his father in the eye.

"Vern?" Mac asked, already knowing the answer. Vern looked a lot like a younger version of his old man, and anyone would be able to tell they were father and son.

"Yessir," he responded and then hugged his father who leaned down to embrace his surviving son. With that, Mac Tate stood up. He didn't want to give the two men in front of him this kind of news sitting down. He folded his hands in front of him and stood as tall as a man his age could manage.

"Gentlemen, ain't no other way to tell you. Rof was on that plane when it went down. There were no survivors." Mac said it as delicately has he could but didn't want to leave room for doubt. Halfway expecting it, but not wanting it to be true, Pops said nothing. His face, already pale, turned ghostly white. Vern could not hold back tears, and they streamed down his face. He embraced his father again, who still had not spoken. The two held each other for several minutes before Pops let go of his son and spoke to Mac, "Thank you, sir. Is there anything you can tell us about why he was on that plane?"

Mac looked at his feet and then back into the old man's eyes. "They told me that it was classified. Rof was on some kind of secret mission. I don't know what and I don't know why. He was one of the few who skipped through AIT just for this particular assignment. I doubt he even knew why or where he was going." His voice grew firmer. "But I promise you this, Mr. Bruce, I will find out more about this. I ain't going to leave it at this. You have my word."

Both Pops and Vern shook Mac's hand and thanked him again as he left. They barely spoke that night even though little sleep occurred between the two of them. He didn't call Patty Lee. He didn't want to say the words aloud. Every time he tried to say Rof's name, no sound emerged. That could wait for tomorrow.

Damn tomorrow, he thought. Tomorrow, he had to start getting ready to bury his only brother or at least an empty box representing his brother. The brother that would not speak to him. The brother that should still be alive. The brother that he would miss for the rest of his life. As the sun came up over the pines, no birds offered their song.

Chapter 6

Pops was never the same after he buried his son or more accurately buried an empty casket. During the funeral, he hovered over the closed empty casket. He didn't shed a tear and there was only the empty look on his face. The only bodies found in or around the wreckage were the pilots. Vern thought that bothered Pops more than Rof dying. Not seeing his son for a final time, seemed to break his father. One day shortly after the funeral, Pops walked into the mill manager's office and retired. On that day, he retired from life. Rare as though they were, smiles became even less frequent on the face of the shell of a man. Laughter was nonexistent. The only time Vern could remember his father pretending to be happy was at his wedding. Pops performed his duties as Vern's best man and seemed to enjoy himself. Even though he put little stock in people other than blood relations, Pops liked Patty Lee. He was proud for his son even as he mourned for the other.

The wedding was about what you would expect for a West Palm debutant. The service on the beach behind the Clark Mansion rivaled any event in West Palm's luxurious history. Vern and Patty Lee recited their vows in front of the rolling waves of the Atlantic Ocean. The royalty of Florida filed in to see one of its most powerful son's only daughter marry an unknown from the Panhandle. The Governor of Florida was there mingling with a couple of congressmen. Vern soaked up every bit of it. He beamed; his chest bowed as he strutted through the crowd, shaking hands with everyone he met. If they didn't know who he was when the party started, they would know Vernon Bruce at the end. Patty Lee enjoyed being the center of attention. She wasn't far behind Vern, shaking hands and soaking up her special day.

The only congressman not there to enjoy the party was Mac Tate's "boss." The rumor held that he was going to retire after this term and didn't need to gladhand with what he considered fake people. He sent Mac instead. Old Man Clark, mentally recording each attendee, didn't miss the slight. He scanned the crowd, making a mental checklist as to who was there, who was invited and who didn't show up. He locked eyes with Tate and the wily old bureaucrat made a bee line to Patty Lee's father. "The Congressman sends his regards. Unfortunately, he was held up in DC." He and Clark shook hands and quickly parted. Tate saw Vern, still shaking every hand in the room and Mac headed his way.

"Congratulations, son," Tate told him as he shook Vern's hand.

"Thank you, Mr. Tate," Vern responded, "and thank you for everything you've done for my father."

"I was glad to do it. It's a damn shame this war keeps eating up our people," he said staring at his shoes. "I don't know how it will end. You can't ever tell with that sneaky ass Nixon in the White House." The two men stood silent for a second and Vern didn't know what to say. Mac noticed the awkwardness and broke the silence, "Let's not get into the problems of the world today, my boy! Again, congrats, and I think you married into the right family." He chuckled. "And you got a good wife in the deal." Vern smiled and snuck a look at his bride. Patty Lee noticed him looking and flashed a pretty smile towards him.

    As Mac Tate walked away and began glad handing with the others, Vern continued to smile. He loved Patty Lee. The fact that she came from money and power had nothing to do with their marriage. He didn't know her at all when they'd met. He expected to be confronted with some kind of prenuptial agreement from her father, but even as the big day neared, neither Patty Lee nor her father mentioned such. Today cemented his position in the Clark family.

    The newly minted Mr. and Mrs. Vernon Frank Bruce did not take up residence near Pops in the small town up the road from the Gulf. Mr. Clark had presented them with a small cottage right on the water in the small town of Mexico Beach, just down the road from Panama City. He offered Vern a place in the real estate business in West Palm, but wanting to make it on his own, he declined. Patty Lee had no intention of living under her father's thumb after experiencing such freedom in college, so she did not object. She loved the cottage. Mexico Beach lay right on the Gulf of Mexico, was home to the same white, sandy beaches as its more famous neighbor Panama City Beach, but still held that small town Florida feel. There were only a couple of restaurants and motels. Most of the people lived there since before the Civil

War and they didn't want their little slice of paradise to become another "Miracle Strip."

Vern also loved his new home and its location. He awoke every morning, walked out onto his back deck and with his coffee, looked out over the Gulf of Mexico. As a boy he'd dreamed of a home like this and now it was reality.

The newlywed couple also had business in the back of their minds in choosing to live on the rural Gulf Coast rather than West Palm. The Gulf Coast was Vern's home, and he saw enormous potential there. The Panhandle coastline was an untapped market. The waterfront properties were owned by people that handed down the land from generation to generation. They didn't know the value of the property they owned. To Vern, these people didn't have vision. Vern knew and his vision of the future was going to make him a fortune.

Often Vern would sit on his back porch in the evening and watch the lights of the fishing boats as they went in and out of the nearby harbor. In these moments, he let visions of Rof reenter his mind. Guilt would trickle back into his thoughts and feelings. The image Vern tried to burn into his memory was his blond-haired, blue-eyed, beach-loving brother at the peak of his youth. But each time the image morphed into the haunting image of his brother's eyes and the hatred they held when they met for the last time.

Sometimes, Patty Lee walked out on the deck at precisely the right time, and break Rof's spell. She embraced her husband during those times, worried he may never shake the guilt of being the older brother and avoiding the draft and shifting it to his little brother. She comforted Vern in the middle of the night when he awoke, sweating profusely and screaming, dreams of his brother slowly sinking to the bottom of the sea, his eyes staring into Vern's soul, raging in his unconscious mind. Patty Lee mentioned it might be useful to talk to someone about Rof and his death, but, like any southern man, he scoffed at the idea. If he had to deal with the death of his brother the rest of his life, so be it.

As time ticked away, Vern became increasingly concerned about Pops. He was not doing well at all. When the boys were home and he had his job to worry about, Pops laid off the alcohol. Each time that Vern remembered his father turning up the bottle for more than a sip, it always ended in one of two ways. Complete and utter sadness or rage. Now with Rof gone, no job, and Vern making his mark on the world, the bottle was all he had.

Pops spent most nights at a little redneck beer joint on the state road near the Alabama line. The establishment was not much more than a shack. It had a couple of televisions, a worn, scarred bar and a pool table. The old man watched the Braves on the television opposite his barstool. Sitting there, speaking to no one, only nodding if someone spoke to him, Pops watched the game and drank his bourbon. Pops still loved baseball, and he felt connected to his lost son when he watched a game. As he watched the shortstop gobble up a ground ball and fire it to first, all Pops could see was the mirror image of Rof doing the same thing on the red clay dirt of the local field. Vern never played the game his father and brother loved so. He was always too much of a bookworm.

On one of those nights, Pops sat down and seemed to stare at the television as if it wasn't there. He didn't react to great plays and nor did any resemblance of happiness cross his face if the Atlanta ball club scored. The broken man drank one bottle and motioned for another. The young bartender hesitated but didn't want to offend one of his best customers. He placed the bottle in front of Pops and told the old man not to drive, he would find him a ride. Pops just nodded, as usual, and began drinking the golden liquor without a glass, straight from the bottle. With each sip, his consciousness slipped a little farther and by the end of the night, his head lay upon the old wooden bar, unmoving. The bartender shook him as it was closing time, but Pops didn't respond. At the end of that night, Pops didn't hurt anymore.

Losing his father and brother, especially so close together, took its toll on Vern Bruce. The mornings spent drinking coffee with his new bride became fewer and fewer until the ritual ended completely. Instead of turning to Patty Lee, like she expected and hoped, Vern turned to work and his pursuit of his own fortune. He started buying a few old houses on the beach near the east end of Panama City along Highway Ninety-Eight westward to what was known as Laguna Beach. Having little startup money and starting to struggle, Vern relented one Sunday, and his father-in-law became their partner in the Panhandle.

Vern didn't want to become just another feather in Old Man Clark's hat though. He and Patty Lee insisted that the newly formed partnership be incorporated and include both their names. Mr. Clark, impressed with the young man's drive and ambition, allowed this concession, only if Clark came first. CB Acquisitions and Holding was shortened to CaBHA, Inc. and then just Cabha. Vern liked it because it sounded kind of foreign, almost Caribbean. Mr. Clark merely accepted it.

Chapter 7

About the same time Pops passed away, a new life burst into the world. Susie gave birth to a healthy baby boy. The blue-eyed infant held a close resemblance to his father. Even shortly after birth, no arguing about who the child's father was needed. Clifford Duane Bruce was a blue-eyed, blond-haired replica of his father.

When the signs of pregnancy could no longer be ignored, Susie had to come clean to her father. The burly, balding man flew into a rage and broke the lamp next to his chair as he struggled to lift his bulk from the chair he occupied. He was none too pleased that his only daughter had gotten pregnant by one of the "beach trash" as he called the young local boys that preyed upon the young girls both local and tourist. His fists clenched, he was ready to strike when Susie's mother rushed in between the father and daughter. She ushered her daughter out the door, pushing cash in her hand as she did.

He never acknowledged he was going to be a grandfather and yelled for her to take care of the problem on her own as her mother slammed the door behind the girl, hoping to spare her the worst of her husband's rage.

Susie only made it through the nine months with help from her mother. Her mother gave her money and support even though her father had forbidden it. They met on a weekly basis and the woman did the best she could for her only child. Susie never revealed to her mother the father of her child. Cliff's maternal grandparents died never laying eyes on their grandson.

Susie only learned of Rof's death though the grapevine. She never met Vern nor Pops and they knew nothing about her. She figured they wouldn't believe her even if she approached them. Her reputation wasn't the best on the beach. Rof wasn't her only *boyfriend* in Panama City. Susie and her son were on their own.

The help from her mother didn't last. As soon as Cliff, as she called him, was born, her father found out about the aid she was being given and flew into another rage. This time her mother was the target, and she ended up in the hospital and her husband in the Bay County Jail. It was the last she heard from either of them.

It wasn't long before Susie worked the tourists that came into town looking for more than just family fun. Even though the small beach town mostly beckoned families, there were those that came into town looking for other types of fun. It was the only way she provided for her son. She tried to get help from the county, but because of her age, she needed her parents and that was not possible.

The pain of getting into this type of life was unbearable to the young girl. She was still a teenager, fallen victim to circumstance repeatedly. First it was the entertainment of gentlemen, then the lure of pain killers took root.

Narcotics were available on the Gulf Coast like never before. They flowed in through places like Gulfport and Mobile with the help of a loosely organized nest of criminals based along the coast and throughout the South. At first, marijuana made its way along the coast and did little harm. Before long, that was not enough for those that fell victim and those wanting a better high began looking for more. The white powder of South America started to creep into the Gulf Coast slowly, aided by those that had brought in marijuana. Cocaine, more addictive and profitable than its predecessor, poured into the region. The disease spread over the beautiful emerald coast and those most vulnerable like a plague. People like young Susie, people that had so much pain in their lives, succumbed to the powder and its effect. Almost at once, she was addicted and her life, already difficult, became nearly impossible for her and her son.

Susie underwent a drastic downward spiral in extraordinarily little time. Her addiction showed on her face. Her eyes sunk back into their sockets and turned black around the edges. Her cheekbones, once hidden by her round face, began to expose themselves. Her eyes glowed red from not only the effects of the powder, but from the massive number of tears she shed on a nightly basis. She became a shadow of her former self.

For two years Susie worked the night and snorted away her life. Her body suffered the consequences and one night she looked in the mirror and hated the person looking back at her. In her frustration, she broke the mirror, and the sound of crashing glass caused her toddler to wander into the bathroom of the seedy motel and he saw his mother in her worst state.

Cliff's life consisted of living from place to place. Most times the mother and son lived out of a motel. Sometimes Susie had enough clarity and money to provide a low-rent apartment in the worst parts of Panama City, not the touristy beach parts. Each time though, the money didn't last, and they moved again, and they ended up at one of the seedier motels than lined the road to the bridge that led to the city. This time, as she picked the glass from the floor, she looked back at her son. The remnants of his tears were still showing on his face, and she pulled him into an embrace. Cliff loved being this close to his mother and snuggled as close as he could. Susie kissed her son on the top of his head and vowed to do better for him.

The same couple of years had been as fruitful for Vern as they had been devastating for Susie and Cliff. The price of beach front property skyrocketed, and his real estate investments paid humongous rewards. He earned his first million in 1973 and directly invested that money into more business ventures. He bought several established businesses along the coast including a movie theater, a car dealership, and a small trucking outfit. His marriage to Patty Lee was flawless. She was enjoying her husband's success. She was a member of the Gulf Coast elite and enjoyed every single minute of it. Even though she earned the same degree as her husband, she didn't need it. She was the vice president of Cabha. In fact, it was her idea to change the name to Cahaba. It didn't sound as stupid as the earlier name. She smiled and agreed when Vern first offered the name, but deep down she didn't like it. When the business started taking off, she pulled her husband aside and whispered her idea quietly in her ear. Her charm always won Vern over and the name change became official.

The Clark Family owned some land and a retreat on the Cahaba River outside of Birmingham. Large oaks lined the property and under the massive tree was a single tire swing. She remembered the countless hours her father pushed her higher and higher. She loved that place. Every time she said the word, Cahaba, she thought of her father.

Vern really didn't care at this point about the name of the company. He was making money, and his greed started taking over his need for acceptance. His wife was happy, the money flowed, and life was good.

Vern was in his office one Friday afternoon gazing out over West Bay and thinking about the money rolling in. As he watched the small boats making their way across the bay, he felt like a titan of industry. He was finally a big fish in this small pond, and he couldn't help but smile.

He chose this location for his office because it looked out over the bay where his father taught him how to catch sheepshead in the salty water below. When he turned in his chair, he looked out of the window and thought of Pops.

Friday afternoons were always quiet in the Cahaba Building. He had a standing policy of letting employees enjoy their Friday afternoons at the beach, fishing, or wherever they chose. He simply liked the quiet. His secretary had gone home about an hour earlier when he heard someone beating on the front door. Mosty everyone knew the building stood fairly empty this time of the week, so Vern sprang to his feet and sprinted to see what was causing all the commotion. Through the glass doors he could see a young girl and a little blond boy standing sheepishly beside her. Peering through the glass before he turned the lock, her face looked familiar. Although her face was weathered, and she had dark circles under her eyes, her face didn't look the same as the one reappearing in his memory. The child stared at the ground. His blond curls looked like they hadn't been cut since birth and it nearly covered his eyes. In fact, Vern couldn't see the boy's eyes but noticed the frown on his face as he slowly opened the door.

None of them spoke when Vern opened the door. The boy's eyes were still locked on the ground and the two adults just looked at each other for a second or two. There was a sadness hanging in the air.

"You don't remember me, do you?" the young lady asked.

"You look familiar," Vern admitted. "But I can't remember your name." He turned his attention to the child and smiled at the boy, but the young kid's eyes locked on his shoes.

"I was a friend of Rof's back in the day. My name is Susie West." She paused, trying to detect if her name sparked any memory, but she saw none. "This is my son Cliff," she told him. Susie finally looked Vern in the eye. Vern vaguely remembered Rof mentioning a "Susie." His brother had so many *friends* on the beach it was hard to keep track.

"A friend of Rof's, huh? I hate to have to tell you, Susie, Rof is gone." Speaking about Rof made the hair stand up on his arms and he took a deep breath, trying not to let the mother and son see his emotions.

"I know. I saw it on the news one night. Couldn't believe it, I just got a letter from him the same day." Susie looked down at Cliff. The child still waiting for his cue, held his gaze downward.

"If you know, why are you here?" Vern asked. A feeling began to creep into his mind. This girl, this little boy, this young lady was up to something. She looked like some kind of addict. Vern didn't have much experience with people like this, but he saw them under the bridge all the time. "Shouldn't you move along?" he asked.

Susie shook her head. "No, sir," she responded. "You're the person I need to talk to." She reached out to shake Vern's hand and he could see her face more clearly as she moved towards him. Her face showed more years than this girl could've possibly seen, and Vern did feel a little sorry for her, but braced himself for the hook. As he took the girl's hand, he noticed the marks on her arm. Needle marks. Vern felt disgusted and looked back at the child and then to Susie. She could see the disgust on his face, but she stood as tall as she could and held eye contact with Vern.

"What exactly can I help you with, Susie, was it? I've got a lot going on this afternoon," Vern lied. Susie looked down at her son and instructed the child to introduce himself. They had rehearsed this for two days and when it was his turn, the boy looked up at Vern, hair still covering his eyes. In a meek voice that Vern could barely make out, the child said, "Hello, I'm Clifford Duane Bruce." Vern took a step back. Blood rushed into his face and rage swelled within him. What was this junkie trying to pull? His anger swelled by the second. Was this trash was trying to use his brother's death and his name to get him to give her money?

Vern managed to keep his cool even as he felt the blood rush to his face. He collected his thoughts and managed to speak quietly yet forcefully, "Now you listen. Get your ass away from here." His anger increasing, he continued, "My brother is gone. If he had a kid, he would've at least told our father and he would've told me. Now Go!" His voice rose with each word until he shouted the last two and the mother and son jumped as if he landed a blow. Vern started to shut the door, but Susie put her hand and foot in the way. It hurt like hell when the door slammed into them, and it took all her might to keep from screaming, but she had to defend herself and the child she and Rof brought into the world, together.

"Look, Mr. Bruce, I ain't trying nothing. I swear it. The night he got his draft card we were together, and I found out I was pregnant after he left. I sent him a letter and..." Susie hesitated and fought back tears. "And at first, he wanted nothing to do with me, but something changed. The day he died, like I said, I got another letter. He wanted his son. This son." She brushed the hair from Cliff's eyes. "He wouldn't have told you because he hated you! He told me that much before he left." Her voice was the opposite of Vern's. She started off defiantly but was nearly in tears when she finished.

Vern finally broke eye contact with Susie and looked into Cliff's crystal-blue eyes and at that moment he knew. His mouth flew open and all he could muster was, "My God." He knew the truth. There was no mistaking those eyes. Vern looked up at Susie and couldn't speak. Thoughts of Patty Lee flooded into his mind, and he knew his life was about to change.

Chapter 8

Vern led Susie and Cliff into his office. She and Cliff walked uneasily behind him, raking their eyes over the well-furnished office. He opened a cabinet, took down a bottle of whiskey, poured a drink and extended the glass to Susie. He handed Cliff some of the candy he had in a bowl on his desk. At first, she declined the offer, but after a few seconds she held the glass with the small amount of bourbon in her trembling hand. She hadn't had a bump from anything in a few days and savored every bit of the soothing drink. Cliff didn't hesitate to accept his offer and worked feverishly at the toffee candy, smacking his lips as he did. Susie glanced at her son and asked Vern if it was okay for Cliff to wait outside. Vern nodded and pointed to the couch next to his secretary's desk.

"Mr. Bruce..." she started until Vern cut her off.

"Vern," he corrected her, and she paused then continued.

"Vern, I need Cliff to stay with you for a little while. I gotta get my life back straight and I can't do that and tend to him. At least not the way he needs."

Vern didn't answer. He let her words hang in the air. He took a deep breath, and Susie saw the concern sweep over his face. This was not something he could agree to without talking to Patty Lee first. He sat down and turned to look out over the bay.

"That's a very big favor," he finally uttered. "Even if what you say about that boy is true." He paused, turned, and looked at Cliff, still content on the couch. "And I'm not sure it is, that's a lot to just show up out of the blue and ask." Vern hid the lie well. In his mind there was no doubt the boy was his brother's son.

Susie tried to keep her composure. "Just a couple of months and I'll come back and get him, I promise. I don't know what you think of me, but I love my son and I'm going to be honest with you," she said and put her head in her hands, her tears no longer holding back. "I'm working the strip. At first it was a high-end hustle but now..." She hesitated. "It's the bottom of the barrel." She hated her life, and Vern could hear the self-loathing in her voice. "I've been doing things I don't want him to know about." Her hands shook uncontrollably, and tears fell between her fingers. The fake confidence she'd mustered outside vanished and the frightened young kid sitting in front of him melted his heart. Vern could no longer hide his thoughts.

"I know that kid is Rof's. Just one look told me that," he finally told her the truth. He stood up and walked to the big window overlooking the cubicles outside his office and turned his attention to Cliff. The child lay on the couch, staring at the ceiling. Vern rubbed his chin, and he wondered how many hours this child spent alone while his mother walked the streets. Cliff noticed him looking in his direction. The kid waved at Vern and flashed a smile. Vern shook his head as Cliff smiled at him. *Rof is alive in this kid*, he thought. He turned back to Susie, walking over to her and offering her a couple of Kleenex he kept on a table near the door.

"Where are you folks, Susie?" he asked, unsure if he wanted to know the answer.

"Turned me out, won't have nothing to do with me. Haven't since I told them I was pregnant. Momma was trying to help but the old man shut that down when Cliff was born." Susie's head was still in her hands and Vern barely made out what she was saying. He heard what he needed, however, and his face didn't hold back the contempt he felt for those two. His eyebrows furrowed and his nose flared.

Damn fools, he thought, turning away their own daughter and grandson. He thought of his own father. There was no way Pops would ever do something like that. Vern exhaled a deep breath and wished his father was still around. He wasn't though, and Vern felt it was his duty to help this girl and his nephew. *Nephew*, he thought and once again shook his head. This was turning out to be a hell of an afternoon.

Vern leaned down and picked Susie's head from her hands and looked the young girl in the eye. "Tell you what. Come back tomorrow. Same time. I'll be here and so will my wife. I want to help y'all more than anything, but she's got to be in. I won't do a thing without her knowing," he told Susie.

Vern knew his wife didn't want kids right now. She was an only child, and she acted like it. They rarely talked about having a baby since getting married. Vern tried to bring about the conversation several times, but Patty Lee was uninterested. Susie smiled as she looked out to her son. He was standing on the couch, looking back through the window and making faces at it. The smile evaporated and her lips trembled. "This is not how I thought this life would go," she cried. "God, I love him, but I can't be there for him until I get myself straight." She fell to the floor, hugging Vern. "Please, Vern. I don't want him to have this life." Vern held her closely and thought about what he would say to Patty Lee.

Vern took a winding path home that night. He didn't go straight home after he left the office after parting ways with the mother and son. How in the world would he even begin to tell Patty Lee about all of this? His wife didn't care much for Rof when he was alive. She had only met him once when Rof came to visit his brother one weekend at school. He didn't end up visiting Vern much at all but ended up with one of Patty Lee's friends after a Saturday night of partying. Just like most of the girls in his life, Rof left and never came back. He didn't see the girl again as she became just another notch on his belt. From that day forward, Patty Lee wanted little to do with Vern's brother.

Even in death, Patty Lee had little use for Rof. The burning words he'd said to his brother made her curse his name and swear to have nothing to do with him. It was something she would never tell her husband, but his dying did not affect her in the least. At the funeral, she stood emotionless. No tears, no frown, no smile, she stood as if cast in concrete. In fact, she was kind of glad that Vern would not have to face him again and hear the words, "I hate you," come from the little brother he loved so much. She knew his death cast a pall over Vern, but in time, the memories would fade, and they could move on. Vern put together a company that even her father was proud of and sometimes too proud. He told his West Palm buddies all the time about the company *he* built in the Panhandle. She winced each time she heard him say this and hoped it wouldn't reach Vern's ears.

As much as she tried to hide it, Vern knew how she really felt about his brother. He could read Patty Lee better than she thought. Now he had to go home and tell his wife he had to take Rof's illegitimate son into their home for a while. Unusual for him, he stopped at a local watering hole for a drink before he made it home. He wasn't looking forward to this.

Patty Lee was waiting in the foyer when she heard the key turn the lock on the front door. Vern was late, uncommonly late. The door creaked open, and she saw the look on his face. There was no smile, no anything. Vern was as somber as he was the day he'd buried his brother and not long after his father. Something was wrong. She could smell a hint of liquor on his breath even as he stood two feet away. She shook her head and started to walk away, but before she took a couple steps, she whirled around and faced Vern once again.

"What is it?" she asked her husband before he closed the door. Patty Lee thought that whatever was wrong, it was business related and she immediately dreaded talking to her father about it. She had never seen Vern in this kind of state before. He had gone through the deaths of his father and brother and yet he hadn't touched a drop of liquor. The liquor he kept in his office was more for show and for clients than himself. Today, something happened that affected him so that he felt he needed a drink. Patty Lee didn't want to drag this out and she pointed her long finger towards her husband, demanding to know what was going on.

"Let's go sit down, Patty Lee," he responded. His voice was weak, and he hadn't yet looked her in the eye. The couple sat down on the couch facing the darkened Gulf. The water was eerily calm. Usually on a summer evening, the offshore breeze picked up and pushed the waves harder inland. Tonight, it was flat calm and clear as a pane of glass. There was no movement in the palm trees that lined the sides of the deck. Everything was deathly calm and quiet.

Vern took Patty Lee's hand, and this startled his wife a little. Vern was never the overly affectionate type, and this gesture worried her even more. She braced herself as Vern took a deep breath. "I had a couple of visitors this afternoon after everyone left," he told his wife. He looked up into her eyes and Patty Lee sensed the dread in his voice. "There was this young lady and her little boy that came to see me." Patty Lee straightened up in her seat and Vern saw the look of concern take over her stone face. If she didn't know Vern any better, she would suspect an old girlfriend, but that wasn't Vern's style.

Vern continued, "This young girl was a friend of Rof's." This got her attention quickly, and the concern evaporated into a frown on her face. Now she understood, and she took her hand away from Vern's. She had often wondered when this day would come. She had half expected it sooner. Rof probably had kids throughout the South knowing how he got around in the summer.

"Let me guess, Rof's kid?" she asked in a sarcastic tone, one eyebrow raised over the other.

Vern pulled his hand back and looked at his wife inquisitively. He wanted to ask her how in the world she would know that, but let it go without a response. He just nodded his head in the affirmative. "She was pregnant with the kid when Rof went to boot camp. She even sent him a letter and told him before..." Vern stopped. He hated verbalizing those words, "Before he died."

"Vern," she said, her tone no longer sarcastic but firm. "Is this girl local or was she a tourist?" Vern shook his head slightly and started to speak but Patty Lee cut him off, "What I mean is, does she know who you are?" She rubbed her fingers together in the air. "To be blunt, how much does she want?"

"No, no, no," he replied. "I mean, she is from here. Mom and Dad ran an old motel down on the strip. They sold it to me a year ago and left. Don't know where they went. They left this little girl and a kid out in the cold. No help. You know which way girls in that situation go." Vern's voice became firm. "Doesn't want money. Girls in bad shape. Strung out, no money, kid is so pitiful but so sweet." Vern smiled thinking back to the little kid waving and smiling at him from the couch.

Patty Lee's expression changed to one of pity. She stood up and put her hand on his shoulder. That was her big-hearted Vern. He may try to act tough sometimes and prove to her that he had the backbone to fit in with the Clarks and she loved him and married the broke young man because he held those qualities.

Patty Lee's family was skeptical by nature. They had to see things to believe them, and they didn't trust people. The Clark's were not loose with their money either. They gave to charities throughout Florida and the Southeast, but they didn't believe in hand outs. Some had called them hard-hearted, but her father preferred "frugal." People knew better than to come to Old Man Clark with a sob story. They wouldn't even get in the door.

She looked over at her husband and tried to smile and reassure him, but the look of pity would not leave her face. "I know sometimes that you can't see things like this, but, babe, I can. I grew up with people like this coming after our money. This girl is scamming you. It happened to my father countless times. Always some kind of guilt trip. That's how they get you," she said as she put her hand on Vern's heart. "I know you mean well and that's one of the reasons I love you so much, Vern, but you've got to be realistic."

Vern put his hand on hers, kissed her cheek and looked at her with the puppy dog look that always washed over his face when he felt like this. Patty Lee couldn't help but shake her head in disgust.

"It's not a scam, Patty Lee. I'm no fool. When I saw this kid's eyes, damn, it was like Rof looking back at me. They're coming back tomorrow. You come over there, look at this kid and you tell me that is not Rof's son."

Patty Lee sat back on the couch. Her mouth was in a frown and lines appeared beside her eyes. Vern did not break his gaze. Patty Lee, relenting against her better judgement, just nodded without saying a word. She agreed and told Vern she would be there. It was more to save her husband from a grave mistake than to see for herself, her mind already made up. Even if this kid was a carbon copy of Rof Bruce, she would say no. She tried so desperately to get Vern to move on and here they were right back in the middle of it. If there was a hell, there was no doubt Rof was there, and he was probably laughing his ass off right now.

After a sleepless night in which both tossed and turned, they were awake as the sunlight peeked into the bedroom. Neither spoke as the rose from bed and the drive into Panama City was silent as well. Vern and Patty Lee usually ate breakfast together each day at a diner just off Thomas Drive. This particular morning, they just had coffee. Neither was very hungry, and they spoke few words to each other, preferring to sip their coffee and stare off into the distance.

Susie and Cliff arrived before Vern and Patty Lee. They found them sitting against a wall by the door when they pulled the Monte Carlo into Vern's spot in front of the building. Susie's face looked even more sunken than the day before and Vern could tell the girl had a rough night. He was also betting that the little boy had taken care of himself all night. His clothes looked like the same ones he had on the day before and his hair had not seen a comb for days. Cliff's hair still hung over his eyes, but Vern could see the boy's blue eyes in his thoughts. Patty Lee looked over the two pitiful-looking souls with utter disgust. She grunted and shook her head. Vern patted his wife on the knee and tried to smile, but neither were in the mood to do so. She had dreaded this moment since last night and just wanted to get it over with. She sat there, rubbing her thumb and finger against each other repeatedly. There was no way that dirty little boy was coming home with them.

Without a greeting, they led Susie into the office and once again had little Cliff wait in the lobby. Vern asked if either had eaten today. Susie told him they had just left a fast-food place and walked over but the sound from Cliff's stomach echoed in the silence and revealed the truth. Vern smiled and went and retrieved the candy dish from his office and placed it on the couch with Cliff. Cliff's hand went instantly for the toffee candy he had yesterday.

Vern didn't sit behind his desk as Patty Lee sat down in his chair. She sat and stared at the frightened girl. Susie could feel her condescending eyes looking her up and down and without her saying a word, she already hated this woman staring at her.

Patty Lee was the first to speak. "That kid out there is Rof's, huh?" Her tone was even harsher and blunter than the night before and dripping with doubt.

"Yes, ma'am," Susie replied, trying to mask her dislike of the woman. Patty Lee had dark, piercing eyes and a fierce gaze that was locked in on Susie, unblinking and like stone. She had inherited this look from her father. It was one advantage the Clarks had always had over their foes. Just by looking at them, they were at the advantage over most others. They thrived on intimidation. Vern wasn't looking at Patty Lee. He leaned on the edge of the desk facing away from her, but he could feel her stare from behind.

"Alright, Susie, just tell us again what you need us to do," he interjected, trying to ease the tension in the room.

"Just take Cliff for a month, two at the most." She glanced back at Cliff to make sure he couldn't hear her. He sat on the couch, digging through the candy dish. "There is a place up in Alabama that can help me get straightened out." She put as much confidence in her voice as she could, but there was no use. She hung her head feeling defeated.

Patty Lee put her hands on the desk and leaned towards the frightened girl. "How are you going to pay for something like that?" she asked sternly. Patty Lee knew what was coming next and a slight grin crossed her face. The other shoe was about to drop, but she was way ahead of this girl.

To her surprise, Susie sat up in her chair abruptly and brushed the hair out of her eyes and stood as straight and tall as she could.

"I don't want any money from y'all if that is what you meant." She held her nose a little higher. "I just need someone to take care of my son. He needs family. I don't want to leave him with just anyone." The gaze she held began to wane and tears began to form in her swollen eyes. Vern looked over at his wife and could sense his wife's resolve melt slowly away. She was no longer staring at poor Susie. She had turned her chair around and looked out over the bay. In her thoughts all she could say was, *I'm a damned fool*. This was something her father would never approve of. It didn't matter about the circumstances. You never get involved with something like this. He always said it is better just to pay for something harmful to go away in the beginning than to let it fester and get in the way. *Don't get involved*, she told herself once again.

As soon as she told herself that, she realized if she intended to handle things just like her father, she'd married the wrong man. Vernon Frank Bruce was not going to turn away someone in need like this girl and her son, especially seeing it was the son of his only brother. A dead brother that Vern felt so much guilt over. Vern felt he owed Rof, even in death. Here, unexpectedly, a chance to make amends presented itself in the form of this poor child. Patty Lee shook her head, more disgusted with herself than anything.

Her resistance, like her resolve, melted away, and she lost the war before the first battle. Cliff was going to be a part of their lives whether she liked it or not. She also realized that like any other stray, he would be with them for way longer than two months. She looked out the office window into the lobby and peered at the boy, his face now smeared with the sticky remnants of candy and bit her lip. It was done. She might as well nod her head in agreement, and she did.

Cliff was watching them, and even the child knew something was up. He knew something was wrong with his mother, but he didn't have the life experience to know exactly what and only his youth shielded him from the reality of their life. The adult voices grew loud and at one point, he was scared. The man seemed friendly enough to Cliff and even gave him some candy. The dark-haired woman, however, scared the child. She was not friendly like the man. She was mean. Even to his youthful eyes, Patty Lee couldn't hide her disdain for the boy. She was the only one not smiling when they called him into the office.

Chapter 9

Cliff looked up at his mother with wide blue eyes. Susie's tears cascaded, and she reached down, picked up her son, and hugged him as hard as she could. The child squirmed under her embrace and tried to wriggle free, but his mother held tight. When the child stopped squirming, Susie placed him back on the couch and kneeled, brushed his unkempt hair out of his eyes and just looked at him for a second or two before speaking.

Susie told Cliff little about his father. He was so young and innocent, she didn't want to burden her son with the truth. She figured he probably wouldn't understand it anyway. She told herself that she would tell him when he was older. All that was revealed to Cliff was his father was gone. The boy lived a hard life so far and probably packed eight years' worth of living into those precious three. His mother only said, "Goodbye," and walked out quickly, not looking back.

Cliff didn't understand the moment but sensed the despair in his mother's voice. He ran to the double doors and placed his sticky hands and tear-stained face against the glass and began crying out for his mother to return. Vern scrambled to the door, picked him up, and pulled the child into his arms, the cries resonating in his ears. He sat back down on the couch, placed the boy next to him and offered him the rest of the candy in the dish, but Cliff pushed it away.

"Son, did your mother tell you who I am?" Vern softly asked the child. Between sobs Cliff managed a weak "no" and

Vern leaned down, so his nephew saw the smile on his face. "I'm your uncle, do you know what that means?"

The innocence showing through in his voice returned. "You spending the night with Momma?"

Vern shook his head and thought about Susie explaining the men coming and going with them being *uncles*.

"No, son. I'm your daddy's brother. I'm family," Vern said, hoping the child would understand. "Do you know about your daddy?"

Without looking at Vern, staring into nothing, Cliff said, "He's gone."

Vern felt tears swelling but fought them back. Patty Lee still sat behind the desk, fiddling with some papers Vern left. She didn't want to hear their conversation and was not going to get deeply involved. As she moved one sheet of paper behind the other, she thought, *This is Vern's mess, let him deal with it.*

The three of them left about twenty minutes after Susie so the boy's mother had time to disappear. Vern hadn't noticed a car parked either day, so he had no idea if Susie was on foot or parked somewhere nearby. He didn't want to risk Cliff running back into her. The child didn't cry. He only sat in the car with a broken look on his face, staring out at the water each time they passed over a bridge.

Vern contemplated stopping by the barber on the way home, but realized it was late Saturday afternoon and wouldn't be open. That would wait until Monday morning. Patty Lee wanted to get home as quickly as possible, but Vern wanted the boy to have a little fun, so they made a slight detour and headed for the Strip. The three stopped at a little arcade newly opened on the touristy stretch of beach. Too young for video games, he enjoyed a couple ice cream cones. Vern hadn't thought to wash his face, and the ice cream combined with the left-over candy to create a sticky mess. Cliff bounced around the back seat during the short drive back home due to the sugar rush, but as soon as they arrived home, he was out cold. Not wanting to disturb him with a bath, Patty Lee made him a pallet on the floor next to their bed. She wasn't about to allow him to foul one of her beds.

 Putting Cliff down for the night, they sat down on opposite ends of the couch and had a serious conversation about the next month or two. Vern wanted to step away from his work just a couple of weeks, making sure his nephew acclimated to his new surroundings. He didn't mention he worried about leaving him with Patty Lee. He knew she would never harm the boy, but his wife would not invest emotions in the child. She would put on a good face, show interest in the boy while Vern was around, but he knew her, and he knew her family. Putting work aside was something her father would never do. Vern looked at Patty Lee, her arms crossed, and he read her face. Apprehension filled him as he spoke.

 "I'm going to take a few days off next week," he said to his wife, knowing that it would be more than a few. She offered a fake smile and nodded her head in agreement as she wasn't surprised.

"Go ahead. You need to," she responded. Vern sat back in his chair and looked at his wife, his face expressing his confusion. All evening he'd prepared for a tug of war. A tug of war he expected his wife to win and somehow, he would have to win over her begrudging support.

Patty Lee was looking out over the dark ocean. The only thing she could make out in the darkness, was the white moonlit foam and distant boat lights that twinkled in rhythm with the movement of the sea. "This boy is your only family. He needs you, but you also need him. Take all the time you need. I'll pick up the slack at work." Her voice seemed sincere, but Vern knew better. There had never been a moment since the day the two met when Vern didn't trust Patty Lee. For a fleeting moment, that feeling crept into his mind. It vanished just as quickly. He saw concern on her face as she broke her gaze on the water and turned her attention to him.

"Are you sure?" he asked. "I've got a lot of things going right now. Staff can handle things while I'm gone if you aren't up to it." Her face hardened and Vern knew that offer angered her.

"I'm just kidding, Patty Lee. I thought that would piss you off." She punched her husband in the arm, and he jerked backwards. When Patty Lee became affectionate, she normally showed it through little things like this. Vern smiled and reached over and pulled his wife to him. Patty Lee offered little resistance.

This would be the last night they shared before the reality of having a kid in the house set in. They made the most of it.

Patty Lee entered Vern's office Monday before anyone else arrived in the building. Vern only employed around five other people, but he was looking to grow. Patty Lee embraced growth and relished this chance to get involved.

The office was dark, and no sound was evident except for the hum of the office equipment left running from the previous workday. She made a mental note for a memo reminding people to shut down non-used equipment. Daniel Clark didn't waste anything, and neither would she. She didn't switch on the main office light, just the lamp on Vern's highly polished, wooden desk. As she sat down in the plush chair and the cushions formed around her, Patty Lee thought about her father.

Each of his days began just as this. He came into a dark office before daylight and devoid of people. He sat in the dark and sipped black coffee. He branded anyone that added any kind of substance to coffee, such as sugar or milk, as weak. He drank at least one pot of coffee a day and always black.

Patty Lee abhorred the taste of coffee, so she found other vices. She reached her slender hand into her purse and produced a pack of cigarettes. Leaning back in the chair, she lit the end of one, inhaling the smoke, holding it for a second and exhaling. She loved the first cigarette of the day. Patty Lee smiled because Vern didn't like them and hated the smoke they put off. She snuck one every once in a while at home, but never anywhere she could be seen. It was her little secret, and she felt better as she took another drag. The end of the cylindrical vessel of tobacco glowed red as she relaxed and blew the resulting smoke into the air. As she released the smoke from her lungs, she picked up the phone. Her father, in his office enjoying his coffee at this exact moment, picked up on the other end. She wanted to tell him the good news. Not that they had picked up a stray, but she was sitting where she was born to sit. The chair of the person in charge. Patty Lee smiled. Vern would have to fight her to remove her from this office.

   Vern spent every day of the first week with Cliff. He let the boy sleep as long as he wanted and when he awoke the two went out to breakfast. At first, the young boy was very standoffish with his uncle. After all, he didn't know him. Each time Vern lowered the three-year-old to the ground, Cliff reluctantly took his hand. Each morning began at this little buffet style restaurant just off the Strip. Always full of tourists consisting of happy families, Cliff seemed to love the place. The little boy enjoyed playing peekaboo over the booths with other kids. Vern grew accustomed to the daily ritual himself. Each morning, he looked around the restaurant, peeking at each family as they enjoyed each other as well as the food. It would take a great effort to win Patty Lee over to this family lifestyle, but he and Cliff would carry out the task.

   Only a short walk from the restaurant, the two of them strolled along the pier jutting out into the ocean most mornings. There were wide gaps in the wooden walkway out over the water so that Cliff could peer down and see the waves crashing against the wooden columns supporting the structure. Every once and a while he could see a stingray swim by or other forms of marine life living around the pier. One morning, the duo reached the end of the pier and Vern held Cliff in his arms, pointing to a large cargo ship off in the distance when the question Vern dreaded came from the child.

"Where's my mommy?" Cliff asked his uncle, his voice breaking and tears beginning to form in his sad blue eyes.

Vern, placing Cliff gently on the pier, lowered himself down to one knee so he could look back into Cliff's eyes. A tear rolled down his pink cheek.

"Son, she has gone a long way away to get better. She is sick and there are people there who can help her," he told the child. Vern looked up to the sky and took a deep breath before he continued. "I'm your uncle." The boy tried to pronounce the word uncle, but he stammered over the word. "Just call me Unc," he told Cliff as he smiled at him. "Your daddy was my brother. Do you know about him?"

Cliff looked down between the cracks and sobbed, "He's gone."

"Yes. He is, buddy." He raised the boy's chin with two of his fingers so he could see Vern as he spoke. "I'm taking care of you now. Me and Aunt Patty Lee." Cliff didn't smile, the image of Patty Lee made him feel uneasy, but he put his arms around Vern and for the first time, hugged his uncle first. Vern wrapped his arms around his nephew and told him how much he loved him.

That Friday afternoon, Vern left Cliff in the care of their next-door neighbor. The boy would be fine as he was content playing in the sand right off the deck, far away from the rolling waters of the Gulf. The neighbor was an older lady who loved children. Even though she was older, at one point in her life, she was a champion swimmer and still in surprisingly decent shape. Vern felt comfortable leaving him with her. It was the first time he had left the boy since they'd brought him home.

He found Patty Lee sitting in his office chair looking out over the bay. He could see smoke rising in the air and held his breath as he walked in the door. He smelled the strong odor as soon as he opened the front door, and he wished she wouldn't do that in his office. He thought he was going to surprise her but just as he was about to say something, she quickly spun the chair in his direction. The cloud of smoke seemed to follow her. She smirked in Vern's direction and exhaled. Vern patted the air, trying to force the smoke in a different direction. Patty Lee's smile widened.

"Figured you would come," she said raising the cigarette to her lips.

"Smoking in my chair?" he asked, annoyed by her habit. He knew and had known for some time, but she never smoked in front of him. This was a new development.

"Just the one," she lied. "Been a good week around here. Hate you missed it, but Cliff needed you." Vern felt the sarcasm dripping from her words as she finally pushed the burning end of the cigarette into the ashtray. Vern shot a fake smile and thanked her.

He could also tell her voice held an added degree of independence. He thought to himself that she was that much like her father. A little bit of power goes a long way.

"What exactly are you so happy about?" he asked.

Patty Lee stood up and walked around the desk to embrace her husband. She loved him even if he was working a fool's errand with this child. She pecked him on the cheek and took him by the hands. Vern braced for the worst.

"We got an opportunity this week. Didn't want to pull the trigger, though, until you decided to show up."

Vern's greed and hunger resurfaced, and he held his out his palm in question. Only one week in charge and here was his wife putting together a business deal. He felt a hint of pride.

"What kind of deal could you have put together in a week?" he quizzed his wife.

Patty Lee bit her bottom lip and flashed her brown eyes before she said, "I know you don't like to do grandiose things. I know you always like to keep it small and local. But this is something we can't pass up. Daddy let me in on it."

So, there it was. She wasn't even going to try and hide her father's involvement. Vern wanted to distance Cahaba from the

Clarks, not position it closer, but he was curious. Once again his sense of greed was piqued, and he wanted more information.

"What, Patty Lee?" he asked, his impatience revealing itself in his voice and his face. She let go of his arm and walked over to the window.

"Right up the coast from West Palm, near Cocoa Beach there is a port. You know it, been there forever. Locals tried to think of ways to get more ships and cargo there for years. Daddy thinks they have been going at it all wrong," she told her husband. Barely pausing between words, she said, "Tourism is getting bigger and bigger. You see it here, down on the Strip. There are more people than just the rednecks from Georgia and Alabama coming here these days. They're starting to come from everywhere. Daddy wants them in Cocoa Beach, and he knows how to draw people there like ants marching from a hill, his words." She laughed at the last part, trying to break the tension and lighten the mood. "He wants the port to expand into cruise ships."

Vern thought for a moment, rubbing his chin and said, "There was already a cruise ship going out of there a while back. Burned up out on the water, killed a bunch of folks. Too much liability." Patty Lee turned from the window and frowned.

"That was small time," she responded. "We are going big. Daddy has already got the ball rolling. Cahaba comes in with...." She paused and braced for the reaction. "Five."

"Five what…. hundred thousand?" he asked. The wrinkles in his forehead tightened.

"Million," she said in a near whisper.

Vern sat down, almost falling into the chair placed in front of his desk. Cahaba didn't have five million dollars. They may have five million in assets but certainly not in cash.

"We ain't got that kind of money!" he yelled at his wife. Patty Lee was not backing down and sat down on the edge of the wooden desk. "We are going to borrow it. Daddy already has us in talks with a bank in Miami. They are thrilled and as soon as our port is a go, they want cargo ships to go out of there too. Expand everything. This could be it, babe." Patty Lee was calm and flashed her brown eyes once more as she called her husband *babe*.

Vern realized he was being ambushed. Ambushed by not only his wife that was right in front of him, but her father, hundreds of miles away.

"Vernon," said a husky voice from the phone's speaker, "this IS it. It's time to stop being small time up there in Lower Alabama." Vern's face flushed with blood. He couldn't believe his wife let her father hear the whole conversation and didn't bother to tell him he was on the phone. Vern chewed his lip. He hated it when Clark called him Vernon and he also despised when the panhandle was referred to as "Lower Alabama." The residents took it as a slight and it burned most to the core, especially those fighting to change it.

"Mr. Clark? Have you been listening to us the whole damned time?" Vern demanded.

"I have indeed. I want you two in on this. This is one of the biggest deals ever in the state of Florida. No time to be timid. I know you like to play it slow, but sometimes Vernon, you have to grab the bull by the horns or else get killed by it." The voice from the phone sounded like a teacher scolding his pupil. Vern didn't say anything for a minute, his face glowing. Patty Lee stared at her husband as if to say, "You are saying yes, whether you know it or not!"

"Son..." He had never called Vern *son* since they'd met. "Need you in this. Need an answer by tomorrow. We are moving forward and either you come with us and end up a billionaire or you stay up there in redneck country and be the king of the Strip."

Before Vern could answer the old man, Patty Lee spoke up.

"We are in, Daddy. We will be down next week to iron everything out." With that she hung up the phone to find Vern standing over her. At that point, he was filled with disgust that she'd committed them to such a gamble. He wanted to raise his fist, yet he did not. He knew he owed that arrogant prick for helping him launch his business. He sighed and stood up from the chair. He wasn't going to be able to distance himself and his company from Old Man Clark. He was neck deep now. He hoped Patty Lee hadn't just drowned him.

Chapter 10

Vern didn't want to go to West Palm to complete the deal. He stalled at every opportunity, and he certainly didn't want to leave Cliff in Panama City. Each time he closed his eyes, he saw visions of Old Man Clark's grinning face. That was something he didn't want to see in person. Since the ambush in his office, each time he encountered Patty Lee there was only the slightest of pleasantries exchanged. Morning breakfast together consisted of a quick cup of coffee, little conversation, and awkwardness. This deal may make them a lot of money, but for Vern, wanting to make his money on his own, it infuriated him each time it entered his mind. He felt like a child being led into a doctor's office with the lure of a lollipop.

One afternoon, having been cornered by Patty Lee as she arrived early from the office, Vern relented and agreed to fly to West Palm with one condition. Cliff was to go with them. Patty Lee tried to lay her charm and flash her eyes, but Vern had none of it. Cliff was going, or he wasn't.

The little boy's eyes widened when they arrived at the airport. Vern thought this was probably the first time he saw airplanes up close, and he hoisted Cliff onto his shoulders as a small Cessna roared down the runway and lifted into the sky. Vern heard the boy utter something about the *coolest thing he had ever seen*. He pulled Cliff down and placed him on the ground, chuckling to himself as he did. This kid amazed him.

The more Vern thought about it, the more he was pretty sure it was the kid's first trip anywhere besides the Gulf Coast. Cliff was young enough that even though he missed his mother, he was adapting. The first month or two, every night was a sleepless one for Cliff. He awakened his aunt and uncle screaming one night and Vern slept next to his nephew trying to calm and reassure the boy. As Cliff finally drifted back to sleep, Vern did too. He didn't notice Patty Lee standing in the doorway shaking her head as she couldn't fall back asleep afterwards. The bond between her husband and this bastard boy grew stronger by the day and she had to find a way to break it.

Nightmares bubbled to the surface and the young boy awakened during the night in terror a few nights a week. Vern was always there, comforting the kid, and he began to pay less and less attention to his wife. Each time Vern left her in the middle of the night to tend to Cliff, Patty Lee felt she drifted farther away from her husband in an empty, cold bed.

The nightmares subsided as the nights away from his mother grew in number. He knew, however, that they would always be there. Just below the surface, waiting to engulf Cliff's developing psyche. That's why moments like this, when Cliff acted like a normal child, Vern was happy. He looked over at his wife and his smile waned as he saw his wife's expression. She looked back at Vern, no smile, no emotion, expressionless.

The twin prop engines on the small private plane roared to life and Cliff sat in his uncle's lap and looking intently out the window. The boy held a wide smile on his face and his eyes were still as wide as Vern ever saw them. Cliff let out a squeal, "*Weeee,*" as the wheels left the ground, and the plan started to climb. He would stare out the window and say things like, "Look, Unc, you can see everything!" or "We are in the clouds!" Vern certainly enjoyed having the kid around, even if his wife did not. As Cliff became quiet, staring out of the window, Patty Lee looked over at the two. The small plane was cramped, and she couldn't even escape the joy of the little boy. Vern even thought she smiled once.

Patty Lee staring at the child, still peering from the window, and Vern holding him tightly in his lap, knew what she had to do. She looked out her window and looked out at a field of clouds below them. She laughed to herself as she remembered her father doing the same thing with her that Vern now did with his nephew. Patty Lee made a mental note to discuss her thoughts with her father.

When Vern looked back over at his wife, the smile, if there was one at all, turned into a look of concentration. He wondered what his wife thought in the moment, but he dared not ask. He just sighed and looked back out the window.

There was only so much that kept a three-year-old's attention during the flight. After the first thirty minutes or so, he was restless and Vern tried reading to the boy, but it didn't work. It took an hour for him to cry himself to sleep in Vern's lap and then they actually had a brief quiet period before he heard the landing gear engage. Patty Lee was clearly agitated when the wheels touched the landing strip, and she swore to herself that they would soon have a jet.

Mr. Clark, expecting his wife and her *family,* welcomed them and his secretary led them directly into his office. The old man loved showing off his view through two huge windows of the Atlantic Ocean. When people entered, he always made sure he stood in front of the windows to draw their attention to the magnificent scenery behind him.

He wasn't expecting young Cliff, however. When the three of them strode into the office, he halfway rolled his eyes at the boy and raised his eyebrow in frustration in Patty Lee's direction. Vern acted like he didn't notice the non-verbal communication between father and daughter, but he felt his own disgust swelling. He placed his tongue in between his teeth and bit down slightly, holding his words within his thoughts.

Patty Lee rushed to hug her father and as she did, she whispered that it was a concession to her husband bringing the child. Cliff was uneasy as he fidgeted at Vern's feet. He picked the boy up and sat in the chair farthest from his father-in-law. He took a piece of candy out of his pocket and placed it in Cliffs little hand.

When Patty Lee sat down, the business meeting began, and the family reunion halted. Vern was amazed how they both could change in an instant. Old Man Clark sat down behind his desk and it was like the flipping of a light switch, all business.

"Well, this afternoon, Mr. Swope from the bank in Miami will be here. Nothing for you to do, really. Just sign the paperwork. That's it. Everything else is done," the old man told them coldly. Vern noticed Clark didn't even look at him, only at Patty Lee. The gesture didn't sit very well with Vern. He had not been a party to all of this and if he was going to sign his name, he had a question or two. He asked how much public and how much private money was involved. Was there a company willing to commit to sailing out of Cocoa before the harbor was even revamped? In the middle of his third question about infrastructure, Mr. Clark cut him off bluntly, waving his hand in the air and a grimace across his face. Patty Lee thew a fake smile and tilted her head in Vern's direction as if to say, *Shut the hell up!*

"Vernon, I've been in many deals like this," the old man, now grinning at Vern continued. "Frankly, you haven't. You are small time right now. Hopefully, you will learn something from this experience. Just let Patty Lee lead on this. We work well together." The old man sat back in his chair and turned his attention back to his daughter.

Vern bristled once again at being lectured in such a manner. He did not ask anything further. He sat in silence, sulking. He bit a little harder on his tongue, stood up, and took Cliff by the hand. Vern nodded to the old man behind the desk and he and Cliff walked out of the room. He wanted to tell that old bastard to take this deal and go to hell, but still, his thoughts did not escape his mouth.

Vern found a path beside the office building and followed it to the beach, Cliff in tow. He hated this beach. It wasn't like the sugar white sands of the Gulf. It was brown, hard, and smelled putrid. The water was not emerald green but a dark shade of dirty blue. He looked back at the office building jutting into the blue sky, perched beyond the single dune. He swore to himself that he wouldn't let that old man get the best of him.

When Vern left the room with Cliff, Mr. Clark motioned for Patty Lee to wait for a moment before they resumed their conversation. From this point forward, their discussion was only for the two of them and he meant to keep it between himself and his only daughter. He watched as Vern and Cliff made their way down to the water and he stood up and slowly walked over to the chair Patty Lee occupied. He didn't break eye contact with her. He grabbed the chair opposite hers and pulled it up close to where the chairs were almost touching. He took his daughter's hand and spoke softly.

"That little boy changes everything in your house," he told his daughter, pausing before speaking again. "He is there to stay. You can bet your life on it. If that girl didn't want money now, she's playing the long game, and she will. He probably isn't even his brother's son. Doesn't matter though. To Vernon he is his brother's son. That's what the girl is *betting* on. He won't let go of him. The guilt inside him over his brother eats him inside. Everything has changed now unless you even the odds."

He stood, walked to the window, and tapped on the glass. He pointed to Vern and Cliff playing in the brown sand. Patty Lee sat and stared into nothing. He continued, "Only one way to go now. I know you aren't going to like it."

Patty Lee interrupted her father, "Have a kid."

Clark turned around and smiled at his daughter. He shook his head and laughed to himself; she was indeed a chip off the Clark block. Always looking at the big picture. Both knew she had to do something to interrupt the hold Cliff put on her husband. Vern wanted children, and she had not. This child coming into their lives like this already drove a wedge between them. Before Susie arrived with this small, pitiful boy at her side, she and Vern sailed through life, happy. Now, the divide was repairable, but the longer she allowed it to grow, it would divide them further and further until repairing their bond was impossible. Since that drug-addicted girl dropped him into their perfect life, the thoughts of division consumed her, and this was the only move possible. She hid her true feelings from her father, however, not wanting to completely show her hand. Not even to her beloved father.

"It's just for a month or two, Daddy. I can see it, though. I do see how Vern changed. He's got to have a kid, one of his own. She will come back, yes, I know, and it will take some money to shoo her away, hopefully with that kid in tow," Patty Lee said, even believing it herself for a fleeting moment.

"Make no mistake," he replied. "She will be back, and she will need money. She won't take the kid. Even if *you* never see her again, rest assured Vernon will. She'll come back to him with some kind of sad sob story, and he *will* give her money. The kid, darling, isn't going anywhere. He'll pay her whatever she wants just to keep that boy with him."

Old Man Clark returned his attention to the two down on the beach. Patty Lee stood up from her chair for the first time since she had been in her father's office, walked over to the window, and gazed out at Vern. He was smiling, laughing, and playing with that bastard child. Her father was right. The only thing to splinter the relationship between uncle and nephew was a child of his own.

The meeting with Mr. Swope ended almost as soon as it began. Both Patty Lee and Vern signed the papers. With a stroke of the pen, they were five million dollars in debt. Vern's hand shook visibly when he attached his signature. Patty Lee just smiled at him and put her hand on his shoulder as he placed the pen to paper. It took every bit of his strength to sign and remain quiet. When he really thought about it, however, his greed surfaced, and he wanted this deal to work, making him a billionaire. He also wanted to pacify his father-in-law. Let the old geezer think he beat Vern and when he had enough money and resources, he would purge the bastard from his business for the last time.

Patty Lee, all smiles, seemed downright giddy as she signed her name and hugged her father. The two of them made quite a pair. Vern and his father were similar, but they were nothing like these two. It seemed they shared each thought, each idea. They shared a bond that could not be broken and it terrified Vern. He loved his wife immensely, but he didn't love the close connection she shared with her father.

The four of them enjoyed a dinner that evening devoid of business discussion. It was kind of like a mafia movie he had seen not long ago, no discussion of business during dinner. After today's events, Patty Lee and her father agreed they needed to let business rest. The pair got what they wanted from Vern and decided to put on a good face for the evening.

Little Cliff was not accustomed to such a formal dinner and Vern took extra time helping the child cut the steak in front of him. Vern held Cliff's hands as the boy tried cutting his steak. Patty Lee had even shown interest in Cliff that afternoon and ensured he was well groomed for the occasion. His blond hair was combed back neatly, and he wore a pair of small khaki shorts with a dress shirt. Cliff loved the alligator sewn into the shirt's fabric and offered no resistance in wearing it.

Her father was wrong about one thing, she thought, there was no mistaking the kid was Rof's offspring. She didn't know him well before he died, but the child looked just like his father. Every picture Vern hung around the house looked just like a larger version of this kid. The blond hair and especially Cliff's eyes. The boy's eyes shone just like his father. Even in pictures, Rof's crystal eyes caught your attention. The fact she knew the truth, however, would never influence her feelings about this child. Cliff was an obstacle and Patty Lee was going to take care of that, sooner rather than later.

Days passed and soon turned into weeks. Vern returned to work, but Patty Lee didn't alter her schedule. She didn't resume her daily life of brunches, lunches, and the like. That was a life to which she would never return. Engrained in the fabric of Cahaba, she made her presence felt on each and every project, big or small. She placed her office right next to Vern's, yet they hardly spoke. Both felt the isolation, but Patty Lee made sure nights were different. She needed a child and sometimes, she just missed the affection.

A nanny watched over Cliff during the day, but each afternoon, Vern put aside his work life and focused on his nephew. Patty Lee's isolation morphed into jealousy as the only times Vern turned his attention to her lay in their late-night rendezvous and only when she came to him.

Patty Lee was in the middle of a call to her father when the secretary stuck her head in the door and told her the doctor was waiting on line two. A smile spread over her face as she told her father about the call and put him on hold.

As the doctor spoke on the other end of the line, Patty Lee exhaled in relief, yet no hint of happiness crossed her face. The tip of her long finger hovered over the flashing button. Before pressing it and reigniting the conversation with her father, Patty

Lee let a slight tear escape her face and slide down her cheek. She brushed it away with her free hand and pushed the button.

Upon hearing the news, Vern grabbed his wife by the waist and held her in the air before putting her down and gently rubbing her stomach. A broad smile broached his face. He was going to be a father. He so wanted this for some time, and he couldn't be happier. When he focused on her face, he could tell Patty Lee was pretending to be happy. She smiled and said the right words, but Vern knew his wife. This was a business thing for her as she didn't do anything without precise calculation. In this moment though, Vern Bruce couldn't be happier. The smile gave way to laughter, and he told Patty Lee that if it was a girl, he wanted her to be just like her mom. That seemed to win Patty Lee over just a little and she nodded and put Vern's hand around her. She enjoyed the attention.

Vern couldn't wait to get home and tell Cliff he was going to have a baby cousin. When the thought of his nephew came into his mind, though, he thought what this might mean for him. He knew Patty Lee only tolerated Cliff. She hoped every day that Susie would appear and take the thorn out of her side and return the old Vern that she loved so.

Vern hadn't told his wife Susie visited him, however. That was a name the two really didn't mention to each other. The mere mention of the young girl's name put a frown on his wife's face. The day she reappeared at the door of the Cahaba building, Vern was glad Patty Lee was out of town. She flew down to meet with her father, on their new jet, and Mr. Swope from the bank. The deal was moving along faster than expected so she spent a good amount of time in West Palm Beach. Vern didn't go unless it was absolutely necessary. Patty Lee thought he would show more interest in her when he found out she was pregnant. The fact of the matter was Vern hated being in the same room as Old Man Clark and even the fact his pregnant wife flew back and forth alone wasn't enough for him to make the sacrifice.

It surprised Vern that Susie didn't want to see Cliff. It was so hard to leave him with Vern and Patty Lee the first time, she didn't feel she could do it a second. Vern understood. He didn't want Cliff to see her either. In his eyes, it was best for the boy and told his mother the child just now stopped enduring his nightly terrors.

Cliff settled into his new life and Vern feared hurting the boy even though Patty Lee treated him like some mongrel pet. Even though Vern's worry over Cliff was very real, however, it was not the whole truth. He didn't want to lose the boy. He not only owed it to his dead brother and felt it was his duty to raise his son, but from the moment he looked into Cliff's eyes, he loved this boy more than life itself. Perhaps even more than his wife.

Susie counted on that fact. She waited to come back so that Vern would think she had been in Alabama at the rehab clinic. In fact, she had never gone to the clinic. She wasn't working the Strip anymore though, as she hadn't been in Florida for several months either. She made her way along the coast to

Mississippi's infamous stretch of coastline and the coastal town of Biloxi.

Biloxi was known to be home of the South's most organized band of criminals known as the Dixie Mafia. The loose band of thugs, bootleggers, pimps, and thieves all called the town off the muddy beaches of Mississippi home. There were other outposts scattered throughout the South. Phenix City, Alabama, the North Georgia Mountains, Memphis, and East Tennessee all housed portions of this violent gang, but Biloxi, Mississippi was the seedy universe's center.

Susie West stripped at some mangy club down on the strip in Biloxi when she met her rescuer. He wasn't some loser that just wanted to be with the young girl. He took her into his home and made her his wife. He was older than her, probably by a decade or so, but she didn't really want to know, nor did she care. Burt Williams owned the club, as well as a couple more on the Biloxi Strip. He was a member of the notorious Dixie Mafia and one that took his job very seriously.

Burt took care of a young soldier that took things a little far with Susie one night. The intoxicated draftee jumped on stage and tried to have his way with the young girl. Burt escorted the soldier out, unharmed, and tossed him in his car and sped away. The soldier was reported AWOL the next day and nobody ever heard from him again. It wasn't an uncommon occurrence for draftees to flee and Burt Williams took advantage. Susie fell for him at once. Nobody ever defended her like that and the next day they said their vows.

When she arrived back in Panama City, the first thing Vern noticed were her clothes. She was dressed to the hilt and her face, now devoid of emaciated cheekbones was round and pretty once again. The bags that had been prominent under her eyes were gone and he could tell she was completely sober. The center in Alabama had worked wonders for her, he thought naively.

He invited her into his office, but Susie declined. She lied and said that she had to get back to Alabama that night as she just had a weekend pass. Vern asked her if she needed money or help of any kind. To his surprise, she declined any money. Tearing up, she asked Vern if Cliff could stay just a little longer. The young woman promised that she would be back, she just needed a couple more months. Even though he knew his nephew needed a mother, as Patty Lee would never be one to the child, Vern was happy she was leaving him. He hugged her like family and promised he would take care of Cliff. He loved the little kid and when he did go home, he would still be an uncle to him and a *father* figure. Susie kissed Vern on the cheek and thanked him once again and walked away. She didn't look back. Vern didn't know it, but their paths wouldn't cross for some time and when they did, things would never be the same.

Chapter 11

Time passes quickly and nine months came and went. A sweltering ninety-degree July day welcomed Casey Jack Bruce into the world. A beaming Vern Bruce, grinning from ear to ear, held four-year-old Cliff up to the hospital nursery window so he could see his cousin for the first time. The little boy pushed his face to the glass and left a small smudge when he withdrew. Cliff looked at his uncle and flashed a toothy grin. Even he, of few years, could tell how happy Vern seemed. He could see the smile, but his eyes also told the story. Little Cliff looked at the baby boy, wrapped up tightly and a small cap upon his head that covered up a tuft of black hair. The little boy thought he saw a smile on his new cousin's face.

Standing right next to Vern, his father-in-law stood with his hands on the glass, admiring his new grandson. Old Man Clark saw the dark eyes when the infant opened them periodically and admired the tuft of black hair. *He came into this world as a Clark,* he thought proudly. The old man glanced over to see Vern holding Cliff in his arms, pointing to the newborn. Without realizing it, the smile vanished, and he pursed his lips. Laying in that small room was the future of the Clark Family. His last name was Bruce, but he was his only daughter's only son. He was going to be a Clark.

Even though the two men stood so close to each other they could touch, they were miles apart. Vern's train of thought steered towards family, not business. Holding Cliff and looking at his newborn son, whisked him back to when he and Rof were kids playing on the beach. The two brothers were only a couple of years apart in age. Being so close in age, they were not only brothers but best friends. When he closed his eyes, the image of himself and his brother turned into an older Cliff and Casey. He wanted them to be close.

Vern cut his eyes in the old man's direction and noticed him sneering in their direction. He realized Old Man Clark saw Cliff as a threat, and so did his Patty Lee, but this was his family. Cliff turned his attention from the nursery and hugged his uncle. *This was his family*, Vern thought. *The old man standing next to him was not going to disrupt that.*

Breaking the silence, Mr. Clark put a fake smile on his face and said, "Good looking kid right there, hey Vernon?"

Vern didn't take his eyes off his son, and just replied, "Yes he is." Mr. Clark mentioned something about the port, but Vern wasn't listening to him, and the old man took one last look at his grandson and walked down the hall. Vern relaxed when the old man left. He noticed as he walked away, Old Man Clark walked gingerly and put his hand on the wall periodically for support. Vern nodded his head and reminded himself, *Just hold on. The old man won't live forever.*

Hopefully, Clark's visit would end when he saw Patty Lee. As the old man slowly made his way down the hall, Vern hoped the Clark jet would be in the air by the time he and Cliff made their way to his wife's room. The birth turned out relatively easy for Patty Lee. There were no complications and Casey's birth came naturally with no drugs of any sort. Vern kind of laughed when she let the doctors know that drugs made one weak and wanted none. When he and his nephew finally made their way to the room and opened the heavy hospital door, Vern couldn't hide the disappointment and resulting frown spreading over his face.

Patty Lee flashed a smile at her husband and said, "Vern, Daddy was just telling me how handsome Casey is." Vern tried to smile back at his wife, but the disappointment kept his face the same. Unfazed, she went on, "He's headed back down to the port. Said he asked you to come down, but you weren't listening." Her own expression changed into one of disappointment with the words.

Vern looked at the old man. "Sorry, no can do. I ain't leaving here until MY family goes home. All of us." Old Man Clark tucked his bottom lip and tilted his head. He understood what Vern meant and in the old man's eyes, that was a declaration of war.

"Look, Vernon, I know you are the ultimate family man, and I realize you want to be here, but I need you down there…" He paused and placed his hand on Vern's shoulder. "…Son."

In his mind, Vern laughed but only a head nod came physically. The Clarks were nothing if not predictable. The old man used language to flatter people and win them over. Vern continued to nod his head while thinking, *It ain't working on me, old man*. Patty Lee often tried the same tricks, but language really didn't work on Vern. She held other arrows in her quiver, but even they were becoming less and less effective.

"I'll come down next week. After they go home." Vern stood his ground. Surprisingly, the old man didn't contest it any further. He just said OK and said his goodbyes, kissed his daughter on the cheek, and left the three of them alone in the room.

Vern hadn't noticed Cliff, but the boy walked around the room, tugging on cords and now quietly sat in the corner. Vern reached into his pocket and tossed Cliff a piece of candy.

Patty Lee grimaced and said, "You're spoiling that boy." Vern didn't want to argue about Cliff right now.

He turned his attention to his still grinning wife and asked, "What the hell was that?"

Patty Lee didn't say anything for what seemed an eternity to Vern. Cliff found the couch and looked out from the high-floor window, smacking the candy around in his mouth, to the other tall buildings surrounding the hospital.

"Daddy just wanted to try and get you involved in the project. He's old, Vern, he can't handle things like he used to," she said.

"Bull. That old man is up to something. Always is," he responded.

"That's all in your mind, Vern. He wants to treat you as a son if you'd just let him." Vern walked over to the window and sat down next to Cliff. He patted the boy on the head, but Cliff didn't remove his gaze from the skyline of Tallahassee. It wasn't the largest city in Florida, but to Cliff, it was New York City.

"Look, Patty Lee, let's just enjoy the day and let tomorrow take care of itself. Plenty of time to worry about business," Vern said as warmly as he could. "After all, our son was just born today." With that she smiled, and Vern authentically returned the gesture. He stood up, walked over and kissed his wife and stroked her hair. Today they were in love again.

When Vern and Cliff left to grab something to eat, Patty Lee lay in the hospital bed with nothing to do but think. She wished things were better between the two, now three, most important men in her life. Patty Lee knew Vern was naturally skeptical of people he wasn't related to, and he wasn't related to anyone except Cliff and now the baby. The thought of her newborn son made a warm feeling spread over her. She hadn't paid much attention to her newborn other than a couple of feedings. She pressed the nurse button and asked for someone to bring Casey into the room. Casey, taking his first breaths and living his first days in this world, didn't know it now, but the future of the Clark Family lay in his tiny hands. If there was ever going to be a bridge between the two families, Casey Bruce held the key.

Vern and Cliff returned, and Vern shook a bag with a fast-food hamburger inside. Patty Lee readily accepted and when Vern handed the burger to her, she held on to his hand a second more.

"In a couple weeks, we will all go to the port. As a family," she told her husband. "I'll call Daddy tonight."

A couple of days later, the young family returned to their home in Mexico Beach. Cliff was already enamored with his infant cousin and held his hand as they made the two-hour drive home from Tallahassee.

Cliff made sure he was the first one up each morning and went directly into the baby's room just to look at him with no one else around. Most mornings, Casey's eyes were open and one morning, Vern overhead the four-year-old say to his younger cousin, "I can't wait to be a big brother." Vern couldn't stop the tear from rolling down his cheek. Cliff looked at little Casey like a brother.

The boy's thoughts of his mother were nearly forgotten. He hadn't seen her since the day she'd left him with his uncle. Now, Unc was his favorite person in the world. The young boy followed him everywhere. When they walked on the beach, Cliff walked behind Vern and put his smaller footprint into each one left by his uncle. He even went to the office with him on occasion. Cliff couldn't wait for Casey to join them. He asked Vern each day about Casey joining them. He couldn't wait to play on the beach with his cousin.

He still didn't feel the same for Aunt Patty. Even the four-year-old felt her cold demeanor towards the child. Nothing changed in the boy's eyes. He was just as scared of her today as the day she'd walked into the office.

In the time he had been with his new family, the image of his mother slowly dissipated and as Vern told Susie during her short visit, the nightmares became few. His mother's face slowly became a faint image upon which he could hardly focus. When his thoughts did turn to her, they faded quickly. Thoughts and images faded faster and faster with each passing day until they seemed like a dream to the child. Vern was the only family he really knew, and he loved living with his uncle. Cliff felt safer with Vern than any other point in his young life.

Patty Lee didn't wait long to call her Daddy and ask for the family jet a couple of weeks after she arrived home with her infant son. As soon as she made the call, a couple of hours later the sleek plane waited for them on the airstrip near the little beach town. Most small towns like Mexico Beach and Panama City didn't have an airport with the capability of handling such aircraft, but the area was blessed with several military installations. The civilian traffic in and out of these bases needed good airports. This one wasn't the grandest in the Panhandle, but it could handle the Clark Jet. It wasn't much to look at, and if you didn't know any better, it looked like one of the several cow pastures surrounding it. It consisted of one building and a narrow strip of pavement pretending to be a runway. The family arrived at the strip in a long Cadillac Old Man Clark sent to Panama City. Vern hesitated in accepting it, but his wife explained her father didn't want her driving around taking care of a baby at the same time. It was for safety, so Vern relented. Patty Lee's secretary drove with Vern beside her in the front seat and the rest of the family, including Cliff, in the back seat.

The jet engines roared as the pilot throttled them to maximum and streaked down the runway. Cliff's eyes were locked peering out the window. As the jet made its climb into the clouds Vern saw his wife already held her eyes closed and hoped for a quiet flight so she could rest. He wanted to talk with her about a lawyer he spoke with a couple of weeks ago about adopting his nephew, but by the looks of it, now wasn't the time.

The attorney told Vern if the parent hasn't tried to financially support the child or reconnect with the child within the past year, he could begin the process. He hadn't discussed it with his wife yet, but he intended to adopt Cliff as his own.

The clouds passed the window, seemingly hypnotizing Vern and his thoughts deepened. If she did show up and want her son back, how would Cliff adjust back into that life? He dreaded Patty Lee's response and his thoughts and his gaze turned from the window to his wife once again. He rubbed his chin and shook his head. He realized the longer he put off holding the conversation, the worse it would go. He decided, when they settled in, he would broach the subject. Cliff's head laid over softly on his shoulder and he joined his family in slumber as the jet screamed its way to West Palm Beach.

Upon landing in West Palm, Patty Lee was surprised her father wasn't there waiting for them to arrive. In his place, two cars awaited the family, one for the children and one for parents. With the child's car, he'd provided a nanny for the boys. The older white-haired lady assured Patty Lee her two-week old son was in safe hands. Patty Lee had no qualms about it, she trusted her father without question, but Vern protested.

"Leaving our son with someone we don't even know?" he growled at his wife.

"Daddy wouldn't send her if he didn't trust her," she said with her beautiful, charming smile. She held her smile as she told him, "Casey is the future of this family." As the words escaped her mouth, she stared directly at Cliff. The boy, too busy watching airplanes moving about the modern airport, didn't notice. Vern did, and he began to speak but decided to leave it alone. For now. He let out a sigh as the glare held purpose and she intended the gesture to hurt. If not Cliff, it was a subtle jab at her husband.

The car picking up Vern and Patty Lee didn't go to the mansion, nor did it take the couple to the Clark Building. They headed straight up the coast to Cocoa Beach. The old man, ready to show off his project and how much money he was going to make off it, waited on Vern and Patty Lee there. When they arrived, the old man sat alone, resting in a chair beneath a single palm tree that swayed in the gentle breeze off the Atlantic.

"Quite a sight, isn't it?" Mr. Clark asked with a smile that was eerily like the one Patty Lee used back at the airport. Vern marveled at how the father and daughter were so much alike.

Vern looked out across the port. The main shipping ports were off to the left and to the right massive cranes were busy putting together a web of iron beams.

"Looks good," Vern said. He really didn't know what he was looking at and felt ignorant. His business consisted of small-time real estate and erecting buildings not more than two or three stories, not something of this magnitude.

Sweat was starting to bead on Vern's forehead, and he hoped asking a few questions may speed this along. "Everything working out good?" he asked and promptly bit his lip in frustration. He hated sounding like a Panhandle bumpkin.

Mr. Clark's head tilted slightly to one side and the smile turned into a sort of grin. His son-in-law didn't know what the hell he was looking at. *This boy has a long way to go,* he thought.

"Main infrastructure is going in now, probably next year or year and a half we will be ready to go." He paused and looked at his daughter. She knew more about what was going on than Vernon. The old man thought to himself that she didn't really need this hick, but that ship sailed, and it looked like he was stuck with him.

"We've already got one cruise line on board. Announcement coming in a month or two. Got another that will be special, but I'm not ready to talk about it yet, lots of dealing to be done."

"When will we see a return on that five?" Vern asked him. At that, the old man eased out of his chair and delicately eased over to the two of them. His limp was more pronounced than two weeks ago, and he used a cane to aid his movements. *Damn*, Vern thought to himself, *he's falling apart quickly*. Old Man Clark hugged his daughter and when he turned to Vern, with a toothy grin he said, "Won't be long."

When Vern and Patty Lee first arrived at the port, the old man sent their car away. They all rode the remaining car to the massive Clark home. Vern suggested he and Patty Lee catch a cab and explore a little bit, but neither his wife nor her father agreed. He smiled and climbed into the front seat, allowing Patty Lee to sit with her father in the back.

Mr. Clark asked one of the staff to bring them some sweet tea to the back and the three of them made their way around the house. The wooden deck that extended from the rear of the two-story house held several chairs scattered about and two swings facing the ocean. Several palm trees lined the perimeter and offered shade from the scorching Florida sun.

They settled into the cushioned chairs under a large umbrella and Vern saw Cliff playing in the sand, accompanied by a member of the old man's house staff. Mr. Clark loved to show off, and he knew exactly what he was doing. Vern watched Cliff fill his buckets and place the sand neatly in the form of a castle. He noticed how much firmer the sand seemed to be here and how it contrasted to the fine, white sand of the Panhandle. Vern smiled as he thought about how the little boy loved the ocean just as much as his dad.

"Go on down, Vernon. Help that child build a proper sandcastle." He winked at Vern and continued, "I'm sure you know how, even with that powder y'all call sand up there." Vern faked a laugh and mimicked the old man to his wife as he walked down the steps to the beach.

Chapter 12

One clear April day a year later found Vern turned in his office chair facing the window. He watched families enjoying themselves on rented boats and fishermen becoming annoyed with them. Each time one of the bulky pontoons passed a fishing boat, he saw the fisherman cuss the wake the pontoons created, at least that's what he imagined. He chuckled to himself. There was a battle taking place on the inlets, bays and lagoons of the area, a battle of old traditions versus new revenue. *The old fishermen of the area were on counted days*, he thought. This part of the Gulf Coast was primed for tourism and not just people from the Southeast. Vern invested in a fleet of brand-new boats for fishing charters. That was the future of fishing and Vern cornered the market before it formed. It may be small potatoes to the old man, but to Vern he was investing in *his* family's future.

As he wheeled around at his desk, his eye caught a glimpse of the color television in the lobby outside his office. Nobody else in the office paid any attention to it, it was on just for noise most of the time, but something caught his attention. A helicopter looked as if it magically hovered over a building and like a stream of ants marching into a discarded cola can, people were trying to make their way up a rickety ladder and into the machine. Vern stood up, opened his glass door, and leaned on the door casing so he could hear but couldn't make out anything. He motioned for his secretary to turn up the volume so he could.

The sharp pointed British accent emerging from the television indicated, as the chopper began its ascent, that aboard, escaped the last American in Saigon. The American ambassador fled the country, chased out by the North Vietnamese Army marching into the city. As he kept watching, he rubbed his forehead and ran his fingers through his hair. A feeling of relief swept through his mind. A relief that now no other family would get the cold news from the government informing them their son or daughter died in combat.

After a few moments, relief gave way to anger. In his mind he pictured the daily newsreels of dead bodies being loaded into helicopters. Men with their heads bandaged, moaning in agony. All those dead American soldiers, all the dead Vietnamese, all of them died for absolutely nothing.

Lyndon Johnson lied to the American people from the first damn place about Tonkin, Vern thought to himself. LBJ whipped people into a frenzy when he announced the NVA attacked one of our ships in international waters. It was a lie. As reporters dug into the incident, the truth came out. The truth revealed the administration didn't know if they were attacked or not, as there were several conflicting reports. It did serve a purpose, however.

According to the Johnson Administration, the main goal lay in stopping communists from taking over Southeast Asia. It was imperative that they not take over South Vietnam. If South Vietnam fell to the communists, as Eisenhower warned in his Domino Theory, the rest would fall like dominoes and LBJ wasn't taking any chances. Vern thought about all the lies concerning the war and he sat down, physically sick at what happened a half-world away.

Here we were after all these years, the NVA was pouring into Saigon, renaming it Ho Chi Minh City. As he sat outside his office, the television playing out Eisenhower's worst fears, Vern once again felt the pain of losing his brother to this mess. The carefree teenager, with blond hair and blue eyes, tanned to the tips of his toes with girls falling in love with him from every part of the country, lost to a lie. Lost to a damn war that in the end, didn't even matter.

Vern got up and switched the television off. He'd seen enough. He told his secretary he didn't want to be bothered right now and shut the door behind him as he walked in and fell into his chair. Every time he thought about the war or his brother, guilt swelled within him. He lied to himself in college that he made a difference. The protests and the anti-war groups he joined only accomplished one thing, and it had nothing to do with war. One particular meeting resulted in Vern bleeding and his future wife falling in love with him. Their first meeting happened at the party, but Patty Lee lost interest in the quiet, bookish Vern quickly. It wasn't until the day she saved his life that they fell in love.

Early March 1969 held not only turbulent times at northern universities, but a few universities in the South also had their share of clashes. A chilly wind whistled through Tallahassee the night Vern attended a speech from one of the nation's harshest war critics. The gathering students wore sweaters and coats rather than the normal T-shirts and shorts. A little over a hundred students gathered eagerly anticipating the speech, but outside nearly twice as many police in riot gear assembled. This was still small-town Florida. Even though Tallahassee was the state capitol it lay in the Panhandle of the state. Those in charge were not about to allow hippies and protesters to take over their town. They didn't care if the university had their own police force, the sheriff of Leon County was a hard-liner, an anti-counterculture crusader and tonight it was his turn to fight for his country.

Just as the speech began in earnest, the back doors to the auditorium ripped open, banging against the wall as the helmeted officers poured through like the Spartan Army of ancient times sacking Troy. They lined the walls, blocking each entrance, pulling electrical cords out as they lined up. The speaker's voice fell silent as the electrical equipment shut down. The only voice was that of the old sheriff, his voice booming through the room. He carried a megaphone in one hand and a cold, black snub nose pistol in the other. Vern's body tensed and he couldn't move. He could only move his head and in any direction, the police blocked the exits. He took a deep breath as the realization that he was trapped sunk in.

The old gray-haired sheriff put the bullhorn to his mouth and in a very thick accent said, "You are to vacate the building. Anyone not doing as told..." He paused and laughed into the device. "...will be dealt with and arrested." Vern thought he heard, "you dirty hippies," at the end but the sheriff had thumbed the switch so he really couldn't tell. It didn't matter. The men surrounding the room began moving in. Vern noticed for the first time not only did they have rifles and nightsticks but also bayonets protruded upward from the ends of the rifles. For the first time he feared for his life.

The jumbled mass of students tried to wiggle through narrow openings like cattle herded though a chute. Vern, in the middle of this mass and towards the back, tried in vain to calm those around him, but panic ensued. He turned around and saw light reflecting off a shiny, sharpened bayonet. *My god*, he thought, *they will really kill me.* The calm he tried to instill in others vanished and panic engulfed him. He tried brushing past the people in front, but they were just as scared as he and trying to fight their way out of the building. As he tried muscling his way around one guy, a bearded kid buried his elbow in his nose, defending his territory. The blow landed directly on his nose but was felt throughout his body, and he tumbled backwards. His knees gave way, and his vision went black. All he sensed was the sharp sting of pain. He stumbled and thought he would eventually feel the hardwood floor smack the back of his head, but he fell directly into the police officer holding the bayonet he tried desperately to avoid.

"You son of a bitch!" the cop yelled at him and in the same motion slammed Vern in the back of his head with a stiff, muscled forearm. Vern's head exploded with pain as he tumbled to the floor. He felt people stepping on his arms and legs as they scrambled away, not wanting to face the same treatment. The cop raised a leg, and Vern felt the air part as the black boot brushed his head. He braced himself for the impact and hoped the blow would knock him unconscious. He could take no more pain; he just wanted this nightmare to end.

The end didn't come, however, as he felt someone's body fall on top of his. His mind raced, and he thought maybe someone else collected the punishment in his place. He opened one eye, his vision returning but blurred, and there, mere inches from his own, he recognized the face of the young girl that had spoken to him at the party a while back. *What in the hell was she doing here?* he thought as his vision faded once again.

The young girl pointed a long slender finger at the cop, whose face held nothing but astonishment. The officer held his posture, ready to strike down this little hippie girl if she kept interfering. She covered Vern's face with her arms and yelled in a strong, yet terrified voice, "MY DADDY KNOWS THE GOVERNOR, YOU BASTARD! YOU KICK US AND YOU WILL GET IT YOURSELF!!"

The police officer recoiled and then placed his black boot right next to her head. She could smell the shoe polish, and it nauseated her. He stood over them for what seemed like hours before shaking his head and moved on.

"To hell with y'all!" he belted as he passed them by.

The rest of the students once outside were promptly arrested. Patty Lee and Vern remained on the floor. Still unconscious and his nose gushing blood, the old sheriff waddled up to them and asked who in the hell she was. Patty Lee looked the old man directly in the eyes and said, "My Daddy is Daniel Clark from West Palm Beach. If you don't know him now, you will tomorrow if you come any closer."

The wily old sheriff knew the name as did most people in Florida. He spit tobacco juice onto the floor, almost hitting the young girl. "Hmm..." is all he said as he walked past her and out of the auditorium. He slammed the double doors as he walked out of the building and into the chaos outside.

Patty Lee couldn't pick Vern up and move him on her own, so she sat down beside him, avoiding the tobacco juice. It took a few minutes for the shock to wane and his vision to blurrily come back into focus. The first thing he saw was the pretty girl's dark eyes. He smiled and said, "I remember you."

Patty Lee took her sleeve and tried to wipe away the drying blood and told him, "You better be glad I remembered you." They both smiled at that. Even Vern's slight movement caused him pain and he winced slightly but couldn't stop smiling back at her.

A flash of lightning and the crash of thunder returned his thoughts to the present and to Patty Lee. The sunny day the tourists enjoyed earlier turned into a torrential downpour. It brought him out of his trance, but his thoughts lingered around Patty Lee.

She detested the war just as much or more as he did in their college days. Once, she wanted to go up north and protest with those college students that were eventually gunned down on their own campus about a year later after the incident in Tallahassee. Back then both wanted to change the world. Vern's quest for money and power hit the back burner, if only for a while. Patty Lee aspired to go to law school after she graduated but her father squashed that goal. Old Man Clark didn't want his daughter to become a lawyer, and he sure didn't want her to be a housewife to a country bumpkin like Vern. Vern rubbed his chin, the thought that everything she did now to please him stemmed from his disappointment in her choice of husband.

Vern grimaced and pressed his head against the back of the chair. Their ideals changed after college. They were not changing the world, only their own bank accounts. In fact, she probably didn't even know that the war ended today. She probably didn't care anyway. Even though the war didn't affect her personally, it did affect her father's wealth, however.

The old man, already rich when the war started, made millions. He invested heavily in "war" stocks, the industries fueling the war and raking in massive profits from the blood of kids. Kids like his brother and countless others. Vern sat up, opened the lap drawer under his desk and slid the picture he kept of Rof out and held it in his fingers. As he glared at the picture, a thought bubbled to the forefront of his mind. Maybe one of the reasons he hated his father-in-law lay not so much with his interference in his and Patty Lee's affairs, but his war profiteering.

Patty Lee didn't know where her father's *real* fortune originated, Vern assumed. While she was a young girl in college, having fun and with lofty ambitions, her father gambled on the war, and it paid off handsomely. He mortgaged nearly everything he owned, personal and business wise, to buy into the war-mongering companies. Companies that many journalist investigations revealed overcharged in their dealings with corrupt bureaucrats. Old Man Clark didn't think anyone outside of his inner circle knew about that and how he did it, but he was mistaken.

On one of his first visits to meet his future father-in-law, Vern sat outside the old man's office when his secretary forwarded a call inside and then took her smoke break. While she stepped outside, he quietly crept over to her phone, still flashing on her desk, and picked up the receiver and eavesdropped in a conversation.

One of the deals Mr. Clark was involved with went exceptionally well. On the other end of the line was Robert McNamara, the Secretary of Defense, who thanked him for investing in one of the companies.

Vern couldn't believe the conversation between the two men. They talked as though profit was the only motivator. To Vern it sounded like they didn't care one bit about stopping communism or keeping Southeast Asia free and democratic. It was all about money to them. Blood money. He hated the war and now he couldn't believe the father of the woman he loved made such profits from young men dying for nothing. As much as Patty Lee hated the war, he couldn't tell her. Her father was her world, and this news would destroy her. Vern swore to himself he would isolate his wife-to-be from this reality.

He put the picture to his forehead, closed his eyes and regret over that decision filled his soul. The rain pelted his window as he continued to think about the past. So many things he regretted not telling her and most stemmed from that war, but not all.

Even though he swore silence to his wife, Vern's thirst for knowledge overwhelmed him. He investigated the old man when found the opportunity, looking for stock transactions and the like. Vern made it a point to rummage through the old man's desk any chance he got. He found out a lot more than just the business deal discovered by eavesdropping on that fateful day. There was so much that he kept buried and quiet and would do so until he needed its use. As much as he despised the old man, he kept his secrets in these years gone by. Not needing it yet, he kept it close, waiting for the right time. Tired and weary of the day's thoughts, Vern locked his office door and went home.

As the sun set on the Gulf of Mexico, white caps crashed onshore and retreated into the ocean. Vern walked onto the back deck of his home. Patty Lee, still in Cocoa Beach, wouldn't be home until the next morning. He slid the glass door open to find the nanny sitting on the couch watching television. He dismissed her for the evening and Cliff, already half asleep when he arrived, crashed on the couch. Gingerly making his way into Casey's nursery, he found the baby sound asleep in his crib. He kissed his son on the forehead and stroked the tuft of black hair on the top of his head. Quietly closing the door, he went back into the den and sat down next to his nephew.

Vern glanced over at Cliff. He looked at Cliff and then at the picture of Rof hanging over the fireplace. Actually, it was a picture of him and his brother. He had it enlarged from a small instant photo they had taken as kids down on the beach. They were almost the same ages as the boys are now, he thought. Cliff looked just like his father and it saddened Vern that little Casey looked nothing like him, Rof, or even Pops. Casey looked like his grandfather Clark. There was no mistaking it but despite the resemblance, Vern loved him just the same. He loved both his boys. Then and there he vowed to protect them both.

He vowed to protect Cliff from the jealousy he knew was coming from Patty Lee and her father. Jealousy fueled from the fact he wasn't their own blood, but Vern made sure they treated him as such.

Thoughts turned to his own son once again. The kid was barely a year old, but the Clarks doted on the youngster. The heir to their fortune and the old man's legacy. He promised himself to protect his son from their adoration. Protect him from becoming a spoiled, rich brat. He wanted to protect Casey from his grandfather and his legacy. He wanted his son to live his own life, not to be an extension of a greedy, unscrupulous old man. Vern hoped the boy inherited the best part of his mother, however the heart of the young girl protecting a young college student from certain death, not the cold businesswoman he feared she was becoming. Sometimes when he looked into Patty Lee's eyes and held his wife close, he saw that protection and love in her again and in those moments, Vern felt hope for the young family.

    Finally, he promised to protect the family from each other. He knew competing forces would pull at them as the children grew older. Once again, he made a promise aloud in the quiet of his home. He promised himself he would be the force that kept them close and kept them together. Vern walked over to the sliding glass door and noticed a full moon glowing over the water. He placed his finger over the moon in the distance, smudging the glass and covering the heavenly body hovering over the water, closed his eyes, and finally his mind rested.

Chapter 13

Even though the first person from the Deep South to win the presidency since before the civil war, Old Man Clark didn't care for Jimmy Carter. Clark detested the path democrats were taking and refused to vote for one in a very long time. Vern, on the other hand, was a democrat through and through. He was thrilled at Carter's election and hoped that the Georgia peanut farmer would do important things in the White House.

The two men didn't discuss politics in each other's presence. In fact, the port deal didn't go as well as the old man hoped, so the two rarely spoke. Patty Lee was the constant go between with the two men. So, when the phone rang one Thursday afternoon, surprise washed over him when it came from the old man himself.

"Vernon how are you, my boy?" the old man bellowed through the solid black receiver. Vern was taken aback; this was not his usual greeting. He felt small beads of sweat begin to form on his forehead.

"I'm fine and you?" he responded with all the courtesy he could muster.

"Son, I'm not going to beat around the bush and I'm going to keep it short and simple..." The old man hesitated. "You are going to get a call tomorrow morning from Mac Tate, you heard of him, right?"

The old man already knew Vern dealt with Mac Tate in the past. The power behind the scenes in the Panhandle had been the one to find out about his brother and he had been a guest at his and Patty Lee's wedding. He hated when the old man patronized him like this and gripped the receiver until his knuckles turned white. Vern wiped the sweat from his brow and answered the old man with a courtesy that sounded at least halfway genuine.

"Yes, sir, I know of him. Maybe talked to him once or twice," he responded.

"I know he is a democrat and all, but he's the right kind of democrat." The old man's voice held a hint of condescension.

Vern knew exactly what *kind* of democrat he meant. Mac Tate was an old style Dixiecrat, the wing of the party holding sway over the South since Reconstruction. Even though he liked the person, Vern utterly despised Mac Tate's politics.

"Well, when he calls you tomorrow, listen to him, carefully, don't ask a lot of questions, son. Could change your life." The old man paused, "Don't worry about the five million, me and Patty Lee worked that out. Came out of my end of things. You kids will still get a cut, though. Call it a gift."

Vern's face reddened. He hated the notion of those two going behind his back. It was happening increasingly these days, and he detested it. He shook his head and continued to wipe the sweat, coming faster now, from his forehead. *But you damn fool,* he thought to himself, *you helped create this monster by staying away from it.* When she flew home from West Palm this weekend, they needed to talk. Right now, however, the problem at hand laid with this mysterious call from Mac Tate tomorrow. He said goodbye and hung up the phone, slamming it as he did and reached for a handkerchief from his desk drawer.

Patty Lee sat across the desk from her father as he talked to Vern. Mr. Clark wanted to put the conversation on the speaker, but Patty Lee knew better. She knew how to handle her husband. It was becoming harder lately, but she could still talk him into anything she wanted. All she had to do was use Cliff as a bargaining chip. She smiled at her father and put her thumb in the air.

"You think he will do it?" the old man asked his daughter.

"He will say the right things tomorrow, but he'll probably not give a straight answer. He'll want to talk to me about it and try to get out of it. By Monday, though, when he calls Mac Tate back, he *will* be excited to say yes," Patty Lee said coldly.

Old Man Clark returned his daughter's smile. His daughter overcame those liberal tendencies that public college tried to instill in her. She grew up to be just as ruthless as her father. The smile turned into raucous laughter. His skinny, frail frame shook all over.

"Damn, little girl," he said. "I raised you right."

Vern dreaded the call he knew was coming promptly at nine the next morning. Mac Tate held the real power in the Panhandle and had done so since before Vern was born. He was an old school Dixiecrat just like Old Man Clark. There must be a crooked deal of some sort the two old pals needed to put together on the Gulf Coast, Vern assumed.

Honesty was a virtue Vern held closely in his business dealings. This was home and he wanted people to know he was a man of integrity. Cahaba owned multiple motels along the Strip in Panama City Beach and a fleet of charter boats. The growing company diversified and bought part of a construction company and owned controlling interest in a bank. Recently he started talks with a small trucking company and hoped to buy at least half of the enterprise. That was a deal Patty Lee was supposed to know nothing about. It wasn't Cahaba, that one was all Vern Bruce. He wanted it for Cliff.

However, when the phone rang exactly as the clock on the wall struck nine, Mac Tate wasted no time.

"How you doin', Vernon?" Tate asked, thickening his southern accent even more. He was well educated, and his mother was from up north, but Tate knew where his bread and butter came from, and he laid it on thick and heavy.

Vern responded with the typical greetings and pleasantries and then Tate went straight to the point.

"I want you to be the first to know," he lied. "The congressman has had enough. He wants to sit out back and watch the waves. Retire. If you ask me, he doesn't want to deal with that bastard traitor in the Oval Office," he said, not letting Vern get a word in. "Your name has come up here and there. I remembered you and your family, son. Bad, bad thing that happened to your brother. Hate what it ended up doing to your father."

The politician paused to let that sink in. Just like the damn crook he is, Vern thought, holding a favor over his head and using his dead brother as leverage to get what he wanted. He and the old man were cut from the same cloth and Vernon's feelings towards Tate grew darker with each word. Clark and Tate knew how to use people, and they knew how to get their way.

"Thank you, Mr. Tate, but why has my name come up?" He asked the question, already knowing the real answer. He envisioned Tate and Clark clinking together two glasses of bourbon in toast, celebrating their idea. Vern also expected the bull Tate spewed next and braced himself.

"I know what kind of businessman you've become, Vernon. Your paw-in-law told me, but I already knew. I know what kind of man you are; your *family* is. You are the kind of man we need up there in Washington looking out for us little people down here in Northwest Florida." In Vern's mind, Mac Tate was slick not only in his dealings, but with his language. He knew how to appeal to individuals. That's why he had lasted so long in the dog-eat-dog world of Southern politics. With his free hand, Vern tapped his fingers on the desk, visions of Old Man Clark's rotten smile permeating his mind.

"One thing though," Tate said in a weird, whispering voice. "We ain't running as a Democrat."

Vern said nothing and his fingers stopped tapping. The entire South, except for the very tip of South Florida and a few minute parts of Dixie, voted Democrat since the South endured

Reconstruction over a hundred years ago. Southern memories faded slowly, and stories were handed down through generations about the evils of the Republican Party.

"Mr. Tate, that ain't possible. There hasn't been a Republican nominated in this area for a long time. For *any* office," Vern finally responded. His voice couldn't hide his surprise.

"Son, times are a changing. If it hadn't been for that son of a bitch Carter, the South would've voted for Ford. You know it and I know it. You know he's the only Democrat to carry the South in a long time. But, even so, the South is primed to change parties. The democrats quit caring about us in the sixties. LBJ screwed us over and we've been leaving the party slowly ever since. We are going Republican, and I want you to lead the change, son." He was nearly shouting as he finished speaking.

Vern sat quietly and motionless. *What in the hell was happening?* he asked himself. Vern, so happy to see Carter in the White House, and now this man wanted him to go against his own convictions and become a rival. Tate wanted him to go against the man that would not only lead the free world, but the South out of its own self-destructive tendencies. He started tapping his fingers again, this time heavier and harder. Once again, however, he knew better. Vern wouldn't verbalize feelings to this powerful man right now and he was damn glad he couldn't see him through the phone. He felt the old man's greasy old fingers all over this and he wasn't going to let him manipulate him. He would simply decline and thank Mac Tate for thinking of him.

Mac Tate, always the wily old politician, sensed rejection coming and interjected, "Before you say anything, son, talk it over with your wife and we will talk again Monday. Take the weekend. Think about the future and the part you could play, not only for the Panhandle, but for our country. We don't want to lose what we have here."

Vern knew exactly what the old politician meant. Control. The old "Southern" way. Those in control didn't want to lose it and they would sleep with the enemy to keep it. Yet, *Tate was right in some ways*, Vern thought and decided he would take the week, talk to his wife, and make the decision of his life. Vern looked out the window, but there were no boats on the water today and oddly no birds floated past. *Just a dreadful day all around*, he thought. Most times he looked somewhat forward to Patty Lee's arrival. Not this time. He and his wife were overdue for an extended conversation.

Vern leaned on the side of Patty Lee's old blue Mustang as the jet taxied to a stop. He looked around marveling at the improvements made to the once ragged airstrip. Mac Tate kept promises, and this was one he made to Patty Lee, even if through her father. They stopped at a roadside hole-in-the-wall for breakfast. He loved the little place with checkerboard tablecloths, an open view of the kitchen, and the greasiest bacon in Bay County. Since she was pregnant with Cliff, the smell of grease nauseated her, and she felt sick as soon as they walked in. Patty Lee hated the place. In fact, she hated every little redneck joint in the area, and she guessed for that reason they sat in the dingy diner. It was crowded on a Tuesday morning with people headed to work or hitting the Gulf in their fishing boats. It was noisy and everybody in the building focused on themselves and what their day would bring. It gave Vern a chance to talk to his wife without the boys and without anyone bothering them.

Instead of waiting on Vern to start the conversation, Patty Lee decided to head him off with a preemptive strike.

"I know you aren't too happy with Daddy writing off that money," she said with a hint of sternness but also with undertones of understanding. "Daddy has this knack of seeing hard times before they hit. He always has. There is going to be a problem with oil coming up—"

Vern cut her off before she could finish, "How in the hell would he know that, or even think that? That OPEC is just trying to make money, same thing he'd do. They know where their 'golden goose' is, right here. He's full of it. The great Old Man Clark is *never* wrong."

Patty Lee didn't retaliate. She just reached out and took Vern by the hand and blinked her brown eyes. "Well, believe or don't. Our money is in a trust, its safe." Vern started to speak, but she cut him off with her palm facing him. "The trust is for Casey, for college or whatever he chooses, when he turns eighteen. So, it was more a gift for his grandson than for us." Vern's face dropped and he stared at the red and white tablecloth. Patty Lee sensed defeat in her husband, and she raised an eyebrow. *That was quick*, she thought.

The young redheaded waitress came by the table, topped off their coffee, and asked once again if they were ready to order breakfast but they both declined. Patty Lee rubbed her husband's hand in hers.

"I know how you want to do things; I understand that and that's why I insisted on Daddy putting the money in the trust. Casey is taken care of and after all, isn't he the most important thing?" she asked her husband in her most gentle voice. Vern nodded in agreement and felt what little fight left in him evaporate. "Now that we've covered that, what about the other?" she asked softly.

"I'm doing it," he said to his wife. Patty Lee's mouth dropped open. Vern happy with finally leaving his wife speechless, grinned, and continued, "I'm not your father nor am I Mac Tate, though. I'm going to do it my own way. I don't want either to interfere and I mean that. Both are pushing eighty and I'll use that to keep them out of it. Even though neither of the geezers will admit it, this is a young man's game, not decrepit old has-beens."

Patty Lee tilted her head and responded, "You *are* running as a Republican though, right?"

Vern grinned back at her and put his other hand on top of hers. "I sure am."

When they arrived home, Patty Lee ran to the phone and called her father. Vern in turn called Mac Tate. They didn't want to wait to inform them of Vern's decision. To their surprise, both men, overjoyed at the news, even agreed to stay out of it. Patty Lee and Vern both knew, however, they would not.

Tate told Vern of an up-and-coming political guru, from Mississippi. A man named Lucious "Lucky" Clay. He would be more than happy to head the campaign. From birth he had gained the nickname "Lucky" mainly because he was born on July 7, 1947. He was only forty, but that was a lot older than Vern. Coming from the Mississippi Coast, Vern suspected someone with a name like "Lucky" may be more than just a *political* operative. He was aware of that part of the Gulf Coast's reputation as the home of the Dixie Mafia. Putting those fears aside, Vern called Lucky that Sunday morning and set up a meeting for the next week. He knew this guy was Mac Tate's stooge, but he figured it was better than the old Dixiecrat being directly involved in the campaign.

With both big confrontations covered for the weekend, the young family spent Saturday and Sunday on the beach in their backyard. The waves gently rolled in and out, and, on this day, the rip currents were non-existent. The beach often gave off a slight pungent smell due to seaweed, but today only the salty air floated on the breeze. Vern took Cliff out beyond the sandbar and gave the child his first swimming lesson. Patty Lee played with Casey in the foamy surf at the water's edge. The toddler loved every minute of it, running away from his mother and falling face first into the salty water. There was a gentle breeze blowing inland and before long the boys were playing in the sand right along where the waves lost their momentum and retreated into the Gulf.

While the boys played, Patty Lee looked over paperwork in the shade given by the umbrella she'd planted in the sugary sand. Vern glanced back over at the boys. Nostalgia overwhelmed him and he thought of Pops.

There were very few days they'd spent at the beach as a family when he was a child, but the precious handful they did contained some of his fondest memories. Vern ran his fingers through the sand as he remembered the time he and Rof wandered too far from shore and found themselves being pulled out to the deeper bluer waters by a rip current. A rip current that rushed the boys from shallow water to water deeper than twice their height. Pops told both of his sons what to do in case that happened, but they were young and scared out of their wits. They forgot and panic ensued. As they struggled against the rushing water, Vern grabbed Rof's arm with a vice-like grip that nothing would break. If he couldn't get his brother to safety, they would both drown. At the expense of his own breath, Vern held his brother's head just high enough to keep his nose out of the water. Just as his head went below the salty water for what he thought was the last time, he felt the rough hand of his father slide under his arm. Pops pulled his sons up out of the water and told him to calm down. They had to ride it out until it dissipated, and he looked both of them in the eye and promised them everything would be OK. Vern saw the love and protection in his father's eyes and stopped struggling. He pulled his brother in close to him and all three rode the rip-current until they could no longer feel its deadly pull.

When they pulled themselves out of the water, Vern gasped for air and every muscle in his body ached. Pops looked at him. It wasn't the cold stare of disappointment Vern expected, only joy and the look of relief.

"Son, you did the right thing. Never let go of your brother. If you're in trouble hold on to family as tight as you can. Don't let go. We're all we got. If you go, we all go," Pops told his oldest son and then he grabbed both of his boys in his arms and hugged them as tightly as he could.

Vern missed his father. He wished to talk to him one more time. He wanted Pops to answer his questions and guide him along. He picked up a handful of sand and let it slowly sift through his fingers. He felt the sun's warm rays on his skin and a calm swept over him.

He let the last grains of sand fall from his fingers and looked up to the boys playing in the surf and looked at his wife, still sifting through a stack of papers. He took a deep breath and turned his focus to the gently rolling ocean in front of him. On this day, family was all that mattered.

Chapter 14

Meeting Lucky Clay was not something Vern was looking forward to. Patty Lee worked in her office next to his own, when the small, bespectacled man showed up unannounced. He looked the part as he wore a plain white shirt and khaki pants with suspenders holding them up. What he needed the suspenders for Vern couldn't guess because Lucky's waist wasn't two feet around.

Showing up without advance notice reeked of Mac Tate. Even though he agreed to stay in the background, this move signaled he was still around and in charge. *So, this was the future of politics in the Panhandle?* Vern asked himself. *This little man?* At first glimpse, Vern was unimpressed, but he did agree to this, and with Clay's appearance, the campaign started today. With the midterm elections only a year away, they didn't have much time to prepare and campaign.

The odd little man approached Vern and ran his eyes over the candidate. He looked a long while at Vern's shoes. He seemed oddly focused on the penny loafers Vern wore to the office every day.

"Gotta change the shoes," the sharp, nasal-tinged voice said in a genteel Southern accent. This caught Vern off guard, and he scoffed.

"What in the hell?" he asked Lucky. Finally Lucky took his eyes off the shoes and turned them upward to Vern, eyeing him through his thick, horn-rimmed glasses.

"Too laid back, too, how do I say, beachy." Lucky stood on his tiptoes as he spoke so he wouldn't appear as short as he actually was. He smacked his lips and finished his thought, "You are a man of power. You hold authority and you have to show it. Starts with the shoes."

Here he was, facing a run for the United States Congress and this weird fellow focused on his shoes. The two men finally broke eye contact and Vern ushered him into his office.

As he entered the room, Vern caught a glimpse of his wife through the glass wall, trying to act busy, shuffling papers and pecking away at her keyboard, all the while watching this strange introduction. She didn't look up, but she grinned, and Vern noticed. He couldn't help but grin himself; it *was* an odd scene. These were the little things he loved about his wife. Even though she played the part of a serious businessperson, she never lost her sense of humor and occasionally, it bubbled to the surface.

The first meeting didn't last long, and Vern happily walked Lucky to his car. He left Vern with a "to-do list" and didn't say a whole lot, other than instructions on shoring up his image. He mostly stared out at the large window while he spoke, enjoying the view of West Bay. The odd little man left just as quickly as he came. The list consisted of trivial things, like shoes, for Vern to correct before their next meeting. Oddly, Lucky paused at each cubicle in the office space outside Vern's office peering at each employee. Vern walked behind him and just shook his head towards each employee when the odd little man walked away. When he finally made it to his car and drove away, Vern put his hands on his hips, raised an eyebrow and whistled. It was one of the most peculiar mornings he remembered and sensed many more on the horizon as the campaign unfolded.

The next few months flew by as the campaign heated up. A Republican previously won the seat only once since the Civil War. That was a fluke of redistricting, and the elected Republican lasted only one term before the state corrected its mistake. Vern ran unopposed in the Republican Primary and tread an easy path to the general election. Several democratic candidates slugged it out in their primary, spending millions of dollars each.

Content to let his Democratic opponents fight it out, he kept his approach low-key. He made few speeches, and the only advertising Lucky wanted consisted of roadside placards with his family plastered on the front with "BRUCE FOR CONGRESS" written on them. Even Cliff joined the family in the advertisements. Patty Lee felt it would show them as a happy family and voters loved happy families. She continued to treat Cliff like the outsider in private, but for the campaign, she treated him like a genuine son. These roadside signs littered Panhandle roads and before long one of them caught attention from the Bruce family's past.

On what was supposed to be a quick trip back to Florida, Susie Brannon, now Susie Williams, saw one of those placards nailed to the side of a BBQ joint that she and her new husband,

Burt Williams, stopped to eat lunch. With the age difference of nearly a decade, Burt's friends thought he would be done with the girl after a fleeting time. Turns out, he wasn't. The two married a few months before and Susie didn't know a whole lot about his past. She knew he was a bouncer in a club owned by a very well respected yet feared member of what was known as the Dixie Mafia. She knew he was a feared man on the Biloxi Strip. What she didn't know was how connected her new husband was to the criminal organization. In fact, it was an understatement calling him a criminal himself. Burt Williams was a product of poverty.

Born and raised in the Mississippi Delta, he knew despair at an early age. The Delta, known for agriculture, held distinction as the richest part of the state. That was until the farms became mechanized and the poor sharecroppers of the area lost their livelihood to massive tractors and modern farming.

Burt's story followed the path of many of the region's poor, indebted sharecroppers. His mother found an early grave, driven to madness by her husband's alcohol-fueled rage. After her premature death, in a drunken rage, his father put a pistol in his mouth.

Burt, only ten years old when he set out on his own, learned he must fight to survive. He became a thief and by the time his sixteenth birthday rolled around, the teenager found himself incarcerated more often than not.

The Strip attracts people like Burt. He worked his way up the ladder in the Dixie Mafia. Most of the rungs of his ladder were stained with blood. By the time his twenty-first birthday came, he held a position of respect, an enforcer, with the loose organization. In these circles, he met different types of people and criminals. It was there he met Lucky Clay. When Burt saw his new wife staring at one of Vern Bruce's advertisements, it caught his attention.

Susie stood frozen in front of the picture as tears began to roll down her round, freckled cheeks. She told Burt she left her son with family over in Florida, but she didn't give him details. But now, there he was, smiling, standing next to Vern Bruce in the picture. Her lips quivered as her eyes focused on Cliff. She stretched out her shaking hand and touched his face on the sign. Nearly seven years passed since she'd left him with Rof's brother. Sometimes she thought about reaching out, but she didn't want to interrupt his new life. She put her tear-stained face into her hands and sobbed. Burt walked quietly behind his wife and put his hand on her shoulder and asked her what was wrong.

"Nothing," she said as she quickly dried her tears with the collar of her dress. "They just look like the family I always wanted." She turned and hugged Burt. He may be a tough-guy bouncer to everyone else, but to her he was a gentle, caring man and she loved him dearly. He was nothing but a big, burly teddy bear. He hugged her back, holding her tightly and wanted to believe her. With his face away from hers, a frown found its way to his lips. It was the first time he thought his little wife lied to him.

He faced the sign himself as he held onto his wife. He studied the advertisement and the family smiling on its face. This sight of this politician affected his wife this severely, and he wanted to know why.

A few years back he did a favor for that odd little guy Lucky Clay. Word in Biloxi was Clay finally hooked a whale and was working in Panama City, Florida with some rich guy wanting to be a politician. By the looks of it, this Bruce guy may be the one. Burt pulled a slender cigar from his shirt's pocket and popped it in his mouth. He didn't light a match; he chewed on it and rolled it from side to side. It was time to see an old *friend.*

Mac Tate and Lucky Clay were just taking their seats at the small conference table inside the rented store-front office space housing the Bruce for Congress campaign headquarters when Vern joined them. The coffee provided tasted awful and burned to Vern, but he forced it down. He needed it just to be in the room with these two politicians. A fake smile adorned his face as he remembered how Mac helped his family years ago. That fact eased his feelings towards him, but his feelings for Lucky hardened each time they interacted. When he glanced at the little man, he shook his head slightly, hoping they wouldn't notice.

Clay ran his fingers up and down his suspenders, adjusted his glasses and leaned towards Vern.

"Alright, Vernon, the real race starts today. You are officially the Republican nominee for the First District." Lucky took little time and offered no pleasantries. "Here is a list of our positions," he said as he slid a single piece of paper over to Vern. The two men noticed Vern's twitching mouth as he read over the paper. Vern hesitated for a second, laid the paper on the table, and tapped his fingers for a minute, speaking very slowly and carefully.

"Gentlemen, this reads like the script Wallace followed in sixty-eight. That was a decade ago; we can't say this kind of thing today. Times have changed." Vern shook his head as he spoke and glared at the two politicians when he finished speaking, awaiting their response.

Mac Tate looked at Lucky and then slowly turned his attention to Vern.

"How many Blacks live in the district?" he asked as if Vern was expected to know the answer. Vern looked back at the old political tiger and shrugged his shoulders.

"No clue," he responded, "what does it matter?"

Lucky smirked, pulled at his suspenders and said, "It matters because there are far more rednecks than Black people living in the Panhandle. Blacks don't elect people here, rednecks do. This paper represents what they want to hear." He reached over and slammed his finger on the paper.

Mac Tate nodded in agreement, but his smirk vanished. His face bore the weight of his concern.

Tate added, "The politicians of the 'New South' paid attention in sixty-eight and especially seventy-two. Nixon ripped the South away from the democrats and they will never get a hold on us again. The future is here and you, Vern, are it. The announcement speech confirmed what I already knew, son, you have *it*. You have what it takes, son, and I'm not bullshittin' you." Vern leaned back in his chair, folding his hands together in front of his chest.

"And what exactly do I have?" Vern asked him.

"You're slick, son. You can bullshit with the best of them and that's what is going to win us that seat. It ain't about ideals anymore. No, no, no, sir. You got to tell people what they want to hear. I know you're figuring that's what politicians have always done, but not like this. Democrats haven't realized this yet. Hell, they may never. There used to be two factions of democrats, and they always balanced each other out, but now, that crap is gone. Tell 'em what they want to hear. Get elected. That's the game, Vern. That's the only game." The old man was nearly out of breath when he finished.

Vern glanced down at the sheet of paper once more. "Lies, just like Nixon, huh?" he shot back at the old man, disgust lining his words.

Mac shook his head furiously. He returned Vern's intense gaze and told him, "Lies built this damned country."

Vern remained quiet as the two politicians did most of the talking. He only offered a nod here or there, consumed in his own thoughts. He placed a large amount of blame concerning his brother's death directly on Richard Nixon, the former president.

Not only his brother's death but the blood of thousands stained the disgraced president's hands and the thought of modeling his campaign after Nixon's sickened him. Once again, he felt himself manipulated by forces he despised and pictured Old Man Clark sitting in his office smiling. He imagined Patty Lee's father laughing, wallowing in delight at how he got Vern to do his bidding once again.

When the meeting finally ended, Vern ran to the bathroom and vomited. He washed his face with cool water from the sink and composed himself. He walked out of the bathroom and Lucky stood outside the door with a towel in his hand.

A couple of days after meeting with his candidate, Lucky got a visit from an old friend. When Burt Williams opened the door and walked into the makeshift office space, he was out of place from the start. The large, hulking, roughly bearded man wore a simple white shirt with noticeably short sleeves and blue jeans. His white undershirt filled in the gap on his chest where his shirt was unbuttoned, and he held an unlit cigar in the corner of his mouth. The rest of the people milling about were dressed in their Sunday best. It didn't take long for the staff to recognize the big man's presence and look at each other quizzically. None of them wanted to approach Burt. Lucky saw him from his corner office window and rushed out to meet him before he told anyone who he was. The last thing Lucky wanted was someone from Biloxi coming through the door.

"Mr. Williams," Lucky greeted him courteously, but in a near whisper. "Good to see you. Let's go into my office." Lucky wasted no time ushering him out of the lobby and into the safety of his office.

As they sat down, Burt turned his attention to his surroundings. "Nice place you got. Should've known I'd find you in the middle of a crook's campaign somewhere." He smiled at a young female volunteer as she walked by the office. "Nice scenery, too." Burt chuckled.

Lucky didn't want to engage in small talk with a known member of the Dixie Mafia. Especially not in his office and certainly not while a *legitimate* campaign was in full swing. He got right to the point, "What's up, Burt? You wouldn't be here if you didn't want something."

"Not even wanting to catch up, I see how it is Lucky," he responded staring at the campaign manager with his wide penetrating dark eyes. Lucky took a deep breath to calm himself and his nose filled with the scent of Burt's overused cologne. The gangster sat back in his chair and a grin showed through his thick beard. "That's OK. I gotcha. Look, all I want to know is who this guy, Bruce, you're working for is. That's it. What's he got going on? Who's backing this cat?"

Lucky eyed Burt suspiciously and tugged at his suspenders, "He ain't going to be a problem for your friends, Burt. That's a promise. This guy is a square. Once kind of a hippie even; I mean a hippie for around here in these parts." Lucky pushed his glasses from the end of his nose and gave Burt a smile. In his mind he wondered just how much Burt *already* knew.

Burt drew his chair a little closer to Lucky and his voice lowered a little as he spoke. "Ain't worried about that. I *already* know who's backing him. Our mutual friend down south." The grin grew wider under his beard as he saw the fear in Lucky's eyes. Burt continued, "But, Lucky, the girl I married took one look at this cat's picture stapled to a wall and started bawling her eyes out. Fed me some bullshit about just wanting a family. I been around too many people and heard too many lies not to recognize one."

Lucky relaxed just a little bit. When he first saw Burt standing at his door, he thought it meant only one of two things. Either the organization wanted a piece of Vernon Bruce, or they wanted him gone. He was relieved that it was personal, and his mind did ease a bit to know Burt already knew Bruce's connection to West Palm. He didn't have to hide it from him. Burt wasn't a man you hid things from. The sweat that began to form under his shirt subsided a bit and he told Burt what he wanted to hear.

"This is just a guy married into money, Burt. Came up broke, but made a little local money, married into a lot more money and power and apparently you already know what money and power." Lucky winked as he talked, but Burt didn't return the friendly gesture.

Burt leaned back in his chair and put one of his massive boots on Lucky's desk. Lucky didn't protest, he knew better. Burt let the words sink into his mind for a second. He was not dumb nor was he just muscle for the machine over in Mississippi. Burt made it this far with his brain not his brawn, even though brawn certainly made it easier.

"There's something else. Something I can't put my finger on, Lucky," he said, "Susie never lied to me and to lie over a picture, don't make sense." He stood up and walked over to the same picture they had seen at the roadside BBQ joint in the middle of nowhere. He looked at each face and studied each feature. His head tilted to one side and his gaze locked on Cliff. The young boy looked kind of different from the other three members of the family. It wasn't much but there was something. He focused as close as he could to Vern's face in the picture and he remembered. *How could I be so damn stupid?* he thought to himself. It all came back to him in a flash.

It wasn't Cliff but Vern's face that sparked his memory. This was the man that he went with Susie to see a few years ago. He sat in the car as Susie walked into an office building in Panama City. Something about tying up loose ends or something like that she told him. They hadn't been together long and at that point she was still just a cute stripper to him.

He turned back to Lucky and this time a tinge of anger showed on his face. He stepped forward, face to face with Lucky, and their noses were nearly touching when he said, "I need to meet with Mr. Vernon Bruce. The man in the picture. Today."

Just when Lucky thought he would escape the meeting without some type of favor or worse yet, ultimatum, here it was. It was one he just couldn't indulge, however. He couldn't let Vern anywhere near a known member of the Dixie Mafia. It was bad enough Burt was in this office. He tried pleading his case.

"Burt, you know I'd do just about anything for you, but I can't get you a meeting with this man. He is a candidate for congress for Christ's sake," he said very carefully, pulling at his suspenders.

Burt smiled and reached into his shirt pocket. Lucky flinched when he quickly removed his hand, which only held a crumpled pack of small cigars. He pulled one from the pack, lit it and blew the resulting smoke in Lucky's direction. The sweet smell of tobacco filled the room. Burt's toothy grin widened into a beaming smile. "You ain't got no choice, partner."

Chapter 15

Lucky chose a little, out of the way, greasy spoon in one of the small border towns near the Alabama line. Located on a narrow, two-lane road leading from the middle of nowhere to the coast. They would probably stick out like a sore thumb, but as soon as they were gone, they would be forgotten. Panhandle people tended to mind their own business. At most, the patrons of the little chuck house would look them up and down at first, wondering who they were, but so many people used this road to travel to the beach from Alabama, that interest would quickly wane. It wasn't the first time Lucky set up meetings like this and with Burt Williams snooping around, it probably wouldn't be the last.

Leaving in what he thought was plenty of time to beat Burt to the meeting, Lucky and Vern found Burt's car waiting in the parking lot. This wasn't the first time Burt held meetings like this either, and he arrived early to scope the place out. Lucky pursed his lips and let out a sigh. *Gotta do better than this*, he thought. The overwhelming smell of the livestock auction across the two-lane road hit Vern in the face upon stepping out the car. He looked at Lucky and said, "Hope that ain't where they get their meat in there." Lucky didn't smile, he just motioned for Vern to follow him in.

The smell of smoke blended with the putrid smell from across the street as the two of them made their way to a corner table. Burt sat in the very corner, chewing away at his unlit cigar.

Lucky said very little to Vern about this meeting, only telling him there was an important person he needed to meet. He assumed that if he were completely honest, that they were meeting with a member of the Dixie Mafia, Vern would have nothing to do with it. Vern could barely see the man in the corner. The place was dimly lit and it being a cloudy day, sunshine didn't complement the sparse artificial lighting. A small light that hung over the table illuminated Burt's face as the two politicians pulled out their chairs to sit down. Vern squinted and faintly recognized Burt's puffy face but couldn't figure out where or when.

Vern eased into the seat across from Burt and Lucky pulled out the chair next to him, but Burt pointed to the empty chair next to his bulky frame insisting Lucky sit next to him. The silence lasted only a second as Burt eased up to the edge of the table. "You don't remember me, do you?" he whispered, winking and rolling the cigar to the other side of his mouth as he spoke.

Vern again strained his memory and only vague familiarness sprung forth.

"No, sir. You look familiar but I can't place you," Vern responded as he glanced at Lucky and asked, "What is this all about, Lucky?"

Burt leaned in a little closer, his mouth in a curt frown. He put the cigar in an empty coffee cup and placed his fat fingers on the table, tapping them in rhythm.

"You can just talk to me," he scolded Vern. "This ain't business today, Mr. Bruce, this is a personal matter."

Vern raised an eyebrow and nodded his head. All manner of thoughts circulated in his mind, trying to pinpoint where he saw this man before. Suddenly the hairs on Vern's arms pricked upward, and a chill ran down his spine, his senses indicating danger. He may not know him, but he knew his type. You didn't grow up on the Gulf Coast and not run into people like this. Against his instincts, Vern decided to tackle the situation directly.

"Just who are you and what the hell do you want?" Vern demanded, just loud enough for impact but still low enough so that nobody close could hear him. Burt leaned back into his seat, taking the cigar from the cup and popping it back into the side of his parted lips. He didn't light it, he just let it dangle from his mouth for a second, holding eye contact with his prey before answering Vern's questions.

"My name isn't that important, Mr. Bruce. The only two names you need to hear from me are Susie Brannon and Cliff Bruce." Burt rolled the cigar to the opposite side of his mouth, holding it between his teeth as his lips widened to a broad smile. A waitress walked towards the table and Burt shooed her away, still focusing on Vern's eyes.

Vern's face lost its color, and the false bravado faded quickly. He expected something to come up about his nephew for some time, although he didn't expect it to come from a man such as this. He hadn't heard from Susie since their last meeting. He figured the young girl started a new life somewhere, and he hoped it was a better one than she lived in Panama City. Vern's eyes lowered, no longer able to return the gangster's gaze. "Is the girl alive?" Vern asked, his voice barely audible.

Burt turned his attention to Lucky, holding back a laugh. The cigar dangled from his teeth as he spoke, "What the hell you tell this cat about me, Luck?" Lucky shrugged his shoulders and tried to put a fake smile on his face. Burt put his hand on Lucky's shoulder and let the laughter escape his mouth. Vern didn't smile, his eyes fixed on the tablecloth. "Mr. Bruce, the girl's alive," Burt said, the laughter still emanating around the café's small corner table.

"What do you want?" Vern asked, his voice quivering and nervously scratched at his thumb.

"Well, Mr. Bruce," Burt responded. "Can I call you Vern? Doesn't matter, *Vern*, now does it? I know 'em. I know about Cliff. Look here, though, I ain't here to cause trouble. The girl, Susie, is a friend of mine; all you need to know. I know she left the boy with you a long time ago. Cute little fella." Both Lucky and Vern flinched as Burt reached under the table. The gangster smiled and laughed again as he pulled out a campaign sign, taking the cigar out of his mouth and using it to point to Cliff.

Lucky didn't move nor did he make a sound. He knew better. He knew better than to interject into a personal situation. He eased his hand to his face, taking off his glasses and wiping imaginary stains from the lenses.

Burt, silent also, held his gaze on Vern and motioned for a cup of coffee as the waitress grew near once again. Burt slid his chair near Vern's and moved his face close to his. "Vern, I know you took care of the boy. I appreciate that. I know you got money and connections, a big shot down in PC. Hell, this time next year it may be Congressman Bruce. I just want you to know that I *know*. Simple as that. Nothing more." Burt patted Vern's shoulder as the waitress placed the cup on the table, and he smiled at her. "Give it to him. Needs it." He patted one last time, this time holding his hand on Vern's shoulder. "I'll be in touch."

    Without saying anything further, Burt nodded at Lucky, still wiping his glasses furiously, laid some money on the table, and stuck his hand in Vern's direction. Vern reluctantly followed suit, and both men tightened their grip. Burt grinned as he released Vern's hand and walked out of the diner, never looking back. When the car pulled onto the country road and was out of sight, Lucky exhaled a breath that he felt he had held for the entire time and slid his clean glasses back on the bridge of his nose. He shook his head as Vern glared at his campaign manager.

    "I'm sorry about that," he told Vern. "I pretty much had no choice but to set that up. He's a person that you really don't say no to. I tried…" He paused and said, "You know."

    "Who the hell is Burt Williams, Lucky?" Vern asked once more hoping for the truth. "I know I saw him before."

    "Burt Williams. Biloxi. Do I need to go any further?" Lucky asked, still shaking his head. Vern's confused expression remained. "Dixie Mafia enforcer. On the news a while back about some young Army guy going missing over there?" Vern's head shook slowly up and down. That is where he remembered the guy from, the news. He stared out the window into nothing, and asked himself, *Why does a guy like that care about my nephew?*

The Dixie Mafia, the Syndicate, the Organization, whatever you wanted to call it, it was bad. Vern continued to stare into nothing as he thought. All sorts of nightmarish thoughts ran through his head, but he gathered himself and looked back at the shaken Lucky.

"How in the hell is Susie Brannon involved with that guy? He her pimp or something?" Vern asked.

Lucky's eyes closed and his head stopped shaking. "Wife."

Vern leaned back in his chair and ran his hands down his face. "What the hell, Lucky? Why didn't you say something?"

Lucky only said, "You don't talk about these guys, or their wives, without permission. You don't talk. Not to you, or to anyone." Lucky looked Vern in the eye. "Cause if you do, you disappear. Like that army kid." Vern looked off into the distance again.

"He'll be back, won't he?"

"Bet your life," Lucky dropped his head and replied.

A couple of days later, Lucky received a call in his office and the caller just left a number and a request to call him back. His face dropped when he read the note. Quietly, he left his office and walked down to a payphone. He called Burt Williams. Lucky expected the call and knew what to expect from a guy like him.

"Lucky, my old friend," Burt greeted him with his booming voice. "How's the campaign going, bud?" Lucky held the receiver away from his ears. He heard Burt just fine without it pressed to his head. He took a deep breath and nervously rubbed his eyes.

"Don't mess with this, Burt, I'm begging you. This cat has got a chance to win this thing. Don't talk to folks down home about it," he pleaded.

"Lucky, Lucky, Lucky. I didn't say a word. A guy over in New Orleans asked around about him. He doesn't want anything with him, just information from time to time. Easy money." The phone went silent, and Lucky started to hang up, but as he began the motion, Burt's voice boomed through once again, "Some folks over here got a call from his daddy-in-law too. He knows the game and the old man likes to play ball with us. Things are in motion, Lucky boy, you just gotta play ball too, *partner*."

Lucky closed his burning eyes when Burt called him *partner*. He knew what Burt meant by it. Lucky realized it was too late to keep the Syndicate's hand out of this pie. As his hopes for a legitimate shot at the big time vanished, he lay his head on the corner of the booth.

Burt continued, "You'll probably get a call from the guy in PC in a couple of days. The old feller down in Florida won't get his hands dirty in all of this but do what Tate says to do. *We've got a lot riding on this now.* Oh yeah, tell Brucie and my stepson hi for me, will ya?"

Lucky could hear the laughter in the background as Burt hung up. He didn't say anything but nodded as if Burt saw his head bobbing up and down and hung up the phone. The enthusiasm and hope for this election disappeared in a single phone call and a feeling of dread crept over him. He stood there, staring at the phone hanging on the hook, dreading the phone call from Mac Tate. Mac swore to him that this was on the "up and up" and now, sharks from his past encircled him. He wanted to ease back into the office, grab his things and get the hell out of Florida, but he knew what happened if he just left. People just didn't leave the Dixie Mafia cold like that.

He slowly started walking back towards the storefront office. The sun's rays warmed him, and he kicked at a rock that lay dormant on the sidewalk. Even though the office stood a mile or two from the ocean, he smelled salt in the air. He loved this place, but he knew now, it wouldn't be home.

He saw a bench in front of the barber shop and sat down. Crossing his legs, he took off his stiff dress shoes and sat them beside him. He rubbed his fingers up and down the suspenders hanging in front of his shirt and thought about Vern Bruce.

If any of Vern's opponents or the press got wind of this, it was over. It wouldn't stop there with this campaign either. Ties to the Dixie Mafia ruined squares like Vern Bruce in legitimate business. *The poor sap*, Lucky thought.

The Organization wouldn't overtly interfere with the election or with Vern, but they had something over him now and

Lucky knew they would use it. Always in the background, like a wolf stalking its prey, stood the criminal organization. Lucky put his shoes back on his feet and rubbed his suspenders harder. The bastards had family in the mix.

Whether he liked it or not or even realized it, blood connected Vern to the Dixie Mafia. Burt Williams would use that blood to squeeze the aspiring congressman as much as he could for as long as he could. Mac Tate would be no help in the situation, he knew the ancient politician owed as much to the criminal gang as he did himself. *Damn, they were all screwed*, he thought.

Discussing the meeting with Patty Lee and the resulting conversation would be no easy task. As Vern drove he tried to focus on the road but as he stared into the black pavement, all he saw was his wife's face. A face that in his mind, held a condescending grin. *I told you* he kept hearing over and over in Patty Lee's voice. Vern's attention snapped to reality when the lights of an eighteen-wheeler topped the hill. Unconsciously, he had drifted into the oncoming lane and snatched the wheel turning the car back into the southbound lane. When the adrenaline waned, Vern refocused his thoughts. He didn't know whether his wife was in town or down south tending to business.

With Vern spending most of his time with the campaign, Patty Lee edged more control of the business than he liked. She was a natural, though. Just as shrewd as her father and twice as tough, in running a multi-million-dollar business. Vern couldn't decide if that was something with which he was comfortable. Vern bit his bottom lip as he pulled into the driveway. Her car, parked in its normal spot, showed Patty Lee was home. The light shining through their bedroom window confirmed the fact.

Vern made sure the boys were in bed before approaching his wife about the meeting with Lucky Clay and Burt Williams. She sat at the small table tucked away in a nook in the kitchen. Sipping a glass of iced tea, she held some papers in her hand and looked up at him through her new reading glasses. Vern thought she wore them just to intimidate people. The tactic worked as the sweat began to form in the palms of his hands. He timidly smiled and kissed her on top of her head.

"Gotta talk to you about something," Vern said in a hushed tone. He didn't know why he talked so quietly. The house was empty save for the two of them and the boys, but Vern, accustomed to keeping things quiet, didn't want to take the chance. Patty Lee looked up at him and tried to smile but she knew her husband well. Vern noticed small lines in the corners of her eyes starting to form and the fake smile vanish as quickly as it appeared.

"Quickly," she commanded. "I've got a lot of work to do tonight. There's some movement on the deal out in Mississippi." Vern sat down and looked at his wife quizzically, his thumb and forefinger rubbing together. Patty Lee let out a deep breath and noticed Vern playing with his fingers.

"What deal in Mississippi?" he enquired.

"We are going in with Dad over in Biloxi. We are getting into the casino business with some partners down on the water between Biloxi and Gulfport. Dad *found* a way to get around those archaic redneck gambling laws down there," she responded matter-of-factly.

"Why am I just now learning about this? This is still OUR damn business, you know," Vern shot back, forgetting the original need for conversation.

Patty Lee paused for a second, stood up and put her arms around her husband's neck, interlacing her fingers behind his head, and said, "Honey, you are in the middle of a campaign for congress. You need to focus on that." She looked into Vern's eyes and continued, "Congressman Bruce."

Vern put his hand on Patty Lee's arm, "You're right, babe, but please, keep me in the loop about things like this." There was still the news of the meeting, but at this moment, he didn't want to stir the pot any further. Patty Lee eased her lips to Vern's ear.

"How did the meeting with Lucky and Mr. Williams go?" she asked flatly.

Vern stood, breaking their embrace. He put his hand to his chin, rubbing slowly, his anger swelling but so far, keeping it contained. He chose his words carefully.

"You were involved, weren't you?" he asked.

Without hesitation, Patty Lee responded in a calm, soothing voice, "Daddy told me. He needed some help down there on that casino project. Daddy called down to Biloxi and *the guy* down there pointed him to Burt Williams. He's a pretty good guy to know down in that area. Gets things done and has some kind of pull with the kind of labor we are going to need."

Vern grabbed his wife by her hands, enveloping them in his. "You know what kind of people these are, don't you?" he asked his wife, genuine concerning coating each word.

She interlaced her fingers with his, kissed them gently and said, "The kind of people you can't be associated with. Don't worry about Williams, he won't bother you again." She stood up so she could look up into Vern's eyes. "Williams knows about Cliff and just wants what's best for him. He won't interfere with the kid, just some leeway for his wife." Patty Lee braced herself for Vern's response, but none came. "Him and his wife, Mrs. Susie, won't bother you or Cliff and his *associates'* presence won't be felt around the campaign. He just wants a promise that you'll consider letting her back into her son's life when she's ready…" She paused and held Vern's hands tighter. "Daddy gave that promise."

Vern pulled his hands away from Patty Lee's and turned his back to her. His face flushed with anger. Cliff was his nephew. He would be the one to make assurances. He closed his eyes, and his breathing grew rapid, but right now was not a time to argue. He did want Cliff to know his mother, but she was neck deep with some very dangerous people and he must protect his nephew from such monsters.

He turned and saw Patty Lee's dark eyes watering and Vern buried his feelings deep inside. Calmly he put his arms around his wife and said, "I love you, Patty Lee. Let's promise right now not to hold things like this from each other." Patty Lee let her tears flow and promised her husband that tonight they began a new life of truth. She rested her head on Vern's shoulder and behind his back, a smile broke upon her face.

Mac Tate didn't waste much time before he called Lucky Clay. Lucky caught the call at his rented house overlooking the still waters of Grand Lagoon as the wily politician made sure these discussions were held in private. Mac laid down the process in which Lucky was to abide. To his relief, the Organization didn't want to interfere with the campaign. The only difference, Lucky was now charged with keeping Vern from any dealings his family had with Biloxi. Lucky was to ensure his election, no matter what. If the campaign trended towards becoming a losing campaign, Lucky was to call for help—help coming in the form of paid off officials. Lucky hung up the phone and took a long sip of the margarita he made in anticipation of Tate's call. He knew what that meant.

If they resorted to old school southern political tactics, Lucky would be the one on the hook. He would be the one left without a seat once the music stopped. He licked the salt from the edge of his glass and continued listening intently, his despair increasing with each word. They were trying something that hadn't been done in the area since Reconstruction and it only worked then because of northern carpetbaggers, electing a Republican in the Solid South.

Right now, though, everything coasted with eagle's wings. Most of the time, in his experience, moments like this held ominous futures, however. Dread locked into his mind with a vice-like grip.

Anytime Burt Williams became involved with something, it never turned out good. Lucky decided after the last conversation with Burt that if things looked like they were going south, he was out of there. He had squirreled enough money away that he could make a run for the Caribbean. Hopefully, though, it wouldn't come to that. Vernon Bruce was a good man and would make a good congressman. Lucky devoured the golden drink remaining in his glass and rubbed his suspenders. The feeling of impending doom lingered in his thoughts.

Chapter 16

In the end Burt Williams or anyone in Biloxi didn't destroy Vern's campaign, his past did. Vern was in a dead heat with his democratic opponent when a small-town newspaper found itself with a picture from the protest rally in Tallahassee. Printed on its front page was a picture of a young Vernon Bruce apparently yelling in the face of a police officer. They were nearly nose to nose and you could almost hear the yell coming from young Vern's mouth. Even though moments after, Vern lay on the ground bleeding, the headline screamed "Political Hopeful Was Once Insurgent." In the very conservative district, it was a death knell for the campaign.

Lucky sat in his office, staring at the newspaper. Always the first one in the office, his eyes saw it first. He walked to the bench in front of the barber shop. The traffic light at the intersection guided non-existent cars through a deserted intersection. Holding the paper in his hand he felt disappointment but also a feeling of relief enveloped him. He pulled a crumpled pack of cigarettes from his pocket and lit one. Slowly inhaling the smoke, he coughed. It had been a while, and he only smoked when things looked bleak. As the sun began to rise over the buildings around him, the disappointment left completely, and he felt truly relieved. He threw the cigarette on the sidewalk and stomped it with his foot. This was his chance.

He sat back and ran his fingers along his suspenders and smiled. He wouldn't have to deal with Burt Williams again. The thoughts of packing up and making a run for it crossed his mind several times upon the entrance of Burt to the political equation. Each time he was close to it, however, thoughts of how the Organization felt about loose ends flooded into his mind. Not really caring at first, the people in Biloxi salivated at the thought of having someone connected to them in Washington. Now that dream vanished, and the blame had to fall on someone, and Lucky Clay presented an easy target. He had to make one call and then he would vanish into the night.

  The campaign wore Vern down more than regular business ever did. His eyes, once vibrant, held bags under them. His stamina seemed to deplete itself and he woke up tired each morning. Sometimes he relished the thought of becoming a congressman and other times the idea revolted him. The phone call from Lucky evoked both of those notions.

  "Vern. Bad News," Lucky said as Vern put the phone to his ear. He never like to beat around the bush when dealing with Vern, so he got to the point quickly. "Where were you on the night you told me everything fell apart in Tallahassee, what the hell did the paper call it..." Vern heard the newspaper rattling on the other end while Lucky searched. He found what he looked for and finished, "*Night of the Bayonets?*"

  "The rally? I told you what happened," Vern responded.

  "Small-time paper, way up in the country, got hold of a picture of you there. Looks pretty bad, and the headline didn't help," Lucky said it so quickly Vern barely understood.

"I know the picture," he interjected. "I've seen it, and I can imagine the headline. Don't tell me. Just tell me what paper and I'll get it myself."

Lucky told him the name of the paper and Vern found a copy in an old hardware store in town. It wasn't good. He took one look and realized the race was over. He felt people inside the small store staring at him. There was one bench in the front where a group of old men always sat and gossiped the morning away. He knew these old men for years and most of the time when he walked in, they all greeted him and included him on some small-time gossip. Today was not one of those days. Not one of them greeted him when he opened the door, and the loud chime sounded. Not one told him good morning. These were old-school country people. It didn't matter if they lived on the coast or in town or out in the boonies. They didn't like hippies and now when they looked at him, the picture from the paper is all they saw. One gentleman cussed as Vern walked by.

He paid for the paper at the old, wooden counter and thought the old man that owned the store grunted when he gave him his change. He didn't read the short story that went with the picture and headline. He didn't have to. He knew everyone saw it and his political life evaporated before his eyes. An involuntary smile came across his face. He said, "Thank God," loud enough the bench riders all turned in unison to see what the hippie said. Vern returned their gaze, raised his eyebrows, and whistled at them. As he walked out the door, he winked at the old man at the end of the bench.

Vern wondered if Patty Lee knew about this. She didn't read many newspapers if Vern didn't bring something to her attention, so he figured she probably hadn't. His wife, however, did put some of her business to the side and became consumed with becoming Congressman Bruce's wife.

Patty Lee even traveled to Washington with Vern a few weeks ago and found them a nice little brick townhouse in which to start their lives in the capitol city. They flew up for the day to check it out. Both boys stayed behind that day, and they toured a little bit of the town while they were there. They enjoyed a nice dinner at a quaint little café and flew home late that evening. Arriving home, *both* went to check on the boys and, finding them asleep, enjoyed the rest of their night together. Now all that too, was gone. He needed to talk to her quickly and jumped in his truck and made his way to her office. He parked the truck and sat there for a few minutes, trying to come up with the right words, but there was no easy way to tell her.

Patty Lee blew the last puff of smoke from her cigarette out the window towards the bay as Vern walked into her office. Vern always looked the other way and pretended his wife didn't smoke even though he knew she still enjoyed a cigarette every once and again. She gently closed the window and turned in her chair towards her husband. She patted the newspaper on her desk as Vern sat down.

"I know. You don't even have to say anything." She flashed her fake smile at her husband as she spoke. "Guess I'll have to get back the deposit we put down on that place up there." She avoided calling the city by name and continued, "Daddy was so looking forward to telling people about his son-in-law, the congressman." Vern took a deep breath and nodded his head, trying to fake disappointment. He wanted to ask his wife if her father knew she was there also but bit his lip.

"Hate to disappoint," Vern responded sarcastically. "Maybe he will get over it one day. With all the money you two are making over in Mississipp—" Patty Lee gestured to cut him off before he could finish his sentence.

"*We* are making," she finished for him, "and now without the pull up there, it may not even happen the way we want it." She reached for her pack of cigarettes and when Vern looked at her with a raised eyebrow, she lit it and blew the smoke in his direction.

The general election, still a month away, wasn't officially over yet, so Vern didn't mention he was thinking about the work situations between them. Knowing it would exasperate the situation, he once again bit his tongue. He decided that conversation could wait until he *officially* lost the election and dreaded it.

Lucky and Burt used the same small diner that held their meeting with Vern to have their conversation. This time, it was only the two of them and the place was empty. The cook plopped a blob of grease on the grill and glanced over towards his only customers. The same as many restaurants and stores lining the blacktop highway, some days were busy, and some days were very quiet. Today appeared to be one of the quiet days. Lucky sat down and looked around constantly, his eyes darting rapidly in each direction. Burt, already seated, laughed at the spectacle. "Nervous, Lucky Boy?" he asked in between laughs.

Lucky's eyes stopped wandering and fixed on Burt, and he responded, "Wouldn't you be?" Burt nodded yes and winked at the waitress that flirted with him as he waited for Lucky to arrive.

"Well, that got messed up in a damn hurry," Burt began, munching on an unlit cigar. "I thought your boy was clean as a whistle, but I guess everyone has some kind of skeleton in his closet." The waitress sat down a full cup of coffee and Burt put his cigar on the edge of the table. He gave her another wink as she brushed his hand when she sat the cup down.

"Yep. I thought I could keep that part of his past quiet. Woulda been better off if he was just a regular old, crooked redneck," Lucky responded, his eyes once again on alert. "People around here don't take to hippies and commies. They are old school redneck conservatives."

"Guess you'll be coming back to Biloxi now. See you packed up," Burt gestured to the back seat of Lucky's car, "Figured you would wait until the results came in, at least," he snickered.

"I'm not going anywhere today," he lied. "Just getting ready. Ain't hanging around after it all goes down tomorrow." He said more, but Burt wasn't listening.

Burt knew he was lying, but there was no point in arguing with a guy like Lucky as there were always more lies waiting. He could lie just as easily as breathing. Burt laughed under his breath as he remembered that it was said Lucky Clay would rather climb a tree to tell a lie than to stand on the ground and tell the truth. He already knew Lucky took some money from the campaign that some people over in Biloxi *contributed*. Burt's poker face gave Lucky no sign that the gangster knew as he just kept nodding and slurping the coffee, paying no attention to Lucky's lies. *The poor sap made himself a loose end and there couldn't be any loose ends running around*, Burt thought to himself. If he wasn't going back to Biloxi, he wouldn't be going anywhere. He knew way too much about a great many things and the money just topped the cake. Lucky finally finished and Burt started chewing on his cigar once again.

"So, you are going to be back in town by the end of the week?" Burt inquired once again. He knew if he didn't get the right kind of answer what he would have to do. He eased his hand below the table and felt the cold steel of his revolver, all the while looking past Lucky to track the cook and waitress. They were chatting behind the counter and weren't paying the two men at the table any attention.

Lucky licked his lips and played with his glasses. "Oh, yeah, I'll be back down there in a couple days. Going up north to visit my sister and then right back down."

"Good to hear," Burt said. His finger slid onto the trigger, but he sat back in his chair and put his hand back on the table. He knew a better way to deal with Lucky Clay.

Lucky wasn't so stupid as to thinking Burt was buying this. He would have to start out heading back down to the coast and change course when he knew Burt wasn't following him. It wasn't his plan, but a plan to escape the Dixie Mafia adaptability. He would take the most backwoods roads he could find so it would be easier to see if someone was tailing him or not. Lucky stopped fidgeting and stood up to leave.

"I gotta get back," he said, trying to end the conversation and begin his run to freedom.

"No problem, Lucky. I'll be seeing you." Burt stood also, and the men shook hands and walked out the door to their cars. Lucky sat in his car, fiddling with his keys so that Burt's car was the first to leave. When his car was out of sight, Lucky started south towards the coast. He drove for miles, checking each dirt road and house, scouring the sides of the road for a hidden Burt Williams, but he saw nothing. Lucky felt the time was right, and he began his backwoods journey to Atlanta. It would take him longer, but he was sure it would be safer.

Lucky wasn't speeding nor doing anything drawing attention to him just in case he met a cop on the back roads. He didn't want to chance getting pulled over. In this part of the country, you never knew who was connected and who was not. He passed a large green sign announcing his arrival in Alabama. The more distance he put between himself and the Panhandle, the safer he would be. Crossing the state line, he picked up just enough speed as to not draw attention but allow him to make his flight to paradise in Atlanta.

He was adjusting the AM radio when he glanced in the rearview and saw the single blue light and heard the siren. For a second, he thought about gunning the accelerator and making a run for it but decided against it. He got the nickname Lucky by taking chances and he decided to play the odds. The cruiser behind him wasn't a local cop, and it was not a sheriff. It was a state trooper who made Lucky feel the odds were on his side. The larger the office, the smaller chance they were connected with the Organization. He pulled over as far as he could manage, and he felt the tires give in the red Alabama clay. The silver and blue police car settled in behind him but not quite as far off the road. This trooper knew his terrain.

Lucky rolled down his window and stuck his hand out holding a card with his name and occupation. The trooper slowly walked up and stood for a second, refusing to look at the card.

"Luck's ran out," was all he said. Lucky knew that indeed it had. He rubbed his fingers on his suspenders one last time and let out a deep sigh and replaced it with a deep breath. He smelled the honeysuckle vine growing on the side of the road. Lucky Clay's time ran out just across the Alabama state line.

Burt Williams took a look at the sign welcoming him to Tallahassee and then glanced at his watch. By this time, he figured Lucky met his old friend in Alabama, and his fate. The gangster had one more meeting to attend before he returned home to Biloxi. Burt refused to fly anywhere. He enjoyed driving through the countryside, enjoying nature and small-town Florida. He held his hand out the window, directing the wind to his face. It even smelled better than Biloxi. Even though the interstates had been around for several years, he didn't like them and refused to ride on them. He took back roads whenever and wherever he could. The ride to West Palm took several hours to complete, and the time allowed him to think.

He mostly thought about his young wife back home. The look on her face engrained in his memory from the day she saw the poster with Cliff's face. Even though word came down that nothing interfered with Vern and his family, he couldn't help but think that Cliff was his family. The boy was his stepson, and he was now a father of some sorts. At a stop sign at a barren four-way intersection he looked over a hay field that swayed in the breeze.

He would bide his time, he thought as he pulled through the intersection and his thoughts turned to Lucky and his unfortunate end. He would follow orders but orders, however, weren't chiseled in stone and they were always changing. Especially in the business he had chosen. He spit into the breeze and continued on.

Arriving in West Palm some hours late, he found Old Man Clark waiting in his office. The old man didn't go to the office much anymore preferring to spend his days at home. He loved watching the waves crashing onto the coarse sand and then retreating into the ocean. It gave him a peace he never knew in the business world. He knew his time was probably running short; he pushed eighty and his health quickly failed him. He accepted these were his twilight years, and he didn't want to spend it in the confinement of an office.

His secretary led Burt into the office and Burt rubbed his hands together and looked back as she made her way out of the room. Mr. Clark was seated in a chair in the corner of the room reading a newspaper and noticed Burt ogling his secretary, shaking his head in disgust. Burt turned his attention to the old man and the paper he held. He could tell it was the paper with Vern's picture and said, "Nice picture of old Vernon," smiling as he did so.

"This is a tragedy," the old white-haired man said in a low tone, but his words dripped with sarcasm. "He was so close," he continued and couldn't contain his himself any longer and erupted in his trademark vivacious laughter.

"If he only knew," Burt replied, moving closer so Mr. Clark's old ears could hear.

"He can't know. Hell, even my daughter doesn't know everything that we have done…" The old man paused and stirred in his chair. He ran his long, slender fingers through the white wisps of hair remaining on his head. "What about the boy? Now, will you go after him?"

"Got orders to leave him alone," Burt responded, "I'm not going against it." Burt reached on the old man's desk and picked up a long, fat Cuban cigar, sniffed it and put it in his shirt pocket and asked after the fact, "Do you mind?"

The old man responded, "You've earned it, but the boy has to go." He leaned in closer to Burt. "One way or another." He leaned back in his chair and turned around so he could see the ocean. "Hopefully now Patty Lee will see the error of her ways, but we got to make sure, just in case."

Burt stood up and shook his head, "Nothing *happens* to the boy. He is my stepson, you know."

Old Man Clark eyed the younger man standing over him. He motioned for him to lean down so he wouldn't have to raise his voice. He didn't want his nosy secretary to hear what he had to say next.

"I pay you for a reason. You follow your orders, but if I tell you to go…" He paused. "You know what I expect. I'll make it right with those boys over there in the Biloxi."

"Does your daughter know what you are planning to do with the boy? Get him out of the picture?" Burt asked, pulling out one of his own cigars.

"Indeed, she does. She is the one who asked me," Mr. Clark responded with a crooked grin. The old man was proud of just how much Patty Lee became just like her father. She was ruthless in business just like he had always been and to her, Cliff Bruce was business.

Burt slid the cigar between his teeth and shook his head and said, "You two are two of the most ruthless sons-a-bitches *I* ever seen." The old man tilted his head and took a picture of Casey Bruce and turned it around to Burt. "This is the future of *my* family."

Chapter 17

Out of nearly one hundred and forty thousand votes cast in the congressional district, Vern only received about forty thousand. It was one of the largest landslide victories in the state. Vern couldn't find Lucky before, during or after the vote and he felt abandoned. He sat alone in the quiet deserted office, staring at the television as the returns came in. Patty Lee, the boys, all the staffers left when it became hopeless.

Usually Vern wouldn't touch liquor, but tonight he broke the seal on an old bottle of whiskey that had been in his office for a long time. He filled a coffee cup on his desk and put it to his lips, taking a long sip of the liquid. It burned his throat, and he held his hand to his mouth, hoping the liquid wouldn't reverse course. He sighed and put his feet on his desk.

This was the first real defeat he'd suffered in anything since he started his own business. It wasn't a feeling he liked or wanted to suffer through again. He took another sip, and his thoughts began to drift. He thought of times before Rof was drafted, time with his small family. They weren't rich, but they had enough, and the father and his sons were happy. He missed his father terribly. He drank down the rest of the intoxicating liquor as he fell deeper into his thoughts and decided he wasn't going home that night. The last image in his mind belonged to Patty Lee, and the scowl plastered on her face as she looked back when she'd left earlier that night.

Old Man Clark summoned his daughter to West Palm a week before election day, but she felt that she shouldn't go beforehand. Patty Lee feared the worst as the results already held low expectations and she wasn't mistaken. The defeat, recorded as one of the worst in the history of Florida politics, shone the spotlight directly on *her* and *her* business dealings. Her father wasn't going to be happy, she thought. She didn't fly. She drove the distance to West Palm Beach and apprehension filled her as she made her way down the interstates and the thick pines lining the sides of the road.

Thursday, a couple of days after the election, she arrived on the Atlantic Coast. She didn't want to be around Vern right now and apparently, he didn't want to be around her. He slept in his office on election night, and she left town without speaking to him. The increasingly strained relationship could become catastrophic with any crosswords, and she didn't want that. Even though they had been at odds lately, there was still love between them and hope.

The old man rested in his favorite chair overlooking the ocean when he heard Patty Lee's car pull into the driveway. The beach was eerily quiet today, not even a gull flew overhead searching for crumbs and the palm trees lay perfectly still. He decided the meeting with Burt Williams was the last time he would go into the office. The old man's home office had everything he needed and staff at his beck and call. Patty Lee didn't go directly inside when she arrived. She walked through the side gate of her father's massive home and stepped up onto the deck. Sadness poured over her when she saw her father. One of the most powerful men in Florida, reduced to an old, frail existence. The old man wrapped a woven blanket around his legs to keep warm as even for southern Florida this November day was cool and crisp.

"Keeping warm, Dad?" Patty Lee asked her father drawing near to her father's chair.

"Hey, little one," he responded as if the small child that he remembered stood beside him instead of his fully grown daughter, "Glad you are here. We've got to talk."

Patty Lee pulled up a chair beside her father and put her hand into his.

"No business right now, Daddy. I just want to sit with you. Like the old days when you would tell me about the ocean," she replied to her father.

He smiled, looked her in the eyes and said, "This won't wait little one. I'm going for a short cruise on the yacht this afternoon. Won't be gone long, but I want to tell you some things before I go." The old man winked at his daughter, and she kissed his forehead.

"OK, Dad. What is it you want to talk about?" she enquired of her father. She stroked the long white wisps of hair on the top of his head and told him she would be at the house in the morning, and they *could* talk then, but the old man protested.

"Probably a day or two out there. I just want to be on the boat for a while. Been a couple of months since I've been out. Ocean is in my blood," he told her.

"I know, Dad, but don't be so bleak about it," she replied. "I'll stay until you get back."

"No, no, let's just talk today and tomorrow will take care of itself."

Patty Lee relented and let her father talk. He squeezed her hand and spoke quietly. He pulled his daughter in closer to him. He wanted to make sure nobody else heard this part of the conversation.

"Look, I know you have a handle on our real estate business, but there are things you need to know." He took a deep breath. "There are deals that you don't know about, but I need you to know. I knew when you came to me about the boy, that you'd be able to handle what I'm going to tell you." Patty Lee looked at her father. A tear formed in her eye, and she continued stroking her father's hair.

Patty Lee sat quietly as her father spoke, only listening. At times, her head dropped, and she shook her head but absorbed each word the old man spoke. He told her of things she'd suspected but never wanted to understand. Her father kept her innocence until this day. On this day, however, she learned how deeply involved her father was with people not only like Burt Williams and his bunch, but others that made the Dixie Mafia look like schoolchildren. It frightened her to her core, but her father didn't hold back, and the end of the conversation found her shaking. Her father reached as far as he could and put his arms around his daughter. He whispered into her ear.

"Patricia..." He never called his daughter by her full name. "You now know that some of our dealings are not exactly *legal*. I figure you already knew that but, today, I just wanted you to hear it from me." His voice became so low that Patty Lee barely understood her father when he continued, "What I'm about to tell you goes absolutely no further." He waited for Patty Lee's nod in compliance. "We have made a lot of money through the ways I just explained to you. There is one association that only *I* know the truth, and now you will know and you alone. Vernon can never know. Nobody knows but blood."

Patty Lee tried to lean away from her father, but he pulled her close once again.

In a voice only she could hear, he continued, "Years ago, I was in Miami. It was right when the first oil embargo hit. Nobody was making any money in real estate. We had invested just about everything on the coast, and it wasn't selling. We invested heavily in the port deal, and it wasn't working out. I couldn't leave you with that debt. You were just out of college and Vernon was broke. I didn't want you to know we were on the verge of..." He paused and looked out over the ocean. "We were almost done, broke." The old man's voice cracked. "I mean, every dime."

Patty Lee squeezed her aging father's hand. She smiled at him and said, "Daddy, you could've told me."

The old man pulled his head back to he could look his daughter in the eyes. He continued, "Not this. Not then. Listen, little one, I had to keep the business afloat, and these people came to me with a deal. They wanted me to send some boats out a couple of miles to meet some other boats coming in from the Caribbean. I brought in bales of marijuana. It paid well, and a partnership blossomed. One that I'm still in. Only..." The old man's voice trailed off and he turned his gaze to the flat ocean. Patty Lee absorbed everything he told her but this she couldn't fathom. She knew her father, a shrewd and ruthless businessman, took risks and at time stretched the law, but she never figured he was a drug runner. When he turned his attention back to his daughter, he noticed the shock enveloping her, but he'd gone too far to stop now. He once again turned so he could look his only daughter in the eye. He owed her that.

"We bring in *everything* now. The coast of Florida is a haven, and we are the only ones connected with the producers in South America," the old man said. Patty Lee turned ghostly white, and she ripped away from her father.

She stood, stiffly, staring at her father as she absorbed his words and realized the ugly truth. Her father was not only a marijuana runner but a cocaine smuggler. Her knees felt weak, and she almost lost her balance, catching herself on the arm of a chair. Patty Lee couldn't speak. She knew her father had connections in Biloxi with some bad people, but a partnership with South American drug lords was more than she could take, and tears flowed down her pale cheeks.

"What happens now?" she asked, sobbing, afraid to know the answer. The old man gathered his strength, slowly rose from his chair and hugged his daughter as firmly as his old, broken body allowed. He moved his hands to her face and locked them on her cheeks, focusing his eyes on hers. He didn't blink, and he didn't hesitate. "It doesn't stop. No matter what. These are people that don't allow you to *resign*. Patricia, Vernon can never know." Patty Lee shook her head free and turned her back to her father. "You want me to lie to him? This is something I won't be able to hide." The old man eased his feeble hand on her shoulder. "You've done it before, little one."

Old Man Clark summoned help and made his way into the house, leaving Patty Lee standing at the railing overlooking the dunes. The afternoon breeze picked up and the cool air made chill bumps on her arms prickle upward. She stood overlooking the ocean and with the breeze blowing onshore, the waves began to swell. She wiped the remnants of her tears, and her face hardened. She knew what she had to do.

The next day Patty Lee arose as the morning sun broke, got in her car and left West Palm Beach for home. Before he left, her father offered her the jet, but she didn't want to fly, opting to drive and take her time. She needed time on the road to digest what her father told her.

She rolled the windows down and the damp, muggy air flowed into the car, and she relaxed just a bit as she drove. She contemplated telling her husband everything her father laid bare to her, but doubts crept into her mind. This was a matter that she couldn't handle on her own, but she knew Vern would never approve. *Hell*, she thought, *he just might call the law himself.* It was no secret her husband never liked the old man, and that dislike could turn into pure hatred if he caught wind of this. She reached into her purse, pulled out a cigarette, and let it dangle from her lips. She didn't light it, she just let it wiggle in the wind coming in from the open window. She thought of one saving grace, however, she wouldn't have to face this problem as long as her father lived. Until then, she would keep Vern in the dark. She lit the cigarette and pressed the accelerator to the floor.

Just as Patty Lee's car pulled out of the mansion's driveway, the old man's yacht was leaving the harbor. Arriving the night before, he'd asked the crew to wait until daylight to set out to sea. He wanted to see the sunrise, so he took up his perch on the vast bow deck and let the salt air blow through what was left of his wispy hair. He enjoyed feeling waves crash into the bow of the massive vessel. The boat lifted with each one and gently settled back down into the ocean as the wave rolled along the hull. In moments like these, he left the cares of the world on the shore. The old man wished he could help his daughter with what she was about to face, but time wouldn't allow it. He had grown too old and too frail. He looked at his slender, freckled hands and smiled, accepting his fate.

His thoughts trailing off as they often did, he seized on a moment of clarity. The tired old man took a deep breath as the sun began its climb over the Atlantic, its rays warming his cold frame. He gathered what strength he had in his bony, tired arms and lifted himself out of his chair. Trying to balance himself as he walked proved difficult. One particularly harsh wave shoved him against the rail of the bow, and he wrapped his long fingers around the iron bar one last time. He wriggled through the double railing and, gathering one last burst of energy, hurled himself from the yacht. He felt the cold, salty water for the last time, and he did not struggle. His body bobbed in the wake given off by his beloved yacht and his eyes remained above water for a fleeting moment before he allowed himself to sink down into the dark, blue depths. He closed his eyes and took a deep breath, filled with seawater. His beloved Atlantic Ocean became his grave.

Old Man Clark's disappearance from the yacht, believed an accident, made it his last act of deception. The police and coast guard searched for days but his body eluded discovery, and the funeral featured an empty casket and a vacant grave. A small group of family and the old man's closest friends gathered near the edge of the frothy Atlantic near the Clark home as the family cemetery overlooked the body of water. Vern stood next to his wife and Cliff and Casey sat near them, confused about the day's events.

    Patty Lee glanced over the gathered faces and one face caught her attention. Among others, his face stood out. He was nearly a head shorter than everyone else and his dark complexion and slick black hair contrasted against the wealthy, mostly fair-haired congregation. She began fidgeting with her hands and looked in her purse for a cigarette, but Vern noticed and shook his head in disapproval. Thoughts of South American drug lords soared into her mind.

    Vern took his wife's hand and squeezed it tightly. He leaned over and kissed her on the cheek and rubbed her hand with his thumb. A priest said a few words and was about to finish when she noticed the stranger walk away. She released a breath she didn't realize she held and smiled at her husband. When the priest made the sign of the cross, the small contingent all filed by, spoke to Patty Lee offering words of condolence and made their way to their parked cars. The stranger reappeared as the last in line and only quietly said, "My deepest regrets," as he shook Vern's hand and bowed in Patty Lee's direction. She didn't notice a business card the stranger placed in Vern's hand as they shook. He patted the two boys on the head and walked up the dune and out of sight, never looking back.

    Vern glanced at the card hidden in his hand and surprise engulfed his face. He looked at his wife and reading the surprise on his face, she studied him, puzzled. Vern just raised his eyebrows in confusion, and she let the matter go, for now. Patty Lee wasn't in the mood to talk about anything, especially business or her father. Vern hugged his wife gently and a sly smile she couldn't see appeared. With Old Man Clark gone, Vern saw peace in their future.

Written on the card slipped to him at the funeral was the name of a Drug Enforcement agent out of Miami. How and why he'd attended the funeral Vern couldn't figure out. On the back was a hand-written invitation to call him, anytime, addressed to Vern. The only reason a DEA agent would have to contact him had to be the guy from Biloxi, Burt Williams. Vern had done nothing wrong in that meeting or in anything else.

He glanced over at his wife and noticed she stood alone, staring over the water. He turned around to see his father-in-law's empty casket, bound by ropes, lowering into the ground. "Sonafabitch," he said aloud.

The flight home, over before he realized it, touched down outside of Panama City at the airport Old Man Clark poured money into so that he could fly in at any time and see his precious daughter and grandson. Patty Lee sat quietly for most of the trip and the boys napped. Vern was surprised that his wife hadn't commented about the stranger at the funeral. Usually, she would question something like that at once, but not today, and it made him wonder what she knew. She caught him staring at her and rolled her eyes. The Panhandle, he realized, would never be home to Patty Lee. A strange feeling came over him and he closed his eyes. The joy he felt in the freedom from the old man's death began to drift away and Vern felt a chill. Old Man Clark gripped his thoughts and emotions from his watery grave. He hated the bastard.

Chapter 18

On Friday afternoon, Vern slipped away from home, unnoticed, and went to his office. He knew it was deserted, he'd be alone, and it would be a good time to call the agent that put the card in his hand at the funeral. Plopping into his chair and wheeling around to look out over the bay, he pulled the card from his pocket, read one side and flipped it over with his fingers. It only had a name, number, and the intimidating words "Drug Enforcement Agency" printed on the front and the handwritten invitation to call on the back. The agent's name, according to the card, was Rafael Demingo and the number placed the agent in Miami.

Vern read a couple of articles concerning Miami and South Florida and the plague of drugs flowing in the tropical paradise city. Vern threw his feet on the window seal and recalled one of the stories, all the while flipping the card from finger to finger. Not only marijuana but now cocaine poured in from South America. Vern knew that Old Man Clark held some high-ranking friends, as evidenced with the call he'd eavesdropped on a while back, and conducted business unscrupulously, but he didn't figure the old man to deal in this kind of stuff. The old man was cold and conniving but, surely, he wasn't stupid enough to get involved with things of that magnitude.

Vern couldn't wait to find out any longer. He picked up the phone and called Special Agent Raphael Demingo. The phone rang a couple of times, and a Hispanic-tinged voice answered.

Demingo wasted little time in getting to the point of why Vern received the card. He was the type of person who didn't waste time. He also didn't engage in conversation without purpose. It was a trait picked up from his father, a Cuban exile, who knew time was a precious thing and didn't waste it.

"Mr. Bruce, there's no easy way to tell you this, but your late father-in-law was a drug smuggler. Cocaine to be exact," he told Vern and waited for his response. Vern said nothing, so Demingo continued, "Has your wife mentioned any of this to you?" That statement stunned Vern, and he tried to speak, but no words came out. Demingo let the silence hang in the air. Finally, Vern found his voice again and responded.

"I don't have a clue as to what you are talking about, Mr. Demingo, and why would my wife *know* about something like that?" he asked into the phone.

Demingo didn't hesitate. "Well, sir, I know for a fact that Patricia Bruce knows all about her father's dealings. He told her right before his, let's say, *accident,*" he said coldly. "Told her everything. Surprised she hasn't mentioned it to you, but I understand you just buried the old guy. She is probably going to tell you. I'd hope."

"Look, I know that old bastard was crooked. He was an asshole, and I didn't like him, and he didn't like me, but, involved in cocaine, and to boot, you're telling me my wife knows?" Vern paused. "What the hell do you want, Mr. Demingo?" Vern's anger grew with each word. An anger not only directed to the other end of the line but also to Old Man Clark.

Vern's defensive mechanisms kicked in and he added, "I think I need to contact my lawyer, Mr. Demingo. If you want to talk to us, contact him. I'm pretty sure you already have his number."

"That's an option, Mr. Bruce, and a reasonable one. If I were in your shoes, I'd probably do the same," he responded.

"Goodbye, Mr. Demingo," he said, hanging up the phone. His office was dark, but by the light of the moon, he saw waves rolling in the bay below. That only meant one thing this time of year, a storm was brewing. Vern looked at his hands and envisioned them wrapped around Old Man Clark's neck, interlacing his fingers and squeezing the old man's imaginary head. He wondered in what kind of danger the bastard ensnared his daughter? Vern wanted to rush home and confront his wife, but shaking his head, he wanted to see if his wife told him herself. He decided to take his time on the way home.

He traveled the long way around and took the road leading him to the pier where his brother, Rof, spent his summer days selling ice cream and flirting with the young ladies. Vern saw in his mind the old ice cream shack, long since torn down and moved away. There was a sign placed next to the pier saying another business was soon to be built, but he didn't take the time to read it. He wanted to walk along their old pier, by himself, with nothing but his thoughts going with him.

He walked near halfway to the end of the pier and stopped, leaned over the railing, and looked back at the dunes lining the beach. He took a deep breath, filling his lungs with the salty sea air. He put his weight against the railing and looked out among the dunes. The sea oats danced in the slight breeze, and he saw a young couple sitting on a blanket enjoying the crisp autumn air and each other. At first glance, he thought the teenage boy looked like Rof, but when he blinked, he realized the boy looked nothing like his brother. The young man's hair was jet black, and he wasn't nearly as tan as Rof. He was so enamored with the couple that he didn't notice the short figure settling in beside him. When the man spoke, Vern jumped slightly as he thought he was alone. He knew the voice from the earlier phone call.

"Nice place to think," Special Agent Demingo said lowly as he turned his body to get the three-hundred-and-sixty-degree view of the place. He stuck his hand towards Vern, but Vern didn't return the gesture. Vern, nearly a head taller than Demingo, looked down into the agent's dark eyes, the surprise showing in his own.

"How in the world are you here?" he asked the agent. "I just called you in Miami."

"DEA, Mr. Bruce. We have ways," he responded with a smirky smile. In fact, the number in Miami was just a call center. The Agency held the power to send the call anywhere in the world. The agent's smirk disappeared, replaced with a blank expression and he continued, "I need to pay your wife a visit.

Thought you might want to see what *is* going on with her before I do. If she gets involved with the things her father was involved with..." He paused and looked around and a frown appeared on his stoic face. "I fear for her safety." Vern looked across the gulf and the setting, bright full moon.

"Give me tonight," Vern said and turned back towards Demingo. "Just give me tonight."

The Special Agent met Vern's gaze and said, "Tonight." He raised an eyebrow and walked away, disappearing into the night.

Vern stood on their pier for a few more minutes, watching the moon illuminate the emerald waters of the Gulf of Mexico. He didn't want to go home; he didn't want to confront his wife about all of this, *but what could he do?* he asked himself. He couldn't let his wife, if she wasn't already, get involved with something like this. But what did her father tell her before he died? Why didn't she tell him? How bad was all of this? The questions raced through his mind as he drove home. "Damn that old man's soul!" Vern screamed into the night and the words disappeared into the wind blowing through the open window.

Arriving home, Vern found Patty Lee in her usual spot settled in the corner nook of the kitchen, her reading glasses perched on her nose, studying a stack of papers. He stood in the doorway until she looked up and acknowledged him standing there. He wasn't going to beat around the bush nor was he just going to take her word and move on.

"You ever heard of Rafael Demingo?" he asked his wife as he sat down across from her. Patty Lee looked up above the reading glasses, slid them from her nose, and stuck the end between her lips, her eyes looking off into the distance. She held the posture for a few seconds and shook her head.

"Don't think so, who is he?" she responded.

"DEA guy down in Miami," was all he offered.

Patty Lee's demeanor changed instantly. She looked down at the floor and uncharacteristically avoided eye contact. "DEA? How do you know him?" she asked, confusion showing in her voice and what little of her face Vern could see.

"The stranger at your father's funeral. Short guy, standing in the back, dark," he responded, standing up directly beside his wife. Vern placed his hand on her shoulder. "He left me a card when he shook my hand. And now he's here, in town, wants to talk to you. Something about your father." Vern offered as little information as possible, studying his wife's reaction.

Patty Lee rose to her feet, walked to the wine cabinet, took a glass from the rack, and opened a bottle. Vern glanced at the sink and noticed a used wine glass already there. She poured a little of the liquid from the bottle into the glass and sipped it slowly.

"We just said goodbye..." She paused. "And you're telling me there was a damned DEA agent at the funeral? Why? He had no business there!" Her voice grew louder with each word, and she wheeled around to face her husband. Vern, taken aback by her last statement, gathered his words.

"Told me that your father was involved with some pretty bad people, Patty Lee. People *we* don't need to be involved with," he replied, his voice remaining calm.

Her face was red, and her voice still raised, "I don't care what he wanted then or wants now."

Vern walked back to the nook and sat down. He looked at the floor and then back at Patty Lee. "Patty Lee, that's beside the point. I know he shouldn't have been there, but he was. He was there. Get mad about that later, but I *got* to know what your father was up to."

"Why? What does it matter to you? He's dead and *I'm* taking over his business," she said. They hadn't discussed the future of her father's company or their own. The revelation didn't surprise him, however, but did wound his pride.

"We haven't talked business, Patty Lee, but shouldn't we *both* decide something like that?" he asked.

"No," she responded tartly. "It's *my* family's company. Not yours and it's none of your damned concern."

Vern, defeated, hung his head and stood up to walk away. He'd heard enough from his wife. He realized she was still in mourning and maybe still in shock. Turning to see his wife's burning face, he realized he lost more than an argument tonight. As he slowly walked from the room, his head shaking, in his mind he heard Old Man Clark's distinct laugh.

The next morning Vern felt Patty Lee's side of the bed. It was cold and the smoothness of the sheets indicated his wife never came to bed. He looked in the usual places, but when he walked down to the garage, her car was gone. He checked in on the boys. Cliff, in his room, slept the morning away but Casey's bed, however, lay in the same state as his mother's, undisturbed.

Vern scratched his stubble, walked into his little home office, fell into his chair and saw a note placed under the picture of his boys. The scribbled note in Patty Lee's hand read, *"Gone to West Palm to tie things up. Took Casey. We will be back Monday."* Vern sighed and settled into his mind. After his conversation last night with Agent Demingo and resulting argument with his wife, he guessed the DEA agent would come calling again today. The phone beside him rang but Vern didn't answer. He didn't want to speak with anyone. He needed coffee and maybe a little whiskey mixed in.

Around noon, there was a knock at the door and Vern, peeking from the window saw who did the knocking. He let the agent stand there for a minute and Vern eyed him through the peep hole. Demingo stood, staring back as he noticed the hole in the door grow dark, with a smile on his face. With a deep breath, Vern unlocked the door and opened it slowly.

"Good morning, Mr. Bruce," Demingo said, still holding the smile on his face.

Vern didn't offer a smile in return. "Patty Lee's not here," he volunteered. "She left for West Palm this morning."

The agent's smile turned into a slight frown, and he responded, "Unfortunate. I was really hoping to talk with her. You did mention that to her last night?"

"We spoke. Didn't go well," Vern responded.

Demingo pointed to the living room visible behind Vern and asked, "Mind if I come in for a moment?"

Vern hesitated but opened the door and motioned for the special agent to come in. He led Demingo into the living room and offered him a seat on the couch. Both men sat down with Vern taking a chair next to the couch. The special agent leaned towards Vern and spoke very softly.

"Mr. Bruce, I don't think your wife wants to meet with me. I don't think she wants to talk with me about what her father told her a few days ago. I could be wrong, but people who want to cooperate usually don't leave when they know I need to speak with them…" He paused and cocked his head. "Unless they have something to hide."

Vern looked past the agent seated beside him and out of the window facing the ocean. He nodded and said, "She is still upset over her father's death. She was really pissed when you showed up at the funeral. I'm sure you can understand why she didn't want to talk to you."

"Just wanted to pay my respects, nothing more," Demingo responded. "Even though I was investigating him, the old man seemed like a decent enough guy. I think he may have wanted out.

Talked to him about it and seemed like he was about to give in. Too bad he felt the *other* choice was best."

Vern grinned. *Old Man Clark sure was smooth*, he thought to himself. Demingo saw the slight grin but didn't explore why.

Demingo stood up, walked towards the window Vern stared at, and continued, "I wonder if he told your wife that."

Vern broke his gaze into the window, stood up, and asked the special agent to follow him into the kitchen. There was a pot of coffee waiting and Vern offered Demingo a cup. Demingo quickly accepted and sat settled into Patty Lee's spot in the nook. Vern took the seat across from the agent, sipping his coffee and tapping his fingers on the table.

"So, the old man wanted to get out?" Vern asked him.

"Hinted at it. Said he didn't want his daughter involved," he responded sipping the steaming coffee. Demingo smacked his lips and held his gaze upon Vern. Outwardly, Vern tried to keep a poker face, showing no emotion, but inside his thoughts raced, and he wasn't very good at hiding his emotions. The agent's wry smile returned as he watched. Vern didn't have experience with people like Demingo, but he watched enough movies to know that someone like him would say whatever they needed to say to gain someone's trust and cooperation. He needed to talk with his wife before Demingo met up with her.

While Vern was lost in his thoughts, Demingo sipped his coffee and let Vern absorb the information fed to him. He hadn't shown his best hand yet and with the game tilting in his favor, didn't think he needed to. Not right now, but it all depended on what Vern said in the next few minutes.

"How about we fly down this afternoon, Mr. Bruce? Your plane is still in the hangar. I went by this morning. Mrs. Bruce used her father's *jet*," he offered, and Vern's face hardened. Demingo sensed the jealousy bubbling just below the surface.

Vern's finger tapping stopped, and he pointed his finger in Demingo's direction. "You already knew she wasn't here, didn't you?" he asked. Demingo nodded and turned his palms in acknowledgement. The agent couldn't help but smile when he was one step ahead and replied, "I cover my bases."

Demingo sensed Vern's willingness to cooperate evaporate. Vern didn't like being toyed with. He wasn't about to fly down and blindside his wife with a DEA agent in tow, especially with how last night ended between them.

"Don't think so, Mr. Demingo," he said angrily, standing up from the nook and motioning towards the kitchen door. "I have things to attend to. My wife will be back in a couple of days. I will make sure *we* meet with you then."

Demingo bowed his head with respect. He expected this response, and his slight grin widened. The agent, trained to read emotion, knew when to leave things be. With one last sip of his coffee he offered, "Fair enough, Mr. Bruce."

The agent rose and said nothing until he reached the door. He reached for the doorknob but stopped and turned slowly. He held up a single finger and waved it towards Vern.

"There is one other thing you might be interested in," Demingo said as he reached into the inside pocket of his sport coat. He pulled out a single sheet of paper. It was folded in half with the blank side facing outward. Vern, peering at the sheet of paper, made out a seal of some sort on the other side. Demingo held it out to him and with a sigh, Vern took it from Demingo's hand. As he unfolded it, he recognized the seal of the United States Army, wings of an eagle outstretched clutching an olive branch in one claw and arrows in the other. A single paragraph typed below the symbol read:

In relation to Private Ronald Frank Bruce, status changed:

Killed in Action removed.
Missing in Action added.

Vern's face turned ghostly pale, and his body trembled, the paper shaking in his hand. Tears formed in his eyes, and he looked up at Demingo.

"What the hell does this mean?" he demanded.

The agent placed his hand on Vern's shoulder and moved in close so he could whisper even though nobody was around to hear his words except Vern. "It means that Rof's body was never recovered. Every other body on that plane *was*..." Demingo looked Vern in the eye, "Essentially what it means is this: Your brother is *suspected* to be alive and held in a prison camp inside

Vietnam or a bordering country. What it means is that finding out for *sure* can become a priority."

Chapter 19

Later that morning Patty Lee arrived in West Palm. After leaving Casey with a nanny, she made her way to the Clark Building. Being a Saturday, there was nobody around and only one car in the parking lot. She pulled into her father's old parking space. He'd designed the lot so that when he parked, he could see through the dunes and onto the beach. Patty Lee sitting in the car for a few moments enjoying the view, noticed something out of place from the corner of her eye. She noticed a car parked in the back corner of the lot. On any other morning, the car wouldn't attract attention, but with the argument between her and Vern last night, she guessed there was probably a connection to the DEA Agent Vern told her about.

She noticed two people in the car. A man occupied the back seat, and another man sat behind the steering wheel. Suddenly, the driver stepped out. He peered at Patty Lee as he stood, nodded at the man in the back seat and opened the door for him to step out. The dark-haired man slowly walked towards her car with the driver trailing behind. Patty Lee double checked the glove compartment for a weapon of some sort since this didn't look like the DEA but found nothing. She started rolling up her window when the man placed his hand inside the car.

"Hello, Mrs. Bruce," he said in an accent she couldn't place. Growing up in West Palm Beach, she recognized most Hispanic accents, but this one escaped her. "My name is Christian Lopez." He bowed his head and continued, "It is extremely nice to meet you at last. My employer, one of your father's closest friends, sends his deepest condolences for his passing."

The hair stood on Patty Lee's neck. This was certainly not the DEA, and she was all alone. Reciprocating the handshake, she glanced through the dunes, hoping to see someone on the beach, but it was deserted. She was all alone. She eased her free hand onto the door handle, just in case the need to escape arose, but realized there was nowhere for her to run. Sensing her apprehension, Lopez retracted his hand, flashed a toothy smile, and took a step back, motioning for the driver to do the same.

"You have nothing to fear, my dear, we are here to help," he said gently. "Why don't we go inside and talk?" Patty Lee stared at Lopez for a few seconds before relenting. For some strange reason, she began to feel at ease and couldn't figure out why. Perhaps it was this man's calm demeanor, or it simply could be that she had no choice.

Walking to the front door, Lopez said something in his accented Spanish and the driver returned to the car. This slightly enhanced her ease and Patty Lee felt less threatened by Lopez's presence.

Alone in the building, she found nothing but alcohol to offer him. He politely refused, and the two sat down in her father's expansive office. Paintings of beach scenes lined the walls and Lopez stopped at each one, studying each stroke. Patty Lee, behind her father's desk watched as he stopped and admired each one and she caught herself admiring his physique. He was tall, maybe a little over six feet, looking every bit a Spanish descendent. His body was trim, and she noticed muscles under his shirt each time he followed a brush stroke with his finger. His tanned skin stood out against the yellow shirt he wore, and his dark hair and eyes were enhanced by the white brim hat. Patty Lee wondered if he looked like that for effect and a slight grin appeared on her face.

"My father loved the ocean," she commented as he peered at the last painting. Lopez looked back at her, with the smile still on his face and said, "As I am learning to." He walked over to a window and glanced around, making sure nobody else would be joining them. Patty Lee eased open the lap drawer and saw the handle of her father's thirty-eight resting on a notepad.

"How do you..." She caught herself in mid-sentence. "How did you know my father?"

Lopez didn't turn his attention away from the window as he responded. "He was a business associate... and a friend. We *helped* each other through some rough times, financially speaking." He turned around and his broad smile turned sly. "We made a *lot* of money together and it is my hope that association continues with you, Mrs. Bruce," he responded, his accent seemingly thicker. *If he was trying to charm her because she was a woman*, she thought, *that just would not do.*

"Mr. Lopez—" she said, and he cut her off.

"Christian, Mrs. Bruce, please call me Christian."

She accepted the interruption and continued, "*Christian*, my father informed me before he passed that he was in league with certain people that do certain things. I'm no fool and I'm no idiot. You should know the DEA contacted my husband." She paused, stood and walked to the window where Lopez stood. "They want to talk to me."

Lopez smiled, stepping forward so that his face and Patty Lee's were within inches of each other. "Oh, yes, we know. We know that right now we are probably being listened to...if not watched," he said as he turned back to the window and gestured. Patty Lee shook her head. The fear vanished completely, and anger filled the void.

"Then why in the world are we even talking? Why the hell did you mention anything if you know we are under surveillance?" she asked. Christian Lopez' face illuminated. "So much like your father," he said. Sitting on the office couch, he offered the seat next to him to Patty Lee. She gently and slowly sat beside him, almost touching.

"Because, Mrs. Bruce, it is inevitable. I am only, however, talking about the *coffee* trade. They *suspect* otherwise, but their racism against my people blinds them to the truth. Just because we are Columbian, they *suspect*. We are legitimate, no matter what they think." The Columbian tried his best to sound offended and in some small way it was genuine.

He placed his hand on Patty Lee's knee and made a gesture with his eyes, lifting them quickly and resetting them.

"Mrs. Bruce, could I interest you with a walk on the beach?" Feeling no fear and interested in continuing the conversation, she agreed.

Burt Williams never expected a call from Vern Bruce. After his failed election, the organization lost interest in him, and Burt's interest was purely personal. His instructions were to stay away from the Bruce family, and he held every intention of compliance. He suspected Vern might try to contact him when Lucky disappeared, but Burt heard nothing. If Vern attempted contact, it was his plan to tell a glorious lie along the lines of Lucky living the good life somewhere and leave it at that.

Another surprise was that Vern found out where and how to contact him. His place of business and phone number were not common knowledge. So, when his phone rang at the little dive bar on the Biloxi Strip, the voice emitted from the other end caught him off guard.

"Well, Vern, always good to hear from family. What do you want?" Burt found that not acting surprised was usually the best course of action. The gangster never tipped his hand.

"Mr. Williams, I know I'm the last person you thought you'd hear from, but I need a little advice," Vern told him.

Burt snickered, "You want advice, son, call a lawyer."

Vern hesitated before responding, "This is something my lawyer really doesn't need to know about right now. I don't know why in the hell I'm calling you, but..." He paused, considering very carefully what he said next. "I need someone who is on the *other* side of the law." Burt chuckled into the phone and a broad smile ran between his jowls.

"So, Mr. Straight and Narrow needs some advice from the *other* side, huh? That's interesting ain't it? Got yourself in some trouble?" he asked, still chuckling to himself. "I am *like* a lawyer, Mr. Bruce, so my advice ain't free."

Vern, in no mood to play games quickly asked, "What kind of money are we talking about and how do you want me to get it to you?" Burt's smile disappeared and even though Vern couldn't see it, his face turned serious.

"I deal in favors with this type of thing, *Vern*, and it's kinda like them old mafia movies. I pick the favor...and time its repaid," he returned.

Vern hesitated and hovered the receiver over the phone's hook before placing it back to his ear and continuing, "Fine. I need some information on a DEA agent."

"Whoa, big fella," Burt responded, shocked. "DEA? Who the hell do you think I am?"

"A man that can get information on most anybody," he responded, pausing for a second before adding, "I hope."

Burt's nostrils flared and his face turned red. Agitated, he said, "Give me the name and a few days. Get out here by the weekend."

"I can't come to Biloxi," he replied knowing he would probably have to.

"Yes, you will," Burt commanded. "Give me the name."

"Rafael Demingo. Said he was out of Miami, and I need to know if he's the real deal."

"Got it," Burt said and hung up the phone silencing Vern.

Vern sat at his desk, once again, watching families enjoying West Bay. He held a glass with a small amount of bourbon inside and sloshed it around. As he turned his attention to the whisky settling in the glass, he wondered what he was getting into with someone like Burt Williams. He had to know, for sure, about Demingo's legitimacy and this was the only way he knew to do so.

He needed to know if the tale of Rof, possibly being alive and in a prison camp somewhere in Southeast Asia, was a lie or truth? If it held any chance of truth, he had to know. Since he'd laid eyes on the memo, images of his brother, clinging to life in a hell that few men survived, filled his mind. He read about prison camps in Vietnam, still holding Americans so many years after the war ended. He took another swig of whisky from the glass. If Rof lived through the crash and a camp like that, time would quickly run out.

While Vern thought about his brother, Burt Williams thought about orders. Orders that told him to stay away from Vern Bruce. No such orders existed concerning the chance Vern contacted *him*. Burt rolled the cigar stuck between his teeth from one side of his massive jaws to the other. *Nope*, he thought, *this stays with me.* He decided Susie shouldn't know of his contact with Vern. He told himself this was all for her benefit, but at the same time, she didn't need to know. If things worked out, he'd call in the favor and it'd be Susie's little boy. He could get Cliff back in Susie's life and Vern Bruce in his pocket. They weren't going to have any kids, and she deserved to have her son in her life now. He tipped the cigar towards the sky and down towards the floor. He would get the info on this Demingo character, and he would get Vern Bruce under his thumb. His body shook with laughter, but not one head turned towards the gangster in response. The patrons of the bar knew better.

Burt knew just the guy he needed to talk to. He looked down at his watch and with it being close to sundown, he knew exactly where to find Ramsay Brown. Ramsey Bown, or RB to everyone on the Mississippi Coast, was one of the few Black police detectives in the state and the entire Gulf Coast for that matter. RB not only held that distinction, but he was one of the few *mostly* honest cops along the coastline. He entered the department in Biloxi as the state desegregated and made a name as a strait-laced cop in a very corrupt town.

In this town, however, strait-laced was a relative term. He did what he had to in order to survive in a place like The Biloxi Strip. Not corrupt by any means, though, he kept his dealings with the Dixie Mafia limited to information peddling on occasion and only with certain people. He considered Burt Williams a friend, even though the two were on opposite sides of the law. If it tipped the scale *too* far, Burt knew not to call on RB. Getting information on someone in the DEA was borderline but Burt had to try.

As he arrived at the fishing pier in Ocean Springs, he saw RB near the end with his fishing rod hanging over the side. After a short walk, Burt stood next to him. RB saw him coming, in fact, he saw him parking his car. If ten years on the Strip taught RB anything, it was to remain aware of his surroundings and the people in them.

"You didn't bring a fishing reel?" RB asked him as Burt took the last few steps.

Burt smiled and replied, "Not this trip, my friend." RB returned the smile and pointed to a rod and reel leaning on the pier's railing.

"Wish I could, but can't stay long," he replied. Burt reached into his pocket, pulled out a piece of paper and handed it to RB. RB didn't immediately take it, instead eyeing his friend. Burt just nodded at the paper and finally RB took it from his hand and read the name Burt scribbled on it. Looking back at Burt, his smile was gone. He crumpled up the piece of paper and tossed it over the side of the pier and into the water.

"How long?" he asked, and Burt told him he needed something by the weekend. RB nodded his head, and the conversation ended quickly. With a nod, the two men parted ways. RB reeled in the fish that he ignored on the end of his line.

Patty Lee slammed the phone down in frustration. Vern wasn't answering her calls. It was Sunday and someone was surely at their house, but the phone went unanswered. She wanted to know if the DEA agent contacted him again and, despite her doubts, she wanted to tell him about Lopez ambushing her at her father's office.

Yesterday, after their walk on the beach, discussing business other than coffee, she'd agreed to meet him again today. She expected Lopez any moment for their *walk on the beach* as he called it. This time however, she'd asked him to meet her at her father's home. The secluded beach offered more privacy than the public beach behind the Clark Building. Her fear of Christian Lopez, first replaced with anger, now turned into curiosity.

Lopez arrived precisely at one as promised the day before and Patty Lee met him at the side entrance. Even though curious about the man and his business, she didn't feel comfortable with him in the house. She led him onto the deck overlooking the dunes and the ocean. As she did, she glanced at her father's chair and remembered their last conversation.

"Mr. Lopez, I'm sorry, Christian, what exactly do you want from me?" she asked.

Lopez gestured towards the sandy beach and asked her to walk with him and said, "So we can be sure we are alone. The beach has nowhere to hide those who would want to hear." He took a deep breath of the muggy, salty sea air and added, "So much different from my home."

To her, Christian Lopez seemed educated and a quite articulate man. He was certainly not what she expected. When her father told her about the partnership he'd entered with these people, she expected quite the opposite. Lopez opened the gate and gestured Patty Lee towards the sand. "As always, ladies first," he told her with a bow.

They walked along the shoreline without speaking for some distance before Lopez broke the silence, "May I call you Patricia?" he asked. "I know most people call you Patty Lee, but I am enamored with your full name. It is a travesty to shorten it."

Patty Lee blushed, smiled and responded, "Let's just keep it, Mrs. Bruce. I want to keep things on a professional level." Inside she felt like a schoolgirl on her first date, but outwardly her face didn't betray her feelings.

"As you prefer, Mrs. Bruce," he replied with his usual grin.

Patty Lee reached down and took her shoes off, holding them in her hands as they walked. "Well, I ask again, what *exactly* can I do for you?" she asked once again, this time in a firmer voice.

Lopez' grin widened. He respected this beautiful woman more each time he talked with her. Just like her father, she was very blunt when speaking of business. Old Man Clark, never one to mix business with friendship, passed this trait to his daughter. This mission would be a challenge for him, but he relished such things. He saw a creature, uncovered by the crashing wave, bury itself back into the sand. "Everything has its instinct to survive," he said as he pointed to the creature, "Which brings me to a conversation we *must* have." He stopped and stepped in front of Patty Lee.

"Mrs. Bruce, we have what you would call an arrangement. Your father provided, what do we say, *transportation* for us. Your business runs a few small fishing boats for charters, yes?" he asked.

"We have a fleet, yes. Mostly small fishing boats and they usually don't go far offshore, maybe twenty miles at the most. My husband does the same thing up on the Gulf." She held no intention of mentioning Vern in this conversation, but it slipped out before she caught herself. She made a mental note not to let it happen again. Lopez moved to the side, and they continued walking along the shore.

"Ahh, your husband," Lopez said playfully. "You were telling me about his visitor yesterday. Someone named Demingo, I suppose," he said, the grin almost disappearing. "A most despicable person, this man, a born liar. I hope you will convey this to *Mr.* Bruce: This man is the son of a Cuban exile and accuses any Hispanic not of his homeland of the worst kind of activities. *Illegal* activities." He stopped once more and peered at the rolling waves.

"Let's get back to the fleet, Christian," Patty Lee said, kicking at a piece of driftwood. "What did my father do for you?"

"He provided transportation, as I said, that's all. Never questioned the cargo. He just let his captains pick up our packages from other boats and deliver them. That's all and we pay very, very handsomely. We will handle everything, just like before. You just get paid." Lopez looked into Patty Lee's eyes and finished, "And we get to allow this newly planted seed of friendship to blossom into a beautiful flower."

Patty Lee looked back and saw her father's home beyond the dunes and concern swept across her face. "I want assurances that if I ever decide to end this, it's over. I don't want this to affect my family and..." She turned to face Lopez. "My husband can never know."

The grin widened into a smile and Lopez offered, "You have my word."

Chapter 20

Burt held early morning meetings at fast-food restaurants because it was the last place anyone expected meetings between a gangster and a cop to take place. He always picked one with a playground so he could watch kids, so when he had a meeting like this, he always picked a booth near the window facing the playground. He loved kids and always pictured having a house full of them, but now as he sipped his coffee, he figured that would never happen. Not with Susie, anyway. Her lifestyle before she made her way to Biloxi made sure of that.

He watched kids climb the hamburger-shaped slide and then pop out the chute on the other side. He enjoyed their laughter and laughed when one tumbled onto the ground. Burt, so enthralled with the playing children, didn't notice RB until he slid into the seat opposite him.

"This place again?" RB asked as he sat down. Burt held up his arms and nodded.

"Love this place, bud, nobody notices much of anything. Watcha got?" he asked.

"Whatever you need with this dude, my advice, just leave it alone," RB said, staring Burt in the eye. "He is legit, DEA out of Miami, but he ain't exactly what I call up and up. He's been on report several times and it looks like he might not be an agent for much longer. He's working on the growing problem down there, the white powder. Nothing really that would affect you, as we don't have that problem." RB leaned in closer to Burt and whispered, "Do we?"

Burt shook him off. "Hell no and don't want it here."

RB pursed his lips, not knowing whether to believe his friend. RB leaned back and bluntly told Burt, "Stay away from this guy, Burt. Trouble follows him."

Burt let the words settle in the air for a second and returned his attention to the kids outside, reached for a cigar, but didn't pull it from his pocket, looked back at RB quizzically, and asked, "Why would he be up in the Panhandle? That powder don't really reach that far." The detective shook his head.

"Can't help you there. That's all I got, and it's all I'm gonna get. Vetted the guy and I'm done. Been a pleasure once again," RB said sarcastically and slid out of the booth. Before he left, he turned slowly and pleaded with his friend, "Don't get in bed with this guy, Burt. Leave it."

As RB walked away, Burt's smile vanished, and he reached into his pocket, this time pulling out the cigar and placing it between his teeth. An older couple in the booth across the aisle looked his way as he chewed on the cigar. When Burt looked back at them, they quickly gathered their food and found another booth. *Why would Vernon Bruce want to know about a corrupt DEA guy*, Burt wondered. Looking out the window, he noticed RB leaving in his personal car. A cop like RB never used his unmarked to meet with a guy like Burt Williams.

The meeting with Vern, set for tomorrow, wouldn't take place at a fast-food joint. Burt wanted the square to see the seedy side of Biloxi, particularly his bar. For Vern to appreciate the type of person to which he owed a favor, he needed to see a harsher side of life. That way, if things went awry, Vern would know a man like himself was not to be trifled with.

Burt slid out of the booth and pulled his wallet from his back pocket. As he passed the older couple that fled his presence earlier, their eyes grew wide. The couple slid nearer each other and the old man took his wife's hand. He pulled a twenty from his wallet and tossed it on the table, not breaking stride but flashing them a wide grin, the cigar still clenched between his teeth.

When Vern opened the door to the bar the next morning, he squinted as the bright sunshine outside contrasted with the dimness of the inside lighting. He barely saw Burt perched on the last stool at the end of the bar and Burt motioning for him to come on in. Making his way towards the gangster, Vern felt this bar closely resembled the one in which his father drank himself to death. The last stool didn't seat his father, watching a ballgame, but a member of the Dixie Mafia, happily waiting to perform Vern a *favor*.

"Vernon, welcome to the glamorous side of the Gulf Coast," Burt said as he gestured around. The bar, even for mid-morning, held several patrons offering their glasses in toast in response to Burt's loud, booming voice.

Vern nodded fake approval and only offered, "Nice place."

Burt smiled and still motioning around the bar said, "I've spruced it up a little since I bought it, used to be a dump."

Vern tried to offer a fake grin at the joke but couldn't muster one.

Vern sat down on the stool next to Burt and wasted no time. "You got something, I hope. My plane is waiting."

Burt, offended, replied, "I was hoping you'd stay the weekend, maybe show you around a little bit. Live a little, Vernon. Some nice girls around here. Better than that stiff you call a wife."

Vern bristled at the insult to his wife but buried it.

"No thanks, gotta get back home. Family coming in tomorrow, and I left Cliff with a friend." He winced as he said Cliff's name. At the mention of the name, Burt sensed Vern's apprehension and couldn't help but stroke his unease.

"Cliff, my stepson, how's he doing?" Burt asked as he took a sip of the drink he held in his hand. Vern's face turned red, and he pointed his finger towards the gangster's face.

"He's not anything to you, you got that?" Vern said, his voice louder than intended, and it drew a few looks from around the room. Burt noticed and pulled in close to Vern's face with his own, pushing Vern's finger down and flashing a smile at his patrons. Burt eased close enough for the cigar and bourbon on his breath caused Vern to grimace.

His voice low enough that only Vern could hear, Burt said, "You remember your place, Mr. Bruce. If I shot you in the head right now, not one soul in this bar would see a thing. This is my place..." Burt put his free hand on Vern's shoulder. "And *my* town."

Vern, knowing when to leave things alone, said, "Look, just give me what I came here for. I agreed to what you wanted," Vern responded in a calm, collected voice and added under his breath, "Pretty much sold my soul for this." Burt heard the comment and shrugged his shoulders.

"Enough with the hospitality," Burt said. "This Demingo guy is legit, but trouble. He's rogue and from what I hear, he's desperate." Burt eased back onto his barstool and asked, "What in the hell does he want with a guy like you?" Behind the look of confusion he shot towards Vern, Burt knew that the agent probably wasn't interested in *him*, but his wife.

Vern fiddled with a napkin laying on the bar and he looked away. Burt noticed his fidgeting and asked, "Not what you wanted to hear?"

"Do you know if he has any connections in DC?" Vern paused then added, "Or the military?"

"From the info I got on this guy, I wouldn't think so. In fact, my guy told *me* to stay away from him and I would do that very thing if I were you," Burt offered with a degree of sincerity before asking, "Why?"

"He..." Vern hesitated, not sure what he should divulge. "He just told me something about an old friend, kinda hard to believe." Vern wanted to keep the information about Rof to himself if possible.

"Men like him," Burt said in a matter-of-fact tone, "they tell people what they want to hear. Truth, hell, don't mean nothing to them. He sees you as a means to an end, my friend. That's it, and I wouldn't trust a damn word he said."

Vern stood up and threw the napkin back onto the bar, shaking his head. Burt's words cut deep into his soul. The thought his brother survived the plane crash gave him hope, but, on the other hand, envisioning Rof enduring torture in a prison halfway around the earth haunted his thoughts. One way or another, he had to know the truth, but, if there was no hope of bringing him home, dead or alive, he hoped his brother found peace.

Regardless, he needed to leave this place. "Thanks. I gotta go." Vern extended his hand and Burt shook it, tightening his grip as they completed the ritual. "No problem, but keep the phone lines open. You never know when family will come calling," He released Vern's hand and as Vern turned to leave, Burt added, loud enough for the entire bar to hear, "And, Bruce, say hello to my stepson." Vern tightened his fists but didn't acknowledge his words and kept walking, making his way out the door, not looking back.

Burt pulled up his stool, pulled out a cigar, and lit it, inhaling a long breath filled with smoke. He held it for a short while before blowing it upwards. "Damn, old man, you left a hornets nest," he said to himself and picked up the phone.

The flight home from Biloxi didn't take long and before he realized it, the tires' loud squeal upon landing jarred Vern from his thoughts. When the steps lowered and he made his first step down, Vern noticed Demingo standing next to his car. Vern stared towards the DEA agent, not expecting an ambush at his own airport. The agent, returning his stare, didn't wait for Vern to make his way to him but marched quickly, meeting him halfway.

"Vacation?" he asked sarcastically as Vern got close enough to hear over the whine of the twin engines.

"Business," Vern replied. "I'm not saying another word to you, Agent Demingo, unless you are charging me with something and my lawyer's present." Demingo flinched slightly and threw up his hands.

"I thought we had a better understanding than that, Vern," he hissed. "All I wanted to do was talk with you and your wife. You are not criminals..." He hesitated. "That I know of."

Vern handed him a card and walked away. As he did, he said, "My lawyer's number is on that. I don't expect to see you again without you going through him."

Demingo bristled, "Mr. Bruce, do you recognize I'm DEA? I don't need to go through a damned lawyer."

Vern wheeled around and took a couple of quick steps back towards Demingo. "You are dirty, desperate, and you fucking lied to me," Vern yelled.

Demingo's face hardened, and he met Vern in his tracks, so they were face to face. "I'm not dirty, but *I am* desperate. I've got to stop the plague invading us in Miami. That's a damned fact and I'll do what I have to..." He paused and stuck his finger in Vern's face. "And I have not once lied to you."

"My brother is dead," Vern managed.

Demingo leaned in even closer to Vern's face, their noses almost touching. Demingo smiled and said, "Pictures don't lie, and I have 'em. When you want me to help *you*, or your *brother*, you know where to find me."

Vern threw his hands up and waved off the information. "Bullshit," he said and left Demingo standing there, the smile still on his face.

Vern retrieved Cliff from his friend's house and the two went home, changed clothes, and took a couple of chairs onto the beach. It had been a while since Vern just sat on the beach with either of his boys and he wanted to spend a little time doing so. Cliff was growing up before his eyes and the boy increasingly resembled his father. He watched his nephew build a castle from the sugar white sand, laughing each time the fine sand fell and ruined the structure. Vern wondered how long it would take before Cliff learned to wet the sand as it was the only way to get it to stick. The child grew tired of failure and sat in the sand, staring over the Gulf, scooping up sand and pouring it back onto the beach. He was tired of that too and ran up to his uncle's chair.

"Unc, I've been thinking about something," Cliff said. "I know my dad is gone, but what about my mom? Is she ever coming back? I don't remember nothing but her face." Vern knew Cliff asking questions about his parents was inevitable, but he just didn't want to face them on a day at the beach.

"I don't know, bud," he replied, choosing his words carefully. "It's been a long time. She might, but I'll never get your hopes up or lie to you. So, son, I just don't know."

Out of the corner of his eye, he saw Patty Lee standing beyond the dunes holding Casey's hand. The child tugged at his mother's hand and pointed to Cliff. She waved towards them and yelled that they'd join them on the beach after changing clothes.

Vern needed to talk to his wife, but things they needed to talk about were not things the boys needed to hear. He decided that, as a family, they would enjoy the afternoon and the evening, and when the boys were asleep, they would talk.

The family enjoyed the afternoon at the beach immensely. Vern gave the boys swimming lessons and Patty Lee watched and yelled encouragement. That evening, the family traveled the short distance from Mexico Beach to Panama City, dining at The Captain's. Both boys were amazed to see the tons of fish laying on the massive dock from the day's catch. They ate, they laughed, and they smiled.

Arriving home and when the boys were asleep, Vern and Patty Lee settled in the kitchen. It was one of the few places where their conversations were always private. After the day the family spent together, neither wanted to have this talk, but both knew they had to.

Vern sat down on the bench opposite his wife in the corner nook. Vern tapped his fingers nervously against the wooden table remembering the last time they'd sat here together. That conversation didn't end well. He took his wife's hand and spoke first, "Rof could be alive."

Patty Lee sensed the tension in his voice, and she put her free hand on top of his. She also felt the tension in his body emanating though his hands.

"What are you talking about?" she asked.

"The DEA agent, Demingo, gave me a piece of paper from the army that his status changed from Killed in Action to Missing in Action," he responded as a tear formed in his eye. Patty Lee closed her eyes and held them closed as she spoke.

"Vern. It's been nearly ten years. Even if Rof survived the crash and was captured, the odds of him being alive right now, well, they are not great," she responded, trying to keep her voice tinged with understanding, "Baby, this guy is trying to get in your head."

The tear formed in Vern's eye quickly disappeared. He expected his wife to react, but hoped it would be different, more supportive maybe. He stood up and walked to the other side of the kitchen, put his hands on the wall and shook his head. "What if it's true?" he asked his wife, his back still turned.

Patty Lee said nothing. She stood and walked over to Vern, putting her arms around her husband. "If it's true, then God help him, Vern. God help all of us."

Chapter 21

Rain pelted Mac Tate's umbrella the next morning as he waited for Vern outside his building. The old politician squeezed under the limited awning and relief swept over him when he saw Vern pulling into the parking lot. He was the first one there and hoped Vern would be the second. The political grapevine told him that Vern received bad information. Mac felt he owed it to Vern to set the record straight.

As usual, Vern arrived before anyone else when he was in town and those days were becoming few. Through his rain-soaked windshield he saw someone standing beside his door. At first, he thought it was Demingo but as he got closer, however, he recognized Mac Tate, and he breathed a sigh of relief. With no umbrella himself, Vern sloshed through the puddles and bypassed a handshake and opened the door.

"Good morning, Vern," Tate said in his usual comforting voice. Vern realized a long time ago that Tate was a politician, and the sly politician knew what voice to use and when to use it. Vern never picked up that trait during his campaign.

"Mac, long time, no see," Vern responded. "What are you doing here?" Both men shook off the rain and made their way into Vern's office. Vern offered him a seat and noticed the old man wince as he slowly settled in a chair.

"Keeping you in the loop..." Mac paused. "About your brother."

Vern wasn't surprised that Mac Tate was still neck deep in everything happening in the Panhandle. You don't become a ringleader in local politics and just give up that power. It was in Mac Tate's blood and Vern suspected he stayed in the loop on a lot of things. Vern decided to play dumb and not say anything about Demingo or contacting Burt Williams. If he didn't already, the old man didn't need to know.

"My brother's dead, Mac," Vern responded. "He's been dead a long time now."

Mac eased his frail body out of the chair and put his hand on Vern's shoulder. "I know about Demingo. Let's not play games, son." Vern didn't look at Mac and instead focused on the bay and wondered why the old man played his hand so quickly.

After a few moments Vern asked, "What do you know, Mac?"

Mac returned to his seat, gingerly sat down and took a deep breath. He ran his fingers across the few strands of gray hair left on his head and looked Vern in the eye.

"Demingo wasn't lying about your brother," Tate said. Vern hid his surprise behind a stoic face.

"So, he *is* alive?" Vern asked carefully.

"He told you the truth concerning reclassification," the older man said. "That's all. To be honest, it's becoming standard procedure. Lots of pressure in DC about those we *may* have left behind."

Vern almost inquired about the pictures Demingo mentioned but wanted to see what the old man volunteered. He decided to focus on the DEA agent.

"What about Demingo?" Vern asked, "He working alone or what?"

"I don't know if I need to go into that," Mac said very low, looking around for good places electronic bugs might hide and motioning around. Vern didn't immediately pick up on the gesture, but suddenly his eyes widened, and Vern shot Tate a look of surprise. The old man just nodded. "I couldn't tell you anything about that even if I *knew* anything."

Vern leaned back in his chair. "Is there anything else you *can* tell me, Mac?" Vern asked and Mac once again ran his hand across his head, his fingers trembling.

"I will tell you this, Vern," he offered. "I've heard of Demingo, don't really know him, and what I've heard is this. Not exactly dirty, not exactly clean. That's all I know." Vern's frustration boiled over and he pounded his fist on the desk, startling Tate. It was the same type of warning coming from Burt Williams. Vern shook his head and stood up.

"Thanks, Mac. You've always been good to me and my father," Vern told him, and the older man got up and put his hand back on Vern's shoulder. "Take care, son." Mac leaned into Vern's ear and whispered, "I know you've got a lot going on. Be careful. If I were you, I'd be very careful trusting *anyone*."

Vern extended his hand, and they shook. Mac Tate let himself out, as people were now starting to file into work on this Monday morning. Vern settled behind his desk. Running through his mind were visions of Demingo and his brother, Rof. Neither image gave him comfort.

Patty Lee left early that same morning before the boys awoke. Arriving in West Palm before the sun broke over the Atlantic, she was seated behind her father's desk before it broke completely. The smell of coffee permeated the building when there was a knock at the front door. Patty Lee took a deep breath and tried to smile as she opened it.

"Good morning, Mrs. Bruce," Raphael Demingo said as he extended his hand. "Such a pleasure to finally meet you."

Patty Lee shook his hand and tried not to let her disgust at his cold, clammy hands show on her face. "Yes, well, I apologize for delaying this meeting. It's been a little hectic since my father's passing and I've been out of town a lot." Demingo once again offered condolences and then a wide grin spread upon his face.

"How is my old friend Christian Lopez?" Demingo asked.

Patty Lee expected him to mention Lopez, but to do so this early in the conversation surprised her and her face couldn't hide it. "I really wouldn't know. I met with him once." Patty Lee hoped the lie didn't show in her voice. "Nice guy, though," she replied, returning the grin.

"Nice guy?" Demingo chuckled, "Your husband know about this *nice* guy?"

Patty Lee leaned in, her grin erased, and responded, "That, sir, is none of your business." Her father taught her about dealing with all types of people and she wasn't easily intimidated.

"You might want to tell Vernon," Demingo said. "You're mixing with some dangerous people. You ever heard of a Colombian necktie, Mrs. Bruce?"

"Don't think I have," she responded and added. "Stylish?"

"That is when your throat is sliced from ear to ear," he said, making the motion across his throat, "and your tongue is pulled through the slit. Kind of a trademark. Ask Lopez about it next time you two talk about *coffee*."

"Might I call your superior down in Miami?" Patty Lee asked. "I'll be a lot more inclined to offer what little help I can if I know the whole deal. Maybe the prosecutor who you are working with or the agent in charge?"

Demingo nodded, his bluff called, but remained calm and kept his emotions in check. "No need, Mrs. Bruce. I'm just trying to help *you* from making the same mistakes your father made." He paused and looked around as if to ensure their privacy. "I guess you don't want the pictures I told your husband about to come to light?"

Demingo sensed surprise in Patty Lee's demeanor. She looked down at the floor and her breathing intensified. Demingo seized the opportunity. "He told you his brother more than likely survived that crash so many years ago, *no*?" Demingo paused for an answer that didn't come before continuing, "He *did* tell you about the reclassification, I hope."

"He told me about it, yes," she offered, looking up towards the agent, her face reddening with anger as each second passed.

"What about the pictures?" he enquired.

"I don't like to play games," she replied coldly. "Just what in the hell are you talking about?"

"Oh, me neither, Mrs. Bruce. Not in the least," he responded, grinning as usual. "I'm surprised he did not tell you."

"Maybe he did, maybe he didn't, Agent Demingo, and maybe it's none of your business," she said, her voice growing louder. "I think it's time for you to leave." Demingo rose from his chair and walked towards the door. As he made his way out, he turned around, his grin spreading into a broad smile. "Maybe you don't *want* him to be alive," he said, and he walked out the door.

Patty Lee locked the door as she watched Demingo's car leave the lot and stormed back into her office, slamming the door. She faced the large portrait of her father and looked into his brush-stroked eyes. She fought back tears and let anger replace them. Patty Lee picked up the phone and dialed the number Christian Lopez left with her on their last visit. Before the line rang, she slammed the phone down and wheeled around in her chair. The sun, fully above the churning Atlantic, made her squint. Shaking her head, she picked up the phone and dialed her husband.

Vern, already in his office back in Panama City, picked up on the first ring. Knowing already who was more than likely on the other end of the line, he didn't waste time on pleasantries.

"How'd it go with him?" Vern asked.

"Why in the hell didn't you tell me how *creepy* he is?" she replied and without waiting for an answer continued, "And it went about like we thought it would." She paused, and Vern could hear her take a breath through the phone. "Pictures?"

Vern raised an eyebrow. He hoped Demingo wouldn't play that hand just yet, but apparently, he *was* desperate just as both Mac and Burt described. "Look, when I called his bluff about Rof, he came back with something about pictures not lying or something like that. Didn't say he *had* pictures, he just said that there *were* pictures. I assumed a lie and didn't want to burden you with it."

On the other end, Patty Lee waited a second before responding, considering her husband's words. "He does *seem* like the type that would use a dead brother against someone." She wanted those words back just as soon as they slid from her mouth, yet Vern said nothing. "I'm sorry, Vern," Patty Lee said quietly into the phone.

"Don't worry about it," he lied, before continuing, "There's more. Mac Tate came around this morning. Told me about Rof being declassified. He didn't say much about Demingo, don't think he could, but he gave me a bad vibe about the guy, just like you got."

"I'll talk to Dad's friends, see if they know anything about Demingo," she said and with that, they said their goodbyes. Patty Lee reached into the lap drawer and pulled out Christian Lopez' number once again. She also pulled out an open pack of cigarettes and lit one, blowing the smoke into the air. She held the number up to her face, pulling down on her reading glasses. Just as she placed her finger on the first digit, she jumped when the phone rang. It turned out there was no need to seek Lopez out as he was coming to her.

Christian Lopez didn't show up personally but sent his driver to pick Patty Lee up at her father's house that afternoon. She was hesitant about getting in the car with the guy but relented knowing that if Lopez wanted her dead, he wouldn't call her and go through all this trouble. She looked the driver over when he stepped out to open her door. He wasn't altogether tall, but stout. His hands, twice as large as a normal hand, carried scars on each. Also visible around his neck and face, were deep penetrating scars. Patty Lee's face must've shown the fear she felt because the driver smiled and nodded as he opened the door.

She tried to bury her fear and smiled back as she took her seat in the back. The road he took hugged the coast up all the way until they neared Cocoa Beach. He parked in front of a giant house that looked out of place amongst the others. It was not a typical beach house but looked more like it belonged on a ranch out west.

Lopez stood alone in the foyer of the gigantic ranch house and opened the door himself to greet his guest. The inside of the home matched the outside. Whoever built and decorated this house, they wanted to be a cowboy and not a beach bum, regardless of being only steps from the Atlantic Ocean.

"Welcome to my home, Mrs. Bruce. Once again, I ask, may I call you Patricia?" he asked as he kissed her hand and motioned for her to come in. Patty Lee finally relented and allowed him to call her by her first name. As they walked inside, she noticed a large painting of mountains mounted over the massive fireplace. Lopez noticed her admiring the painting and motioned for her to sit down.

"When I heard you were back in town, I knew I had to set up a meeting of some sort and I thought, what better than to welcome you into my home," he said.

"This is yours?" she asked, her amazement telling in her voice, as she looked around.

"Yes. I bought it when our business began with your father. You see, my home, in the mountains, is surrounded by giant ranches. I grew up on a ranch in Colombia. We didn't own it, but I worked on it. Same as my father and his father before him. I like the ocean and the beach, but not as much as your father." He stood up and looked at the painting in front of him. "I wanted my home to remind me of where I came from and..." Lopez looked out a window. "Where I shall return."

"It is beautiful," Patty Lee said as she scanned the home once again and looked up to where Lopez stood.

"Thank you, *Patricia,*" he replied, smiled, and added, "I continue to love your full name." Patty Lee felt her face turning red and quickly looked away, trying to hide her face. Lopez noticed at once, but didn't push the issue. He sat down next to her and offered her a cigarette. She accepted, and he struck a match, lit it, and watched her intently, enjoying her blushing face. Patty Lee turned away, exhaled the smoke from her lungs and spoke without looking at her companion.

"I want to ask you about Rafael Demingo," she said and as Patty Lee mentioned his name, Lopez' nostrils flared, and he clutched his fist. "He's been harassing my husband with nonsense about his brother that died in Vietnam. He's trying to convince him that Rof isn't dead and he's a POW."

"Dreadful person, Rafael Demingo," Lopez said waving his fist in the air. "He will lie, murder, and steal trying to entrap people. He's done it before and he's doing it again, to you. If he wasn't the son of a Cuban pig, they would've fired him years ago. But alas, the DEA feels they owe him. Bay of Pigs never goes away, does it? That fiasco saves the bastard because his father died there." Lopez calmed himself, took a deep breath, and apologized for his anger. Patty Lee waved it off.

"He's kept around by the DEA because of his father?" she asked.

"Unfortunately, yes, and most of the time, he does what he *wants*, not what he is *told*," Lopez responded still gesturing in disgust as if Demingo was some toxic odor he fanned from the air.

"And he just gets away with it? No consequences?" she asked, her curiosity aroused.

"Most of the time..." Lopez looked skyward and then back to Patty Lee. "Oh, for sure, he gets reprimanded and slapped on the wrist but nothing with *real* consequences. It's my understanding that the DEA wants someone else to, how do I say this? Do *away* with him. They even contacted my government concerning the assignment and they, of course, declined."

Patty Lee stood up and felt her palms fill with sweat as panic overcame her. Fear came over her as she realized that she was in a Colombian drug smugglers home, listening to him speak about *dealing* with DEA agents. "I have to go," she said and darted for the door. Lopez blocked her way, and he grabbed her by the hand, turning her until they were face to face.

"My dear Patricia, do not worry. I apologize, now is not the time to discuss such things. I didn't invite you to my home to scare you with tales of rogue DEA agents, but you asked for truth. I should've been more discreet, and I apologize." Lopez, still clutching her hand pulled her towards the dining room. "Come and let us have dinner. Our own *business* relationship needs to be nurtured and cared for, as I've said before, as if it were a tiny plant. Let us plant the seed of a long friendship tonight. My personal chef prepared us cuts of steak imported directly from my country. Let us enjoy."

As Patty Lee and Lopez enjoyed their dinner, Demingo, parked far enough away as to not attract attention, sat in his car down the street. He followed Lopez' car and didn't care what was said inside. His purpose was to confirm his suspicions that Patty Lee wasn't being completely truthful about her visits with Lopez and that purpose was now fulfilled. The breeze, blowing in off the Atlantic, offered little in the way of comfort as the days became warmer and sweat dripped from the end of his nose.

Starting the car, he eased by Lopez' ranch style home and as he did, the driver stood outside the gate. As Demingo rolled by, the driver peered into the car and the agent waved and smiled. It was time to let Mrs. Bruce know that she held a choice in her hands, drug smugglers or the law. Demingo laughed as he wondered if her husband even factored into the equation for her.

Chapter 22

A couple of days after dinner with Patty Lee, Lopez decided the time was right to pay a visit to Special Agent Demingo. Demingo didn't leave town after he finally met Patty Lee and Lopez kept tabs on him. He knew where the Cuban, a creature of habit, ate lunch while in West Palm and decided to pay him a visit.

Demingo, not expecting Christian Lopez to walk into the restaurant, hid his surprise well. He didn't look up from his plate and continued enjoying the sandwich in his hand. He only looked at his visitor slightly when he spoke.

"Special Agent Demingo, how is that Cuban sandwich?" Lopez asked him as he slid into the seat opposite Demingo in the cramped booth. "Don't look so surprised, my old friend, it is my lunchtime also."

Lopez' placed his hands on the table and looked at Demingo with delight. The DEA agent shook his head as he lifted his eyes and peered into the eyes of a man he despised. Demingo remembered the promise he made the last time the two men were in the same room, a promise that would leave either Lopez in handcuffs or lying in a pool of blood, but right now he didn't want to see the drug smuggler.

"Get out of here, Lopez. Nothing we need to talk about," he admonished Lopez.

"Quite the opposite," Lopez responded, his voice calm and void of the hate in Demingo's. "I know you are alone, and you've been told to leave us alone. I know you have been told to leave well enough be as it relates to my business."

"I may be alone," he admitted, "and I know you have some sort of deal with those in charge, and I mean *really* in charge, but I will never let it go," Demingo responded his voice growing in volume. "You are a savage bastard, Lopez, and I *am* going to send you back to Colombia in a body bag."

Lopez laugh began deep inside and grew until his slender frame shook all over. People sitting on the other side of the bench took notice and offered a glance towards them. Lopez apologized and contained himself. He gestured mockingly at Demingo with his hand in the form of a pistol. "How long has it been since you've been back to Cuba?" he asked, still chuckling under his breath.

"Go to hell.," Demingo said. Lopez stopped laughing and a grin replaced his broad smile. "You first," he responded. He placed a hundred-dollar bill on the table and said, "Lunch is on me." Lopez slid from the booth and tipped his broad hat before walking out of the cafe.

Demingo slammed what remained of his sandwich onto the plate and pushed it away. It wasn't the first time the two adversaries played this game and Demingo didn't fear Lopez, but, in that moment, he tipped his hand, admitting he was working the Bruces against orders. Christian Lopez spread the deadly scourge of cocaine throughout and for years the snake evaded the consequences. For some reason, however, his superiors didn't want the same, but he tired of playing by their rules. He picked up the hundred-dollar bill and peered at the face of Benjamin Franklin staring back at him. He carefully placed his fingers on each end of the bill and ripped it in half. It was time to up the ante with Mrs. Bruce.

A couple of days passed before Demingo showed up, unannounced, at the Clark building. Before entering the front door, he sat in his car, with the engine running and cool air blowing in his face. He loved air conditioning, and it didn't matter what the president said about conservation in directives handed down from Washington. The peanut farmer from Georgia was on his way out and the tough talking actor seemed poised to take his spot. Demingo felt that it was pretty much the farmer's fault what was happening in Miami and quickly spreading throughout the land. Liberals, always too soft on crime, played games with these thugs, but if his father taught him anything, was the fact you had to play by thug rules to win. If he waited for people like the farmer to give him a green light to take down Lopez, old age would kill him before Lopez did. Demingo adjusted the vent and directed the air to blow directly into his face.

He grabbed a manilla envelope from his glove compartment, turned the key and started inside. As he approached the doorway, a security guard stopped him. "Mrs. Bruce isn't allowing any outside visitors in the building right now," he said pointing his crooked finger towards the parking lot. Demingo reached in his back pocket and produced his badge. "She will want to see me," he replied. The guard held up his hands and opened the door for the DEA agent.

Patty Lee grimaced noticeably as the guard led Demingo into her office. Still in the process of making it her own, she replaced the large painting of her father but left his paintings of the ocean. They soothed her, and she needed as much comfort as she could get right now. She stood in front of one of the paintings as Demingo sat down without an invitation to do so. Patty Lee turned, sighed, and took her seat behind her father's old desk.

"Why am I not surprised?" she asked. Demingo shrugged his shoulders and fanned the envelope in the air.

"Just dropped by to show you these," he said as he leaned forward, holding the envelope towards her. "I think you may like what you see..." He paused and raised an eyebrow. "Or you may not, whatever the case may be." He placed it on the edge of the desk and Patty Lee slid the envelope over to her, eying it for a second before breaking the seal and carefully removing the contents.

Inside she found a picture of several men, more than likely POWs, inside a cramped hole in the ground. The men looking up into the camera wore ragged, torn clothing and she could see through the torn garments, emaciated bones protruding from their skin. She winced and pulled a cigarette from the desk. "What the hell am I looking at?" she asked. She lit the cigarette and blew the smoke in his direction.

"Look at the man on the far right. Looks familiar, doesn't he?" Demingo asked. Patty Lee focused as best she could on the picture in her hand. It was blurry, and she envisioned whoever took the picture did so quickly. She could not for the life of her make out the man's face, but she did notice the shaggy blond hair and the shape of his head. "I suppose you're telling me this is Rof Bruce?" she asked, tossing the picture in his direction.

"Looks like him, doesn't it? Or it does from what few other pictures I've seen of him," he replied. "Perhaps, take a look at the other picture." She pulled the remaining picture from the envelope, pulling her reading glasses from her hair to the brim of her nose. She looked at the picture, focusing on it with her glasses and then without. The picture, much clearer, appeared as same blond man, but he stood alone. Even though it was clearer, the picture wasn't clear enough to be sure, and she tossed the picture on top of the other. She hoped it wasn't Rof, but the man, she admitted to herself, looked a lot like him.

"Mr. Demingo, I'll agree this man looks like Rof Bruce, but these pictures hold absolutely no proof its him. How many blond-haired young men went over there? How many didn't come home?" she demanded, waving the cigarette around in the air.

"That *is* Rof Bruce, I assure you. It was taken a little over a year ago. I'm sure in the eight or so years, his looks have changed slightly, but you can't deny the similarities," he assured her.

"You want it to be him so badly, don't you?" She paused and peered out the window, watching the breeze from the ocean whip through the palms in the parking lot. Patty Lee stood up and walked over to Demingo, her hands placed on her hips, but her voice softened. "Please don't do this to my husband. Even though these are no proof, they *will* be to him. I know how he will take it." She walked past the agent and peered into the painting again. "What do you *really* want?" she pleaded.

"You want to spare your husband pain, I understand, and I can help. Help me, Mrs. Bruce. Help me take down a criminal that preys on the weak. *He* is your enemy, not me. I know this is Rof Bruce. I have connections I've been assured of this from someone that knows." Demingo stood up, standing behind Patty Lee. "If you help me take down Christian Lopez, I'll make sure your brother-in-law comes home..." The agent paused and put his hand on her shoulder. "Or goes away for good."

Patty Lee brushed his hand from her shoulder and sneered at Demingo. "What do you think I am? Of course, I want my husband's brother home, alive." The steel returned to her voice as she spoke, and her face reddened.

"Very well, Mrs. Bruce, but I warn you, the longer you wait, the less chance he will survive," Demingo said coldly.

Patty Lee sensed his desperation and opened the door, motioning for him to leave. He returned to the desk and slid the picture back into the envelope, bowed and walked out, waving the envelope in his hand. Patty Lee said, loud enough for several of her people standing near to hear, "Don't give this to my husband." The people standing near turned their attention to her reflexively before quickly shuffling away. Patty Lee lowered her voice, "Let me talk to him."

Demingo smiled; his usual grin not showing up in this encounter until this moment. His grin betrayed his thoughts as he felt this family within his grasp. The DEA agent knew when to back off and let things simmer and he'd reached that point.

"I'll give you a couple days, Mrs. Bruce," he said, bowing his head. "I'll show myself out."

The first call Patty Lee made after Demingo's departure wasn't to her husband, but to Christian Lopez. She picked up the phone with every intention of calling her husband, but as her finger dialed, she realized it wasn't his number but that of Lopez. She didn't want to lie to Vern, and she couldn't tell him about the pictures. If Rof lived and was now held as a POW, it was best if Vern didn't know. Relief spilled over her when Lopez answered the phone in his strange, but charming accent. His pause indicated to Patty Lee his surprise.

Finally, after a few seconds, he greeted her. "Patricia, so good of you to call," he said into the receiver.

"How about a walk on the beach?" she asked. The words escaped her mouth with a tint of girlish curiosity that she didn't intend.

"This evening," was his reply and with no further words, both ended the call. Patty Lee left her office and walked onto the second floor overlook. The wind blew through her dark hair, and she leaned against the railing, turning her back to the ocean. Her husband's sanity should be the *only* reason she decided not to tell him about the pictures, but she knew it wasn't. The call to Lopez wouldn't leave her thoughts and she didn't really know what she felt. Her feelings towards the Columbian should be strictly business, however, she felt excitement when he agreed to meet her. She wheeled around, facing the ocean, and watched the waves crash onto the beach and took in the salt air. She felt like a woman again.

As the sun disappeared under the peninsula that afternoon, Christian Lopez arrived at Old Man Clark's house. Despite the number of invitations he'd received from the old man, he never made it inside the enormous home. The meetings between he and Old Man Clark were always held outside, in the open. The daughter displayed a lot of her father's mannerisms, and, in a lot of ways, Patty Lee reminded Lopez of her father. However, the old man was friendly with Lopez, but they were not friends. He hoped to change this with *Patricia,* he thought to himself and smiled. He loved hearing the name, if only inside his own head. He smoothed his dark mustache with his fingers and pressed the doorbell.

As usual, the short, stocky driver leaned on the car as Patty Lee greeted her guest. They shook hands and followed the path beyond the gate to the beach. As the breakers made their way on shore and retreated into the foam, Patty Lee stopped before the two of them reached the shore. She stood close to her companion and fought the urge to step closer.

"Christian," she said, using his first name without being prompted to do so, "I need help with something."

"Anything, *Patricia*, just name it," he responded. "We are friends, just like your father and I."

"Special Agent Demingo brought me some pictures today. Pictures I don't want my husband to see." She looked away from Lopez's dark eyes and over the blue water, "They would only cause him pain," she told him. Lopez joined her gaze over the ocean and noticed the moon starting its climb. He already knew about the pictures and their origin, but it was a secret he must keep, for now.

"Are these pictures of you?" he asked, and she blushed but didn't let it last long. Lopez's eyes widened as he realized his implications and shook his head, embarrassed. Patty lee smiled, and the two shared a laugh.

"No," she said through her smile. "They are *possibly* my husband's brother." Patty Lee moved her foot in the sand slightly, digging in her heel before continuing, "He got drafted and his plane crashed going to Vietnam, but these pictures show someone that looks like him in a POW camp, alive." The Columbian pursed his lips and gently took Patty Lee's hand.

"Hmm," he said softly. "Vietnam. I am so sorry. It is truly awful, please relay my condolences to your husband." She recoiled at Vern's mention and pulled her hand away from his.

Lopez held their eye contact, however, and said, "I understand. You don't want your husband, Vern is it, to worry about something he can do nothing about." Patty Lee's demeanor calmed. She smiled back and nodded at Lopez, feeling relieved that he sensed her motive.

"Yes, exactly," she said, more at ease, "If Vern sees them, he will become obsessed. He'll put it before everything, our son, our company, even that little bastard nephew of his." Lopez raised an eyebrow. He knew Old Man Clark's feelings towards the boy, but to hear it from Patty Lee, he shook his head. She was certainly her father's daughter.

"My friend," he said as he wrapped his arms around her, "I will do what I can." Patty Lee, at first, felt uncomfortable in the embrace, but she allowed it to continue and after a few seconds, enjoyed it and pushed her head into his shoulder. He felt the reciprocation and closed his eyes tightly.

The two strolled through the sand back to the gate. Their embrace lingered in their thoughts, but they didn't speak of it, nor did they speak of Vern or the pictures. They talked of the ocean, moon, and the starry night instead of business or Vern. Before he lowered into his seat in the back of the car, he tipped his cap and said his goodbyes again promising to do whatever he could. He told her it could take a couple of days and to be patient.

The taillights faded into the night and Patty Lee stood, unmoving beside the gate. Closing her eyes, she felt the embrace she shared with Lopez in her mind and a warmness fell over her.

Turning around, looking up to the moon that now hovered just above the water, thoughts of Vern faded.

When he returned to his ranch house on the beach, Lopez's dilemma weighed on his mind. If he went after the pictures for Patty Lee, there was a good chance blood would be spilled. If he did get the pictures and give them to her, there was little doubt in his mind that there were other copies, and, by now, they would be in military hands. The military of this country didn't want pictures such as these to get out into the open and perhaps, they would be grateful to someone making sure that didn't happen. The best bet was to get the pictures away from Rafael Demingo. He stared at the painting over the fireplace, rubbing his chin and his thoughts darkened. He knew the stupid agent, with his idiotic ideals, would try to use them on Vernon Bruce. An idealist like him didn't see future consequences, only blind devotion to a cause. He turned and summoned his driver. The Cuban had served his purpose.

Demingo worked alone, and he admitted such when Lopez interrupted his lunch a couple of days before. He would not be able to sneak up on the agent again. Lopez was sure that put him on alert and that's why he used the pictures. Unfortunately, this time if he were successful, it would take the involvement of the lovely Patricia. Each time her name found its way into his thoughts, he couldn't help but smile and he felt the intoxication each time. He intended their relationship as strictly business in the beginning, but each time he met with her, he felt a little bit more for her.

Lopez sat in the darkness, alone, and slowly rotated the wine in his glass. Holding the glass to his nose, he inhaled the rich aroma, put his lips to the edge of the glass and took a sip. He released a loud breath and thought that he would have to be even more careful with her than with the DEA agent.

He'd killed men like Demingo before and the thought of doing so again didn't bother him. He was, however, bothered by the fact that success hinged on Patricia's participation. Lopez pondered this for a moment and asked himself, *What would be so bad about it?* At present, Patricia was only ankle deep in the life he'd led for more years than he could count. She appeared to enjoy each step she took as he had not pushed very hard, and she fell, lockstep, into their partnership. Lopez took another sip and said aloud, "*Patricia,* my dear, perhaps you want to step a little deeper."

Patty Lee waited patiently for the pre-flight checks to end as she pushed her head back into the cushion. She and Vern spoke very quickly on the phone, and he agreed to take point on the deal in Biloxi. Infatuated with the situation in West Palm, she didn't care that he agreed so quickly.

She mentioned nothing of Demingo, Lopez, or Rof in their conversation. Trouble grew by the day, but, to some degree, she enjoyed the excitement it brought. Special agents and Colombian smugglers seemed right out of a James Bond movie. She felt the surge of adrenaline, but it waned quickly as Casey wiggled in his sleep in the seat beside her.

Patty Lee thought about the kind of mother she was to her son. He tagged along when she went down to the Atlantic Coast, and as a result, he was out of school a lot. She vowed to do better with her son, but Cliff was Vern's baggage. As she peered from the window, she thought back to the Sunday they'd spent on the beach, as a family. She enjoyed the day and the excitement she felt was quickly replaced with feelings of confusion. She felt confused a lot these last few weeks. She closed her eyes and thought to herself, *Slow down Patty Lee.*

Before they began their taxi to the runway, the pilot stepped through the narrow cockpit door. Patty Lee instantly thought that something was wrong with the plane but before she could ask a question, the pilot informed her that a call waited for her in the hangar. The tower radioed him that Mrs. Bruce had an emergency call and to abort takeoff. She hurried out the door and, in a run, made her way into the hangar.

"Yes, what is it?" she nearly yelled into the phone.

"Ahh, *Patricia*, so glad I got you before you took off," Lopez calmly said from the other end.

"Christian, I mean, Mr. Lopez, what in the hell?" she asked.

Lopez, his voice still calm, responded, "I need you to do *me* a favor so I might perform the one you asked for."

Chapter 23

Vern didn't fly to Biloxi this time. He drove. Like the old drives to and from college, these long distances helped him think. He was going there to check on the hotel construction down on the Biloxi Strip. Vern smiled as he thought about the hotels. They were just the start. Casinos floating on giant barges was phase two of the plans and he'd already started counting the money.

Patty Lee called him before he left on his road trip. She met Demingo down in West Palm and was flying home so they could meet face to face. His wife wouldn't tell him on the phone what she found out so this trip to Biloxi needed to be very quick. The smile left his face when he thought about the *other* reason he was making the trip. He needed to talk with Burt Williams once again.

To Vern's surprise, his meeting with Burt didn't happen at the seedy bar on the strip. This time Burt insisted on meeting at a fast-food joint just outside Biloxi in the working-class town of Gulfport. As he drove through the small coastal town, he felt like he'd arrived in a different country. Gone were the strip clubs and beer joints of the Biloxi Strip and replaced with business more in line with his beloved Panama City. He felt more at home and relaxed, but that was probably why Burt wanted to meet here, so that Vern would feel more at ease.

When he parked his car, he saw Burt through the window. He occupied a booth near the window. Walking towards the booth, he noticed something different about Burt. He couldn't quite place it, but it seemed Burt's expression wasn't the same as at the bar. Vern stopped, trying to figure out what the difference was. He stood for a few seconds before it dawned on him. Burt seemed happy. Not the mischievous kind of happiness he put forth in their brief meetings before, but his smile seemed genuine. Vern, already thrown off by the location of the meeting, closed his eyes and gathered himself before sitting down.

Burt wasted no time in starting the conversation. "I like it here, especially early in the morning," he said, still staring out the window. "I love to see happy kids." Vern felt a chill run down his spine. Instantly his mind flashed to Cliff and Burt's ominous words about cashing in favors.

Vern, trying to hide any emotion showing on his face and in his demeanor, replied, "This isn't about Cliff. Let's keep it business this time if you don't mind." Burt finally turned his gaze from the playground and faced Vern.

The genuine happiness disappeared in an instant and the mischievous gangster Vern knew previously returned. "We are family, Vern, all of us. One big...happy...family." Burt's eyes locked into Vern's as he tossed the verbal daggers, and he eased a cigar into the corner of his mouth.

"Well, what can I do for you, *brother,* on this fine Mississippi morning?" he asked Vern.

"I need more info on Demingo," Vern replied as turned his attention to the playground and away from Burt's dark, piercing eyes.

"I told you to stay away from him," he scolded Vern. "Nothing but bad news." He shook his head in disgust and moved the cigar to the other side of his grinning mouth.

"I didn't want to meet him again, but he ambushed me at the airport, told me about..." He paused as a vision of his brother entered his mind. "...about some pictures that proved Rof was, or at least had been, alive in a camp over there."

Burt pursed his lips and leaned back in the booth and said, "So ol' Rof could be alive." He put his hand on Vern's jaw and pushed his face back into eye contact. "How'd *our* boy take the news his daddy might be alive?"

Vern pushed Burt's hand away and stood up to leave. "I knew this was a damned mistake."

Burt, ignoring Vern pushing his hand away, motioned for Vern to sit down, "Little early in the morning to get upset," Burt told him, grinning so wide the cigar hung precariously from his mouth. Vern, once again, gathered his emotions and eased back into the seat.

"From what I hear, you ain't the only *Bruce* Demingo's been talking to," Burt volunteered. "Heard he met with your pretty wife down in West Palm." Vern didn't say anything but wondered to himself how in the world Burt Williams knew about Patty Lee's meeting with the DEA agent. He decided to deny knowing anything about it and hated that Burt was always one step ahead.

"What are you talking about?" he asked Burt, "I don't know anything about that." Vern tried to put on his best poker face, but Burt was an expert at realizing deception. You don't get this far in the Dixie Mafia without knowing how to spot a liar.

Burt didn't hesitate. "You're a bad liar, *Vern,*" he said, laughing as he spoke. "Maybe you shouldn't try anymore." He slapped the table, and the jolt made Vern jump slightly. Burt placed the cigar between two of his thick fingers and motioned for Vern to lean in towards him. "You know how I know you're lying? That's because I tell nothing but the truth, my friend. When you are always truthful, you know when someone else isn't. Now...let's cut the bullshit. You know they met. What happened?"

Vern, out of his comfort zone, tried to limit what he told the gangster. "I know they met, but honestly I have no clue what they talked about," he said, halfway telling the truth.

Burt nodded and plopped the cigar back into his mouth, leaning back into his chair, "More like it," he replied, his grin widening. "You see, Vernon, we're family. Let's be honest like a family should." The gangster paused, gleefully watching Vern's face redden before continuing and anticipating observing his reaction to what he told him next.

"What about her meeting with a guy named Christian Lopez? You know anything about that?" he asked Vern, trying to keep a poker face. Burt couldn't hide his smile as he watched Vern squirm in his seat. He wondered if Vern saw the slight shaking of his head when he realized, by his reaction, the fool had no idea who Christian Lopez was.

"Who is Christian Lopez? She hasn't mentioned anyone by that name," he responded. This time he knew Vern saw him shake his head as his disappointment in him grew. *What a damned fool*, Burt thought to himself.

Burt sat, shaking his head and chewing his cigar. "Only a Colombian drug smuggler operating in South Florida. From what I hear, he's met with your wife a couple of times." Burt's sly grin erupted into a toothy smile. "Even took a couple walks on the beach, so I hear." Vern's nostrils flared and he balled his fist tightly. Burt noticed and shook his finger at Vern. Taking a deep breath, Vern relaxed, if only slightly,

"And just how would you know that?" he asked through clenched teeth. Burt's whole body shook as he started laughing.

"Don't you come to *me* for information? This is information I'd want to know if my wife were meeting with a guy like that," Burt responded, raising an eyebrow.

Vern's mind raced and he found it difficult to concentrate on why he initially wanted to meet with Burt. He thought maybe Burt was lying, but what would he gain lying about something like this? But his mind couldn't fathom this was the truth. He took a deep breath and mustered all his courage.

"You're lying, Williams," Vern said in his toughest voice, but Burt only smiled.

Burt didn't get upset at that; he was expecting that kind of reaction. Every man he ever knew that got bad information about his wife, information in which he had no clue, always reacted in the same way. Fake toughness. It was like a dog getting kicked. Men's reactions were the exact same as a dog, show their teeth, or tuck their tail covering their genitals. Once again, he shook his head. Burt knew from Vern's reaction; he just tucked his tail. Gathering all the information he needed about Vernon Bruce, he said, "Well, ask her. See what she says." Burt looked around, making sure nobody was close enough to hear. "That little bit of info was free. If you want me to find out about these pictures, it will cost. Upfront."

"Name your price," Vern told him. "I'll pay you whatever you want. I have to know."

"I ain't wanting money, *Uncle* Vern," he responded. "I want Susie to see Cliff...beforehand."

Vern shook his head furiously and stood up to leave but Burt grabbed him by the arm. He tugged him back down into the seat. "All I want, and all she wants, is for him to know her. That's it, Vern. Ain't too much to ask."

The hair stood on the back of his neck as he peered into the dark eyes of Burt Williams. He wanted to fight, he wanted to tell him to go to hell and walk out but he couldn't do that. A defeated expression took over Vern's face. This was the only man that could help him.

Burt leaned in once more. "She brought him to you in faith."

Vern sighed. Burt was right. As she promised, she didn't interfere with Cliff in all these years. "What are we talking about, Mr. Williams?" Vern asked.

Burt stood up and motioned towards the playground. "Let's talk."

After the meeting, Vern stopped at the first payphone he saw and called the office. He expected to talk to Patty Lee and let her know that he would be back in Panama City in a few hours. Instead, his secretary told him that Patty Lee called from West Palm. Something came up down there and she was going to be delayed a couple of days. He slammed the phone down and kicked at a pebble. He needed to talk to his wife now, not later, so he dialed the number to her father's house. Letting it ring for a couple minutes, he once again slammed the phone down in frustration. Shaking his head, he tried to reach her at the Clark Building, but the secretary there said she hadn't been in the office today and she hadn't called in. Worry enveloped his mind, and he couldn't get the words "Colombian drug smuggler" out of his thoughts. He stood outside the little open phone booth and once again picked up the receiver. He called his pilot and instructed him to get the plane ready to fly to West Palm in a few hours.

As Vern ticked off the miles on the way back to Florida, he wished he would've just flown to begin with. He couldn't stop thinking about everything that was going so wrong in his life right now. He couldn't believe how his small, quiet, life in the Florida Panhandle turned so chaotic, so quickly. As the stunted, scrubby oak trees and long lanky pines whizzed by, his mind alternated visions of his brother, his boys, and his wife.

He thought back to the days of his youth, playing with Rof on the beach. The two brothers often hitchhiked down to the coast and spent countless days on the beach. He wished that for his boys. His thoughts turned to Cliff and what lay ahead for the young boy. Even though he was an innocent bystander in all of this, his life was about to be turned upside down.

Vern rolled down the window and let the wind from the road fill the car as he thought about the questions Cliff asked on the beach. Questions to which he would soon find answers. On the one hand, he felt joy in Cliff's opportunity to know his mother, but there was always the specter of Burt Williams. He leaned over, opened the glove compartment and pulled out the small bottle of whiskey. He carefully opened the bottle and took a sip, afterwards returning it to its hiding place. He laughed aloud as he saw Patty Lee's disapproving face slide into his mind. She loved her cigarettes and wine but looked at Vern's sip of whiskey every now again as immoral.

He gnashed his teeth when he thought of his wife. He wondered how he should handle asking her about this Lopez character, if he even existed. Trust was something Vern didn't hand out easily these days and Burt Williams certainly hadn't earned it. As the miles passed, Vern's thoughts did not, and he found his hand slipping back into the glove compartment every few miles.

It didn't take Burt long to call on his old buddy RB. He knew Old Man Clark was in business with some very dangerous people towards the end of his life. He didn't know a whole lot about the old man as their business was confined to Cliff, but if his friends loved one thing more than breaking the law, it was gossip. He needed RB to clarify what was real and what was just talk. He knew RB kept his ear to the ground all over the Gulf Coast and sometimes beyond. Living near and dealing with the Dixie Mafia, you pretty much had to, even somewhat strait-laced cops.

Burt asked his old friend to meet him on the pier across the bridge in Ocean Springs. RB agreed, not only because he didn't want to be seen in Biloxi with Burt, but it'd give him an excuse to bring a fishing reel. When Burt walked up, RB already had his line in the water.

"Christian Lopez?" RB asked rhetorically. "Cold-blooded killer. Only thing you need to know," RB told his friend. "You messing with Demingo and now Christian Lopez? You gotta a death wish?" RB asked, not taking his eyes from the water.

"I ain't messing with anybody, buddy. I just need to know for someone else," he responded, grinning and holding his hands up. "You know me."

"I know you've brought up two people to me that I wouldn't mess with, and you know *me*," RB warned him. He took his eyes from the water for the first time and looked at Burt. He saw the concern in RB's eyes. "Let me tell you a story about Christian Lopez. Before he was running drugs down in Florida, he was running the show in South America. Everywhere. One local cop thought he was going to take him down. Even arrested him at one point. All the dude did was smile the entire time he was in the guy's jail, not saying a word. While this cop thought he had him caught, his men were mutilating his wife and kids. I mean his kids!" RB put his hand on Burt's shoulder and said slowly, "Burt, he cut them up into pieces." RB looked at a young family enjoying their pier. "His damned kids," he repeated. "He chopped them up and had his men bring the pieces of his family to the jail. Didn't kill the cop, let him live to tell people what happens when you cross Christian Lopez."

Burt's face turned a ghostly white and he put his hand on his forehead. "This guy that I'm asking for, he damn sure ain't ready for this. Hell, he ain't even ready for *Biloxi*."

"Well," RB responded, "you better get him out of it."

"Ain't really him in it with Lopez. It's his wife."

"Won't be long before, well…" RB paused and raised an eyebrow. "From what I've heard Lopez is a ladies' man. If you follow me." RB chuckled slightly when he said it, but quickly turned serious. "You got some folks in some deep shit."

Burt heard all he needed to hear. He thanked RB and the two parted ways. There had to be some kind of way he could use all of this to his advantage. He knew what he wanted. He had been thinking about it for some time. How to get to that point was something he knew he had to figure out. *Burt Williams always comes out on the best end of everything and this time*, he told himself, *would be no different.*

As he sat in his car, the windows rolled up and the air conditioning blowing full speed, he thought about what angle he needed to play with this. Vern and his wife wouldn't last in all this. Maybe his wife could, hell, at least she knew a little about underhand dealings, but Vern was like a lost sheep amongst a pack of wolves.

Burt pulled out a cigar and cracked his window. He lit this cigar and exhaled a big puff of smoke. There were a couple of guys in New Orleans that owed him a big favor and as he dangled the lit cigar from his mouth, decided it was time to cash it in.

First, though, he needed to beat Vern to South Florida. He knew that there were daily flights to Miami out of Mobile and looking at his watch, figured he could make the last one if he hurried. He stopped at a *connected* hotel and called Susie. Burt told her he was going out of town for a few days. She'd learned not to ask questions early on in their relationship, so she just told him she loved him and to be careful. He did volunteer that he was headed to Miami, though, and if everything went well, she might make the next trip with him to Florida, saying something about "business opportunities."

While Burt made plans in Mississippi, Vern made good time getting to the airport and on his way to South Florida himself. He left word with Patty Lee's secretary that he was on his way, so when he arrived, he felt slightly disappointed his wife wasn't there to greet him. He stopped off at her office and not finding her there, unsuccessfully tried to call her at the house once again. It seemed as though she'd fallen off the face of the earth. He didn't know where to look nor who to ask. The only thing he could do was wait at the Clark house and hope she would show up.

As night fell, he started to really worry. Hopefully, he wished to himself, it was only his imagination running wild. He'd heard a lot of things in the past few days and weeks, and he feared for his wife. Surely, she would've told him if she was in danger. Hell, Casey had been with her every day lately. She even took him out of school to come down here. Their trust had been strained lately, but it had not been broken. He trusted Patty Lee and knew that she would do nothing to endanger herself or her family. Especially her child, or at least he hoped.

When he saw the taxi pull up to the house that evening, he wiped the bead of sweat from his brow and finally took a deep breath. His wife and son climbed out of the back seat, and he finally knew for sure they were alive and well. He met them at the door and when he opened it, Patty Lee took a step back, surprised to see her husband standing there. Casey ran up to his father and hugged his leg.

"Hey sport," Vern said as he lifted Casey into the air. He reached with his free hand as he let his son dangle on his hip to his wife and hugged her around the neck.

"You don't know how I've missed y'all," he said as he let them both go.

Casey peeked around his parents, scanning the house and asked, "Where's Cliff?"

Vern told the child that Cliff stayed in Panama City with a friend. He told them he left in a hurry, wanting to get down to see them and that he didn't want to take Cliff out of school. He didn't mean to look at his wife as he said this, but she didn't seem to notice the veiled barb. Vern kissed his wife on the cheek, but she didn't return the gesture and seemed to not want to look at him. Vern shrugged it off.

"Oh," Casey responded dejectedly.

"When did you get here?" Patty Lee finally gathered herself and asked.

"About an hour ago. Where y'all been? I've been trying to call you all day," Vern asked.

Patty Lee looked away and replied, "I've been out meeting with some people about business. Been mostly lunches and drinks. I did find a school nearby that will let Cliff sit in from time to time. Costs a lot, but it's worth it." Vern motioned for them to go on inside and Casey found some toys on the living room floor as his mother and father sat down. "We need to talk, Patty Lee,"

Vern said, "but it might be better to do it outside." He nodded towards Casey as he spoke.

"Sure," she responded, "about what?"

Vern moved in so he could whisper into her ear, and Patty Lee's heart fell into her stomach as he said, "Christian Lopez."

Chapter 24

Rafael Demingo hung up the phone and sat there, motionless, for a few seconds. The call was a surprise, and he needed a few minutes to digest what he heard. He pulled at the stubble sprouting from his chin and wondered if it was too good to be true. The fear in Patty Lee Bruce's voice sounded real and in his line of work, he often heard voices that weren't. The only thing giving him pause was how quickly she decided to work with him. Most times it took months, if not years to turn someone, yet with this woman, it only took a gentle prod.

He stood up and flipped the light switch. The drive from Miami to West Palm would give him time to think. In these moments, he wished he still had a partner, but with the way the last partnership ended, he vowed a long time ago to always work alone. "Fuck it," he said aloud to no one, lit a cigarette, and slammed the door.

The drive to West Palm didn't take nearly as long as he thought it would. In a rare instance the interstate was nearly clear of traffic and Demingo arrived early enough to scout the area. He parked up the road from the harbor and hid his car amongst the scrubby bushes as best he could. One last check of his weapon and he walked the short distance to the entrance. He traversed the hill leading from the road and as he did, scanned the darkness for anything out of place, but saw nothing unusual.

The night felt strange, however. Already protected by a couple of long jetties, and with the air completely still, the water was more akin to a fishing pond than a part of the Atlantic Ocean. The boats, tied up along the long rows of docks, were motionless as if they were on land rather than water. Tonight, it was deadly calm and even the fish that lived in the waters around the docks seemed to go to sleep as Demingo saw no ripples indicating their presence. There was absolutely no movement anywhere.

He carefully made his way past the small supply shack, looking in each window, and towards the row of boats. He swept his eyes over each one and eased his hand from his weapon and leaned against the railing at the edge of the water. Demingo turned his back to the water and a feeling of hope enveloped him. Perhaps this time, Christian Lopez would face true justice.

A car stopped at the end of the gravel path leading to the main road and Demingo tried to focus, but the headlights beamed towards him, and he couldn't make out what kind of car, but he thought it resembled the old man's Monte Carlo. He eased his hand around his back until he felt the steel of his revolver, but as he reached his fingers around the handle, he felt a cold hand on his shoulder. He didn't need to turn around. Demingo closed his eyes and cursed his stupidity.

Realizing Lopez snuck up from his rear, Demingo wished he would've paid more attention to the boats, but it was too late. He could feel Lopez's breath on his shoulder and the drug smuggler leaned in and spoke in his ear.

"Let's just put that gun you have in your hand there, well, just toss it into the water my old friend," Lopez said, his voice oddly calming.

"I see your charms worked. Got to her, didn't you?" Demingo asked him as he felt the cold end of Lopez's gun on the small of his back.

"I guess the name on the boat there, says it all," he replied as he released his shoulder and pointed to a boat on his right side, about halfway down the dock's middle walkway. *Daddy's Girl* written across the fishing boats stern. Demingo slowly turned to face Lopez and the two, nose to nose, locked eyes. Lopez smiled and took a step back. "You know how these American women are all over *my* kind of accent." He tried to suppress his glee, but his smile widened, and a quiet laugh escaped his lips.

The DEA agent shook his head and raised an eyebrow. "What do you want, Lopez? You and I both know the rules."

Lopez's smile disappeared, and he nodded in agreement. "Yes, yes my friend, I know the rules, but you forget how the game is played," he coldly replied. His eyes widened, and he tilted the gun in his hand. Demingo looked to the stars and slowly began to shake his head. He looked back at Lopez and for a moment, he thought he saw a sadness in the Colombian's face as he said, "My friend, I was truly shocked when I got the…how do the American's so colorfully put it? Ahh, the *green light*."

Demingo spit into the water, watched the ripples spread through the calm water for a second before responding without looking up, "You don't care who you hurt, you're a damned monster."

Lopez's demeanor turned cold and his face like stone when he said, "Not a monster, Rafael, a businessman."

Demingo once again closed his eyes and slowly looked back at his adversary. He felt adrenaline surge throughout his body, yet he couldn't move. His muscles tensed and he wanted to run, but for some reason, his legs became as though they were encased in concrete. He even glanced at his feet, but nothing held him in place but fear. In that moment, knowing that it may be his last, he tried the one tactic he never thought himself capable of, but death's door grew near.

"Well, *businessman*, I guess she sent you after those pictures," Demingo said, his voice calm. "Let me go, I tell you where they are, and we both live to fight another day."

Lopez's laughter began small but soon echoed off the motionless water and nearby vessels. "I already have them, Rafael. I had them before *she* called you. I have *always* had them."

The realization that he had been set up from the very start began to ring home in his mind and his thoughts filled with the smiling image of his old partner and there was a smile on his face. His thoughts began to race, grasping the truth that the information, the photos, they were all just bait. Bait that brought him to this very moment, bargaining for his life. Demingo straightened himself, took a step and came face to face with Lopez. "You better not tell the bastard I tried to bargain," he said, his voice emitting no emotion, the same as his face.

Lopez, the veiled sadness returning, said as he raised his weapon, "I wouldn't give the fucking gringo the satisfaction."

Before the bullet ripped through his head and ended his thoughts, the last one entering his mind was that there was no difference between Castro's Cuba and this place. It all ended the same. He wished he could tell his father.

Lopez stood over Demingo's lifeless body for a moment before motioning for his driver. As he waited for him to make his way down the gravel drive, he leaned on the railing, looked towards the heavens, and said a quick prayer for the dead. He wasn't a monster, as the DEA agent said, Lopez lied to himself once more as he turned his attention to the task at hand.

They picked up Demingo's limp body and very carefully wrapped his head in a towel. He had fallen perfectly, his head hanging over the seawall and his blood spilled into the bay where the salty water told no one of its secrets. After they secured his body and made sure no trail was left, they boarded the *Daddy's Girl* and made their way out the harbor.

The night was dark, as there was no moon, and the stars seemed brighter in the darkness. Lopez admired them as the craft made its way through the jetties and into open water. Far enough offshore, they could barely see lights shimmering on the shoreline and Lopez tapped the driver on the shoulder. He nodded and eased the throttle to neutral and turned the key. They tied concrete blocks, which they had stashed on the boat before Demingo's arrival and pushed him over. They both leaned over to watch the body sink into the dark blue water.

As the body sank out of sight, and the two men were just about to lean back over the railing, Lopez eased his small revolver from his waist and silently as he could, cocked it. With one motion he placed the gun to his driver's head and with a bang that faded into the night, the driver arced over the side of the boat. As he went limp, Lopez pushed him over the side and let the weapon sink behind him.

There could never be a witness tying him to his deeds and if he lived, the driver's knowledge lived with him. Lopez didn't like loose ends as they always tended to unravel. It also provided a bit of insurance. If anything were found, the blame would befall some nameless Brazilian. Nobody in the states knew him or more importantly knew his face. He'd hired him for those explicit reasons and now his duty fulfilled may one day serve another purpose.

Lopez reached over and started the boat. The wind had picked up and now the boat rolled over gently rolling waves as he made his way towards the harbor. Patrica was the only person that knew the driver's face, but he wasn't worried about her. Her sweet smile penetrated his thoughts, and he thought it would be a shame to kill her. He shoved those thoughts to the back of her mind. Tonight proved she was her father's daughter. He grimaced as the boat lurched through another wave and he thought about hiring another driver.

    Patty Lee spent most of the next day avoiding her husband. He tried to talk with her early that morning, but she insisted she needed to run to the office, and she'd be right back. Vern sent the Clark jet to Panama City where it picked up Cliff and by that afternoon, both boys played on the beach together. Vern waited patiently, enjoying the sun, but a short trip to the office turned into an all-day affair.

    It was fairly late when Vern finally sat down with Patty Lee. Cliff flew in that afternoon to reunite with his family. Cliff and Casey, exhausted from a long day on the beach, went to bed early and Vern sipped a small amount of bourbon whiskey as his wife slid through the glass door. He sensed disappointment in her glance as he put the glass to his lips, but his patience depleted, he didn't care.

    "Christian Lopez," he said, sloshing the remaining liquor around in his glass. The first sliver of a new moon produced a glimmer over the water and only a slight ripple appeared every now and again. Patty Lee gazed at the sliced moon and held her breath. Her life drifted towards a pack of lies, but she couldn't tell her husband the truth about Lopez. She finally let the breath go and sat down next to Vern, placing her hand on top of his.

    "He is a business associate of my father's, Vern. I just met him a couple weeks ago. I didn't see the need to tell you about him." She didn't exactly lie, but her next words danced around the truth. "Coffee. He's a Colombian coffee dealer. My dad helped him bring in some products without going through the proper channels. Wasn't exactly on the up and up, but he made pretty good money with it." Patty Lee could taste the lies as they escaped her mouth.

Vern rolled his eyes. "Do you know how ridiculous that sounds, Patty Lee? Coffee? You aren't stupid," Vern shot back and shrugged his shoulders. "Or maybe you are."

Patty Lee absorbed the insult and responded with steel in her voice, "No, Vern, I'm not stupid. I know my father did business with some *questionable* people. That's a fact. This guy is just interested in continuing business as usual. I'll really have little to do with it and we will make a lot of money." She paused and took her hand from her husband's. "You said before we were married you wanted money, respect, power. Well, Vern, this is how you do that, *honey*. You can't be a small-time Panhandle real estate agent if you want more."

Vern hung his head, stood up, walked to the edge of the railing and said, "I did, but I don't know anymore, Patty Lee. I hate it down here. This isn't my home, it's yours." Vern tossed the drops of whiskey in his glass over the edge. "Let's just sell all this," he said motioning to the house. "Let's just live our life in little old PC. We're on our way to royalty up there."

Patty Lee crossed her legs and shook her head. "Queen of the rednecks? Is that how you see me?" She motioned around, mimicking Vern. "I'm more than that."

Vern turned back to the ocean and the salty breeze floated past his nostrils. "This place reeks of your father's ghost."

"Fuck you, Vern," she replied.

Vern took a few steps and stood over her, "Your father risked your life, Patty Lee, with these people. Do you realize that? Now you are going to risk ours? Our boys?" When Vern mentioned the boys, Patty Lee snorted under her breath and Vern grabbed her arm, "You hate Cliff, I know that, but risking Casey's life?" Vern tightened his grip. "No. Fuck you, Patty Lee."

Patty Lee leaped to her feet, grabbing Vern by the shoulder and pushed him backwards. Vern caught himself on the railing and she put her slender finger in his face. "Now you look here," she said with tears in her eyes. "I don't love him, but I feel sorry for the boy. Dead father and a junkie, whore mother. He's not my son and there is no blood there, but for you, and for Casey, I'll tolerate him, and I'll pity him," Patty Lee said coldly. She left Vern, stunned, leaning on the railing. Still holding his glass, he rolled it in his hand and wished he had the few drops back he'd tossed into the sand.

They didn't speak again that night, sleeping in separate rooms. Patty Lee to her father's old room and Vern to a guest room beside the boys. Thoughts of the other and their shared words haunted both. They loved each other, but the ties binding them faded slowly and in their own way frightened them both.

Vern's thoughts focused on the past. Idealists in college when they met, both wanted to change the world. Vern thought about how he strayed from that path as his quest for money and power escalated. But now, he realized it brought him nothing but pain. As he tried in vain to go to sleep, he thought about the night they'd met once again. In his quest to protest the war, Vern almost lost his life. It was her face that saved him. Lying there, his head gushing blood, he wanted to die, but her soft hands held him and the steel in her voice that saved him from the trooper's boot. By God, he thought, she saved me, but she also may be the cause of my death.

Patty Lee also tossed and turned in her father's old bed that night. She missed him so much and thought about him often, yearning for his wisdom. She was proud to walk in his footsteps, even if Vern didn't follow. Vern was the one that distracted her from that path. He changed her, but blood is blood, and they grew so different now. The distance between their paths widened with each step. She sat on the edge of the bed and reached for her pack of cigarettes.

Chapter 25

After the argument and sleeping in separate rooms, Vern arose early, woke the boys up, and took one of Old Man Clark's smaller boats, enjoying a day out on the water. He loved the smell of the ocean. After you made it out a few miles, all oceans smelled the same and if he didn't know any better, he thought how much it seemed like the Gulf.

He laughed as Cliff and Casey argued over which rod and reel each would use. The two boys, arguing back and forth, reminded him of his childhood and the arguments he used to have with Rof over the same type of things. Back then, he wondered why Pops didn't intervene but now, he understood. Pops enjoyed the limited time he had with his boys and Vern was determined to enjoy today. He slowly helped each to put their lines in the water and then he sat in the sun, waiting for one of them to get a bite.

They didn't have a boat like this back when he and Rof were growing up. Their boat was half the size, but they ventured beyond sight of the coastline when they went out. Pops knew where the fish were and most times they came back with a cooler full of snapper, grouper, or whatever was biting. Pops was a heck of a sailor as it just came naturally to him. He told the brothers when they were young that he had served on a submarine in World War Two, but he never really elaborated on it. Pops didn't become emotional much, but if he tried talking about that, he did. Sometimes they pressed him for more information but all he would say was, "One day," but the day never came.

The sun beamed high, and the temperature began to warm. What was a cool morning turned into a ridiculously sweltering day and Vern coated his boys in sunscreen so thick, they looked like ghosts. The boys turned their attention from fishing and began to play in the sunscreen. With no fish in the boat and the boys playing more than fishing, he decided to call it a day.

The smiles on their faces and the sound of their laughter showed the ride back was their favorite part of the day. A storm brewed above the ocean behind them. Lightning streaked across the sky and wind blew from the clouds. In turn, the waves picked up and the small craft bounced high as it crested each one and flopped to the other side. Vern knew he had to be careful, and he was kind of weary, but to Cliff and Casey, it was a ride at the fair and they saw no danger. They sat on the bow and yelled out with joy after each encounter with a wave.

Despite the storm chasing them, they made it into the harbor easy enough and tied up the boat in its usual spot. Vern made sure to tie it up more securely than normal and took his time. As soon as the job was finished, the boys jumped up on the dock and ran towards the supply shack that also doubled as a small store for some refreshment. Vern was just about to follow them when he saw something from the corner of his eye. A small, square object squeezed between the hull of the boat and a bait box right up against the hull. He walked over, reached down and saw it was a wallet. He figured it had been left by one of the fishermen who often rented the *Daddy's Girl,* or it might even be Kennedy's, the often time skipper that ran the boat. He opened it and the license had a picture of a dark man with piercing eyes. He was not smiling, and Vern thought that was odd. It looked more like a mug shot than a driver's license photo. "Miguel Jose Chatom" was the name on the card. "Chatom" Vern thought, strange damn name for a Hispanic. Lightning flashed nearby and thunder exploded nearly at the same time. It was close and Vern stuffed the wallet into his pocket and ran to catch up with the boys. He would call Kennedy and run it by him sometime before he left. Another flash and Vern hustled the boys inside, forgetting about the wallet.

After Vern left with the boys that morning, Patty Lee hoped for a normal morning at the office. That hope shattered when she pulled into her parking spot and Christian Lopez leaned next to the building's door. She put out the cigarette and blew the smoke away with a long sigh. This is not what she needed this morning. Seagulls flapped above her head and begged for a crumb as she walked towards her early morning visitor. Right now, she wished she was one of them.

"Good morning, Patricia," Lopez greeted her, stepped aside. "Hope all is well."

Patty Lee tried to sound halfway friendly as she invited him inside the building. She led him into her office and glanced to where the painting of her father once hung. Each time she looked in that direction, she regretted her decision, but this morning, as she led him in, she told herself to start thinking of this place as hers, not her father's. She didn't sit in her chair behind the antique wooden desk but in one of the two chairs on the other side of the desk. Lopez claimed the other. In his hand he patted a large manilla envelope against his leg.

With a smile, Lopez held the envelope up in the air for a second and then placed it on the desk. "The pictures," he said calmly, as if it were just a picture of a sunset contained within. Patty Lee didn't move, she couldn't. She tried to breathe, but that became difficult as well. Lopez noticed her hesitation and motioned towards the envelope. "Please," he said. Patty Lee turned her eyes to Lopez and his dark eyes and wide smile seemed to put her at ease. She gathered herself enough to speak.

"I take it you were successful," she said sheepishly. Lopez widened his arms and then clasped his hands together.

"Yes, very much so," he said as he looked through the window making sure they were alone before leaning closer and whispering, "I also convinced Demingo to give up his fantasy. Go home. Leave you alone, my dear." Lopez smiled as he spoke. He reached out, placing one hand on top of Patty Lee's and with the other, picked up the envelope. "What will you do with them, Patricia? We can destroy them right now if you wish." Patty Lee didn't remove her hand. Instead, she grasped his hand and held it for what seemed an eternity before she spoke.

She held up her hand. "I don't want to see them again. I want them gone. Vern can't know about any of this..." She hesitated "And..." she said looking him in the eyes while their hands were still entwined, "he asked about you. I don't know how he found out, but he knows."

Lopez's smile widened, and he said very softly, "It was inevitable, my dear Patricia. Your husband is caught up in this just as much as anyone else. I have it on pretty good authority he has talked with someone in Biloxi, *Mississippi*, I love saying *Mississippi*, about you and your business."

"Vern is such a damned idiot. He's probably been talking to that Burt Williams. He's married to his nephew's mother. Came by to see him during the campaign. He's a shady son of a bitch," she said. "What does he know?"

Lopez squeezed her hand, delighted she wanted to know more. Patty Lee didn't hesitate when she found out he was investigating *her* business. She was shrewd, just like her father. *Business first*, he thought. As he held her hand and looked into her eyes, he realized for the first time he loved this woman. She wasn't just another mark, a pawn in the game. He had fallen for her. This was unfamiliar territory for Lopez. It wasn't his style to fall for someone he was manipulating. He was going to have to be careful. As his father told him as a young man, working on that cattle ranch in the Colombian mountains, women kill. Looking at Patty Lee, he knew what his father meant.

Chapter 26

Burt tried to fold the map, failed, and threw it in the empty seat next to him. He whistled when he pulled up to the front of Old Man Clark's house. The air was hot, but a cool breeze blew through the palm trees as rang the doorbell. Burt spread his arms wide when Vern slowly opened the door, a cigar dangling from his lips.

Vern, not sure what to say, stood motionless for a few seconds, then looked Burt up and down. He noticed Burt wasn't wearing his customary jeans and white shirt, unbuttoned at the top with a V-neck undershirt. Vern couldn't help but shake his head as he studied the figure standing before him. The gangster wore a Hawaiian style shirt, shorts, and, when he glanced at his glowing feet, Vern chuckled to himself when he saw sandals replaced the cowboy boots. If he didn't know that round face, he would've mistaken him for an average tourist.

Burt wiggled his toes and proudly held up one foot, slightly, as he said, "Morning, Vern. Heard you wanted to see me and well, I was in the neighborhood." Vern's amusement dissipated, and he slowly looked back into the house, making sure the boys hadn't followed him to the door.

"What in the hell are you doing here, Williams?" he asked, shock taking over his expression.

"I thought you could tell me, buddy," he responded. "I'm on vacation."

Vern doubted that Burt Williams was *just* on vacation and *happened* to be in the neighborhood. "Sure," Vern said trying not to sound overly sarcastic. Vern did need the oddly dressed figures' help, but the surprise of his presence in the doorway wouldn't go away.

Burt grinned and spit the cigar into a bush. "Let's talk. But first, friend, you gotta invite me in." Vern hesitated but opened the door wide enough for Burt to walk past him. "Let's go out on the deck," he told him. Burt admired the home as he walked. "Nice place," he said. "Your wife's father had some kind of style."

Vern's ears pricked and his eyebrow raised in confusion. "You knew him?"

Burt backtracked his admiration for the old guy. Vern didn't need to know about his past with Old Man Clark. "Read about him in the papers a little bit," Burt said, and he looked back at Vern with a half-cocked grin. "And he was pretty well known in the circles."

Vern pointed to the glass doors and Burt looked around one more time and just said, "Damn." Vern laughed a little to himself and thought, *That old man would have no association with such a redneck wannabe gangster.* Once on the deck, Burt admired the view. He stood there, his flower-covered shirt blowing in the breeze, slightly exposing his oversized belly.

"You folks sure know how to live," Burt said finally and looked at Vern, the half-grin still adorning his face, "and *who* to get hitched to." Vern's expression darkened, and Burt's grin spread across the whole of his face.

"I'll remind you, Mr. Williams, I made my *own* money," Vern responded.

"You made money, but this *is* money," Burt snickered as he spoke. Burt allowed his large frame to fall into a nearby chair and motioned for Vern to take the one next to him. As Vern stewed, Burt closed his eyes and held up his chin, basking in the bright Florida sun. He didn't change postures as he said, "Anyway, let's talk business. Vern, remember you called me." He lowered his chin and opened his eyes, squinting. He pulled a pair of horn-rimmed sunglasses from his shirt pocket and slid them on, looked at Vern, and asked as a father looking after a lost child, "What have you gotten yourself into this time?"

Vern looked down at the wooden deck and picked at some of the splintered wood with the toe of his shoe. "You been watching the news any?" Vern asked him.

"Sure, all the time." Burt rolled his eyes as he responded, "I watch the sports returns," he said. "I've always got a little money on a game somewhere." Vern grimaced, shook his head and asked, "You know any Hispanics with the last name *Chatom*?"

Burt took off his baseball cap and ran his fingers through his hair and brought it back down his chubby face, rubbing his chin. "Chatom? Beaners? What have you been smoking Vernon?"

he asked Vern, rolling the halfway chewed cigar to the other side of his mouth.

"Hispanic guy with the last name Chatom washed up in the bay the other day." He pursed his lips and continued, "You telling me you haven't heard? Someone in your line of *work*?"

Burt shrugged his shoulders and shook his head quizzically. "Got a picture of him?" Vern told him to wait a second, walked into the kitchen, grabbed the newspaper that held Chatom's picture on the front page and tossed it into Burt's lap. "Here," he said. "You do read don't you?"

Burt let the insult go with just a tilt of his head and picked it up off his lap. He peered at the picture and saw the headline above it. "Drug Smugglers in West Palm" the headline screamed. Of course, the story was all speculative and assumption, but Vern couldn't help thinking this was somehow connected to the Old Man, and in the back of his mind Patty Lee. He watched Burt's reaction, trying to read the gangster body language, but he offered very little.

Burt made a clicking sound with his mouth. He knew the guy faintly. He had done a little business with him in New Orleans once. He worked for the new guy in the Big Easy. He wasn't Hispanic but from Brazil and spoke with a strange accent. Burt wasn't familiar with Portuguese but heard it around the coast every once in a while. This guy's accent was like that but with some sort of twang. He threw the paper down and shook his head.

"Don't know him," he lied. "Just another dead beaner is all I see." Vern asked him to wait and walked back into the house. He strode into his bedroom and grabbed the wallet he found on the *Daddy's Girl*. He didn't toss it like he did the newspaper, but gently handed it to Burt.

"What the hell is this?" Burt asked as he reached out, taking the wallet into his stubby fingers.

Vern collapsed back into his chair and asked loudly, "Chatom's wallet?" Burt slammed it down on the table between them. Vern put his finger to his lips with one hand and pointed back to the house with the other. Burt treated the wallet like a rattlesnake, ready to strike, and leaned away from it.

"What the hell, Vern? Why do you have it?" Burt's voice still raised, and he lifted his bulk from the chair. "I'll slit your throat right here and now if you're trying to pin something on me by getting my prints on it!" he yelled.

Vern waved his hands. "No, no, no, Burt! I found it on one of Old Man Clark's boats," he responded, purposely lowering his voice.

"Found it on one of yall's boats? How the hell did it get there? Why in the hell do you still have it? In your fucking house? Are you crazy?" Burt's words flooded Vern's ears, and the gangster moved towards the door, but Vern jumped in front of him.

"Calm down, Burt. Damn, I called Kennedy just to find out if he knew about it and then I reached out to you because

Kennedy wouldn't say a word, seemed scared as hell. I figured you would know what to do."

Burt stopped and looked Vern directly in the eye. "*Do?* You have a dead drug smuggler's wallet in your house. What did you want me to do? Bury it in the sand out there?" he asked as he pointed towards the beach.

Vern shook his head and in his calmest voice replied, "No. Help me find out why it was there."

Burt took a step back and his panic eased. The smile that disappeared in the past few frantic moments returned. There it was. The opportunity Burt waited for. He rubbed his meaty hands together and after a few moments, removed his sunglasses. He erased the step backwards and leaned in so close to Vern that the gangster felt his breath.

"If I help you, Susie gets regular visits." He found another cigar in his pocket and eased it into his mouth. "Starting tomorrow." There was no hesitation as Vern agreed, but stipulated the visit wouldn't be here, at the Clark House. There was a fast-food joint, out near the Cape, and he would meet the Williams there around three o'clock the next afternoon, with Cliff in tow. Burt agreed, but he held a finger in the air as if he just remembered something. "Just remember, *Vernon*, if you try to screw me over, well…" Burt stopped mid-sentence and just threw Vern a toothy grin. "I'll show myself out."

Burt stopped by the dingy motel's office before going to his room and asked if anyone came around looking for or asking about him. He didn't expect anything, but in his line of work, he never left anything for chance. To his surprise the weaselly looking guy behind the desk said in a Jersey-style accent, "Williams…" as he fumbled through a stack of papers. "Here you go." Burt snatched the note from him and snorted. He always hated Yankees. His eyes widened, and he felt sweat bead under the brim of his ball cap. The note signed C.L. held directions and a time. Burt, glancing at his watch, took a deep breath. Looking back at the Yankee behind the counter, he pointed to the directions and asked if he knew where the place was. The guy winked at Burt and said, "Better take your swamp boots."

There were plenty of places out in the swamps and back roads of South Florida where someone could be miles away from anyone else. Burt drove with the windows down, but he couldn't stop the sweat from rolling down his cheeks. His shirt, saturated with perspiration, made him shiver. It was an odd sensation and as he glanced at the black water lining both sides of the dusty road, he wondered how many bodies the alligators feasted on each day.

The bad thing about working in this part of Florida was that the Dixie Mafia didn't have a whole lot of reach down here. The drug runners, working out of Miami, didn't like his kind and only worked with each other when they must. Burt pulled off his sweat soaked ball cap and tossed it out the window. At least, with the backing he had from New Orleans, he might make it out of this alive, but he hoped he didn't have to play that card just yet.

He needed to think. He stomped on the brakes and slid to a dusty stop on the side of the road. It amazed Burt that it no matter how much water these swamps held, the road was as dry as the Sahara Desert. As the dust settled, he sat there, still sweating and rubbing his head. "Why the hell are you doin' this?" he asked himself aloud.

Taking chances was really his thing. His risks were always calculated. Mixing in with the likes of Lopez, no matter his backing, played against the odds. He closed his eyes and felt the sweat burn, and a vision of Susie filled his mind. Never mix business and your personal life, he kept thinking, but he loved Susie and wanted her to be happy. If this is what he had to do to make that happen, then damn these sons of bitches.

Burt felt his pockets. He made sure he had two things before he left, his cigars and his little .38 he carried to meetings like this. Small and easy to conceal, it was insurance against ending up between an alligator's jaws. He stuck a cigar in his mouth, lit it, and put the car in gear.

He rolled up to the meeting with his lights off. The moon was bright, and he could see for miles. Lopez stood in the middle of a bridge, alone, but inside the car parked on the edge of the wooden structure, he made out someone behind the steering wheel. He checked to make sure the .38 was loaded and ready before stepping out.

Lopez didn't look at Burt as he slowly made his way where the Colombian stood. He stared out into the darkness and said, "I love it out here." He motioned towards the swamp. "The sounds, the smells, it may not be the jungle, but it's certainly *alive*." Burt looked out over the swamp and listened to the sounds of the night. It sent chills down his spine, but he didn't show that to Lopez.

"Yeah, kinda peaceful," Burt responded, "but look, I don't want to be out here any longer than I have to. What can I do for you, Mr. Lopez?"

Lopez took his gaze from the darkness and focused on Burt. He raised his eyebrows. "Learn anything from Mr. Bruce today?"

Burt squinted and held up his hands. "Friendly family visit. You know we're kin."

Lopez slowly made his way and stood beside Burt. "Mr. Williams, let us not start our relationship with…half-truths." He smiled at Burt. "Let us be friends. What did you learn, my *friend*?"

The hair stood on Burt's neck, and never before had he feared for his own life as he did in this moment. He decided to come clean.

"Vern Bruce has the wallet of the guy they found floating. Found it on one of his boats and he doesn't know what to do with it," Burt offered. "Wants me to handle it."

Lopez smiled, turning his eyes over the black water. He stood there in silence as the water seemed to rise and fall as if the swamp were truly alive. "Hmm," he replied, nodding in acknowledgement, "Seems like Mr. Bruce has gotten himself in a predicament." Lopez chuckled slightly. "I know he has it, or at least *hoped* he would find it, or someone would. I know the men running the boats for my old friend, Daniel Clark. If one of them found it, they would take it to Vernon, or Patricia. Either way, it works to *our* advantage." Lopez turned toying with the gold cross hanging around his neck. "Tell me, Mr. Williams, what does Vernon Bruce suspect?"

"A lot. But he hasn't been to the cops because he knows his wife is in deep with something, mainly you," Burt said kicking at the dirt and wiping his sweaty hands on his shorts, drying them the best he could.

"Come here, Mr. Williams, Burt, if I may?" Lopez gestured towards the rear of his car. Burt kept a close eye on the driver who hadn't moved a muscle. He opened the trunk, and Lopez motioned to a chrome pistol, gleaming in the moonlight through the plastic enveloping the weapon. Lopez picked it up gently, admired it, and said, "Keeping people in line with *my* thinking is what I do, Burt."

"What in the hell is that and why would I care about staying in line?" Burt asked as he carefully reached in his pocket, wrapping his hand around the tiny revolver. He saw the driver's eyes in the car's rear-view mirror, trained on him.

"Did you know a man called *Lucky*?" he asked coldly. Burt furrowed an eyebrow, and he gripped the revolver's handle tightly.

"I *know* a man named Lucky. Lucky Clay, from back home. He's in the Bahama's from what I hear." Burt couldn't suppress a mischievous grin.

"Come now, Burt. We both know the truth. We know *exactly* where he is," Lopez said, glancing towards the stars.

"To be truthful, I don't have a clue," Burt responded, and it held truth. It was a hit, and he paid a lot of money for it. Lopez laughed and rubbed his thumb and forefinger together as if reading Burt's mind.

"You pay well, Burt. I pay *better*," he said through his laughter placing his hand on Burt's shoulder. "My friend, this is just an insurance policy as it is the weapon used to take poor *Lucky's* life. Came at a steep price up in Alabama."

He closed the trunk, and the two men stood face to face. Burt, cornered with the truth, pulled his fingers away from the revolver and used the newly freed hand to wipe the sweat from his forehead. "What about Vern Bruce?" he asked the Colombian.

Lopez looked skyward once again and then across the black water. An owl screeched in the distance, and he replied, "Do what he asks. Give him help. Lead him to water, but don't let him drink." Lopez, his hand still clasping Burt's shoulder, lowered his head until their eyes were directly aligned. "I'll make sure you become a very, very rich man. My pockets run deep, and I help those that help me."

Burt's greed overwhelmed him, and his thoughts centered around money with Susie placed in the distance. He agreed and the two men shook hands. He noticed Lopez wiping the sweat garnered from Burt's hand on his pants leg as he lowered himself into the back seat. In an instant, the taillights disappeared into the night and Burt realized he was alone. The owl screamed into the night once again, and by the time it finished, Burt was slamming his car door.

The moon was high in the sky now and the light the glowing orb provided could almost pass for dawn as he sped down the gravel road. For the time being, the old gangster decided he would play along with the Colombian's game. He'd show sympathy for Vern, convince him of his sincerity. Burt chewed on a cigar and tapped on the steering wheel to the music flowing from the car's speakers. Vern Bruce, the gullible square, will fall for it all. But, taking the wallet from him, putting Burt's ass on the line… There could be no mistakes.

The fact Lopez knew about it and admitted he planned for it to be found, made Burt nervous. Lopez didn't take risks and if he *wanted* it to be found, you could damn sure figure there was a reason behind it. For men like Lopez to gain the position he had with the Cartels, he was a survivor and smart as hell. Burt would never trust him, and he opened his grin wider, rolling the cigar to the other side of his mouth, thinking to himself, "*This asshole doesn't know Burt Williams.*"

Chapter 27

Vern woke up early the next morning. Before the sun rose, he had a pot of coffee going and sat in the kitchen, looking out the window, watching the first glowing rays of the sun cast its orange glow over the Atlantic. In the past days, Patty Lee started a habit of rising early and leaving before anyone else was awake in the house. He wouldn't allow her to bypass him today.

Patty Lee might've started keeping things from him, but he wouldn't do the same. Vern decided, alone in his bed again, during the night he would tell her about Burt and the afternoon meeting between Cliff and his mother. As he sipped his coffee, he still contemplated telling her about the wallet. That might wait, but only because he hadn't decided what to do with it yet.

Patty Lee stepped quietly on each step coming down the stairs and easing into the kitchen. When she flipped on a light, she jumped slightly when she saw Vern standing there.

"What now?" she asked as she sniffed the air, the coffee's aroma filling the room. Vern poured her a cup of coffee and she lit a cigarette to go with it.

As the smoke mixed with the smell of the coffee, Vern winced. "Smoking a lot now?" he asked. Patty Lee shot him a look and shook her head, muttering something under her breath that Vern couldn't make out. She took another long drag from the cigarette and blew the smoke from her lungs slowly. Vern thought he caught a slight smile as she did.

"Why in the hell are you ambushing me this morning?" she asked coldly. Vern put the mug to his lips and slurped the remaining coffee. There was no use sugar-coating it. He waved the smoke away from his face and sat back in his chair. He didn't know how she was going to react.

"Cliff's mother is going to visit him this afternoon. Her husband and I talked, and we agreed the boy needs to see his mother," Vern told her. Patty Lee put the cigarette to her lips and inhaled. The resulting exhale fled her pursed lips in a straight line, nearly in Vern's direction. "Figured this would happen sooner or later," she responded. "Husband, huh, more like thug."

Vern knew she was right, but he didn't want to be lectured about friendships by his wife. "I'd be very careful about casting aspersions my way, Patty Lee," he said sternly, "after the company you've been keeping."

Patty Lee rolled her eyes. "We've been over this. Several times in fact. My business is my business."

Vern stood up and walked over to a large bay window facing the swaying palms beside the giant house. The sun, halfway over the horizon, made him squint. He lifted the window slightly, hoping Patty Lee's smoke would escape. He picked up a newspaper and laid it on her lap.

His willingness to talk to her about *his* business drifted away and his anger towards his wife bubbled to the surface. The conversation he hoped to have with his wife gone, he now wanted to know more about *her* business.

"You recognize this guy?" he asked as he turned, facing the ocean once again. Patty picked it up, glaring at the picture in front of her. She recognized the face as Christian Lopez's intimidating driver. She already knew about his fate because, along with her new friends, she'd picked up a new habit. She followed the news religiously. She noticed Vern staring at her over the top edge of the paper and wondered why he would ask her about this guy.

"I've seen him on the news and in the paper," she told him, placing the paper on the table and tapping the picture with her finger. "What do you know about him and why are you asking?" she asked, trying to turn the conversation.

Vern turned around and faced his wife. "He's been on one of your father's boats." When the words left his mouth, he instantly wanted them back. He sat down across from his wife and tried to match her gaze, but she smiled gently. She didn't want to laugh in his face, but she found it amusing when Vern tried to *act* tough.

"Kinda strange that he was on your boat, left his wallet, and turned up dead..." Vern paused for a second and considered his words. *What the hell,* he thought and said, "Maybe your friend Lopez knows something. Looks like they are in the same line of business."

Patty Lee's nose flared at the accusation and her voice grew louder, "A lot of people charter our boats, *dear,* and people die all the time. Probably went for a swim and drowned, something took a bite out of him, or just got drunk and fell in. Hell, Vern, he might've felt depressed and took a walk into the waves. Take your pick."

Vern nodded his head and for a second thought about how the conversation morphed into the direct opposite of the one he'd intended. Both forgot about Cliff and instead here they were, knee deep in something both wanted to deny, however, neither could. He pushed the envelope. "Kennedy hasn't taken him out. I asked."

Patty Lee turned away from her husband, choking back at the impulse to curse him for talking to *her* employees and instead focused on the implied accusation. "So the first thing you think is Patty Lee. You son of a bitch, what kind of person do you think I am?"

"Patty Lee, I didn't want this to go like this, but we need to talk about what you've gotten yourself into. I know about Lopez, and I know what he does. Let's just get it in the open. Stop all these damned lies."

Vern reached for his wife's hand, but she snatched it away. "Fuck you, Vern."

Vern swung across the table, hurling her coffee cup into the wall. Thousands of fragments littered the kitchen and the coffee left in the bottom plastered the wall, dripping to the floor. A tear escaped his eye as he grabbed her shoulder, spinning her around in her seat. Her eyes wide and her eyes halfway closed, she braced for the blow, but it never came. Vern made no move, he just looked her in the eye, "I don't know, anymore," he said as released her shoulder.

"You gutless coward," she said between clenched teeth. Vern shook his head and walked slowly out of the room.

Patty Lee sat in silence, coffee pooling at the base of the wall. She hadn't really lied to her husband, but she did hold back the whole truth. When all of this started, after her father's funeral, she hated each lie that escaped her lips, but now, the sting faded so much that she barely felt anything.

She lit another cigarette, inhaled the smoke, and held it longer than usual. When she finally exhaled, she realized she didn't understand the feeling inside her. She felt sorry for her husband but at the same time, something else mixed in. She thought about Christian and her thoughts turned to how safe she felt with him, and she realized the other feeling inside her. It was love. Not for her husband, she knew that love had turned into pity, but love for someone she knew she shouldn't.

She tapped the cigarette on the ashtray and the realization that their marriage ended with that conversation settled in. Her father was right. She shook her head and remembered their conversation and his reluctance in accepting Vern. He knew. He knew back then he wasn't fit for *real* business, but her youthful love blinded her. There wasn't much she could do, though. She couldn't just divorce her husband. She pounded the cigarette into the glass dish and ran her fingers through her hair.

When they married, she was so in love with Vern that, against her father's wishes and advice, they'd signed no prenuptial agreement. If she tried to divorce him, Vern could possibly take a large amount of money from her. She stood up and glared at the drying coffee on the floor. She didn't want him or his bastard nephew to walk away with any part of what her father built. They didn't deserve it.

She didn't want Casey raised by such a weak man as Vern either. *Her* son wasn't going to be weak; he needed a real man to be a father to him. She bent down, carefully avoiding the splintered glass and started cleaning up Vern's mess. She picked it up, piece by piece, inspecting each one and discarding it in the trash. With each shattered part, her future became clearer.

When each piece of glass was safely in the trash, Patty Lee stood over the phone. Several times she picked up the receiver but each time she placed it back. The last time she dialed the number and heard Lopez's voice. She told him what happened.

Lopez flew into a rage on the other end of the line. She heard him curse Vern's name, and he told her he would come to her. She didn't want him at her home, not right now. Patty Lee told the Colombian she was on her way to his place in Cocoa Beach. She left a note to the nanny letting her know that she would be late and not to worry. She didn't leave any type of note for her husband. He was quickly becoming none of her concern. She put on her shoes and quietly slipped out the back door.

When Patty Lee arrived in Cocoa Beach, the first thing drawing her attention was Christian Lopez's new driver leaning on his car. He nodded towards the house as she pulled into the drive. It hit home at that moment that his former diver, Chatom, no longer lived. She read his name and gazed at his picture, but his replacement drove the point home. She sat in her car for a few moments and caught herself staring at the driver. If he noticed, he didn't show it. He stared at the road as if he expected an armada at any time.

Patty Lee closed her eyes and took several deep breaths. This was the point of no going back. If she got out and went through with this... She stopped herself. She replayed the coffee mug smashing into the wall through her mind over and over until her mind was made up. She opened the door, stepped out, and felt the determination in her steps as she made her way to the door.

She hadn't noticed Lopez standing just inside the open door. He watched her every move and noticed she moved with a resolve he hadn't noticed in her before. As she approached, he saw fire had replaced the timidness in her eyes and he fought the urge to throw his arms around her in a fierce embrace. Even with the fire burning inside him, his voice remained calm.

"Patricia, don't get me wrong, I'm delighted to see you, but I must ask, why?" Lopez questioned her.

Before he finished his inquiry, Patty Lee wrapped her arms around him, kissed him on the cheek and asked to come inside. As she released her embrace, she whispered, "Chatom."

Patty Lee sat down, and Lopez eased onto the seat next to her, their legs touching slightly. "Vern has this guy's wallet somehow," she started, not wasting time. The Colombian nodded his head and put his fingers to his lips.

"Hmm," he responded as he always did in conversations such as these. "How would he have that?" he asked, already knowing the answer.

Patty Lee gently placed her hand on his leg, and he reacted slightly. "Said he picked it up on one of our boats. Had to be *Daddy's Girl*. He mentioned the guy that usually works that one."

He looked up at Patty Lee as her hand had drawn his focus and replied, "Interesting. What does he plan to do with it?"

Lopez stared into her eyes and placed his hand on top of hers. He could feel her pulse race and he wondered if she would tell him the truth, or would she lie? In his mind, he thought he already knew the answer, but he had to know for sure.

Patty Lee didn't hesitate. "He isn't taking it to *anyone*, at least I don't think he is. Not right now, anyway."

Lopez interrupted her, "You mean Demingo?"

She looked at the floor and thought it better not to mention Burt Williams and asked, "Where is he, Christian?"

Lopez squeezed her hand tightly. "Demingo is no longer a worry, my dear. He went *home.*" The tone in which he said "home" made the hair stand on the back of her neck, but Patty Lee accepted the response for what it was worth. She didn't have much experience in this life, but her instincts told her to leave it at that. Besides, she already knew what he meant.

She just offered him a warm smile. Christian Lopez was the direct opposite of her husband, and to her that quickly became welcoming.

"Enough about business," he said as he pointed to the dining room. "I have an early lunch for us." Patty Lee smiled, nodded, and put her lips to his. He pressed hers in return and placed his hands on her cheeks. When they separated, both smiled, and she put her head on his shoulder. Her mind held no thoughts of her husband, Cliff, not even of her own son.

Vern spent most of the morning alone until the time came to fulfill his obligation to Burt Williams. As they drove, Cliff was unusually quiet as well. Occasionally, Vern glanced over at his nephew, riding along quietly, and thought how different he was from his father. Rof was never one to let a quiet moment last, but his son seemed to know when to talk and more importantly, when to keep quiet.

Pulling into the parking lot, he noticed Cliff's confusion in his nephew's face. Cliff looked over and asked, "I thought we were going to take a look at the shuttle."

Vern sighed and pulled into a parking space. "I need you to meet someone, Cliff," he told the eleven-year-old. "You remember a while back, you asked about your mother?" Vern watched the color drain from Cliff's face. The boy just nodded as it dawned on him what was happening.

Vern looked up and saw Burt's massive bulk peering at them through the window. Cliff didn't say a word as they got out and walked into the restaurant. Vern motioned towards the booth and Burt stood up. Susie didn't move.

Susie couldn't hold back tears, and her mascara streaked down her full cheeks when she laid eyes on her son. Cliff, always alert, noticed and offered her a napkin from the table. Burt motioned, and they all sat down. Vern and Cliff sat together on one side of the booth opposite Burt and his wife. Burt's smile seemed authentic, but Vern couldn't tell for sure.

Susie, her face still stained from tears and mascara asked him, "Do you know who I am?" Cliff didn't know how to react, so he peered into his mother's face. What only took a few seconds seemed an eternity to her.

"I know," he said, his steely gaze fixed on her face. "I remember your face. I remember your face from the day you left me. I can't forget it," he said and turned his attention to Vern. "Why, Unc? I don't want to see her."

Vern looked his nephew in the eye, put his hand on his shoulder and told him, "It's time, Cliff. Your mother is better. Took a long time, but she is ready to see you. I promise you, she ain't here to hurt you."

If there was one person in the world Cliff trusted without question, it was his uncle. He looked back at his mother and a tear began to form in the corner of his eye. He fought the urge to jump across the table and hug her. He'd never stopped loving his mother or missing her, but he didn't want to hurt like that again. Even though he was young, and he didn't remember a whole lot about when she left him with his uncle, he remembered the hurt. He remembered feeling as though his heart was ripped from his chest. That feeling haunted him, so, for now, he kept his composure.

"I've missed you," he said, in a muffled voice but loud enough for Susie to hear.

Her tears didn't hold back and streamed from her eyes. "I've missed *you*, baby," she sobbed, and she reached her hand across the table. Cliff stared at it for a moment before putting his hand into hers and with his free hand tried in vain to wipe away the tears. Burt touched Vern on the arm and motioned outside to the playground.

As Cliff and Susie continued their reacquaintance, Vern and Burt walked outside. It was hot and humid and neither man wanted to be outside for long. Burt took out a cigar and began chewing, "I'll take care of that wallet. Bring it to me and I'll get rid of it. No questions, no problems," Burt said as he wiped a bead of sweat from his forehead. Vern, surprised by his sudden eagerness to help, took a step back.

"So, just hand it over and its gone," he replied. "What kind of fool do you take me for?" Vern's eyes began darting around the playground and he half expected Lopez to jump from around one of the bushes lining the property. Nothing happened.

Burt laughed. "What the hell do you think, Vernon? I'm setting you up?" The gangster eased forward and almost poked Vern's face with the cigar. "You asked me, buddy. Remember?" Burt, remembering that he was dealing with a square, eased back a little.

"Look, you want this taken care of for your wife, or what?" Burt asked, his patience weakening.

"My wife?" Vern asked, shaking his head. In the moment he had forgotten their encounter a few hours ago. "What did you find out about her?"

Burt poked his short stubby finger towards Vern's heart. "Only what you already knew. She's in deeper than I thought with some bad people. Lopez is dangerous and she's jumped in headfirst."

Vern hung his head. Burt was right, and he already knew the truth. He just didn't want to believe it. "What do I do?" he asked, not specifically to Burt but into the air.

Burt responded, "You kept up your end of the deal, Vern. You keep Susie happy, and I'll find out more when I can. First, I need you to get me that wallet."

Vern's indecision on whether to trust the scoundrel faded quickly. In his mind, there was no other choice. "I'll get it to you tonight. Come by the house, I'm sure Patty Lee will be late," he said, the defeat showing in his voice.

Cliff didn't say much on the ride home. He just stared out the window and let the wind blow his blond hair. They were about halfway home when he broke the silence, asking only one question, "Do you think she actually loves me, Unc?"

Vern looked at him, nodded his head, and replied, "Yeah, I *know* she does, son. But you've got to be careful. Trust is earned. Right now, love her, get to know her, but don't trust her. Let her earn it." He paused, looked out his window, and said, "Her husband is not to be trusted. You gotta be careful with him. He's not family, but, for now, you treat him like it. Treat him like family, but again, never trust him."

Cliff's face tightened in confusion. "Why not? He seems like a cool guy," Cliff asked.

Vern looked at his nephew and focused on his face. "Do you trust me, Cliff?" Vern asked. Cliff nodded in agreement and Vern continued, "Then just listen to me and do what I say."

Vern wanted to tell his nephew that men like Burt Williams aren't around for long. They play a dangerous game and usually wind up in an unmarked grave somewhere. That thought made the hairs on his arm stand at attention. He never intended to get this deep with Burt Williams. All that he had sought, to begin with, was information and now he was handing over a dead drug smuggler's wallet to him. He knew better, but, as he told himself earlier, there wasn't much he could do right now. He couldn't keep the wallet and he damn sure didn't want to get caught with it.

He looked back over at Cliff and shook his head slightly. The thought that he was using his nephew as a pawn made him physically sick and he chewed back the bile forming in his throat. Cliff could never know. Burt Williams may be a rough and tumble kind of guy, but Vern didn't think of him as very smart, and he intended on using that against the gangster. He punched Cliff jokingly in the shoulder and smiled. "Ice cream when we get home, kid."

After they got home and ate their ice cream, Cliff went to his room to play the new video game console Vern bought the boys. Casey was already in the room playing as he and the nanny had been home for hours. She told Vern about the note, so he didn't expect Patty Lee home any time soon. That turned out to be a good thing because as darkness fell, Burt Williams pulled into the driveway.

"Everything ready?" Burt asked without getting out of his car.

"Here. I have your word, from this point forward, this is done?"

Vern asked hoping for reassurance from him but Burt just grinned and said, "Sure. You'll never see this thing again." He moved his cigar to the other side of his mouth. "We will be expecting Cliff for a visit before school starts, right?"

Vern bristled but, as usual, remained calm. "Call me when we get back to Panama. We'll set it up. Just don't let the boy get hurt."

These two men were playing a dangerous game with Cliff at the dead center. Burt sneered when he told him, "My *son* will be fine."

Chapter 28

Burt held no intention of disposing of Chatom's wallet. In fact, the next morning, he was pulling up to Lopez's home in Cocoa Beach to hand it off. Vern Bruce was a fool for trusting him. If he didn't already know it, he would soon. He was getting used to the life in South Florida. Burt liked the area and most of all he liked that there wasn't a big presence of his people down here. Here, he could make his own mark.

As he was turning down the narrow road leading to the ranch house on the beach, he eased to the side of the road for an oncoming car to pass him. As the Lopez house was the only one on this road, he figured it was either Lopez or one of his people and rolled down his window to speak. The car didn't stop. In fact, it slung gravel in his direction, and it pinged off his car. Burt only caught a glance as the car passed by him and he only saw the driver through a cloud of dust and debris, but something did catch his eye.

He could make out a woman driver, but her head was covered with some type of bonnet, and she had on dark sunglasses that obscured her face. He figured it was one of those dancers down in the club he heard Lopez liked to frequent. He grinned as she passed. He couldn't wait to get in on that action. He liked the car too; he liked the Monte Carlo body style, and the color was red just like he liked them. Burt loved everything about South Florida and as he drove began making plans to stay.

When Burt eased up to the front of the house, he saw Lopez standing there waiting on him. The driver, at his usual spot, leaned on the parked car. It wasn't the same car he saw when they'd met in the swamp. Burt didn't see the usual calm and collected Lopez, but one that looked at him nervously and fidgeted with the hat he held in his hands. Obviously, he saw something he wasn't supposed to. He'd cheated with married women so much before and hadn't really stopped with his marriage to Susie. He knew the look of a man who'd just slept with one.

Lopez tried to act as if everything was normal, but Burt really noticed the shifting of his eyes as he walked up. He suppressed a laugh.

"I did not expect you here so early, Mr. Williams. But, since you're here, perhaps some breakfast?" he asked. Burt, still amused that a woman affected the Colombian to this extent, readily accepted, and the two walked into the kitchen where the chef was wiping the countertop clean and frowned when Lopez and his guest walked in.

Burt couldn't help himself as he sat down at the kitchen table and said, "You roll with some good-looking women, Mr. Lopez, if you don't mind my saying."

Burt smiled towards Lopez, but he didn't return the smile. His face hardened, and his voice turned to ice. "That was none of your concern, Williams." Burt could feel Lopez's eyes focused on him and the cold look on his face told him to move on.

"No problem. I didn't mean any offense or anything," Burt scrambled to say. Very obviously, this had struck a nerve with the South American and Burt filed it away. He took the cup of coffee offered by the chef and Lopez shooed him away. When the chef disappeared through the doorway and shut the door behind him, Lopez turned towards Burt. He no longer fidgeted and the cold, calculating Lopez returned.

"Business, Mr. Williams," Lopez said. "What can I do for you this early in the morning?" Burt pulled a cigar from his pocket and began chewing. "This," he replied as he plopped the wallet down on the table. Lopez didn't move, he only stared at it.

"So, you were successful?" Lopez asked, his eyes focused on the wallet. He reached for the intercom on the wall and said something in Portuguese. Burt made a mental note that he needed to learn a few words of the language. He already knew just a little Spanish. A few moments later, the kitchen door opened, and the driver appeared with a stack of cash. "As a thank you." The Colombian smiled and slid the money over to him. The driver picked up the wallet with only two fingers, holding it by its edge and walked back through the door.

Burt fanned the cash in his hand and smiled. "This is nice, but I'm looking to maybe make a move down here. Lot nicer than Biloxi. You could probably use someone like me," he said. Lopez's expression didn't change, he only nodded slightly. He leaned in and motioned for Burt to do the same.

"What does *he* know?" Lopez asked, avoiding Vern's name.

Burt leaned back and moved the cigar from one corner of his mouth to the other. "He knows his wife is in bed with you," he said, and Lopez face dropped slightly, but noticeable to a man like Burt. Burt didn't expect it and was taken aback. Burt's eyes widened and inside his mind an explosion of reality invaded. The only reason he would react like that was if they were *actually* in bed together. As the Colombian stared at him, the gangster held eye contact, but the initial shock wore quickly on Lopez's face. Burt let the silence linger for a moment or two before continuing. He'd found the smuggler's weakness.

"I mean in *business*, in bed together, you know, old redneck term," Burt said.

"Of course," Lopez replied. "Does he think his wife had involvement with Mr. Chatom's demise?"

Burt rolled the cigar around a couple of times and grinned. "Why else you think he gave me that? He wants to protect his wife." Burt shook his head. "Not like the bitch needs it." As he spoke, he watched Lopez's face fill with blood. Burt only allowed his lips a smirk as he affirmed to himself, he had in fact found a pressure point. He never thought it would be Patty Lee Bruce.

Lopez thanked Burt and once again called his driver to the room, and he escorted the gangster to his car. As Burt climbed in under the driver's watchful eye, he turned the air conditioner to full blast. He let the cool air pour over him, pulled out the wad of cash and thought about which fancy hotel he and his wife would enjoy tonight.

He waved to the driver as he left but he only glared at Burt as he drove by. He thought about Lopez's reaction to the "bed" comment as he let the cold air blow over his face. He lit what was left of his cigar out and blew the resulting smoke out of the window. He rubbed the hair on his chin with his fat, stubby fingers and tried to remember what the woman he encountered coming from Lopez house looked like, but he remembered nothing but sunglasses and a bonnet. He just hadn't seen enough of her face and hair to be sure, but what he was sure of was the car she drove. That red Monte Carlo. He took a ride by the Bruce residence before picking up Susie at the mom-and-pop motel.

He didn't pull up to the giant home's gate but parked down the street in front of another house. He walked the short distance down the street to where he could see inside the gate and saw two cars parked. Sure enough, there sat a brand-new red Monte Carlo and Burt wanted to dance, but all he did was smile. There was no mistaking it. It was a beautiful car, and the new paint dazzled in the bright Florida sun. He slowly walked back to his car and thought to himself, *So, Lopez was literally in bed with Bruce's wife.*

He whistled as he walked, and thoughts cascaded through his mind. Not only was this leverage on Lopez, but Vern Bruce too. He stopped, looked back at the gigantic home and thought about how nice it would be for his new *family* to live somewhere like that. *Damn,* he thought, *he loved Florida.*

He walked back to his car and fell into the seat. He cranked the engine and once again, let the air conditioning pour over him. Biloxi was hot and humid most days, but here sweat seemed to consume him from early morning until late evening. Even the nights were uncomfortable.

He closed his eyes as the air cooled his body and when he reopened them, the red car had left the driveway and was headed right towards him. He lowered his big frame as much as possible in hopes the driver wouldn't see him. He could see her, and this time, without a doubt it was Patty Lee Bruce. Same bonnet and same glasses. He laughed to himself and thought this could be a goldmine. But he had to play his cards right. Lopez may've found himself blinded by his attention to her, but the man was dangerous and more importantly deadly.

Patty Lee strained her eyes to see the driver of the car without turning her head. There was no mistake, however, it was the same one that nearly ran over her this morning in Cocoa Beach. Her first thought was that it could be one of Lopez's men and she was being followed. She wouldn't blame Christian for that, but after last night, the mistrust, if any, should be gone. She felt her heart race as thoughts of the previous night rushed upon her.

She pressed the brake, thinking about turning around, lifted her foot from it, and continued driving down the street, her eyes glued to the rearview and the car she saw in it. If she turned around, surely the driver would catch on to her. She decided to leave it alone.

Another thought entered her mind, and her lips pursed. The last time she and Vern were in the same room, he'd exploded, hurling the coffee mug into the wall. That outburst was something she wasn't used to from Vern, and it surprised her then and continued now. She reached into her purse, pulled out a long, slender cigarette and lit it. It had to be Vern. Her husband must've hired someone to follow her, and if that was the case, she hoped he got the information he craved. She had to know if that was the case.

Against her better judgement, she circled around the block but when she rounded the corner, the car was gone. She stopped in front of her father's house and flipped the ash from the burning cigarette out the window. She rolled it between her fingers and glared at the lipstick smeared on the filter. She and her husband were about to have their last argument.

After confirming his suspicions about Patty Lee, Burt sped back to his motel and, pulling into the parking lot, he saw Susie in a chair beside the pool. When he walked up to her, the smell of suntan oil and her glistening skin almost made him pick her up and take her to their room, but he fought the urge. Instead, he kissed her cheek, told her to come up in a little while but to give him some time. He had business first.

Burt took one last deep breath and whistled as he made his way to the room. He picked up the phone and, pulling a folded piece of paper from his wallet, dialed and asked for Darryl. It took a few minutes, but a male voice answered on the other end.

"Beck," the voice said and waited for a response.

"This is Williams," Burt replied and continued. "We need to meet. I'm out of town but I'll meet you at the BBQ joint down the road."

The voice didn't respond for a second and Burt sensed his apprehension by the deep breaths in the silence. Finally, he asked when. They finished the plan to meet, and Burt hung up the phone. Susie expected a nice waterfront dinner, but he had to go break the news that their date had to be postponed. As he walked back to her outstretched body, still glistening in the sun, he hesitated. It would be a lot more fun to take his wife to dinner and back to bed, but he shook his head. Business always came first. He leaned down and whispered in her ear that he had to go up the road for a while. She sighed and let out a deep breath, but she wouldn't make a fuss, though. She knew better.

The drive North to Lake City took each man about four hours and they arrived at the BBQ joint at about the same time, parking their cars next to each other. Neither was happy to see the other, and they didn't waste much time on pleasantries.

Darryl Beck didn't know why Burt needed to see him, but if he had to guess it was something to do with the hit a while back. He walked behind Burt as they made their way into the BBQ joint, and he eased his hand to the small of his back and felt better about the situation. His backup pistol was secure.

"What's going on, Burt?" Beck asked as he slid into the booth. Burt glanced around and made sure nobody was around them.

"Anybody talk to you about that job you had a while back?" he asked.

"Talk to me? Hell, no. I took care of it and that's it," he said with both fear and aggravation mixed in. "You know me."

Burt nodded and saw the waitress coming towards them. He smiled at her and asked for a couple of sandwiches and cokes. When she walked away, he glanced in her direction and raised his eyebrows. Beck didn't care and held his palms up, becoming annoyed. Burt just grinned back at him. Deep down the gangster hated cops. Any cops. Even those that were on the Dixie Mafia payroll. Especially those that killed without question. He didn't like Darryl Beck.

"This guy I'm working with, he knows," Burt said coldly, looked around and said in a low voice, "He claims to have the tool you used and kinda holding it over my head, so..." He paused and tapped the table with the revolver that he held under it since he sat down. "How would he know?" Beck stretched out his arms and tried to ease one behind him, but Burt tapped the table again and the crooked police state trooper knew he had messed up. The only way out of this was to talk his way out.

"I know one thing, Burt, he ain't got the tool. It's in my car. I used my own personal *tool*," he said and pointed to the car. His hand shook visibly as he did.

"You dumb son-of-a-bitch, why in the hell would you use your *own* with something like that?" Burt's voice was calm and collected.

"Because they'll never find anything, and I keep all my secrets," Beck said and tried once again to reach his gun, but like the other times, he heard Burt's barrel tapping the table. "Look, I don't know how this guy knows *anything*, but it didn't come from me, I AM LOYAL," Beck said and started to get up. Burt grimaced and motioned for him to sit back down.

"I believe you, Darryl," Burt said, still nearly under his breath, trying not to draw any attention. The restaurant was empty save for the waitress, and he didn't want to have to kill her and whoever was cooking in the back. "Only one thing, Beck, I need that tool."

Beck continued to get up and shook his head. "I can't give you that and you damn well know it. That belongs to the department and another thing, if you have it, that gives you *all* the advantage over me, Burt, and that ain't happening."

The waitress burst through the back door with their sandwiches and Cokes on a platter. Burt threw a hundred on the table and told her to keep the food and the money and apologized that his friend wasn't feeling well.

Burt got up, eased his revolver inside his jacket and motioned for Beck to go ahead of him. "Let's go for a ride," he told the cop and Beck grimaced.

"You bastard."

Burt's smile returned to his face. "I'll need your keys. We'll go in mine. Let's go see old Lucky and see how he's doing." Beck thought about making a run for it but realized he was cornered. He cursed Burt's name and vowed the gangster wouldn't get away with this. Burt laughed as he winked back at the waitress. "Already have my friend," he sneered.

Vern jumped when the glass door slid open, and Patty Lee bounded through the opening. "Got somebody following me?" she asked her husband as she marched onto the deck.

Vern, taken by surprise, lifted his hands in the air and responded, "No clue what you are talking about."

Patty Lee stood over him, her hands firmly on her hips and shook her head. "Bullshit," she said, her tone growing angrier with each word. "I saw the car, Vern, in two places on the same day."

Vern looked up at his wife, his face showing no emotion. "Where were you, Patty Lee?" he asked.

She leaned and he could feel her breath upon his face. "With Christian Lopez," she said, and she smiled as she said it.

Vern sighed and stood up, brushing past her before turning around and pointing his finger in her face.

"You're screwing a cold-blooded killer and putting all of us in danger, you know that?" Vern stood up, his voice matching Patty Lee's in anger. "What the hell has happened to you?"

Patty Lee just smiled and took a deep breath. Her tone lowered, and she stepped forward until her chest touched Vern's pointing finger. "I wised up. You are not the man to lead my father's company. You never were, you fucking coward. You let your brother die in your place, or at least *suffer* in your place." She paused and turned her back to Vern. "I had the pictures, Vern, had them in my hands and *I* destroyed them. I did it because I didn't want you to suffer, but now, honey, I don't give a damn."

Vern's face turned a fiery red, his hand transformed into a fist and before he realized it, he struck her, and she tumbled to the ground. Patty Lee caught herself, turned over, and Vern saw blood dripping from her nose. He fell to his knees and reached for her, but she picked herself up. When Vern looked up, she stood over him, the blood still oozing from her nose, and smiled. "Thank you," she said defiantly, and Vern knew what was about to happen.

Police response in the Clark's part of West Palm was lightning quick and in mere minutes, two policemen arrived and handcuffed Vern, placing him in the back of their patrol car. Patty Lee told the police officers how Vern attacked her, and they took pictures of her bloodied nose.

Vern sat in silence peering out the window, watching his wife explain things to the officers. As he sat there, he thought of Pops and how disappointed he knew his father would be if he were still around. Vern wanted to cry but held back the tears. This was his fault. He let Patty Lee goad him into striking her and he would deal with the consequences. All his life, Pops told him to never, ever strike a woman no matter how much she may ask for it. He saw Patty Lee look at him and when she did, she shot a wry smile in his direction. Vern's head dropped. He wanted to die.

The police booked him at the station nearest the Clark home. The two cops, exceptionally large men, manhandled him as much as they could. Each time one touched him, he felt it to his bones, and it made him feel that much smaller.

Booked into jail, complete with mugshots and fingerprints, all he could see in his mind was Patty Lee's bloody face and all he could hear was his father's disappointed voice.

When the barred door slammed shut and he eased down onto the cold bench inside of his cell, he remembered his brother's pictures and Patty Lee's confession of their destruction. Tears that he held back flowed freely, and he cried out into the silence.

Chapter 29

"I will kill the bastard," Lopez said as Patty Lee replayed the events of the day. After the police hauled Vern away, she cleaned herself up, went straight to Cocoa Beach and directly into his arms.

"Just leave him there," she said, her head tucked into his shoulder. "He's got a couple of days to think about what I told him. I don't care what happens to him now. But I'm not going to press charges. I don't want him in jail. I just want him to get his bastard nephew and go back to Panama City." She stretched her reach and kissed Lopez on the cheek.

"Certainly, he cannot get away with this," he fumed, "My honor as a man will not allow it."

She held him and kissed him passionately but this time on the lips. A feeling of safety, security, and love emanated from her body, and her whole body quivered. She never had these feelings with anyone else, not even Vern. She pulled away slightly, looking into Lopez's dark eyes. What she saw in those eyes frightened her, however. She didn't want Vern dead.

"No," she said, as she pulled back from him completely. "Nothing happens to him."

Lopez grimaced. "I will not kill him, Patricia. I just want a message sent."

"The same message you sent that DEA agent?" she asked, turning around so she wouldn't have to see his eyes when he lied.

"Patricia, I will not lie to you. He is gone. You asked, I delivered." He paused for a second or two before continuing. "Whatever you ask, my dear, I will deliver," Lopez told her.

Patty Lee realized the hard truth confronting her. Vern knew too much. She turned to face the Colombian. "How can we get rid of him...without killing him?"

Lopez put his finger to her lips. "Shh, Patricia, the *how* doesn't matter."

She released a tepid smile and put herself into his arms once again. The feelings flooded her again, and she wrapped her arms around him. *Here is a man that would kill for me*, she thought. She felt empowered. She felt like a princess, or more, a queen.

For the first time, she had brought Casey with her to the Lopez home. He was watching an old cowboy movie on the television in the living room and the two of them entered the room quietly, not wanting to disturb the child. She and Lopez sat down on either side of him, and Lopez rubbed the boy on top of his head. "Welcome, *home*, dear boy," he said as he smiled at Patty Lee.

As they sat, watching the cowboy in white fighting the cowboy in black, he thought about how much he respected this woman. He wouldn't take all her innocence, but if he couldn't kill her husband, Vern certainly couldn't be allowed to run free. Lopez didn't like to leave loose ends and Vernon Bruce would be a very loose end. He glanced over at Patricia, her son's hand in hers. She caught him looking and flashed a beautiful smile. He felt his heart melt and for a second, *he* felt fear. This was unfamiliar territory for him as he had never fallen for anyone like he had this beautiful woman sitting beside him. But he had to be very careful with all of this. This was the first time he needed to balance his personal life with business and as he looked at Casey, Lopez realized all that came with that balance.

"Excuse me for a moment," he said as he stood up and walked over to the intercom and spoke a few words in Spanish. A few moments later, the driver stood in the doorway, and he and Lopez walked out onto the foyer and shut the door behind him.

Lopez spoke in Portuguese because he didn't know if Patty Lee knew Spanish but surely, she didn't know the Brazilian language. "I need Burt Williams to meet me in the same place as last time, tomorrow night." He pulled the driver in closer. "Get this request to him, *personally*." The driver nodded in agreement.

Susie waited patiently for her husband to return from his trip *up the road* when there was a heavy knock on the door. She squinted one eye and peered through the peephole and saw a Hispanic gentleman peering back at her. The driver stood perfectly still with his hands exposed where she could see them. There were many non-verbal signs in the world she occupied with Burt, and this one was the first she'd learned. It meant the man was not compromised in any way and to open the door, but she hesitated. Her breathing became heavy, and a cold fear ran though her body. Susie realized she made a mistake just looking through the peephole. The man knew someone was in the room by the darkening of his side of the hole. Just as she was about to speak, she heard Burt's voice, and her breath escaped her lungs for the first time since the knock on the door.

"How can I help you?" Burt asked with his hand inside his pocket, loud enough for Susie to hear on the other side of the door. He clutched the revolver resting in his jacket.

"Hello, Mr. Williams," the driver said in a thick accent. "Our mutual friend requests your company. He instructed me to tell you the same spot." Burt eased his finger from the trigger but kept his hand wrapped around the gun.

"When?" he asked. The driver told him tomorrow night, same time. Burt nodded in agreement and allowed the driver to slip by him and down the steps. He leaned on the railing of the second-floor walkway and watched until the car disappeared into traffic. When he opened the door, he saw his wife sitting on the edge of the bed, visibly shaking. He rushed to her, plopping his bulky body on the bed and wrapping his arms around her.

"Who was that?" she demanded, irritated.

Burt hugged his wife and said, "Just a guy that works for another guy, you know the drill." He looked around the room and said, "Pack your things, we're out of this joint."

They checked out of the mom and pop and drove over to the old Colony Hotel. Susie's face, even in the dark, lit up when she saw the magnificent old building. Burt noticed her reaction as he pulled up to the valet parking and told her, "Baby, this is just the start."

They settled into their room and spent the night in each other's arms. The next morning, Burt was up early and went down to a coffee shop near the hotel. Someone had left a newspaper on the counter, and he picked it up as he walked by and placed it on the booth's table as he fell into the seat. He ordered a coffee from a young flirty waitress and Burt, always ready to return the gesture with a pretty woman, winked at her as she walked away and unfolded the paper. Vernon Bruce stared back at him from the front page. It was a mug shot, and the headline read, "Former Congressional Hopeful Jailed." Burt pulled out a cigar and chewed it between sips of coffee. Shaking his head, he said aloud, "Son of a bitch, what did I miss?"

He finished his coffee quickly and skipped breakfast. Nobody knew him down here, so he just walked into the jail and asked to see Vernon Bruce. The police officer at the desk grimaced and growled, "Lawyer?"

Burt smiled but held in his laughter. "Family," he responded.

Burt wanted to laugh as the first thing he saw was the bright orange jumpsuit he wore when they brought Vern into the room and sat him across from Burt, but he held it inside. A thick pane of glass separated them but there were holes in the middle for conversation. Burt couldn't hold in his laughter any longer. He burst out with a laugh that developed deep within him and escaped his mouth, echoing off the walls.

"What kind of damned mess are you in now, Bruce?" he asked when his laughter died down.

Vern didn't look up, he just stared at the small sliver of a counter in front of him. "You didn't hear?" Vern said with a slight shake of his head. "I'm surprised. I thought you knew everything."

Burt's laughter stopped, and he leaned in close so only Vern could hear him. "Picture's in the paper, hotshot." Vern didn't expect this and put his head into his hands. He began sobbing and Burt popped the glass. "Act like a damn man," he admonished Vern. Vern tried to stop the tears and managed to slow them but his eyes, still watery, asked lowly, "Cliff, who's got Cliff?"

Burt leaned back. "I guess he's at your wife's place. I don't know."

Vern's tears stopped. *"She's* with *him?"* he asked. Burt shook his head, as he really didn't know, but Vern asked again, *"She's with HIM?"*

Burt stared at him and raised an eyebrow. "What are you gonna do? And why haven't you bonded out? You have the money," he said, bluntly.

"I haven't bonded out because I deserve this," Vern told him, and Burt just shook his head. "Go get Cliff. Patty Lee won't give a shit. Go get him and take him to his mother until this is over. I'll get him in a week or so." Vern finally looked up and said, "If he doesn't know, don't tell him. Just tell him I had to go away on some business, you're good at lying." Burt let the insult go without response. "Tell him I wanted him to spend time with his mom."

Burt wanted to smile and enjoy Vern groveling and plotting like this, but he had a part to play, and he played the sympathetic buddy role brilliantly. "Sure, you got it," was all he said, and he got up to leave.

Vern called to him and said, "When I get out of here, I'll be in touch." Burt nodded and walked out. He couldn't force the smile off his chubby face.

Vern used his phone call and dialed the Clark house. He told the nanny that Burt Williams was coming to pick up Cliff and to call his lawyer in Panama City. He found out from her that Patty Lee left after the chaos and hadn't returned. She took Casey with her. Not only was Patty Lee with that maniac but now his own son was with him.

The nanny did exactly as instructed and within a couple of hours Vern gained his freedom. After his release, he called home again to make sure Burt had picked up Cliff and taken him to his mother. He didn't know what to feel when she told him he had. Cliff was safe, and now his attention fell to Casey. He wasn't as weak as Patty Lee thought he was and now he had work to do. He took a cab first to a liquor store and then, ironically, to the same small motel Burt and Susie had used.

Susie and Burt dined at one of the most expensive restaurants in West Palm that night. Cliff went with them. Still unsure about his mother, he remembered what Unc had said about her husband and what he told him about trust. He did enjoy himself though, as they all did. Susie felt as if they were just any other family out on the town for the night. When the meal was complete, Burt dropped Susie and Cliff back at the hotel. The gangster smiled as he leaned on the railing outside the pool area, watching Cliff enjoy the pool and the smile on his wife's face as she also watched her son. He patted the railing and left for his meeting with Chrisitan Lopez.

The drive out to the middle of the swamp didn't feel as eerie to him this time. This time, he held the upper hand on Christian Lopez. Burt knew he was bluffing about the gun; he knew it for a fact. What he didn't know was how the Colombian knew about Lucky Clay. That part bothered him a little bit, but just knowing Lopez's bluff, Burt felt he held the advantage. His lit cigar dangled from his mouth as he clicked off the miles and blew the cigar smoke out of the window.

He pulled up to the same spot he had last time, and Lopez stood in front of his car. Burt glanced around and realized the driver was nowhere to be seen. He was not behind the wheel, or anywhere near the car. Burt hadn't removed the gun from his pocket since putting it back after leaving the police station. He figured Lopez knew he'd picked up Cliff and with a man like him,

Burt didn't know how to predict his reaction. As he got out of the car, he made sure he was alert for any sound that didn't belong in the swamp. All he could hear was the common sounds of frogs and night animals. Thankfully, no screech owls made their presence known. The frogs were particularly loud, and it would make someone trying to sneak up on him hard to hear. But, he figured, if Lopez wanted him dead, he'd probably never hear the shot or feel the blade until it was too late.

"Mr. Lopez," Burt said, looking around, "beautiful night."

Lopez didn't smile and ignored the comment. "Vernon Bruce is a loose end to our business. He cannot be tolerated any longer."

Burt crooked one side of his mouth and in the distance an owl screeched through the noise of the frogs. He eased his hand to grab a cigar from his pocket, raised an eyebrow slightly and said, "Mr. Lopez, with all due respect, I don't think that will help my business or yours right now. If you take this guy out, what will his wife think?" Burt put a finger to his head as if in thought. "What about his kid? Kids have a way of finding out shit like this and you don't want to *complicate* things."

Lopez took a step towards him. "He cannot be left to meddle in my affairs, business or…" He frowned at Burt. "Personal." His words cut through the diplomacy Burt tried to convey to him and the gangster had to think quickly.

Burt put his hand to his chin and rubbed the little bit of stubble that had grown in the past few days. "There are other ways," he said, looking over the swamp below the bridge. He strained his ears and tried to keep a watchful eye around him as he expected the cold steel of a blade in his back at any moment, but none came, so he took a deep breath and continued. "What if he were to be, let's say, in prison for a long time?" he asked, and Lopez tilted his head and shrugged his shoulders.

"Go on," the Colombian replied and moved ever closer to where Burt stood.

Burt rolled the cigar in his mouth and eased his hand into his pocket. He felt sweat bead on his forehead as he was about to lay his cards on the table. It was a gamble he was willing to take. "You have jack shit on Lucky Clay. I know it and you know it. It's bullshit. Let's get that out right now.," he said without flinching or hesitating.

Lopez wasn't used to people speaking to him in such a manner and he shot a glance out into the swamp, pursing his lips. Burt figured he lost this gamble. He watched Lopez closely and looked for a signal so he could prepare to defend himself. He felt his heartbeat through his trigger finger, and squeezed it ever so slightly, "Just tell the guy out there to hold off a second, you'll want to hear this."

Lopez motioned to the tree line, and the driver stepped out into the light coming from the two cars' headlights. "Good," Burt said with as much confidence as he could muster. "We are all on the same page now. Like I said, jack shit. I have it from the *best* authority where Lucky Clay is, where the gun that killed him is, and where the assassin is."

Lopez grinned for the first time that night. "You've been busy, Burt. First you gain all this *information* and then you visit your *friend* in jail, take his nephew, and now plot to send him to prison for the rest of his life." His grin turned into a broad smile. "And they call me cold-blooded."

Burt had not taken his eyes off the driver since appearing from the trees, but now he diverted his attention to Lopez. "I'm a big picture guy and I'm starting to like it down here," he said as he returned Lopez's smile.

Lopez nodded in agreement and extended his hand. The two men squeezed the hand of the other and the Colombian laughed for a split second and his face then turned deadly serious. "That's all I need to know for now. Get it done. Get this man out of the picture. Your thoughts have merit. If he goes to prison, no telling what could happen," he said, sliding his finger across his throat. "Say hello to your dear wife and young Clifford for me, will you? The pool is enormous at the Colony, and I know they had fun tonight."

Burt knew exactly what that meant. He had to be careful around this man. He couldn't let things go wrong because, if it did, it wouldn't be him that suffered. His death would come quickly, but Susie and Cliff would be delivered to him in pieces if things went off the rail.

Burt, releasing Lopez's hand, nodded in understanding. He stood in the faint light of his headlights as Lopez and his driver got in their car and left. The red lights from the rear of the car faded into the distance on the dusty gravel road and he stood there amongst the swamp for what seemed like an hour. The frogs were as loud as ever but he couldn't hear them over his thoughts. Even when the owl screeched into the night once again, it didn't faze him. This was a dangerous game he played. The tables always turned quickly. He wiped the sweat from his brow, got in his car, and turned on the air conditioning.

Night in the South Georgia swamp was just as hot as it was in South Florida. Just off an unpaved country road in the middle of nowhere, a group of teenagers were setting up camp. Their intentions were to drink the night away next to the black water of the Okefenokee River. The moss hung from ancient oaks and cypress stumps littered the shallow water next to an old cabin, but the teens decided on tents.

Nobody intended to sleep, just to drink the two coolers full of beer in the back of their pickup. They paid a random guy ten bucks to buy it for them from the small store about a mile back on the main road. It was something they did nearly every weekend.

One of the teens wandered down to the water's edge to find some wood to build a fire and took one of the flashlights. The banks of the slowly flowing river were notorious for housing cottonmouths and getting bit by one way out here was flirting with death. As he shined the light back and forth on the bank, something caught his eye. At first, he thought it was an alligator, lying in wait on the bank for its nightly prey but, as he eased towards it, he saw it was a human, not an animal.

He figured it was one of his buddies, already passed out, and began walking softly in the spongy ground hoping to yell and make him jump in the dark water. He eased the light along the bank until it illuminated the person's face, and the teen stumbled backwards, tripped over his own feet, and yelled for his friends. Darryl Beck's body had been found and next to him was the severely decayed body of Lucky Clay.

Chapter 30

Vern wheeled his car into the parking lot of the hotel and laughed. He thought about how the tables had turned. Here he was, looking for Vern Bruce in the small, seedy hotel and Burt, along with Susie and Cliff, were living it up at the Colony Hotel. He slipped the clerk a twenty, and he gave up Vern's room number. He knocked on the door and a red-eyed Vern opened it slowly, wincing at the intrusion of sunlight.

Burt drew back when the stench of cheap whiskey and body odor hit him. Vern didn't handle substantial amounts of liquor well and it was clear when Burt found a pool of vomit in the doorway into the bathroom. Vern was barely coherent, stumbling over not only his feet but also his words and Burt, for a second, felt sorry for the man. At first the gangster didn't recognize the sentiment as it was one he didn't have often. Burt sat on the edge of the bed and chuckled under his breath as Vern stumbled into the bathroom and missed his target once again.

"Vern, Vern, Vern, you look and smell like shit," Burt said loud enough for Vern to hear over his heaves. He finished and crawled out of the bathroom, leaning on the door casing.

"How did you find me?" Vern asked, slurring his words.

"You ain't hard to track, my boy," Burt responded. "But we need to get you back to Panama City and fast." Burt started looking for any type of belongings to pack up. There were none.

Vern waved his finger in the air. "No, sir, I ain't leaving until I get my son away from them. Both of them." He made it to his feet, his knees wobbly under him, and started looking around for the bottle of whiskey he'd drained in the hours before. He found a little drop at the bottom, and he turned it up to finish it off, but the bourbon fell free from his mouth, dripped down his chin and he slid back down to the floor.

Burt shook his head, stood up, and grabbed Vern under the arm, lifting him from the floor. "Vern, you gotta get out of here. You don't mess with men like Lopez. I know, trust me," Burt said trying to steady Vern on the edge of the bed.

"I'm going to get my son," Vern replied. "I'm going to get my son, and I don't give a damn who Lopez is, or what the bastard is capable of. Casey is my blood." He became silent, his nostrils flaring, stood up on his unsteady legs, and faced Burt. "Cliff's with his mother, right?" Burt nodded and told him the boy was safe.

Vern released a deep breath. "Thank you, Burt. Thank you for that." In his drunken state, his emotions fluctuated wildly. Tears tried to form, but he held them back. With Cliff safe, his thoughts turned quickly back to his son and visions of him walking, hand in hand, with Lopez filled his mind. Vern saw the whiskey bottle lying near the spot where Vern picked it up, kicked at it, missing it completely and fell to the floor once again. This time he just laughed as he lay face down on the cold tile.

"Go home, man, let this settle. Go after Casey *your* way, through the law," Burt tried to reason with him, but Vern only laughed.

"The *law*?" Vern released a deep guttural laugh, "The *law* ain't going to help me."

Burt fell to a knee, turned him over and pulled him in close, flinching from the smell of Vern's breath. "You damned fool. Going to get yourself fitted with a pair of concrete shoes if you go after him. Guaran-damn-tee-it."

"I don't need a damn thing from you, Williams." Vern paused and closed his eyes. "Except one thing." Vern seemed to sober up very quickly. "I need a gun. I'm going to kill them. Both of them. I'm going to get my son."

Burt stood up and rubbed his chin. "Son, that's the liquor talkin'."

Vern stood up, his knees finally supporting him, steadied himself, and looked Burt in the eye. "I need a gun." Burt had seen that look in many men's eyes before and nodded.

"If you are dead set on this, I'll help you this one last time and we are done. Susie gets the boy, no questions." Vern closed his eyes again, wiped his eyes, and remembered the promise he made Cliff as a small boy. The promise to protect him and love him like a son. He lied to himself that this would protect him, but he knew better. He was trading his nephew for revenge. He nodded slightly, agreeing to the deal.

Burt turned around and put his stubby finger in Vern's chest. "If you let it out that I helped you, I'll kill you myself."

Vern placed his finger to his lips. "OK" he said, and Burt walked out of the room. With Burt gone, he couldn't hold back his tears any longer. He sat on the floor, back to the end of the bed, sobbing as Burt reemerged in the room. He carried a shirt, wadded in his hands, and placed it on the bed next to Vern.

"We are done," he said coldly and left, this time for good.

Vern stared at the end of the gun protruding from the dirty shirt. He picked up the whiskey bottle, still laying on the floor, and shook it, but it was bone dry. Once again, his drunken emotions changed direction and anger swelled replacing anguish.

He pulled the gun free from its soft enclosure and envisioned pulling the trigger and Lopez crumbling to the ground. In the same vision, he turned the gun on Patty Lee, the woman he'd loved for so many years, the mother of his son. He was going to need more whiskey.

Burt leaned on his car in the parking lot, smoke lifting into the air from the end of his cigar. This job rubbed Burt the wrong way. Vern was a square and he kind of liked him, or maybe he just felt sorry for him, but he *had* warned him about getting involved with all of this to begin with. He understood Vern's feelings and he would probably feel the same way if it was his wife. Vern took a long puff from the cigar and let the smoke blow into the air. He wouldn't be that stupid, though. Lopez was not the kind of guy that tolerated ex-husbands. He was an all-or-nothing type of guy, and as far as Burt knew, the Colombian never ended up on the "nothing" end.

He leaned down and pressed the burning end into the pavement and put the extinguished cigar in the corner of his mouth. Realizing that, now, he was neck deep with the drug smuggler made him just a little nervous. It was a calculated risk, and Burt made all the calculations. In the Dixie Mafia for a long time, since he was a young teenager, he'd previously only heard of South American gangsters and what he'd heard scared the shit of out him. He would never have gotten involved with them if it hadn't been for Chatom and the other guy, he couldn't remember his name, but his face was burned into his memory, coming up to him in Biloxi.

They were strange anyhow, their accents a blend of Portuguese and, strangely enough, redneck. They didn't tell him a whole lot, but they came with a lot of money. Now, Chatom was dead, and he hadn't seen the other guy since that day in Mississippi.

Burt fell behind the wheel, took one last glance at Vern's window, and drove off. Vern wasn't thinking this whole thing out. Burt was. He had to stay two steps ahead, or he may end up like Vern Bruce and that wasn't going to happen. Poor guy, he thought as he rolled up the windows and turned the air conditioner to full speed.

He saw the car as soon as he pulled into the shopping center's parking lot. Underneath a couple of large, swaying palm trees in the corner of the lot sat Lopez's new driver. Burt headed towards him and placed his fingers on the headlight switch, but he hesitated. If he went through with it, if he gave the go-ahead, he was taking Vern Bruce's life. Maybe not directly and probably a while down the road, but Vern's life would be decided with a flick of the switch. *The dumb sonofabitch did it to himself*, Burt thought, and flashed his lights.

Alcohol from the second bottle of whiskey flowed though Vern's veins, clouding his mind and influencing his judgement. His tears were long gone, and the demon liquid amplified his rage. His eyes were barely able to focus, but somehow, he kept the car between the lines. He knew Lopez lived somewhere in Cocoa Beach and pointed the car in that general direction.

He coaxed the location of Lopez's ranch house from the local guy running the liquor store. It only cost a hundred dollars, and he bought another bottle. Everyone from Cocoa Beach knew the house because the style simply didn't belong. It was out of place. The only reason he knew of the house was a slip of Patty Lee's tongue a while back describing the beauty it held to the nanny. She didn't tell her who owned the house, but Vern figured it out.

He reached over to the passenger seat, picked up the gun and wrapped his finger around the trigger. The steel felt cold and ran a shiver throughout his body. He let it go, opening the bottle and turning it up to his lips. Soon, he would end all of this, or at least, he would be dead and Lopez with him, maybe even Patty Lee. He twisted the cap back onto the bottle and pressed the accelerator. He needed to get this done as fast as he could. No more thinking, all he saw was red.

Vern's ears picked up a sound coming from the rear of the car, but he couldn't place it. His mind, clouded by the alcohol pulsing through his system, passed it off, but when he looked in the rearview mirror, through blurry eyes he realized what the sound was.

The rotating blue lights filled the mirror and Vern, a sudden panic enveloping him, tossed the gun to the floorboard. For a fleeting moment he thought about running and just as his foot became heavier on the accelerator, saw a horde of flashing blue lights directly in front of him. The panic overwhelming his drunken mind, he looked for a side street but only houses lined the street. It was the perfect place to enclose someone, and Vern slid to a stop in the middle of the road, black lines and white smoke trailing him. He slid his hand onto the door handle, thought about the gun resting on the floorboard, and flung himself towards the weapon. His hand mere inches from its goal, he saw the barrel of a gun from the corner of his eye and a booming voice told him to put his hands in the air.

A sudden will to live chased any thoughts of going for the gun and Vern put his hands as far in the air behind him as he could, his head careening into the gun. He felt the blood gush from his nose, and he tasted the iron in his blood.

In a matter of seconds, he was pulled from the car through the window and thrown to the ground, face first, opening a new wound on his face. He felt gravel working its way into the cut and asked himself, *All of this for drunk driving?* He tried to free his mouth enough to speak and yelled, "What the hell did I do?" Two officers were on top of him now, forcing his hands behind his back and slapping him in handcuffs. He could barely breathe.

"Vernon Frank Bruce?" one of the burly officers asked into his ear.

Vern took as deep of a breath as he could and answered, "Yes," he took another breath and it felt like his lungs would burst, but he had to ask, "What the hell is this?"

The officer rolled him over as the other released his knee and the pressure behind Vern's neck eased. The officer leaned down and told him, "Vernon Frank Bruce, you are under arrest for the murder of Lucious Clay and Darryl Beck." Both officers placed an arm under his shoulders and picked him up. "Fucking cop killer," one of them said. Blood covered his face, and his eyes burned. He wished he had reached the gun.

"Yes, sir," said another officer, searching the car. "Here it is." The officer picked up the revolver that was on the floorboard with a gloved hand and held it up for all to see. Vern tried to see what he held, but the blood kept pouring from his wounds and into his eyes.

A voice came from behind him. "Is it a forty-five?" The voice belonged to a man in a suit and tie with a badge hanging from the pocket. The officer looked at him, smiling, and said, "Yes sir, Detective. Looks like that tip worked out."

The realization of his alleged crimes hit home, and Vern yelled, "I ain't killed nobody!" He struggled in the two large officer's grasps. "I don't know what the hell is going on. I ain't seen Lucky Clay since the election!"

The detective walked over towards Vern, paused at a squad car, pulled a towel from the back, and tried to wipe some of the blood from his eyes. "Nobody had, son," the detective said, "until they found his body up in a swamp in Georgia, along with Trooper Beck."

"What the hell has that got to do with me?" Vern asked, calming down and trying to understand what was happening.

The officer pointed to the gun laying on the trunk of Vern's car. "Both shot in the head with a forty-five, not at the same time, but for some reason somebody put them side by side on a riverbank. Takes a sick bastard to do something like that but I'm sure you'll fill us in on some of the details when we get you booked."

Vern dipped his head, and tears burned his eyes. He danced with the devil and that devil turned out to be Burt Williams. He had told Cliff not to trust him, yet he didn't follow his own advice. Once again, he wished he had reached the gun or at least another drink of whiskey.

Christian Lopez nodded his head and put his hand on the driver's shoulder. He leaned in, told him something in his ear, and it was the driver's turn to nod, and they parted. Patty Lee, drawing the curtain back slightly, watched through a living room window from the "Hacienda." She started calling it that, and Lopez loved it. He wanted it to be a home for his new family and today was a big step in that happening. He knew she was watching and as the driver walked away, turned slightly and a look of concern showed upon his face. As soon as he walked in the door, Patty Lee stood in front of him. The concerned look on her face matched his.

"News," he said, shaking his head in fake disappointment. "Your husband has been arrested for murder." Patty Lee felt her mouth drop involuntarily and then she laughed. She didn't mean to as she didn't think anything was funny, but she wouldn't believe for a moment that Vernon Bruce murdered someone. Lopez's bewildered glance at her made her laugh even harder.

She gathered herself slightly and said, "Vern? Murder?" She spoke with a hint of laughter remaining in her voice.

Her dark eyes looked up at Lopez and she noticed he had stopped shaking his head as there was no use in trying to act sympathetic. *His* Patricia was not stupid, always practical, and quickly learned how the game was played. He placed his hand under her chin and kissed her softly on the lips, thinking how much he loved the woman.

He pulled away slightly and whispered into her ear, "Would you like to know?" Patty Lee thought for a moment, rung her hands, and sat down in the nearest chair. Her eyes darted around the room, making sure no one else was around, especially Casey. He was still in the other room playing a video game.

"Yes," she finally said under her breath. Lopez kneeled beside her and placed his hand on top of hers and told her, "Vern killed his campaign manager after the election. It looks like he met with him and shot him in the head. "

Patty Lee laughed once again, catching Lopez once again off guard, and thought there was no chance Vern shot anyone, he didn't have it in him. Lopez cocked an eyebrow and continued, "A police officer, from Alabama, investigated, found, somehow, that your husband became involved with the vile *Dixie Mafia*. At some point after he killed poor Lucky Clay, he killed the officer, a man named Beck, with the same gun. From what I'm told, Beck was spotted up north with a man in a café. They left; Beck never went home. Someone found him with Clay's body."

Patty Lee put her head into her hands and said through a muffled voice, "And they are saying Vern did this? Vernon Bruce? Pansey Vernon Bruce? Coward Vernon Bruce?" she asked with her laughter growing louder.

Lopez kneeled in front of her, and she picked her head up from her hands, again flashing her big dark eyes. "There is more, my dear Patricia, and this may be hard to hear," Lopez cautioned. "Just a couple of hours ago, the police received a tip. They caught Vern, drunk, with a forty-five in his possession."

Patty Lee asked a question that she was not prepared to have answered. "You drove him to kill himself, didn't you?"

Lopez stood, turned away, and said with his back turned, "No, my dear, he was coming to kill you."

Patty Lee stood up in a burst, anger enveloping her mind and body. "That bastard, more of a coward than I thought. Drunk you said? He never could handle liquor. Yellow asshole had to be drunk to do anything."

Lopez turned back to her, put his arms around her, and her head onto his shoulder. The Colombian smiled as he hugged her. She kissed him passionately and said, "Thank you."

Lopez, the smile growing broader, looked directly into her beautiful eyes, and said, "My dear, I will move mountains for you." He paused. "And *our* son."

Chapter 31

The sandy-haired, middle-aged detective pulled his glasses down to the end of his nose and slowly lifted his eyes from the papers in his hand to look Vern in the face. "My friend," he said in a crisp accent, "you are in up to here." The detective motioned with his hand above his head. He just finished telling Vern the version of the story as he knew it. When he placed his hand back on the table, he looked to Vern to fill in the blanks, but all he did was shake his head.

"Burt Williams," Vern responded, "Burt Williams set all of this up. Wouldn't doubt if he wasn't working with a man named Lopez. Christian Lopez."

"Never heard of either of them," the detective lied. "We got the gun that killed those two men..." He paused for effect and leaned ever so slightly towards Vern before continuing, "Ballistics is going to prove it, in your possession I might add. If I have my way, they are going to light you up." He started laughing as he leaned back and stood up. He started towards the door but stopped suddenly and turned, "Other than the call to your lawyer, any family we need to contact?"

Vern dropped his head onto the iron desk, and instantly regretted it. His already throbbing headache grew much worse. The alcohol had worn off and his head was throbbing with pain. He felt his heart pulse each time it beat throughout his body. "I have no family left," Vern said more to himself than to the detective.

"Suit yourself," the detective mumbled and continued walking.

The door shut with a metallic thud and Vern sat alone, his hands still handcuffed and his head pounding so hard it seemed it would soon explode. He wished it would. The room was dark with one light bulb dangling from the ceiling on a long cord. The wind from the slamming door put it in motion and it swung above his head, compounding his pain. He wanted to cry, but he wouldn't allow himself to succumb to the emotion.

As he sat, alone, hurting, and wishing he was dead, all he could think was this was poetic justice. This was his punishment. Since the day he'd handed Rof the draft card, this was his fate. He hadn't only failed his brother, but he now failed his brother's only son. The light began to slow to a stop and finally the shadows grew still. He picked his head up and for a moment a vision of Rof, hands tied, and mouth gagged, seemed to form on the wall.

He wanted nothing more than to reach out and put his arms around his brother. He wanted to tell him he was sorry. Not only for failing him, but now his son. A son Vern swore to protect was in the hands of a man like Burt Williams. He had made so many wrong choices and so many mistakes that he couldn't even count them anymore.

Vern looked up at the light and closed his eyes. He tried to pull his hands apart, but the cuffs only left a small amount of movement. He wondered if Williams had played him all along or did Lopez get to him? The gangster claimed he was just trying to help Susie, but to place trust in a man like him, Vern cursed aloud. He was stupid to think that it was strictly personal, and he held no other motive but his wife. He cursed again and put his forehead back onto the table. This time he didn't slam the table but eased his head onto the cold steel desk.

Minutes turned into hours and Vern still sat in the small, dark room. He had fallen asleep as his body took over his mind, trying to repair itself from the onslaught of the whiskey. The door creaked open and Vern, expecting the detective, opened one eye, but in the brightness of the door stood the silhouette of a woman.

"You son-of-a-bitch," Patty Lee said as she stood in the doorway. She muttered something under her breath as she walked in. The door remained open and out of the corner of his eye, Vern caught a glimpse of Christian Lopez.

"Why are you here?" he asked. He couldn't mask the hatred in his voice as he still wanted to kill her.

"I just wanted you to know something," she said as she walked over to him and leaned down close enough for Vern to feel her breath on his ear. He pulled at his restraints to no avail. They cut into his wrist, and he felt blood dripping from them. If he could only break free, they wouldn't have to frame him.

He couldn't see her, but he felt her smile. "Casey and I will be in South America for a while." She stood back up and turned to walk away and flashed her beautiful smile back at Vern as she walked out. When the door slammed shut, Christian Lopez looked through the small pane of glass and smiled and nodded. Vern wanted to die now more than ever.

Later that evening, after dropping Patty Lee off at her father's house to gather her and Casey's belongings, Lopez met Burt Williams at the Clark Building. The Colombian occupied Old Man Clark's chair as Burt strolled into the office.

"I've done everything you asked me to do," Burt told Lopez, nodding his approval to the sight of him in the chair. "Every single thing."

"And I thank you for it, Mr. Williams," Lopez replied as he leaned back in his chair. "I hope you understand that in *my* organization, there are no foreigners allowed in positions such as you ask." Burt reached into his shirt pocket but paused and looked at Lopez for permission. Lopez nodded. "Of course." Burt continued and placed a cigar in the corner of his mouth.

Lopez looked at Burt and a sly grin appeared on his lips. "Perhaps, something else."

"I'm listening," Burt told him.

Lopez pointed his finger in Burt's direction and said, "Your wife, she is Cliff's mother, yes?"

Burt nodded and slid his cigar to the other side of his mouth. "What's that got to do with anything?"

Lopez stood, walked over to the picture of Patty Lee that had recently replaced her father's, looked intently, and ran his finger along the brush strokes. "Our organization needs to expand its footprint here in this country. Young Cliff will soon inherit a part of his uncle's part of Cahaba and when he does..." Lopez turned suddenly and again pointed his finger in Burt's direction. "You will be allowed to run the entire business, until he is of age, of course. It is also my understanding that this nephew will inherit a transportation company in which his aunt and cousin will hold no ownership. *This* will be beneficial to us."

Burt looked surprised. "Vernon Bruce ain't dead. He can run it outta prison and second, is his wife all right with that? She owns half of everything." Lopez rubbed his eyes. *This man has no vision*, he thought to himself. He held his doubts, but this was Patricia's idea, and he didn't think the gangster needed that information at this time.

Lopez stepped closer to Burt and lowered his voice. "Vernon Bruce will not see his trial; I will make sure of that. My honor as a man will not allow it. As for the second question, s*he* wants this."

Burt, caught off-guard by this offer from Lopez, took the cigar from his mouth and a frown replaced it. "I don't know anything about running a company like that. I'm just a small-time *businessman* from Biloxi. They are talking about building legitimate casinos. That ain't my game."

Lopez's smile widened, "Don't worry, Mr. Williams, you will have help. I assure you and I forgot to mention, you will be paid handsomely." Burt thought about the consequences if he declined such an offer. Loose ends did not last long as Chatom's fate quickly entered his thoughts. That wouldn't be his fate, at least not because of turning down a man like Christian Lopez. He wasn't that stupid.

Burt extended his hand. "Deal," he said. "When can I expect the wheel to get to turning, if you know what I mean?"

Lopez's grin turned to stone in a heartbeat, and he motioned into the air. "It already is." Lopez looked at Burt's hand, but the Colombian embraced him, kissing him on the cheek. Burt tried to pull back, but Lopez tightened the hug. "You will be richer than you could ever imagine, but, if you betray me in any way, I will slit your throat and pull your lying tongue through the hole." Lopez let him go and the look in his eye sent chills down Burt's spine. Burt could only nod. He was in it to the death, now, and so was his family. The chill turned into cold, dead fear and already Burt regretted dealing with this man.

Burt slowly made his way down the blacktop highway. He lit the remains of his cigar and blew smoke out the window. Needing the wind on his face, he resisted the temptation to switch on the air conditioner. The look Lopez gave him with his piercing, cold eyes wouldn't leave his thoughts. For the first time in a long time, he thought about an exit.

Perhaps it was time for him to try and succeed where Lucky failed. Escaping this life. Escaping with Susie and Cliff to a life in the Caribbean. He had enough money stashed away and they could try to make a run for it. Even with the windows rolled down, he began to sweat, and he hated sweating. In the Florida humidity, your clothes stuck to you when perspiration mixed with the cloth. Biloxi may be just as humid and just as hot, but sometimes it gets cold. Burt loved the cold. Maybe they could run to Canada. The Dixie Mafia didn't have any presence in the cold, dark north.

Burt forgot the burning cigar in his mouth, and he felt the heat as it burned towards his lips. The sensation brought him back to reality. If he ran, it would just be a matter of time before they were dead, all of them. If the Dixie Mafia didn't kill them, he knew about loose ends and how much Vern's wife hated Cliff. She would jump at the chance to do him harm. For a second, he wondered who was more vicious, Lopez or her, as he flicked the cigar out the window.

Before long, he was back at the hotel, turning the key to open the door. As he did, he took a second before he pushed it open and took a deep breath. He had placed his family in terrible danger, and he knew that he could never get them out. Once again, however, he thought about what someone had said, or maybe he saw it in a movie once: "This is the life we have chosen."

When he opened the door, Susie was seated at the table in the corner of the spacious room and Cliff was nowhere to be seen. There was another person seated at the table with his back to the door. When he turned around towards the door, Burt at once recognized him as the quiet guy that came into the bar with Chatom when all of this started.

Burt realized that involuntarily, his hand had made its way to the gun slid into the waist of his pants. The man sat motionless and slowly held up his hands. Susie smiled and Burt knew they were in no immediate danger.

"Burt Williams, nice to see you again," the man spoke, his Brazilian accent complimented by a twang. Burt eased the hidden pistol from the small of his back and held it beside him, tapping the barrel on his leg. He wasn't going to leave anything to chance.

The man waved his hands. "No need, Mr. Williams, I am not armed." The man rose and lifted his shirt and rotated.

"Then you are a fool," Burt replied. The man completed his rotation and faced Burt.

He bowed his head and said calmly, "I apologize for not introducing myself to you when we met sometime back. My name is Antonio Jefferson Black. You can call me Jeff. I come here to ask something of you. I mean no harm to you or your family. In fact, I offer salvation."

"Salvation?" Burt returned and tapped the barrel on his leg a couple of times more. "What kind of salvation?" he asked as he noticed a shadow pass behind him. He spun around but realized he had not shut the door, and someone simply walked down the hall. He walked over and eased it shut. Black motioned as if asking permission to sit back down. All the while, Susie sat quietly and said nothing. She didn't fidget, and she offered no signals that something was wrong. "Where is Cliff?" Burt asked her.

Susie, still offering her smile, said, "The pool. That is where I met Jeff. He needed to see you and he told me that everything was *peachy*." Burt looked back at Black. "Peachy" was a code word used in the Dixie Mafia relating that a person was a friend. It wasn't handed out to just anyone and if compromised, the person didn't last long.

"I don't know you." He looked at Black and squeezed the pistol still in his hand.

"No, my friend, you do not. But we know some of the same people," Black replied. "I, along with my *family*, are from Brazil. We have been exiled there for quite some time, but we prepare to come home, and..." He held his palm out to Burt. "We need your help to do that."

Burt shook his head and cocked his head to one side. "I don't have a damn clue what you are talking about. Exiled? Coming home? Who the hell are you?"

Black bowed his head slightly and pointed to the door. "If we may walk, Mr. Williams." Before he started towards the door, Black turned and offered his hand to Susie. "Thank you for the hospitality, Mrs. Williams." He released her hand and once again gestured towards the door. Susie winked at Burt, and he reluctantly followed the Brazilian outside.

Jeff Black was tall, and his skin reflected at least slight Hispanic heritage. His facial features, however, were strictly Caucasian in nature. His narrow, pointed nose rested between the high cheekbones. As Burt studied him, he thought how strange this man not only sounded but looked. The two men walked towards a grassy courtyard as the sun began to set across the peninsula.

There was a bench centered in the rectangular area between buildings and Black offered Burt a seat before finding his own beside Burt's bulk. "Mr. Williams, I can't explain everything right now and for that I apologize. I was hoping to meet with you a little later, but things have happened to make *our* timeline advance."

Burt held up a single finger, waving it in the air and leaned in close to look Black in the eye. "What did you mean *salvation*?" Burt asked again.

Black smiled but Burt couldn't tell if it was a genuine smile or some kind of act. He could usually tell if someone was lying within a few minutes of talking with them, but this man was different. Burt couldn't tell and that gave him pause.

"All in due time, Mr. Williams. I *will* tell you this, that if you help us, you will be helping your own kind, not that Colombian dog, Christian Lopez."

Burt once again held a finger in the air. "Who is *us*?" he asked. He looked around and he reached over, patting around Black's midsection, "If this is a setup, you can go back and tell Lopez I passed." Black didn't flinch and a broad smile broke over his face.

Black's smile gave way to a deep laughter and when he settled down said loudly and emphatically, "I am in no way connected to Christian Lopez." He spit on the ground in defiance.

"I know what Lopez has offered and I know what he has threatened," he told Burt in a calmer voice.

Burt pursed his lips and watched a young family walk by. He knew better than to double cross a killer like Lopez, but deep down, he knew that no matter what happened, eventually, he would be a loose end, and he knew what happened to those. He patted Black on the shoulder. "Let's talk," Burt told him, and Black's smile reappeared.

"The other Brazilian is in town," the driver whispered into Lopez's ear as he was eating dinner with Patty Lee and Casey. The news was something that he didn't want to hear but he didn't let that show on his face. He picked up his wine glass and rotated the small amount left. The driver stood beside him, awaiting his command.

"Where is he?" he asked, loud enough for both Patty Lee and Casey to hear. The driver whispered into his ear once again and this time Lopez couldn't hide his reaction as his face turned blood red. He glanced back at his driver. "How unfortunate."

When he'd killed the other Brazilian that night on the *Daddy's Girl*, Lopez knew this day would come. The two men didn't want to go into business with a Colombian in the first place, but they relented in order to push their agenda forward. He felt Chatom's disdain for him each time the Brazilian looked at him, so when the opportunity presented itself, he didn't hesitate and ended the situation.

Now here was his partner interfering with his business. *No matter*, Lopez thought, he would take care of it. He was saddened though to hear that Burt Williams had talked with him, however. Perhaps Burt was faithful, but he *was* a member of a bunch that really didn't have loyalty. They often turned on each other. They killed and robbed each other, and Burt Williams was no different. He had heard of his exploits before their association and Lopez knew he took a risk bringing in Williams. but he liked him, and he was connected to several people that he needed. No matter how much he liked him or wanted him to be *somewhat* loyal, Burt Williams was now a risk, and he didn't like risks. Just like Columbia, he thought, people make me hurt what they treasure the most. He shook his head in disgust and noticed both Patty Lee and Casey watching him. He smiled at them and winked at Patty Lee. "Just business, dear Patricia." She released a deep breath and nodded, patting Casey on the head. The child, unfazed, returned to his cheeseburger.

The driver had taken a couple of steps back, but Lopez motioned for him to return to the table. There was no joy in his face when he looked up at him and simply said, "Take care of it."

The driver nodded and as he walked out of the room started whistling. Lopez could feel Patty Lee's gaze upon him and when he looked in her face, he saw worry.

"The guy in jail?" she asked him, not wanting to say Vern's name in front of their son.

Lopez motioned with his hand. "No, my dear, just some *other* business."

She trusted him and at the same time thought about her husband, or soon to be ex-husband. Vern was right where he needed to be, rotting behind bars. She wanted his thoughts to be consumed by her and Casey, living a life of luxury in the Columbian countryside. She wanted him to think about Cliff, riding on a white horse, held in place by the hands of Christian Lopez. She laughed and motioned for her glass to be refilled with wine. As she put the glass to her lips, she laughed again.

After they finished their meal, Lopez and Patty Lee strolled on the beach, their feet barely touching the water. She pulled out a cigarette and Lopez lit it for her. The wind blew slightly, and a brightly shining moon hung over the Atlantic. Lopez clicked his lighter shut and placed it back in his pocket.

"We have to leave this week," he told her. "Business has arisen, and we must go." He was not looking at her, but his glare trained on the glowing moon.

She put the cigarette to her lips and drew in the smoke. As she exhaled, she asked, "Will we come back here?" That was a question he had been expecting.

"Perhaps," he said as he took her hand. "Colombia will be too beautiful for you to leave."

Patty Lee flipped an ash and turned her focus from the ocean to Lopez. "Maybe, but my business is here." Lopez smiled, his heart almost bursting with love, his beloved Patricia, always thinking business. She was the first woman he knew that did so. He loved the fact Patty Lee knew when to talk, when to shut up, and when to interject.

"I don't want to fly," she informed him. "Let's take the boat, the big boat of my father's."

Lopez pulled her close and said, "Nothing would make me happier. Day after tomorrow, yes?" Patty Lee put her arms around him and her lips to his. He had his answer.

Chapter 32

Both meetings Burt was involved in today confirmed one thing: he had to get Susie and Cliff out of South Florida. He needed Vern Bruce's plane to get the job done. The next morning, he was the first visitor at the Brevard County Jail. When the door opened and Burt stepped into the visiting room, Vern banged on the table with his shackled hands and called for the guard. He had nothing to say to Burt.

Burt furiously shook his hands and stared down at Vern, trying to get him to calm down, but Vern had none of it and continued calling for the guard. A slender guard burst into the room, baton drawn, but Burt lunged forward, hugged Vern tightly so he couldn't move his arms and pinned his hands to the table.

Burt played the only card he held and whispered the words, "Cliff's in danger," into Vern's ear. Burt released him and just as he did the scrawny guard was about to crash down upon Vern's arms with the baton and Burt stepped between them. "I'm sorry, officer," Burt pleaded, "My brother-in-law and I have personal business, he's alright now." Burt reached in his pocket and pulled out a hundred-dollar bill and slid it into the breast pocket of the guard's shirt. The guard frowned and pointed the baton at both of them.

"If I have to come back in here, I'll bash both of you sons a bitches."

"I know I'm the last person you expected, but look, your nephew needs to get out of town…" Burt spoke in a tone of voice that Vern had never heard from the gangster. Fear coated each word, and Vern raised an eyebrow while Burt pleaded, "You gotta trust me."

"Trust you, huh?" he asked as he raised his hands as high as he could and motioned around the room.

Burt leaned back in his chair and took a deep breath, shaking his head once again. "No, trust him." He motioned for the door to open. The guard appeared in the doorway and looked up and down the corridor before guiding Cliff into the room. It had cost Burt a lot of money to get him in the visiting room and he hoped he wouldn't need him, but as always, Vern needed a push. He walked through the door, his eyes wide and each cautious step seemed to take forever. When he got close enough in the dimly lit room and he could see his uncle's face, his eyes widened even more.

"Unc!" he yelled and ran towards Vern. He wrapped his arms around the orange jumpsuit, and Vern felt the tears pouring onto his shoulder. Burt pulled his chair beside them and forced Cliff into it.

Vern didn't know if he felt happy to see Cliff or livid that Burt was using him as some kind of pawn. "Why did you bring him *here*?" he asked Burt through gritted teeth.

Burt patted the boy on the head. "I want you to see him, Vern. You never know when it is your last chance." Burt's fear had receded, and a crooked grin replaced it.

Vern's gaze stiffened. "Threat?" he asked calmly.

Burt looked hurt. "Vern, you know I care about *my* family. They gotta get out of South Florida, today. Him and his mom need to go back to Biloxi where I *know* they will be safe."

Vern's anger overtook any joy he felt in seeing his nephew. "What the hell have you done, Williams?"

Burt's eyebrows furrowed, and he said, "What have *I* done? Buddy Boy, I ain't the one behind bars. The gangster looked over at Cliff. The tears weren't flowing as much as before, but his eyes were still moist and trained on Vern. "I ain't gonna rehash it in here, but, what you did, you did on your own. Nobody forced you, *asshole*."

Vern looked at the floor. Every word he said was true. "I don't have much time to make up my mind, do I?" he asked without looking up.

"Look, if you help me get them up there, I got friends *everywhere*." Burt was using his convincing, best friend voice now. Vern was starting to be able to tell which manipulation Burt used, but again, he didn't see another choice.

Vern may be able to change his voice at will, but he saw the fear in Burt William's eyes. It was something he had never seen before. Burt always seemed in control, but this time, his eyes just wouldn't lie.

"Save it," Vern said. "Get me a phone call and be at the airport at three." Vern narrowed his eyes and said, "If something happens to my family, I'll spend the rest of my life hunting you down." Burt snickered but knew when a man meant what he said.

"It's done," Burt said, remembering the hundred Vern's temper tantrum cost him and hoping he had enough cash on him.

Vern looked over at Cliff and smiled. "Love you, Cliff, you take care of your cousin. If something happens to me, your mother will take care of you. Life changes every day, son." He motioned for Cliff to come to him, and the boy leaned over and hugged his uncle once again. Vern closed his eyes, wishing the embrace would last longer. "I love you. Don't forget what I told you about trust." He pushed his head against Cliff's and held it there for a few seconds before turning his attention back to Burt, nodding to take the kid out of the room.

"But, Unc!" Cliff yelled as Vern told Burt to get him out of there. Burt grabbed the kid by the shoulders and pulled him towards the door. Vern dropped his head. In his heart, he knew that he wouldn't see his nephew again.

After he watched the plane float into the clouds, Burt drove to the ocean. He parked his car on the brown sand and sat down on the hood, his feet resting on the chrome bumper. He watched waves crash onto the beach and the seagulls floating in the air, riding the invisible currents in the sky. A lit cigar dangled from his lips and his hand clutched a beer with beads of condensation rolling down its sides. The only sound filling his ears was the crashing waves and the gulls over his head. As far as he could see to each side, the beach lay barren. There were no tourists, there were no locals, there was only him and his solitude.

He watched the sun behind his back cover the blue water with a golden hue and as it faded below the dunes behind him, watched the water turn back to its usual blue. He took a long drag from the cigar as his eyes adjusted to the darkness. He had a choice to make. One that was likely to get him killed if chose wrongly. The important thing was he made sure Susie and Cliff were on their way to the safety of Biloxi.

A trusted friend was to meet them at the airport and make sure they were taken care of. He took a swig of his beer, hopped off the hood of his car, took one last look at the waves as they found their way onto the sand and retreated into the ocean, and got in the car. He turned one of the control knobs all the way to high. He let the air conditioning blow over him, and he held his head back, enjoying every second. He didn't want to move. If only he could sit there and enjoy the cool air blowing over him forever, but his mind was made up. There was a job to do, and he put the car in drive and headed back out to the road.

He went back to his room at the cheap motel near the cape and waited by the phone. A couple hours later, it rang three times. He didn't answer, but he knew his family was safely back home. He finished off the six-pack about an hour before the phone rang and the alcohol started leaving his body through his sweat. In order to do this thing right, he needed to be completely sober and decided to wait about another hour before leaving. He plugged in the small coffee maker and thought to himself that it wasn't going to be enough.

All of his belongings were in the car except one thing. The old hunting knife his grandfather left him after his death. It was probably a lie, but his grandfather told him as a child the handle came from an Indian one of his ancestors killed in the Creek War over in Alabama. Burt ran his stubby fingers along the smooth handle and wanted to believe it was true. It was his only possession passed down from his actual family. He left him the sharpening stone to go along with it. He waited in the darkness, scraping the edge of the blade against the stone, one side, then the other. The process repeated over and over again. He placed his chair so that he could see out of the large window in the front of the room. The clock on the wall ticked louder as each minute passed and the coffee's aroma filled the room. He dialed the number and the voice on the other end told him tomorrow evening. He hung up the phone and held his grandfather's knife in his hand as he slept.

The setting sun's rays glittered through the water as Patty Lee and Casey boarded the yacht. She glanced at the bow where her father chose to end his own life. Lopez went to "tie up some loose ends" as he put it and would be there within the hour. She was somewhat surprised to see the car pull up only a few moments later and a different driver open Lopez's door.

"Everything ready?" he asked as he scanned the deck and kissed Patty Lee's cheek.

She looked around and replied, "We are ready. Captain Moore has his instructions; everyone is here that you said would be here except your driver." She pointed to his car that was pulling away from the harbor.

"He will fly down, hard to find a good *driver*," he said with a grin.

Patty Lee accepted it without question. She took Lopez by the hand and looked into his eyes, accepting any truth he offered. Her body tingled with excitement, and she couldn't wait to be at sea with her new life on the horizon. *This is a life I was born to live*, she thought and let go of her lover's hand and told him, "I'll meet you up on the bow, Casey is already there."

"As you wish, my dear," he said as he kissed her cheek once again and started walking towards the front of the boat.

Lopez stopped halfway along the boat's railing while Patty Lee continued on. He placed both his hands gently on the smooth wood and looked over the small port. He flashed a broad smile and savored his victory. By now, Burt Williams was surely dead and the wife and nephew in Biloxi would soon follow. Lopez's smile narrowed into a slight grin as he thought about how much he liked Williams. *Too bad*, he thought. *Had he been born in Colombia, he could have served as my right hand.*

His thoughts of Burt Williams fading, he made his way to the bow. He patted Casey on the head, took off his hat and enjoyed the warm sun beaming down onto his face. The passage into open water didn't take long and by the time they were on the high seas, Patty Lee joined them.

She caught Lopez's eyes staring at her. She changed into her two-piece bathing suit and eased into one of the lounge chairs. She threw a wry smile in his direction as she rubbed one of her feet on the opposite leg. The Colombian thought his heart would explode.

The seas were gentle, and the boat hardly rocked in the waves. Casey threw his arms into the air and yawned deeply. The excuse Lopez looked for presented itself, so he motioned for one of the stewards to take him inside for a nap.

Lopez took Patty Lee by the hand, lifting her up and the two walked to the back of the boat. They stood, her arms wrapped around him and her head on his shoulder as they watched, together, as the Florida coast faded.

"Welcome to a brand-new life, Patricia," he said as he took her face into his hands. "There is nothing we can't accomplish. The world is ours." He leaned down to kiss the woman for whom he'd waited an eternity.

Suddenly, her head jerked backwards, and a blade slid across her throat. The wound opened and the only sound she made was a gurgle as she choked on her own blood. Her eyes, wide in fear, slowly closed as her life faded.

In the same moment, an arm wrapped around Lopez's neck and slid him backwards. He wanted to cry out as he watched

Patty Lee crumple to the deck, but a hand covered his mouth. He struggled to see the man holding him back and he could see only the dark of a mask covering his face. The smell of cigars betrayed his identity beyond the mask.

"Williams," he said defiantly as the masked assailant wheeled Lopez's body around to face his him, "and Black, I presume."

The two men pulled off their masks. Lopez's body stiffened and his eyes narrowed. "If I die, you will never be safe. I..." As he tried to finish his sentence, Black stuck a knife deep into his heart. Blood poured from his mouth instead of words. His limp body fell alongside his dead lover and the last thing he saw before he faded to black were her closed eyes.

They picked up Patty Lee and tossed her over the rail and Lopez's body followed. The two lifeless bodies bobbed in the wake of the propellors for a moment before they were lost to the darkness of the sea.

The two men quickly and quietly launched the life raft that served as their shelter for the hours until the ship steamed out of port. The night hid their escape, and they waited until the ship was almost out of sight before cranking the small gasoline engine. Slowly they made their way back to the shore. They remained silent since they'd escaped the yacht with their own lives.

It would be some time before the discovery of the two bodies. Black guessed it would be the next day or perhaps sooner depending on the currents. Before they parted, Black told him,

"There will be no reprisal. I have that on the *highest* of authority. My people have taken care of it. Lopez had to die because he betrayed trust. Patty Lee died so that you can do…" He paused. "…what you have to do." The two men shook hands and parted, each going a different direction. As Black glanced back, he saw a flash, but thought perhaps it was only lightning on the horizon.

Burt, back in his room before sunrise, cleaned his grandfather's knife and watched the blood drain down the sink. He made a phone call to Biloxi, let it ring twice, and knew that Susie and Cliff would be back in West Palm by the next afternoon. He wasn't so sure about there being no revenge for the Colombian. That wasn't the way this world worked, and he knew it.

Burt didn't trust Black, but he knew he needed to work with him to get out of the situation he was in. Black had taken care of the driver, just as he'd said. He wiped the blade on a towel and admired the steel. He had made the right decision. If he chose differently, the driver would be on the boat heading to South America, and *he* would be the alligator's dinner.

If Black was true to his word and everything went like it was supposed to, he was going to end up a very powerful and rich man. He eased the blade into its sheath and placed it in the small of his back, looked around, and nodded. He eased the door closed and when it clicked he looked around and breathed easily for the first time in days.

Chapter 33

Patty Lee was reported missing by the captain the next day. Casey woke up and asked for his mother. When the Nanny informed the captain she wasn't to be found and after Old Man Clark's suicide, he at once stopped the boat and assumed the worst. He radioed the coast guard, but only reported Patty Lee's disappearance. He didn't mention Christian Lopez and his man on the boat slipped off into the night when the boat returned to port.

When the news reached Vern, it was delivered by the same detective that interrogated him after his arrest. This time, he felt the satisfaction emanating from the cruel man when he told him his wife was missing. Vern asked him about Casey. He wanted to know what would happen to him. The young boy had no other family and neither did Patty Lee. She was the last of the Clarks, besides Casey.

"Little fella is a ward of the state now," the detective said devoid of empathy. "They picked him up at the harbor this morning in West Palm." Vern's head dropped and the detective stood, walking towards the door.

"If they don't find Patty Lee, or..." He raised his head. "If she's dead? What happens to my son?"

The detective smiled and said, "You have to talk to Child and Family about that." Vern sighed and begged the detective to make that happen. He didn't say anything; he just nodded and whistled as he shut the door.

After a few days, Vern figured the detective, in his callousness, didn't call Child and Family. He paced as far as the confined cell allowed for hours at a time. He didn't know where his son was or what was happening. Several days passed and the detective finally came to his cell and told him there was no sign of Patty Lee or Lopez's bodies. As with most "accidental drownings" at sea, as the media and authorities were calling it, most bodies were never found if they were not found within a day or two. There were many hungry creatures lurking off the Atlantic Coast in Florida.

Vern asked again about Casey and the detective only shrugged his shoulders and walked away, leaving him to wallow in his misery. On one of the early, deathly quiet pre-dawn mornings, he found himself scanning the room for anything he could fashion as a noose, but he quickly snapped out of it. If he was dead, Casey's fate was sealed. He imagined the vultures coming after the Clark's fortune and became physically sick.

Finally, after several agonizing days, Vern received a visit from a social worker about Casey. He was direct and to the point and held a poker face, showing no emotion when he spoke. Vern guessed in his line of work, he had to remain all business.

Instead of going to the regular visiting room, the two were allowed to use the interrogation room. When Vern came in, the social worker was already seated and had a briefcase open. The guard stayed in the room with them as the guy was visibly nervous. After all, Vern was suspected of shooting two people in the head with no remorse.

"Mr. Bruce," he said, "I'll get right to it. Your son, Casey Jack Bruce, is in the custody of the state of Florida. Currently, he is housed at a facility in Orlando." The man licked his lips and for a split second, Vern saw concern spread across his face. Just as quickly it vanished, and he continued. "Seeing that you are residents of the Panhandle area, arrangements are being made to get him closer to home. Dozier School for Boys has an opening." Vern's face turned pale, and he felt his heart drop into his chest.

Dozier School for Boys was well known around the Panhandle and throughout Florida as a death camp for teenage boys. The school paraded itself as a type of place to help boys that ran afoul of the law and others that had no other place to go, but Vern knew better. He'd heard stories of beatings and other unspeakable things going on there.

Vern shook his head and pointed his finger towards the man. "That is no place for my son! He isn't a criminal!" he shouted. The guard hurriedly stood beside Vern, his hand on his baton, ready to strike, but the social worker put up his hand.

"That is not for boys in Casey's situation," Vern said, his voice lower but still tense.

"Well, it *is* right now. We've got a problem on our hands in South Florida if you didn't already know. We have a flood of kids with nowhere to go and your son is no exception, no matter his last name or family line." The man stopped, noticing the anguish in Vern's eyes. He ran his fingers along his pencil-thin mustache and said, "Hopefully, his stay will only be as long as it takes to find a foster family. Maybe that won't take long, but you know how it is." Vern wondered how many times he'd repeated this same lie to other parents.

The man leaned in and shot a glance at the guard who really wasn't paying attention. "Of course, I've been instructed to tell you that cooperation greases wheels," and he stood to leave.

"That's it? No more choices? No deals?" Vern pleaded.

The social worker stopped and ran his fingers along his mustache once again, walked back over to Vern, and whispered, "It is within your rights to sign over custody to *anyone* you choose but not many people in your situation seem to have many friends, I've found. You might have *one*."

He walked over and the guard opened the door and let him out. Before the door shut behind him, the social worker looked back and said, "The clock is ticking," and walked out of sight. The guard unlocked the chains holding Vern's hands on the desk and walked him back to his cell. The door slammed shut, leaving Vern alone with his thoughts. *One friend*, the words the social worker said, ran through his mind over and over. Vern fell onto the slender mattress and couldn't believe what he was about to do.

In Vern's mind there was only one thing to do. Something a couple of weeks, even a couple of days ago, would've been unthinkable. He had to contact Burt Williams. Susie seemed like a good mother to Cliff; maybe she would be so for Casey. At least for a little while, until he could clear his name. He stared at the bare, gray wall in front of him and thought how insane this sounded, but he couldn't let Casey get shipped off to Dozier.

Tonight, he got his phone call, and he had until then to make up his mind for sure. He had two choices for his son. Doom him to a prison for boys or give him life. A life with a Dixie Mafia gangster. It was a hell of a choice.

That evening, he made the call. He had sat in silence and thought about it for hours. He hit his head on the concrete wall when he'd finally realized he had no other choice.

He didn't speak with Burt directly but left a message with the guy at the bar that he needed to see him. Vern didn't know if Burt would show or not, but he made sure he knew that the meeting was urgent. He had gotten word later that day, after the meeting with the social worker, that it would only be a couple days before Casey was shipped off to Dozier. Time was something that he didn't have.

Hoping this was the last time he would have to meet with Vern in the county jail, Burt sheepishly walked in and requested visitation. This was the last time he was going to give his real name in this place. Even though nobody knew him down here, he was not going to chance it. Cops were stupid, but like major league hitters and fastballs, give them enough chances and they will connect. The guard led him down to the visitation room, and he sat down and waited for Vern.

He didn't wait long as Vern, in his ridiculous orange jumpsuit, was led through the door and took his usual seat. Vern eyed the gangster as the guard locked him into place.

"What can I do for you now, Vernie boy?" Burt asked.

Vern looked at him without speaking for a moment or two and finally said, "Look, I've got a proposition for you." He looked around as if to keep the conversation private. "It involves Susie too."

Burt looked confused, and replied, "This about Cliff?" He held up his hands and continued, "Look, Vern, he's with us. Nothing you can do about that right now. Susie *is* his mother."

Vern shook his hands and head. "It's about my son, Burt," Vern said, still not believing the words coming out of his own mouth. "He needs to be with Cliff. At least until Patty Lee is found, or—"

Burt held up his hand and cut him off. "Sorry to tell you this, bud, but they found her this morning. Washed up on some beach between West Palm and Cocoa. Guess news is slow in here." Burt tried to be as sympathetic as he could. Vern looked at the ceiling and held in tears. He knew that he would eventually get this kind of news, but still, he was shocked to hear it. His tears began to flow and streamed down his face. Burt, surprised to see him crying over her, shook his head slightly.

"After the way she did you?" he asked Vern. "You still give a shit?"

Vern turned his gaze to the gangster. "Nothing to you," he shot back. "How did she die?" Burt's sympathy evaporated with Vern's curt reply. He told him how she was murdered and slid his finger across his throat. Vern just shook his head and tried to choke back his tears.

He gathered himself enough to speak and said, "You and Susie have got to get Casey. They've got him in some kind of facility now over in Orlando, but they threatened to take him up north, to Dozier." Even in Mississippi, Burt heard about that place and winced.

"Damn, that place is bad, heard a lot about it over my way. In this line of business, you hear a lot about places like that. Talk in the bar and such. Criminals love to gossip," he replied.

"I give you two custody, and you keep it until I get out of here. He and Cliff need to be together. They are like brothers. And Burt, I'll be honest with you, I don't trust you as a father, but I do trust Susie. No offense." Burt wasn't particularly stung by that statement and just nodded. Then it hit him. They were the only heirs to *both* companies. That damned Jeff Black came through, just as he'd promised.

"You realize what comes with that right?" Burt asked him.

"I'm getting out and I'll pay you," Vern said. "But yes, I know what that means if I *don't* get out anytime soon. I don't expect bail. Beck sealed that," Vern replied. His lawyer already told him not to expect it being an accused cop killer.

Burt grinned. "Yeah, killing a cop, even a dirty cop, will do that to ya." Burt winked at Vern. Vern wanted to say something, but Burt shook his finger as if to say, *Careful, bud, people are listening.*

"Deal is," Vern continued, "y'all get the boys and control of the business down here, but everything else is in a trust. When I get out, you get paid, and I'll pay generously either with money or favors." Vern hesitated before continuing. "You can live in Clark's mansion and work out of his office; god knows I hate the place."

Burt grinned. "You know me, Vern," he replied. "Money talks."

"That's it then. Get up with my attorney in Panama City, get him down here. We will get things done before Casey is shipped to that damned place."

"I'll get on it as soon as I leave. Family is coming back to town today. I'll tell Susie the good news. She always wanted a big family." Burt's grin was a full-blown smile, and he reached for a cigar, but he remembered where he was. *It can wait*, he thought.

Vern looked Burt in the eye and warned him, "If you double cross me, dammit—"

Burt cut him off with laughter. He had heard that one before. "You'll what? Hunt me till your dying day?"

"We got a deal?" Vern shot back and Burt reached down, grabbed Vern's hand, and winked at him.

Burt Williams walked out of the Bevard County Jail in a lot better mood than when he'd walked in. He sang along with the radio as he drove out of the parking lot and made his way back to West Palm. He drove by the Clark mansion and parked in front of it. There was no activity there. Patty Lee's wake would probably be held there by *friends* of the family, but there was no family left. Soon, it would be empty. Young Casey Bruce would own it, his father on death row for double murder, and the Williams Family would probably have to move in permanently. Burt couldn't stop smiling and he once again reached for a cigar but decided to wait. He wanted to wait until Susie came back to celebrate. He started the engine and moved on.

As Burt admired the Clark mansion, Vern sat in his cell, contemplating what he had done. He may have saved his son from harm physically, but what was he being subjected to? Vern lay back on his bunk, but he couldn't get the vision of Burt Williams, cigar dangling from his mouth, teaching his son and nephew how to survive in the Dixie Mafia.

He thought back to the day that Rof got that damned draft card. It was a day that changed all their lives. His, Rof's, Pop's, hell even Patty Lee's life changed that day and she didn't even know it.

If Rof wasn't drafted, Vern wouldn't have gone to the meeting on that fateful night in Tallahassee. He was against the war but hadn't really been involved up until then. They would probably never have gotten involved with each other if it hadn't been for that particular night. They were both young and wanted to change the world. and now, she was dead and here he sat awaiting his fate.

He had pledged to take care of Cliff, and he failed. Hell, he couldn't even take care of his own son. He knew, deep in his guts, that Burt was the one that set him up, but Susie was the key. He had to get to her somehow and plead with her for the boys' safety. Burt was doing this strictly for the money. Vern knew that. Susie, however, loved her son. Anyone could see that. He hoped she would learn to love Casey as her own. He hoped she was a better mother to him than Patty Lee. His anger swelled. It was her damned lies that got them into this. That and her coward father killing himself leaving her to pick up the pieces.

He closed his eyes, and his mind wandered. Maybe, in some other reality, she was in congress, and he was raising the boys. Perhaps they were all together and happy. Thoughts of happiness consumed him, and he had all the time in the world to think.

He slapped himself. He couldn't allow this dream about what might have been. If he had time to do that, he could be working on getting out of here and fixing everything himself. Somebody, somewhere, knew what happened to Lucky and Beck. There had to be.

Burt found himself in the Clark Building parking lot just as the sun set beyond the row of swaying palms lining the street in front of the Spanish-style structure. He sat with the windows rolled down and enjoyed a cool breeze coming in from the ocean. He admired Old Man Clark's style. It was a hell of a lot more sophisticated than Vern Bruce.

To Burt, Vern was just a simple redneck from the backwoods of North Florida. He wasn't much more than Burt except for one thing. Burt knew which horse to hitch his wagon to. He knew how long to ride it out and when to jump off. Vern was just gullible. He was, if nothing else, easily manipulated. His wife manipulated him from the start. It was kind of like that old saying, she did nothing but feed him lies from the tablecloth. From the very start, that woman knew what she was doing. She knew what she was doing right up until the moment she fell in love with the wrong man. She could never really love a man like Vern, so undoubtably she felt sorry for him for some reason unknown to Burt. He laughed at the image that popped into his mind of that orange jumpsuit. *Dumb bastard*, he thought. He admired the view for a few more minutes before he left for the airport.

The funeral for Patty Lee happened quickly. Casey attended, escorted by a social worker. His face held no expression and no emotion. He didn't say a word until he saw Cliff and ran to hug his cousin. Burt leaned down and introduced himself and Susie to the young kid. Casey, overjoyed to see his older cousin, held him tightly with tears streaming down his chubby face.

The cemetery was crowded as Patty Lee took her place in the family plot beside her father and mother. Burt looked at Casey. He still had tears in his eyes, and he could tell the boy was timid around the social worker who brought him.

Burt empathized with the young boy as he had been in his shoes once. Left with nobody to care for him after his grandfather died, the state of Mississippi took him. They put him in one of those places that make good kids into criminals. It did it to him and he had to fight for every inch he gained for the rest of his life.

Vern did the right thing, he thought, not letting that kid go up there to meet a dark fate. There was no way the kid would make it. He was soft, just like Cliff. The boys, raised in fancy cars, nice houses, and fast jets, could never survive like he did. They were lucky to be with him. He'd make real men out of them.

Susie introduced herself to the social worker and explained the situation. She then bent down to one knee and told Casey he would soon be going home with them, and he would be going home with Cliff. She hugged the little boy, and they separated as the funeral ended. Burt held his wife's hand as they made their way. Susie smiled at him and squeezed his hand. At last, she had a true family.

Burt waited until everyone left the building. He glanced around one more time and then popped open a window and climbed through. He walked around the office for a while, admiring the paintings on the wall. He finally made his way to the Old Man's personal office; the one Patty Lee took over after his death. The only real change he noticed was her picture replaced her father's. "The bitch didn't waste time," he said aloud.

He had met with the old man right before he died, he remembered. He thought about how much had changed since that meeting. He laughed to himself; Old Man Clark got what he wanted. Cliff and Vern were definitely out of the way, just not his daughter's way.

The door wasn't locked, and he walked inside and found his way behind the desk. He ran his fingers along the back of the dark leather chair as he sat down. He laughed again as he imagined what Old Man Clark would think about Burt Williams sitting in his chair. He propped his feet up on the desk and reached into his pocket.

As he lit the cigar and rolled it around his mouth, a grin formed in the corner opposite where the burning stogie came to rest. Smoke rose heavily and eventually filled the room with a slight haze.

That meeting with Clark had set the stage for all of this. With his feet still perched upon the desk, he gazed at the portrait of Patty Lee and imagined it was still the old man's. Burt wondered if he knew. Did he set his daughter up with this destiny? Did he know it would go as far as it did? He blew out another wisp of smoke and swapped which foot supported the other. It didn't really matter, Burt thought, as he looked around. Here he was, Burt Williams, dirt poor kid, Dixie Mafia, and all-around hoodlum about to be in charge of one of the most powerful companies in Florida. Not to mention, he thought, become one of its biggest smugglers. He smiled, puffed his cigar, and thought about the future. He had danced with the devil and got the better of him. He picked up the phone and checked in with Black.

Chapter 34

The months since Patty Lee's funeral passed slowly. Vern, still in jail, found the wheels of justice turned slowly. The judge refused bail and progress on his defense pretty much halted. His attorney, for some reason, seemed unconcerned and Vern found trouble contacting anyone about a new lawyer. Accused cop killers weren't granted many favors, and he spent most of his days and nights alone and lost in his thoughts.

While Vern rotted in jail, the Williams family occupied the Clark Mansion. On the surface, they seemed the perfect family. Burt was introduced as a family friend from Biloxi asked to cover things at the office until Vern proved his innocence. The employees, knowing better, but with no other choice accepted him at face value. Susie spent her days enjoying her new role as a stay-at-home mom. The boys, enrolled in a private school nearby, adapted to the new arrangement quickly. Cliff asked about his uncle often but focused much of his attention on his cousin.

The body of Christian Lopez never washed ashore so Patty Lee was never implicated in any wrongdoing. The media chalked up the murder as an act of piracy and since they were in international waters, no real investigation took place beyond the coast guard. Some journalists did note nothing was taken yet the story never found traction and was soon forgotten. It would be one of those things never solved but people would gossip about for years.

Christmas was almost upon them, and the Williams family looked forward to spending their first Christmas together in their new home. The tree was placed near the front, for all to see and the outside was immensely decorated. Susie made a fine homemaker, and the family was accepted as one of the community. Nobody knew a whole lot about the husband and wife, but all knew about the Bruce boys and where the real money lay.

On one unusually cold December day, as Christmas neared, the doorbell rang. Susie didn't want the staff retained when they moved in, so she was alone. She peeked through the window in the doorframe and a well-dressed man of Asian descent smiled back at her. Even though they lived a new life, in a new home and town, she remembered the way things happened in the Dixie Mafia. The man saw the concern in her face and in a heavy Vietnamese accent he said, "Mrs. Williams, I have a message from Rof Bruce," as he continued smiling.

Susie took a step back and stood in silence. Nobody had told her of the turmoil behind the pictures or that Rof could still be alive. Burt had thought it wise to keep it from her, not for her sake but for his. He feared the ghost of Rof Bruce as a threat to his marriage. Susie knew he hated each time she spoke of him and how stupid it was of Burt to be so jealous of a dead man. She reached for the door, but stopped, her arm suspended halfway through the motion. This was a chance she had to take.

She completed her reach for the door and opened it slowly. The man's still smiling face greeted her. Her voice shook noticeably as she asked him to repeat what he said. The man bowed and once again told her of his message.

"If I may come in, I will explain," he responded and motioned with his hands.

In the back of her mind, all the alarm bells sounded. She still had the mindset of a Dixie Mafia wife, so she didn't trust anyone. She ignored the red flags. This was something she was not prepared for. The boys were safe at school, and the danger would only encompass her. She motioned for him to come in.

He took off his shoes upon entering the house and Susie looked intently, not sure what to do.

In his heavy accent he said, "Out of respect for your home," and bowed once again.

Susie led him into the expansive living room and offered him a seat on the sofa. As he sat down, he asked Susie to take a seat beside him. Her mind raced with confusion and her breathing intensified. The man gently put his hand on her knee when she finally took the seat next to him and told her he meant her no harm, only good news.

"Rof?" she asked gently. "He's been dead for years. I don't understand what kind of message you have from him." Tears began to swell in her eyes, and she remembered the night on the beach that gave her Cliff.

The man noticed her tears and patted her knee. "My dear, you do not know?" he asked as the tears began to flow in earnest.

"Know what?" she asked, her voice quivering.

"My dear, we have a lot to talk about." He realized he forgot to introduce himself and said, "Please forgive me, my dear. My name is Colonel Duy, formerly of the Vietnamese Army." Susie shook her head as her confusion grew.

The man took off his hat and pulled a tattered, stained envelope out of his coat's pocket. He wiped sweat from his brow as the room was warm. Susie took advantage of the usually chilly weather to use the often-neglected fireplace.

"May I?" he asked as he motioned to take off his coat and Susie nodded affirmatively.

She couldn't take her eyes from the envelope and once again her breathing grew rapid. She felt as though she would faint, but Duy, sensing her apprehension, hurried to his mission.

"This," he said as he held the envelope to her, "is to your son." Susie couldn't move. She wanted to take it, but her body was paralyzed. Duy place it gently on the sofa between them, "It is from his father."

"His father is dead. I just told you that, died over ten years ago," she said, her voice steadying with anger replacing the uncertainty and apprehension.

Duy held up a finger. "No, Mrs. Williams," he responded. "He did not die all those years ago." Susie shook her head and put her hand to her forehead as he continued. "I *was* a colonel in the

Vietnamese Army, one that I'm afraid to say, still holds prisoners from the war. I worked at one of those *prisons*." He paused and let Susie's mind absorb the words before continuing. "The prison that held Rof Bruce."

She buried her face in her hands and a deep, loud cry came from within, at first low but grew slowly into a piercing scream. Susie couldn't believe what he was saying. Duy reached over and put his arm around her. He felt her trembling.

"There's no way," she said. "No way!" Her head was still buried in her hands.

He reached into his coat, hanging on the arm of the couch and pulled a picture from the same pocket from which he had produced the envelope. He placed his finger under her chin and pulled her head from her hands and handed it to her. She knew from first glance that it was Rof. She could see his blond hair and his eyes were unmistakable.

"How can this be real?" she asked through her sobs. "Why didn't anyone tell me?"

Duy shook his head. "I know the information was presented to your husband. Why he didn't tell you, I cannot say." He leaned back and put his back against the cushion, releasing his arms from her trembling shoulders.

"I know this is hard to hear," he sympathized. "I sent pictures to your government a long time ago. Many have known, including Vernon Bruce, his brother." Susie shook her head and tried to speak, but her tears returned.

"Every damn body knew he was alive but me and his own son?" she said through angry tears. She had felt sorry for Vern, but now she hated him and wondered how much Burt knew.

Duy patted the letter. "This is a letter to your son. Rof and I became *friends* of sorts." He took a deep breath. "Because of our friendship, my own escape became necessary. I had to do things, evil things, and I could do it no longer." He stared at the floor as his mind drifted to the past. "I couldn't help Rof in any other way, so I promised him I would get this to his son."

"He knew about Cliff? How? He knew I was pregnant, but he didn't know..." She couldn't finish the sentence as memories of her time with Rof flooded her mind and her emotions overwhelmed her.

Still staring through the floor, Duy continued. "The Vietnamese, unfortunately, can be cruel. They provide the prisoners with information and then twist it to inflict pain. They told Rof of his son." He looked up at Susie and placed his hands over hers. "They gave him information, giving him hope. Then they told him lies. Lies that caused him pain, so much pain." Susie could see the pain in the colonel's eyes, but he shed no tears. Years in the prison camp made him shed such luxury as tears. But in those eyes, Susie saw the truth.

"Is he alive?" she asked sheepishly.

Duy shook his head. "I don't know," he responded. "He was alive when I made my *escape* last year. He has lived longer than most in those conditions. I believe he is, but I don't know for certain."

Susie took the envelope and started to open it but stopped. "This is for Cliff. I don't want to know what it says," she said. Duy smiled for the first time since his smile faded as his story unfolded.

"I would love to meet the son of Rof Bruce one day," he said, "and tell him of his father."

Susie nodded in agreement. "I think that would be nice." He patted her hands and bowed once again.

He stood to leave and unexpectantly, Susie jumped from her seat and embraced him. "Thank you," she said into his ear. He squeezed her in their embrace, let go, and took a step back.

"We will meet again, Mrs. Williams," he said quietly and began walking towards the door.

"Thank you, Colonel. Thank you from my son," she said, drying her tears with her hands.

He nodded one last time and walked out the door. Susie watched as he got into the taxi that had been waiting for him and as quickly as he appeared, he was gone. She held the envelope in her hands, running her fingers along the creases and all she could see was Rof's smiling face. In his face, she saw her son's. She went upstairs and put the envelope on Cliff's pillow. She slowly touched her lips and placed the same fingers on the envelope.

"I love you, Rof," she said in a whisper and left the room, closing the door gently behind her.

Cliff ran up the stairs as soon as he got home from school. Usually, he stopped by the kitchen for a snack, but with it so cold outside, he wanted to grab a book he had been reading first. He and Casey couldn't go to the beach, and he didn't really want to play the video games in Casey's room, so he decided on the book. It just so happened the book was about a man, wrongly accused, and languished in a hellish prison. It kept his uncle in his thoughts.

He burst through the door and reached for the book on his desk. He didn't notice the envelope at first and started to head back downstairs. As he rushed by the bed, the envelope brushed the side of his head and fell to the floor. He saw it out of the corner of his eye, stopped, and picked it up.

He held it in his hand and wondered where it came from. It looked dirty, and he ran his fingers down the crease in the middle until he reached the top. He opened it with his finger, ripping most of the envelope in two. He pulled out a single piece of paper, unfolded it and started reading.

Son,

I know this comes as a shock, but I'm alive. I don't know what to say or how to say it. I hope your mother told you about me, and I hope this letter finds its way to you and you are happy. I've been here for a long time. These people told me about you. They told me about your life. A week or so ago then they told me you were killed. I don't know what to believe, but I have to hope you're alive. I can't think that something happened to you or your mother. I want you to tell her I love her, I always did. She was always there for me, and she'll always be for you. That's the way she is.

I wrote you a letter on the day I left for the war. I often wonder if you got it. I was a different person then. I was an angry person. Your uncle and me parted ways with some bad feelings, but I've been told he's helping you. I want you to thank him for that. Tell him for me.

I love you, son. I wish I could watch you grow up. I don't even know what you look like. I picture you in my mind, playing on the same beach I did. The way me and Vern played on the beach. I miss my dad. They told me he died, but I hope they were lying. If he did, just know Pops was the best man I ever knew. I hope Vern becomes more like him. I know this is rambling, I just don't know what to say. I won't get another chance, I know that. Just know, that I fought to get back to you. I just don't know if I ever will. I love you so much.

Tell your mother that I'm sorry. I put her in a bad spot with you and I know she has done the best she can. Whatever happens, remember I love you. I love you, son. I may never get a chance to show you, but life changes every day, and I'll never give up fighting to get back home. I will always try to get back to you.

Your Father,
Ronald

Cliff's tears rained onto the faded paper. He read it over and over. His thoughts raced. Questions like how did the letter get here? How was his father alive? Is this real? His young mind couldn't fathom the notion that perhaps he *did* have a father after all, and he was *alive*. He read it once more and carefully folded the paper, placing it gently into the now torn envelope.

He wondered about the bad feelings mentioned in the letter between his father and Unc. What was his father talking about? Unc never mentioned anything like that. Now, sadly, he was gone too. He opened a drawer on his dresser, moved aside the clothes and placed the letter under them, placing the clothes back over it.

Cliff sat on the edge of his bed, wiped his tear-stained cheeks, and peered at the swaying palm tree outside his window. If this was true and his father was alive, he would move mountains to find him. He needed his uncle's help. It would be up to them to set him free. But it was up to him and only him to free his family from the everything holding them apart. He picked up the book, sat back on his bed, turned the page and read.

Pelham Pugh

The Bruce Family Story Continues:

Last Castle in the Sky (August 5, 2025)

If you enjoyed *Perfidious Tides* please leave a review on Amazon and/or Goodreads.com

Thanks,
Pelham Pugh

Made in the USA
Columbia, SC
17 August 2025

e10e9f24-b1b3-410d-9667-41a7cfe944d5R02